So Wild a Dream

Also by Win Blevins

Stone Song

The Rock Child

RavenShadow

So Wild a Dream

WIN BLEVINS

A Tom Doherty Associates Book
New York

This is a work of fiction. All the characters and events portrayed in this novel are either fictitious or are used fictitiously.

SO WILD A DREAM

This book is printed on acid-free paper.

A Forge Book
Published by Tom Doherty Associates, LLC
175 Fifth Avenue
New York, NY 10010

www.tor.com

Forge® is a registered trademark of Tom Doherty Associates, LLC.

Library of Congress Cataloging-in-Publication Data

Blevins, Winfred.
So wild a dream : a novel of frontier America / Win Blevins.—1st ed.
p. cm.
"A Forge book"—T.p. verso.
ISBN 0-765-30573-9
1. Rocky Mountains—Fiction. 2. Mountain life—Fiction. 3. Fur trade—Fiction. 4. Explorers—Fiction. 5. Trappers—Fiction. I. Title.

PS3552.L45S6 2003
813'.54—dc21

2003046854

First Edition: September 2003

Printed in the United States of America

0 9 8 7 6 5 4 3 2 1

To Meredith, my partner in the great dance,
turning, turning forever

Note to the Reader

AT THE TIME this story begins, in 1822, the vast reach of plains, mountains, and deserts penetrated briefly by Captains Lewis and Clark was still mostly unexplored. In St. Louis, on its eastern edge, some men felt a great yearning to venture westward. Mountain men, they called themselves.

Their excuse for westering was the prospect of fortunes in fur. This spring of 1822 saw the launch of the first big fur-trade enterprise into the Rocky Mountains. Most of the men were new to the mountains—so much to see, do, learn. The plains, rivers, mountains, and deserts themselves. The Indians and their ways. The ways of the animal creatures as well, from the magnificent buffalo to the wily beaver, both prized for their fur. The newcomers had to learn to trap, trade, get along with the Indians, live on the land itself.

The risks were terrible. The country or the weather was apt to kill them, as was starvation, or mishap, or Indians. Yet these men relished the mountain life.

Why did they go? Why did they stay? Less for profit than for adventure, a seductress often underestimated. Also, perhaps, for a boon they didn't know how to explain. The old ways seemed dead. Out with European ideas like royalty, the class system, and Original Sin. Out also with past American ways—the conventions of the industrial Northeast, dictated by family, church, and the law; and the traditions of the plantation South, darkened by slavery.

Yes, you might die. But, if you dared, if you freed yourself, you might instead discover your true nature. You might invent a new, American way of living.

Mountain men like Sam Morgan bore these hopes into the mountains unconsciously. . . .

Part One

VENTURING FORTH

Chapter One

EDEN.

Sam always took a long time looking down into it first, and listening. His eyes would sweep up every detail, his ears soak up every breath of sound and silence. The sounds would be songbirds, this early in the morning chickadees and blue jays, when the sun was higher, cardinals and song sparrows. Silence would mean something out of order, an intruder. Perhaps himself, if he was careless. Perhaps a bear or other danger. He stood still and let himself taste Eden's climate before he eased off the trail, onto the slope below the ridge and down to the creek, where limestone outcroppings offered a lookout. He slipped down, like descending into another world, an enchanted place.

Eden.

This was a childish fantasy, he knew. Eden, where the human race was born, where the first man saw all the things of the earth—the fliers, bird or bee or wild turkey or screech owl; the four-legged, squirrel, coon, deer, bear; the crawlers, snake, worm, snail; the rooted grasses, wild roses, beeches, poplars, the great oaks, the rambling vines; the swimming fish, and myriads more, beyond knowing and again and again beyond. The perfect place, Eden, and at the same time the home of the snake. Sam was deathly afraid of snakes.

Now he stepped softly into the little hollow, putting his foot gently on the winter-dry leaves to lessen the noise of his passing. He padded softly down the long slope. When he got to the limestone, he climbed the jutting he knew would give him the best view up and down the stream. He set down the long rifle he inherited from his father and stretched out on the rock. In a few minutes the forest would accept him, and again would breathe normally.

Sam came here to remember and to balm his loneliness.

Two years ago on Christmas Eve, an afternoon nearly as warm as this one, his father came to Eden to die. Last year and this year Sam came down here the day before Christmas, his own seventeenth and eighteenth birthdays, to be alone with his father on the day of his death, as near as could be.

Lewis Morgan, who liked to call himself the Celt, didn't say anything about dying that pleasant winter afternoon, said he was feeling better and wanted to get out of the house for a while, walk around his own place, smell the air and feel the fragile sunshine. No one suspected, though they should have, since the stomach trouble had been eating at him so many months. Lew's wife pooh-poohed the idea—you need your rest. The Celt's other son and his daughters shook their heads at such foolishness. But the Celt asked Sam to walk down to Eden with him. It was their favorite place, their father-son place. Nothing much really, a dip between two hills with some limestone outcroppings and a creek. But it was graced with a kind of beauty, and it felt like theirs.

The Celt had spent hours and hours, days and days here, teaching Sam to see a forest, how life circled through it in a thousand ways and back again. Owen, the Celt's eldest, had no interest in such things. To him the forests of young America were a blackboard left blank by the Creator for men to write on. Owen was eager to get on with that job. The Celt had founded a mill. Owen was bringing in a blacksmith, a tinsmith, a cooper, and a store for the far-flung farmers. Lew Morgan's little clearing was now a town. The twenty-mile track to Pittsburgh was becoming a road. Soon all things would be decent, and civilized.

Other times the Celt would tell Sam stories about his Welsh ancestors. Sam liked those stories, but he liked even more the tales of Daniel Boone, and especially Simon Kenton. Kenton fought with Boone in Kentucky, and fought the Shawnees across the river in Ohio. Kenton came to be the kind of man people looked up to and told tales about, even tales that couldn't be exactly accurate but in some way said some truth about the man. Or Lew Morgan told stories about the boatmen who first floated down the Ohio River from where it started at Pittsburgh, down to the little settlements as they grew along the river, Cincinnati and Louisville and the others, all the way to New Orleans. The way the Celt told it, those alligator horses were real men.

On this day, their last afternoon together, Lew Morgan didn't expand on his usual talk about the ways of the grasses, the bushes, how these made small leaves that fed the grazing and browsing animals, and these fed the flesh-eating animals, and all gave their bodies back to the earth, which gave root to the mosses and grasses and bushes and produced once more the small leaves. Nor did he speak of these limestone outcroppings, and other rocks, how they rose from the earth here and there, great and small. They covered themselves with soil in places and gave birth to grasses. In other places they took the warmth of the afternoon sun and held it into the evening. Slowly, ever so slowly through the wind and rain, they changed back to soil and sand and returned to the earth they came from. He didn't mention how human beings rise and return to earth in a short time, how the stones rise, spend centuries wearing away, and then rise again.

Instead the Celt looked and listened and held his face up into the sun. After about an hour of talking, he said he was going to take a little nap and stretched out on the limestone in the sun there in Eden. He never woke up.

So Sam came back to this little place two years later to remember. He didn't think about Eden's snake. Instead he recalled when he was little, the Celt let the boy give names to the citizens of the forest, childish names Sam no longer remembered. Then, slowly, he learned their real names, and began to learn their ways. Where the mosses grew. What time of evening the moon rose in its fullness, and what time of night in its crescent newness. How long a day was in summer, in autumn, in winter, in spring. When the creatures moved about and when they didn't. When berries were ripe. Where wild onions could be found, and chestnuts, hickory nuts, and walnuts. When the deer came to the creek, and the hunter might take one, so that his children might grow . . .

"DAYDREAMING?"

Sam jumped, whirled, and grabbed his rifle.

Katherine giggled. "You don't need The Celt for me." That was the name he used for his rifle, after his dad.

He flinched. He could hardly believe he'd let anyone, especially a white girl, sneak up on him in the woods. He could hardly believe Katherine had come down here. Wanted to come down here. Was with him alone.

"You were daydreaming, towhead!"

He wished for the thousandth time his white hair would turn dark.

She sat down. What the devil was she doing here?

"We all know it's the day your dad died." She waited, but he didn't know what to say. The Turleys lived a few steps down the road from the Morgans, but Sam had never been alone with Katherine. He'd wanted to. He'd looked at her whenever she passed. When her family visited, he couldn't keep his eyes off her. She knew it. He couldn't guess whether she had similar feelings.

Her mother wouldn't like them being alone together. His brother, if he judged right, would like it even less.

"Happy birthday!" she cried.

"Thanks." A good feeling began to warm his belly.

"What kind of day is it for you? Happy because it's your birthday? Good because it's Christmas Eve? Or sad because it's the day your dad died?"

"I remember, mostly."

She gave him a look he couldn't read.

"I brought us some lunch."

She stepped back along the rock, dropped to the ground, and returned with a basket and a big blanket for a tablecloth. Napkins were folded on top of the blanket. She set out a loaf of pumpernickel bread, some headcheese, a wedge of cheddar, and a small flask. "Applejack," she announced. There was one package wrapped in napkins that she didn't open.

She handed him the flask and said gaily, "Happy birthday, Sam Morgan!"

He swigged. She swigged and handed him back the flask. "You are not," she announced, "going to be sad on your birthday."

THEY TALKED THE sweet nothings of the courting young. A day later, even an hour later, neither would remember a word of it. They touched each other in small ways. They held hands. They looked into each other's eyes, searching for answers that could never be there. Yet Sam thought he saw all—the future, set out not as a progression of human strivings, but a delightful bubble of colors, and a melody that made his heart dance.

The first moment of importance, the first Sam remembered clearly later, came when something arose deep in Katherine's eyes, dark, still, unfathomable, something he didn't understand, didn't expect, and couldn't account for. Afterwards he put it down as his first experience of the mystery of woman.

Suddenly, she announced that she had a present for him. She handed him a cloth bag filled with pieces of brown waxy paper that held . . . taffy!

Sam laughed and popped one into his mouth. He loved taffy. He clamped his teeth on the sticky pull, grinning, and mouthed "Thanks!" through the goo.

They jumped in like kids. When it was gone, Katherine brought up the second matter Sam would remember afterwards. "What are you going to do now that you're eighteen?" She hesitated and then blurted, "You're going away, aren't you?"

He felt all a-mumble. "Owen wants me to help in the mill, take it over really, and I think Ma needs me. . . ."

She gave him a look. "Seems to me you want to be a, what do you call it, alligator horse."

He puffed up. "Whoo-oop! Lookee here! I'm an alligator horse—I'm a snapping turtle—I can whip ten times my own weight in panthers. I use up Injuns by the cord, and swallow 'em entire, either raw or cooked. I can out-run, out-dance, out-jump, out-fight, and out-drink any white man that's ever took breath within two thousand miles of the Ohio River. Whoo-oop!"

He grinned at her, but noticed that her eyes didn't smile as big as her mouth.

"Pretty tempting, life on the river, free, rambling. Wild nights in port."

Sam chastened himself. "Could be a hard, lonely way to live."

He kept his eyes down a long time and looked up only when he felt her hand in his hair.

"I love your white hair." She lifted her face to his and kissed him.

When he started kissing back with enthusiasm, she stood, spread the blanket, on the dry grass, and drew him down beside her.

What they did over the next infinity or two seemed to Sam the most spectacular thing that ever happened to him, or probably happened to any man. They didn't speak, because their understanding of each other soared to a perfection beyond words.

An hour or two later Katherine stood up and put her clothes on. Sam did the same. He felt woozy. She took him by the hand, led him back to the ridge trail, and along it ten minutes until they neared the Morgan house.

Now she stopped. For a moment she buried her head in his chest. Then she looked at him seriously and said, "That's all." For a moment she held his eyes. "That's all. There's nothing else to say." Then she kissed him hard but quickly, and ran toward her own house.

Sam felt . . . everything . . .

Chapter Two

ELLIE MORGAN HAD a world of things to do before Christmas dinner. Not only were her daughters coming and the Turleys, but . . . It would be special even beyond any other Christmas Day.

Daughters, her mind moaned. Babies. Pain . . .

Ellie shook her head hard, like she was shaking a fly off her nose. With exaggerated vigor, she stoked the fire in the stove to get the double ovens nice and hot. Aloud, in an odd singsong voice, she said to whoever might be listening, "I'm going to make this day . . . one to remember."

Suddenly she thought, We need a plucked hen. Ain't I something, forgetting that? I'll get the fattest one.

She got a ham from the smokehouse too, the last one. Owen loved ham.

When she had the head off the chicken, Ellie sat and made feathers fly. The air of this Christmas Day was mild, perfect to cool things without freezing them.

Ellie jerked out a big handful of feathers.

Christmas. Another winter. In the summer, garden things gave her a pang of hope, a feeling that was otherwise gone from her life. She didn't quite know how it happened. How did I turn out like this, a crazy old lady? I was wife to a successful miller!

Their business had been good. Lew Morgan chose wisely in building the mill at this spot. Every farmer for miles around brought a little grain for grinding at Morgan's mill. Over the years the trade grew. Husband, wife, and the children were always well fed—local folks didn't have much in the way of cash money, so they traded chickens and hogs, sides of beef and flour, headcheese, butter, fresh milk, and every imaginable garden product in exchange for the milling.

Ellie went over the bird once more with her hands, feeling for even the tiniest pin feather. She whispered, "I'm going to make today perfect."

She stood awkwardly, bird in hand, and the baskets hanging on her back porch caught her eye. Herbs, they were, though dried and dead now. The baskets were arranged in such a shape, and colors painted onto their bottoms, that they made a strong hex of protection for the house. Ellie didn't have the power to make a hex like this, but her mother had made one at both of the doors, front and back, to ward off anything harmful that might come this way. Mother, God rest her soul, also knew how to do beseechings, charms, go-aways, findings, sealings, remindings, and the like. Mother was mistress of the ancient powers.

Ellie hadn't learned such power. Maybe that was why she felt so weak now. All she could do was plant the proper herbs, front and back, come every spring. But what use was warding off outside harms when something harmful lived in Ellie?

Gwen came out the back door and smiled at her. "I thought you'd like some help, Mother." Gwen didn't have any children yet, just the one on the way, and it was easier for her to get away than Betsy.

"Score the ham on the counter," Ellie instructed hesitantly. She heard her voice and wondered why she couldn't manage a normal tone to her own daughter.

Gwen disappeared into the kitchen. Ellie knew her daughters didn't like being around her much anymore. She couldn't blame them. Crazy old lady.

She thought but didn't say, Make a diamond pattern to keep the outside fat from rupturing in an ugly way. The same way each of you kids ruptured me, when you came out.

Ellie set the basin down with its chicken and limped toward the root cellar—they needed apples and pumpkins, and cheese from the springhouse, too. Oh, don't I wish we could have greens fresh from the garden and slices of ripe Indian tomatoes! When she got agitated, her arthritis bothered her and one leg didn't work right.

Back in the kitchen she looked over Gwen's shoulder. "Ham looks good," she said. "Tie up these legs and squeeze the chicken and ham into the left-hand oven. They *will* fit."

Not even Gwen's body language talked back.

"First, would you get parsnips? I forgot them."

Gwen headed for the root cellar without a word.

Ellie got bread pans out, and two canisters of flour, one white, one pumpernickel. The Welsh Morgans preferred the light, the Turleys the dark, since the mother was Pennsylvania Dutch.

She whacked the white dough flat, flat, flat. Then she realized. I've made pie dough instead of bread dough. She put it into a pie pan, mixed more white dough, balled it up and plopped it into a bread pan. She did the same for the pumpernickel and slid both pans into the other oven.

Ellie took in a big breath and let it out slowly. One tear trickled down the side of her nose. "Oh, now what?" she brayed loudly. "I have no time for this."

Lew's face flashed here and there in her brain, like lucifers spurting into flame. She always told people, truly, that he had been a good man, never beat her. They grieved together when the first child was stillborn and the last died young. They suffered together through every childhood illness of the other four. They put up with the cramped cabin until they could add a second bedroom. Though he was not educated, nor raised much of a Christian, Lew liked to tell Bible stories every Sunday evening, and she thought he walked through life as much a Christian man as most. When he died two years ago, she, well, she'd been a little off ever since. She didn't know where she'd put herself, or how long she'd been gone. And she didn't know where to begin to look.

She had no complaint about her four children. Owen was one go-getter. He'd seen several years ago that they should add a store to the mill, and trade manufactured goods for flour and cornmeal, which they sold in Pittsburgh. Now the store made more profit than the mill, and had turned the ramshackle cluster of houses and businesses into Morgantown. Ellie and her children were as prosperous as anybody, their buildings in good repair, the smokehouse, root cellar, and springhouse full of food.

Gwen? Well, Gwen would make a fine wife and mother, which was exactly what she wanted. Same with Betsy. Sam? She worried about her younger son. He wanted the book learning she couldn't give him. Where Owen loved the family business, Sam hated it. When Owen told Sam to do this or that (in Owen's bossy way), Sam just moped. He liked to roam those woods, and he learned by hearing stories and retelling them. Her mother said he was a natural-born druid, like back in Wales. Ellie was just afraid he wouldn't find a place in the modern world. But Sam was Sam. There was a hunger in him, a big ache. For what? She'd never known. She didn't understand her younger son, but she loved him. She supposed he'd search till he found . . . whatever it was.

She'd always regretted especially that Coy died. Sam loved that baby. He needed a brother, and Owen . . .

"But what about me?" she said much too loud, and was taken aback at the querulous bitterness in her voice.

She was a good wife—she scrubbed and rubbed every surface in her house, she cooked and cleaned, she bore children and reared them up good, even if she couldn't teach them book learning. She kept them healthy with wardings, the way her mother taught her. She'd wanted to do all those duties. But somehow along the way she'd scrubbed her hope in life down to a nubbin. Though she'd gone hopeless before Lew died, it didn't chafe at her then like it did now. These last two years she went about her rounds like a phantom. Her children murmured together about her, probably speculating whether she was tetched or just hadn't gotten over their father's death. "Both!" she bellowed to the empty room. Then again, softly, "Both."

All this just made today more important. She was going to do right by her first-born, however much a mother could really do that.

"Gwen, put extra cinnamon and sugar in that pumpkin filling. Owen likes it that way."

Just then Gwen came in the door with the parsnips.

They studied each other. "Oh. Well, remember, lots of cinnamon and sugar in the pumpkin pie," Ellie said apologetically.

VERY EARLY THAT same Christmas morning, going back into Eden, Sam felt like he couldn't do anything right.

When he put his foot down, seemed like a rock would turn under it. When he bent beneath the branches of a tree, seemed like a branch would flip his hat off. Thorns scratched at his eyes. Now he stepped on a patch of snow and his foot went out from under him and he landed hard on his back and his rifle butt hit a rock—CRACK!

Some way to ease through Eden silently.

What was going on with him? Hadn't he had the best day of his life just yesterday? Wasn't he going to see Katherine in just a few hours? Wasn't he doing what he liked best, hunting? He told himself he was as contented as a young man could be. Visions of Katherine danced in his head. Yep, he sure was.

Sam put his mind back on what he was doing, moving down to the creek silently. There he would wait for the deer and then the sun. His mind drifted back again to the Eve he'd gotten right here yesterday. He couldn't believe it, not yet.

Whoa! This morning was no time for dreaming. Owen had objected to Sam going into the woods on Christmas Day. Ma overruled the older brother, saying the family always needed meat in the winter. So Sam would ease up the back side of his favorite lookout, sit completely still, and deer would come to him. He would keep his mind off what happened yesterday and keep his eyes on today's deer.

SCRATCH-SCRATCH-CRACK-SCRATCH-SNAP-SWOOSH!

Sam jumped backward and fell on his butt. The Celt's barrel banged a limb.

A huge, dark blob dropped from the tree, scarier than any snake he ever dreamed. It hit the ground right in front of him and roared like the boom of thunder.

Wild with fear, Sam threw up the flintlock.

The dark blob bounded away.

Shivers ran up and down his legs and trunk and neck. Goose bumps prickled his arms.

He watched the blob run off, its hind end bouncing up and down with every step. Then he laughed. He broke the silence again with another low chuckle. Damn. A cinnamon bear! It spied Sam, but Sam, his eyes ranging the ground for deer, didn't pick out the bear in the tree, a dark ball of fur against the pearly pre-dawn sky. And then the bear's man fear overcame all, and lickety-split it rammed down that trunk as fast as falling and skedaddled. Scaring the bejesus out of Sam.

A man stood up right in front of him. An Indian. Above the bush he held a rifle, and he was grinning.

THE INDIAN SAID, "You scared off my bear."

The Indian was speaking English. For that matter, he was wearing white-man clothes, or half white and half Indian.

"You could say you're sorry." Said with a big smile, like he was one of those fellows who finds everything funny.

"I'm sorry."

The Indian stuck out a hand to help him up. Sam got to his feet without using it.

He studied the Indian. "You're not pointing that rifle at me."

"Not a bit," said the Indian.

"You're not mad."

"Some days I'm mad, some days I'm crazy, some days I'm a pretty good fellow. This is one of the pretty good days."

Sam nodded to himself. He could understand that. The Indian was much older than he was, thirty or more, fleshy-faced, tall, put together stockily.

"I was hunting that bear. Unusual to see one this late in the season. Warm winter. I played a game with myself, seeing how close I could get without spooking him, before I took the shot. He sure skedaddled away from you."

Now Sam knew what was odd, or one thing that was. The Indian spoke regular English, no accent. You didn't hear "Heap big" or "No want" from this fellow.

"What do you want with the bear?" The Indian wasn't from around here—Sam would have known him. And there wasn't much a traveling man could do with hundreds of pounds of bear meat.

"My folks live up the river, below the ferry." That was a couple of hours' walk. "They need the meat."

"Old man MacKye?" MacKye—pronounced to rhyme with *sky*—was a white man, his wife a squaw, Delaware as Sam recalled. Because of that, no one really knew them.

This Indian—Delaware, apparently—nodded and stuck out his hand again. "Hannibal MacKye."

Sam stopped gawking long enough to shake it. *Hannibal*? A Delaware?

"The usual way is to say your own name," said MacKye, grinning again.

"Sam Morgan."

"I know. Saw you here yesterday. Knew your pa a little."

"You were here yesterday?"

"Scouting for that bear. You ran him off two straight days."

Sam felt his flesh go hot and knew he must be the color of a tomato. Yesterday he and Katherine, he and Katherine . . .

"Nothing wrong with young love," said the Delaware. "Good sight to see, matter of fact."

Sam kept flushing, and it all flooded back on him, the looks, the feelings, the touches, the heating of the senses. *Our first time together. Oh, Katherine . . .*

"Want to smoke?"

At first Sam thought maybe the Delaware meant a peace pipe—Sam had never done that, or even seen one for real. But the man whipped out a corncob pipe and a leather pouch and started fingering the tobacco into the bowl. He sat on one end of a boulder and Sam took the other end. Without hurrying, the Delaware readied the pipe, struck a lucifer, and got the smoke going. A lucifer—the latest thing, and from an Indian. One strange Indian.

He offered the pipe to the east, south, west, and north, and handed it to Sam.

"This smoke is a ceremony?"

"All smoking is. No big thing."

Sam puffed on the pipe and handed it back.

"Don't come tomorrow and I'll get that bear."

He could figure why MacKye was doing the hunting. Old man MacKye was *really* old. As far as Sam knew, he and his squaw had no one around to help them.

"I could take your folks some meat," Sam ventured. He didn't know why he hadn't done it before. Well, yes, he did know—the white man and his Indian wife, they weren't accepted. Squaw man, people called him.

The Delaware handed him the pipe. Sam pulled hard on it, hiding his shame behind a cupped hand.

"It would be good if you went to see them. My old man knows a *lot*. But I'll take care of the meat for a while. May I see your rifle?"

Sam handed him The Celt. The Delaware turned it over and over, inspecting. "Jacob Schmidt, a Lancaster gunsmith. I've seen this rifle before. Your father's, wasn't it?"

"He willed it to me." Only thing his father left him, but Sam didn't say that.

"I heard he passed. We made a trip together. Buffalo, to see the western end of the Erie Canal."

Sam didn't like to think about that trip. Three years ago—he was sick and didn't get to go. Owen went. "My pa and brother were keen on progress," he said. "Owen still is. You?"

"I'm curious and curiouser. I like to see what human beings decide to do, the good and the bad. You take care of that rifle. Good piece of work."

It was the only rifle in the family, a tool worth a month's wages. "I treasure it."

They looked at each other through an awkward silence. Sam felt like he'd known this man a long time.

"Why don't you take supper with me tonight?" said Hannibal MacKye. He sucked on the pipe and puffed smoke out. It shimmied upward from his face. "My camp is at the mouth of the creek."

Sam felt embarrassed again. "All right, Mr. MacKye. May I bring . . . the young lady you saw me with yesterday?"

"Call me Hannibal. Bring anyone you want. Come about sundown."

Tongue-tied, Sam nodded yes. I don't know any Indians, really. Why do I feel sheepish about this?

"You still want a deer?"

Had Sam told the Delaware he was hunting deer?

"There's two bucks over that rise, in the bottom." He nodded toward the low hill in the east.

"Thanks."

Hannibal handed him the pipe. "Offer those bucks the last of the smoke."

OWEN CAME INTO the kitchen like the man in charge, as was his way. Ellie cast a fond eye on her eldest, but she had long since lost control of her son, her self, her life. Welcome to it, Owen, she thought.

Owen marched around the kitchen. How odd it was, she thought, that for a small man, he bristled energy at you. While her youngest, far bigger, was shy and standoffish.

Owen took the lid off the pot of boiling redskin potatoes. "I'll scallop them," she assured him.

"And don't forget to sprinkle bread crumbs on top," he said briskly.

"The ham and hen are in the oven," Ellie said meekly.

"And the pies are cooling on the window sill," put in Gwen, stepping through the back door. Gwen didn't allow for Owen's bossy manner the way Ellie did. She studied Gwen's face to see if she was standing in dread too. No. That was just as well.

"Gwen, would you slice a saucer full of cheese?" Keep her busy, that's the solution. "Oh!" Ellie nearly startled herself, exclaiming like that. "I almost forgot the coffee." She got the hand grinder out and took down a canister of beans she'd roasted herself.

Owen stepped into the parlor where the grandfather clock stood. "Eleven minutes," he called. "Eleven minutes and they're here."

Ellie stifled a sob.

SAM LABORED UP the last hill as fast as he could. It's past noon, I'm sure, damn it. Owen will be upset.

He'd done the work as fast as he could. Clean head shot. Buck gutted quickly and steaming innards left on the ground. Then he shouldered it and trudged toward home, feeling guilty. He was at least an hour behind what he'd promised.

He hung the deer in the icehouse, washed at the pump, got the blood off. He stripped off his deerskin jacket outside the kitchen door and hung it on a peg, his shirt being much more presentable, and turned into the wide opening to the dining room.

They were arrayed around the gala table, the Turleys, Betsy and husband, Gwen and husband, his mother. Katherine, though, wasn't sitting with her family. She was standing at the head of the table. And holding hands with . . . Owen.

Sam's head swirled.

"Towhead," said his older brother, giving his fierce, public smile, "you have missed our great announcement." He lifted Katherine's hand high and declaimed, "Katherine and I are betrothed to be married."

Sam could see nothing in her face. She was smiling broadly at everyone in the room and no one in particular, looking at everyone in the room and no one special. Not at Sam.

Bile came up his gullet.

He tried to fix her eye, but she beamed wider and cast her gaze about the room democratically.

Words rumbled in the bottom of his brain. 'Katherine, yesterday, *just yesterday* . . . I was going to ask you to . . .' Unspoken words, ones to strangle on.

His mother poured applejack into the heavy glasses, her best.

He staggered but recovered his balance.

His mother set the jug down and stood next to him. He could feel her, willing him to be calm.

"A toast!" cried Arthur Turley. "Many happy years to the new couple, and many, many children!"

Owen led the cry of "Hear! Hear!" Only Sam and Ellie were silent, the mother looking with panic into her youngest's eye.

Sam lurched backward, tripped on the door sill, and tumbled into the kitchen. His head hit the floor with a resounding *crack*!

Ellie gasped.

Owen looked at Arthur Turley with a knowing smile. "Just like my little brother," he said, "to try and outshine me."

After a long moment of fussing with him, Ellie said. "It's not a bad cut, but I'd best put him to bed."

With her support he got up dizzily.

Anything to get out of here, he thought.

LATER, MUCH LATER, his bedroom door scraped. He blinked his eyes open. A shaft of twilight showed Katherine's figure. She closed the door and stood with her back against it. "Yesterday," she said softly, "yesterday I told you, 'That's all.' You were my first. But I meant it. I have no more to give. That's all."

She looked at him hard, stepped back through the door, and closed it.

Chapter Three

SAM SLIPPED OUT the window into the night. He could hear them all, still celebrating. He'd be damned if he'd join in. He'd be damned if he'd act sick either. He needed to roam.

He opened the porch door quietly, got his jacket, and brought down his father's rifle. Not that he knew what he might shoot at night. He also took his bundle of taffy. He crossed the yard, going around a shaft of light made by the candles—Owen was burning all the candles tonight. As he passed the parlor window, he did not look in.

The darkness made no difference to him, nor the lack of help from the new moon. He knew his way to Eden in the dark, in the light, in his dreams.

Beyond the barn he looked for the place where the bare branches of the trees showed an opening. At the edge of the wood he felt the path with his feet. He took a deep breath and let it out.

Quietly, he stepped into the forest.

Something hit his shoulder.

Sam whirled.

"Easy," said a voice he recognized. Sam realized it was a hand on his shoulder. "It's Hannibal."

"What are you doing here?"

"Waiting for my dinner guest."

Sam burst into laughter and at the same time felt tears spring into his eyes. He was glad Hannibal couldn't see his tears in the darkness.

"You missed your Christmas dinner and didn't have any supper either. Come down to my camp and eat."

Sam searched Hannibal's face, but could see it only dimly. Suddenly he was ravenous. "How'd you know I missed meals?"

"Been waiting for you. Your brother and his fiancée came outside and talked together."

So Hannibal knew. "They hug and kiss a lot?" In the chill evening Sam felt the hot blood rush to his face.

"They hugged and kissed and did more than that."

"What else did they say?"

"Nothing that matters. Let's go, I'm hungry too."

Hannibal moved out through the darkness, his feet sure on the path. Sam followed behind him uncomfortably. What the hell am I doing? They padded for ten minutes and came alongside Eden, now dark and impenetrable to the eye. Ten more minutes and they came to the river, the Allegheny, a minstrel ditty of little whooshes, gurglings, and gulps in the night, and a breath of cold air.

Hannibal's fire and lean-to were between the half-fallen-down cabin and the little dock. Staked near the fire was one of the handsomest horses Sam had ever seen, a glossy-coated sorrel, beautifully conformed, and looking like he was built to run.

Hannibal pulled the stake, moved it away from the fire, and put a feed bag on the horse. "Funny animal," he said. "He likes to look at fires."

Sam looked around. He knew this place well. Once it belonged to a Delaware Indian family, but they'd moved on before Sam was born. Owen had bought the forty acres to have a good place to build a dock, so he could float sacks of grain down to Pittsburgh. Having an interloper, even a temporary one, made Sam uncomfortable.

"This is our land," he said.

Hannibal put kindling on the fire and sat on a log before he replied. "Seems like every inch around here is owned by somebody now. Wasn't that way when I grew up. People built this cabin were my aunt and uncle, the Walkers."

"Walkers? That's a white name."

"Like MacKye," Hannibal said, and chuckled. He dipped a tin cup into the pot over the fire, drew up whatever mix was in there, and dumped it onto a tin plate. "The Walkers were full-blood Delawares, good people. Somebody gave them the name Walker as a joke, because of the Walking Purchase." He handed Sam the plate and a spoon.

Sam welcomed the diversion. "What's the Walking Purchase?"

Hannibal chuckled, and now Sam could see his teeth and eyes flash in the firelight. "Now that's a good story. When William Penn came into this country, the Leni-Lenape, the Indians you call Delawares, were a big tribe. We hadn't done the big fight with the Iroquois yet. Damned Iroquois whipped us so bad, they told the Leni-Lenape we couldn't speak of ourselves as a tribe anymore, or call ourselves men."

Sam was eating hard at the stew. The coals had done well—it was still warm.

"Anyway, we Delawares were real friendly to William Penn.

Way later, his son Thomas came up with the Walking Purchase. Claimed he'd found an old treaty said the Delawares gave William Penn a big piece of land, from the fork of the Delaware and Lehigh rivers as far as a man could walk in a day and a half. That meant as far as a good man would normally walk, maybe thirty, forty miles. But Thomas came up with a trick. He hired three fast walkers to go as far as they could, took the distance of the farthest one, and claimed all that land for himself. It was about twice as much land as the treaty meant, if there ever was any treaty. We Delawares got so mad about it, we left that part of the country and came to the Ohio River, here and on west. Raided hell out of the Pennsylvania frontier for a long time, on account of that."

Sam said, "So this was Delaware land once."

"People think land belongs to them. Some live on it a while, then they leave or get pushed off and others live on it. Sometimes the others are critters, not even men. Process goes on forever. The land ignores the ones who say they're owners, keeps on making grasses and trees and birds."

They sat in silence, eating. Sam wanted more stew, but he didn't want to eat what might be Hannibal's breakfast. Suddenly he thought, got out his birthday taffy, and handed Hannibal half.

"Ummm, dessert," Hannibal said with a smile.

"How come you dress like a white man?" He looked at his companion's outfit—pants with the crotch cut out, a breechcloth, a fine-looking cotton shirt with a pleated front, bearskin coat with the fur on, a derby hat, and moccasins—a bewildering combination.

"Since my father's white, my mother's Delaware, I dress however I want." Hannibal spooned more stew onto Sam's plate. "You want to tell me what happened up at the house?"

Sam felt his throat tighten up, so choked he couldn't eat, maybe couldn't even talk.

"Katherine got betrothed to Owen."

"The girl you were loving down here yesterday and your brother."

The two men ate in silence, then stared into the fire.

"You know they were sweet on each other?"

Sam shot the words out hard. "It was me and her, I thought it was us, we always looked at each other like . . . something special, and we . . ." The silence felt like a big lump. Then, slowly, like a question, "We did love each other down here yesterday."

"First time you did that?"

"Mmmm." Hannibal knew that meant yes.

"You didn't notice them making eyes at each other the same way?"

"She never!"

"You two make any promises yesterday?"

"Everything was plain enough."

"Maybe not. She say anything to you today, explain?"

"She came to my room. When they gave me the news of the . . . betrothal, I pretended to trip and went to bed. Later Katherine slipped into my room. What she said was, 'Yesterday I told you, That's all. You were my first. But I meant it. I have nothing more to give. *There's nothing else to say.*' "

They both pondered the words, like turning a coin over and over in your hand to feel if it's real silver.

"Sounds like she was saying, 'That's once and for all.' "

"Guess so."

They pondered that.

"I don't get it," said Sam in a hurt tone.

"Me neither."

They sat.

"Any ideas?" asked Hannibal.

"Too mad for ideas."

They sat.

"You want to hear any ideas?"

Silence. Finally Sam muttered, "I guess."

"O tiger's heart in a woman's hide."

"That the Bible?"

"Shakespeare. It means a woman can be fierce about getting what she wants."

"Does it apply?"

"Maybe. Suppose Katherine was attracted to you, or you and Owen both. Suppose, for whatever reason, she thought Owen was better husband material."

"That's stupid."

"He's older, has a good living. Her parents would point such things out to her. You're handsome, but you have a footloose way about you."

"Hmmph."

"An unmarried woman might consider herself at liberty until she's betrothed. But not after."

Sam appeared to be considering that. Hannibal thought it appealed to him.

"Then she played swift and loose with me."

"Maybe she did."

"You believe that, what you said?"

"Might be true. Might not."

They gazed into the fire.

"Any other ideas?"

"One."

"Let's hear it." Sam sniffed, and kept his head down toward the fire, so Hannibal wouldn't see the quick tears.

"Did you declare yourself?"

"No."

"Tell her you wanted her?"

"No."

"Mmmm. Let's say she felt a spark for you. But she'd made up her mind for Owen. If I guess your ways right, maybe it was because he spoke up and you didn't. Maybe because he was the more sensible choice. He won her head, you had her heart."

Hannibal let that sit. "She thought she had to tell you about the betrothal. Even though you hadn't spoken to her, she knew from your eyes how you felt, and she felt the same way. So she sought you out, privately, to tell you there in the woods yesterday. Maybe she got mixed up. Maybe she hadn't made up her mind all the way. Maybe she was beginning to feel trapped—just one man for her whole life and all that. She was afraid she was making the wrong choice. And you still didn't speak up. Maybe all those things put together."

He waited, pondered. "Anyway, when she found you yesterday, she couldn't bring herself to say it. Instead she gave in to an impulse—she kissed you. Did she start the kissing?"

"Yes."

"Her heart got wild in her. She wanted one adventure in her life, and you were it."

"Her adventure, but not her life."

"Yeah."

Sam looked up from the fire into Hannibal's eyes, and saw that his brown face was wet with tears.

"How come you're . . . ?"

"Nothing like watching people." Openly, without embarrassment, Hannibal wiped his face with his bare palms. "What do you think about that guesstulation?"

"Sounds good."

"But it's all guessing. Here's what's real. She's made up her mind and she'll stick to it."

Sam choked back a big, ugly, throat-blocking sob.

"You know that, Sam. You can drive that stake in the ground and measure from it."

Sam hid his face in his hands.

Hannibal watched the fire.

"Tell me, what do you want?"

"Katherine."

Hannibal waited. Then, "Set that down. What do you want that you might have?"

"Katherine. And . . . I want out of here."

"Because you're embarrassed in front of your brother?"

"No, I been thinking on it a long time. This country's changing. My pa, he took me into the woods to teach me the ways, help me see how things work. All this land, its shapes, its waters, its critters . . . I liked that.

"Know what? Not so much of it left. More people moving in, chopping down the forest to make fields, using the word 'wilderness' for what feels like home to me. Pittsburgh is cutting the hills away for coal mines. A man even built a blast furnace there. When the Erie Canal is finished, settlers will flock in and make a civilization, they call it. Not my kind of world. More machines and more people and especially more people who work the machines, and are even turning themselves into machines."

Sam stopped, surprised at himself. He'd never said so many words in a row all his life.

"You know what you want, then?"

"Go west. I was planning to take Katherine west. Go down the river and look around. . . . I don't know what all. I want to *go. Look.*"

Hannibal listened to the meaning behind the words. "Yes, you do. That seems not so wild a dream." Then he judged carefully and took the risk. "When are you going?"

"Real soon."

Hannibal let that sit with Sam, and then let it sit some more.

"Why don't I just go now?" Sam blurted out.

"Why not?"

Sam snorted. "Why not?" He lifted his head and looked at the infinite stars. "No reason why not."

Hannibal listened to the words and the heart behind them.

"I want to go. Now. Tonight, to the Ohio and head west."

Hannibal followed Sam's gaze into the stars. So many more stars when the moon is new.

"Oh, hell, I'm not ready."

"What do you need?"

"I don't need one damn thing!"

They searched the stars for a sign, a voice, an answer.

"I'm wearing what clothes I need. Got Pa's rifle, and my shot pouch." He went glum. "Got nothing to eat, got no money."

"How will you get to Pittsburgh?"

Sam's voice began to sound excited now. "I could take the small flatboat. I can float at night, I know the river. Boat belongs to the family, though."

"What the family owns, is it part yours?"

"Half mine, I guess."

"If you go away and leave Owen the mill, the house, the whole place, is that worth more than the boat?"

"Hundred times more."

"Then can't you honestly take the boat?"

"And sell it in Pittsburgh. Are there flats and keels heading downriver now?"

"Always are. And always a way when you aim for what you want."

"By God. By God." Sam searched Hannibal's face. "Am I crazy to do this? Do it right now? Tonight?"

"Everything worth while is crazy, and everyone on the planet who's not following his wild-hair, middle-of-the-night notions should lay down his burden, right now, in the middle of the row he's hoeing, and follow the direction his wild hair points."

But Hannibal saw he'd lost Sam's attention. The young man was thinking of . . . Pittsburgh? The river? Boats? St. Louis? New Orleans? Katherine?

Hannibal stood up. "I'm going to bed now. Up early to get that bear." He padded to the lean-to. "Here's some dried meat for when you get hungry." Hannibal handed Sam an oilcloth wrapped around brittle sticks of meat.

He stepped to the good-looking horse, took the feedbag off, and stroked its muzzle.

"It's a clear night," Hannibal went on. "You won't get rained on. Here's an extra blanket." He tossed it to Sam. "Use it while you sit by the fire and think. Or sleep in it tonight and go home in the morning.

"If that's not your true home, set out to find it. If you go, tell people on the river you know me, especially in St. Louis. Take the blanket with you. That and the meat are my gifts for your adventure."

He squatted and lit his small lantern. He rolled into the lean-to, wrapped himself in his thick, wool blankets, and fished his book out of his carry bag. Out of the corner of his eye he watched the young man sit gazing into the fire. He wondered what Sam Morgan saw in those prophetic tongues of flame. Then he opened *Don Juan* and tried to concentrate on it. He liked the rhymes of this Lord Byron.

Sam sat. He stared. He thought about it. Then he stopped thinking, and only sat and stared. Before long he knew.

He rose and stretched limbs stiff from sitting too long, and from the cold. He jumped up and down lightly on the balls of his feet. He gathered the blanket, dried meat, and rifle and strode down to the dock.

The blackness was almost perfect, but Sam knew the boat. He brought it flat against the dock, wrapped the Celt in the blanket, tied thongs around the oilcloth, and stowed them both behind the middle seat. He looked back at the forest where he grew up, then shook his head. His mind was already on forests of the future.

On the bank, from behind the horse, Hannibal MacKye stood watching.

Sam took the big step into the bottom of the boat, and flinched at the thump of his own foot. He walked to the bow and untied the painter, a knot he'd tied himself dozens of times. He took his seat in the middle and unshipped the oars.

Then he noticed. Before he'd taken a stroke, the current gently pulled him away from the dock, the haven his family owned. It drew him away from the bank, the place he'd lived all his life.

Without any effort on his part. When he'd got ready, something pulled him.

He took several strokes toward the current, the river's muscle.

On the bank Hannibal MacKye listened to the rhythmic creak of Sam's oars, once, twice, three times, forever. His lips murmured a language he did not speak often enough anymore, his mother's language, a prayer for the well-being of a young man off on the adventure.

Chapter Four

IT ALL FLOODED in on Sam, hard. The sour smell of ale, beer, and whiskey. Of sodden sawdust. Of a hundred dirty, sweating bodies, white, red, and black. Of clothes seamed with perspiration from laboring backs and arms and legs for weeks, unwashed. Of sooty oil burning in the lanterns hung high overhead. Of smoke from leaky stove pipes. Of stew bottom-burned on the stove. The brew of smells was almost stomach-turning.

The sound was a low rumble, like standing next to a shoal. The ingredients were the sounds of normal conversation, the tinkle of coins, the cry of toasts and mugs clanking against each other, the soft snick of cards dealt from a rough hand, the anger of arguments, the bray of boasts, threats, and rancor.

It was a topsy-turvy sight. A seething jam of men lifting their mugs and glasses, staggering, gesticulating, throwing darts at a circle on a board, gambling at cards, bumping, crowding, and clapping backs. Bed rolls thrown against the walls, many men's beds for the night. Doors to rooms where the better-off slept, always two to a bed, often strangers.

A rank air of roughness about the drinkers, men who would be found at night in any waterfront dive, added a sense of hazard. Something about that Sam liked.

It was his first time in a tavern. To make the adventure more delicious, it was a waterfront tavern, the roughest sort.

Two dollars and twenty-five cents nestled in his hunting pouch—most of a week's wage for those foolishly willing to hire themselves out. He was following his wild hair, as Hannibal said. Tonight he meant to find out what ale tasted like. Or beer. Or whiskey. Or all three. Everything stretched out in front of him, all of life, to be slurped up.

He went toward several planks that were slapped across barrels to make a crude counter. Behind the planks and in front of the casks was a man wearing an apron and exchanging drink or food for coin. He was doing a lot more business in drink, from the look of it. Sam traded a half dime for his first mug of ale.

He turned to find a round, cherubic gray-haired man smiling up at him from a seat at a barrel serving as a table. The round fellow and his hulking companion sat on kegs. "Come," said the aging cherub, "join us."

Sam said to himself, 'Why not?' and did.

"Grumble is my name," said the round man, sticking out a cordial hand. "This here's Hiram, another new friend."

Sam propped The Celt between his legs to free his right hand and shook with both of them, mumbling his name. Then he tried his first sip of ale. Thick, yeasty, nutty—not half bad.

"Are you from here?" asked Grumble with an amiable smile.

"Near," said Sam, "but I'm on my way . . . somewhere else."

"Where to?"

"Wherever the river takes me." Sam was feeling his freedom.

"Young or old, a man should have some adventure," allowed Grumble. "I'm headed down the river myself."

Sam saw now that the cherub wasn't a small man at all, in fact was substantial, but his size was round-about instead of up and down. Grumble's hands drew Sam's attention. They were small, delicate-looking, and wonderfully clean, with clipped and polished nails. Grumble had a bald head with a monkish fringe of hair and a grandfatherly smile. Sam put him at about fifty.

Hiram, on the other hand, was a monster, well over six feet, bear-built, and hairy as a bear too.

"Hiram and I are playing a little game," said Grumble. He showed three face cards, gentleman, lady, and boy with a hoop, and began to shuffle them. His shuffling was so clumsy that Sam realized he must be arthritic, or his hands somehow crippled. He interleaved the cards slowly and painfully. Then he spread them on the barreltop facedown. "Go at it, Hiram." Aside to Sam he said, "Hiram wins by picking the boy with a hoop. For a half dime."

Hiram and Grumble plunked half dimes next to the cards. Hiram reached out and tapped one card with a huge, hairy hand. Grumble turned it over. The lady.

Merrily, Grumble turned over the boy with a hoop, which was the middle card. "Hiram, you've got to keep an eye on that boy." Clumsily, he picked up the two half dimes.

This time Sam watched carefully as Grumble shuffled. Keeping track of the boy with a hoop was easy, the dealer's hands being so slow and fumbly.

This time Hiram picked the gentleman.

Sam knew where the boy was, and sure enough, Grumble showed it, before collecting the half dimes.

They played another hand, and this time Hiram won.

"Mind if I try it?" said Sam.

"Welcome to it. Both of you. Win and you play again. Lose and the other man gets a turn."

Sam put down his half dime. "No bet until you've caught on to the game," Grumble said.

He watched carefully as Grumble shuffled the cards. When the cherub laid them out, Sam knew right where the boy with a hoop was, and picked it out with a grin.

"Very good," said Grumble. He picked the cards up clumsily and began to reshuffle.

Sam put the half dime back down. "For real this time."

He followed the boy through his changes again, and when Grumble laid the cards down, reached straight to the youngster.

"Impressive," said Grumble.

Sam picked up Grumble's half dime and left his own. His concentration got even sharper now. If this old man thought he was going to cozen a rube . . . Sam's eyes followed the boy with a hoop through Grumble's awkward shuffle like he was a gold dollar. Right in the middle it went.

Except that it was the gentleman.

Grumble giggled like a school child as he swept away one half dime. "Your turn," he said to Hiram.

"I need a drink," said the big man, as he got up and stepped to the improvised bar.

Grumble cocked an eye at Sam.

Glad of the chance, he plinked down his half dime.

He lost it.

And the next one.

And the next.

Sam was frustrated. Grumble was shuffling those cards slow as can be with those cripped-up hands of his. This wasn't a hard game. Sam just had to sharpen up his eyes. He put down another half dime and concentrated.

He lost it.

Sam looked challengingly into Grumble's eyes. "You're running a streak of bad luck," the elderly cherub said. "Perhaps you should take a . . ."

Just at that moment a man as big as Hiram loomed between them. "Sam Morgan?" he said in something like the voice of God.

Before Sam could open his mouth, Grumble said mildly, "This is my son, Jonathan Grumble, Constable." Sam noticed the fierce glint in Grumble's eye, but the The Voice seemed to miss it. "What business could you have with us?"

Now Sam saw the badge of office pinned to the man's waistcoat and the pistol held high and pointed toward the ceiling. He also saw a squat constable and a tall, thin constable behind The Voice. The squat man also held a pistol high, and surveyed the room against danger. Sam kept his mouth shut.

"What's your name, boy?" rumbled The Voice.

"Jonathan Grumble," Sam replied without hesitation. He saw Grumble's eyes smile at him.

"You fit the description of one Sam Morgan," said the officer. Then to his companion officers, "You think so?"

"Absolutely."

"Yep."

"Jameson, go get Carter." The tall, skinny one left. The squat one kept eyeing the room. "I have a warrant for the arrest of Sam Morgan, sworn out this afternoon by Owen Morgan."

Sam felt his blood rise. Owen?! Out to get me arrested?

"That's nothing to do with us, Constable," Grumble put in smoothly. "We're just having a drink in peace."

"You from Pittsburgh?"

"Just passing through," said Sam.

"How'd you get here?"

Grumble shook his head slightly and Sam took the cue not to answer.

"Flatboat, was it? A fourteen-foot flatboat rowed down from Morgantown? One you stole from Owen Morgan?"

Sam thought, Damn you, Owen. But he didn't say a word.

Watching Sam's face, Grumble saw the truth.

"Let me see that rifle," ordered the Constable.

"You have no call for that," said Grumble quickly. "It would be an unreasonable search."

"He even quotes the Constitution," mocked The Voice. He instructed the squat constable, "Show him what that means to us."

The man ripped The Celt out of Sam's hands before Sam could even flinch.

Over Squat's shoulder Sam saw Hiram give him a wink.

While Squat held the butt in front of him, The Voice read the engraving on the plate aloud. "Jacob Schmidt, Lancaster, gunsmith. That's the information we have."

"Give that rifle back," Grumble snapped. "You have no right . . ."

The Voice slapped his face so hard Grumble's keg rocked. "Speak when you're spoken to," he said. He held up the pistol and glared menacingly.

Half the eyes in the room were now on The Voice. The barkeep was fixed on him.

Grumble started standing up. To Sam the constable said, "What caliber is this rifle?"

As Sam opened his mouth to lie, Grumble whacked the constable's arm upward like a club. The man's pistol sailed away.

Hiram kicked The Voice ferociously in the tailbone. The man flew forward and plowed sawdust with his nose.

Leaping at Squat, Sam seized The Celt at both ends and turned it hard full circle. The short constable hollered out in pain.

At that instant Jameson barged in the door with another officer and the man Sam had sold the boat to, Carter. The officers were shouting, "That's the culprit! Hold him!"

Grumble stepped between Voice's legs, cocked a foot far back, and kicked him smack in the balls. Voice made a pig squeal of anguish.

Hiram grabbed Squat by the seat of the pants and the shirt collar and threw him through the air into the middle of a table where men were playing euchre. Cards, mugs, glasses, and men scattered in all directions, sloppy with ale, beer, and whiskey.

Two of the euchre players attacked the intruding Squat. The other two went after Hiram, who appeared to welcome their entry into the fracas.

Any number of men swarmed on the incoming officers. "Throw the damned law out," somebody yelled.

Grumble grabbed Sam by the sleeve. "Run!" he growled.

Sam followed Grumble, ducking under the improvised bar. The barkeep was lifting a handsomely polished walnut club and showing his teeth fiercely. Swiftly he pointed to the left and back.

"In your debt!" yelled Grumble. The barkeep rolled into the turmoil with a fighting grin. "I'll get the booly dogs," he growled.

Sam and Grumble ran past the casks of liquor, through a hall with a desk, and out a back door into the night.

"Wharf!" shouted Grumble.

Through the dark streets they charged toward the Allegheny, stumbling, sprinting madly, and stumbling some more. Occasional bars of light angling out windows showed the way.

The wharf area was darker even than the town. Grumble caught Sam's sleeve and led him nimbly between stacks of barrels and boxes toward the water. Soon they clambered into a rowboat. Several quick strokes and it was under a dock. Dexterously, Grumble tied the painter around a piling.

They settled into the bottom of the boat, rocking on the river and scraping against piles deep in the shadows of the dock. Breath came easier to Sam.

Grumble whispered, "Fun, wasn't it? For now they'll be searching. Best get comfortable."

"What's a booly dog?"

"Rough talk for a police officer."

Sam scooched down into the bottom of the boat. It was going to be a long night. He slid back up onto the seat. Damn, the water in the boat's bottom was cold.

By a shard of light from town he could see Grumble had settled all the way to the floorboards, water and all. "Miserable doss, isn't it?"

"What's a doss?"

"Rough talk for a bed."

Sam wasn't sure he wanted to learn rough talk. But he settled down into his wet, cold doss.

"ONLY THE YOUNG sleep like the dead."

Those words woke Sam. He didn't think he'd slept at all. His whole back side was cold, stem to stern. He shook his head and rubbed his eyes against the dawn light.

"Behold, lad." Grumble was doing something with his fingers. "And learn." Now Sam could see. The cherub had a coin in each hand, held between fourth and fifth fingers. Then he slipped each coin merrily from fifth-fourth to fourth-third, then to third-second and second-thumb. And back, without dropping either coin, or even hesitating.

Sam caught on, but Grumble continued the demonstration. He held up a deck of cards and shuffled them as nimbly as ever anyone saw. Then he made them shoot through the air from one hand to another like a flock of ducks in close formation. He did another trick or two Sam had never seen. The man could do anything with a deck of cards.

"Sorry for the deception, young Sam. If we're going to be fugitives together, we should be honest with each other."

"Who are you anyway? What are you?"

"I am a man of many names. If I had a title, it would be trickster."

"Way you took my money wasn't honest."

"I hope you learned something, gambling with strangers."

Sam felt peevish. "You take Hiram's half dimes too?"

"He was my shill." When Grumble explained this, Sam began to see humor in the situation.

"How about giving my money back?"

"Better, don't you think, if I teach you to survive in this half-crazed underworld you know nothing about? That's worth more than a few half dimes."

"Don't want to be a card sharp."

"You'll find I have knowledge far more valuable than that. For instance, how are we going to get around the law now?"

"Guess I'm in pretty big trouble."

"Owen Morgan—is he your father or your brother?—probably would have dropped the theft charges. But the constabulary doesn't take lightly to assaults on officers or resisting arrest."

"How come half the men down there helped us? Wasn't their fight."

"Ruffians. They hate all authority. Once you were the coppers' enemy, you were their friend."

"Still . . ."

"Still, we must take measures. Do you truly want to go down-river?"

Sam regarded his new friend. "Nothing could suit me better."

"We'll both use my escape hatch," said Grumble.

Chapter Five

IT WAS THE movement that woke Sam. At first he didn't know what it was. He'd slept a couple of hours, maybe more, and the noise and bustle didn't wake him. Plenty of loud activity—the crew hauling the downstream cargo on board the keelboat, flour, salt, iron, bricks, barrel staves, and more, in crates and barrels. Chairs, tables, rugs, brooms, beds, tick mattresses, uncrated. He'd tried to wrap his mind around the idea that someone might need to buy this paraphernalia from a boat, of all things, but he wasn't up to it.

What woke him up?

Fortunately, Sam and Grumble didn't have to help with the loading. In the dawn light Captain Stuart had swept the fugitives to the back of the roofed hold, well out of sight of the constables, and told them to lay low. Which Sam did until now, when the movement itself woke him, teased his mind out of sleep and into awareness of . . . he didn't know what.

He stood up and stretched. His body creaked, stiff from his awkward position in the rowboat. And his bones still felt chill from the water. Next to him Grumble's wide back and butt made a wall. Grumble was rummaging in a trunk next to them. "You travel with luggage?" Sam asked through a yawn.

"Tools of my trade, lad. You'd be surprised what I carry."

"Up your sleeve?"

"Among other places."

Sam got to his knees and peered into the trunk. A fiddle case. A dozen decks of cards. At least two wigs. A pile of official-looking papers. Stacks of clothes, including at least one woman's dress. "The boat has been my hotel for a couple of days."

"What's in the fiddle case?"

"A fiddle. You needn't be suspicious of everything. And drop the Friday face. I got you out of a pickle."

"What's a Friday face?"

"Hangings are on Friday."

The boat lurched, and Sam knew what motion woke him up.

Sam picked up The Celt and walked through the stacked barrels and bricks and out into the sunlight—the noon sunlight, it turned out. The sun had climbed only halfway up the sky from the south. It glinted sharp off the water—he visored against it with a hand.

Right now they were floating past the Golden Triangle, a piece-of-pie-shaped point of land where Fort Pitt sat in the midst of a clutter of streets and businesses and homes. Just ahead the Monongahela joined the Allegheny from the left to make the Ohio, one of the two great rivers of the United States. Four men pushed hard on the great sweeps mounted starboard and larboard on the cabin roof, shoving the boat from this slow water into the current. Captain Stuart was at the helm, and another man in front keeping lookout. The eddy line jostled the big craft, and the main current swept them away from the wharf and toward the wedding of the waters.

A great voice roared behind them. "You son of a bitches, get back here. You son of a bitches . . ."

Sam jumped, it sounded so close.

"Tethered men complain when free men rise and go," said Grumble, stepping up beside Sam. He waved off-handedly back toward the shore.

The Voice stood there, the sun flashing off his badge of office. He gesticulated wildly. "Stop them, they're escaping," he boomed.

Grumble waved sweetly, almost like a girl. "We'll miss you too."

Captain Stuart walked up smiling. "Leave off, boys. You wouldn't want to find warrants for your arrest in Cincinnati or Louisville."

He strode into the shade of the hold and was back in a moment. "Mr. Grumble says you never let go of that rifle." He stuck out a hand to Sam. Earlier they hadn't introduced themselves properly. "Sly Stuart, captain and merchant navigator of this vessel."

Sam shook his hand, hoping he'd eventually learn what "merchant navigator" meant. Captain Stuart looked a fine figure of a fellow, the sort of man who bears himself like he's in uniform even when he's not, and he carried a don't-mess-with-me look. "My father heired the rifle to me, Sir," he said. "Sir" didn't feel comfortable on his tongue. He hadn't often said it.

"You might get a chance with it. We got another man, though, says he can shoot a bee on the fly and clip just a wing off."

Sam felt better when Grumble and the captain laughed at this.

"What's your name, towhead?" He touched his hand to the top of his short-billed sailor's cap. The gesture made it look like he had papers or something else hidden in the cap.

"Sam Morgan, sir. Not towhead."

Stuart smiled at this. "Sam, you are on board the new flatboat *Tecumseh*. We stop to deliver and pick up at several cities, and we'll make port in New Orleans in about a month."

Sam was just glad to be on a flatboat, now a river man, ready to work his way up toward alligator horse.

"Mr. Grumble is signed on as the boat's cook," said the captain politely. "We have myself, a pilot, four deckhands, and Mr. Grumble. Cook of salt pork and burned bread, if experience tells."

"And what's my job, sir?" Sam asked.

"Job?" The captain looked embarrassed. "You don't have a job. You're our paying passenger."

Sam flushed. A passenger, not a river man? He searched for Grumble's eyes, but the round trickster was staring off in another direction, any other direction, Sam guessed. "How much am I paying you?"

"Two dollars to Cincinnati."

"Two dollars? That's every cent I've got."

"Mr. Grumble and I determined that before we decided on the fee. Not bad for a fugitive."

"You searched me?!" He fished in his hunting pouch with two fingers. He pulled out a note instead of the coins. He opened the note and stared at it. "Can't read." He handed it to the captain.

Without taking it, Captain Stuart said in a don't-challenge-me mode, "It promises you passage and room to Cincinnati for the two dollars, and further without charge, if you contribute by hunting."

Sam regarded Grumble, but saw only his back.

"Or we can give you to the constables," said the captain.

"God love the booly dogs," said Grumble.

Sam was thinking, I'm going to get even with Owen.

"I'm not getting paid either," said Grumble.

"Can you hunt?"

"I can," Sam said sullenly.

Captain Stuart smiled like that was that and strode away, and suddenly Grumble was facing Sam.

"You got some nerve!" Sam exclaimed.

"Enough to rescue both of us from the clutches of the law."

"I wish we were going to St. Louis."

"You seem stingy with gratitude."

Sam gave him a sharp look. "St. Louis seems the new world, New Orleans is the old."

"I confess I look only for opportunities to practice my craft."

"How'd you know I could hunt?"

"A shrewd guess," said Grumble, "and the way you never let go of that rifle. Even if you can't, you'll be a long way from Pittsburgh when the captain puts you off." He winked and walked away.

"Try not to get us in water that's too damn deep," Sam called after him.

But he wasn't really angry. A start in the river trade. A chance to be a hunter, what he loved best in the world. Hunting the grounds of Virginia, Kentucky and Ohio, which he'd heard tales about his whole life. Going to New Orleans on a flatboat.

Sam walked to the larboard beam. The four men on the sweeps were pushing the boat into the main current. Sam walked up along the bow. "My name's Sam," he said to the little fellow.

"I'm Frenchy, the pilot," he said cheerfully. He wore a red flannel shirt and a black sailor's cap—looked like the outfit was practically a uniform for the crew. "Zis is easy water so ze captain steers and I keep lookout."

"How much we keep a lookout?"

Frenchy looked at Sam with surprise. "Always. Snags, rocks, bars, everything to watch for."

"Damn. This happen much?"

"Oh, ze river, she is a temperament. You take your eyes off her, she slap your face. But look at zis boat, brand new. A beauty, no?

Stout capstan and snubbing posts, new hawsers, gouger" (here he patted the short oar next to him), "thirty-five-foot sweeps." He pointed to the huge oars manned from the top of the hold. "Truly a beauty."

It looked like a huge, floating freight wagon to Sam.

In front of the hold was a big box of sand where Grumble was bending over something. "Playing in the sand?" Sam asked.

"We cook in the sand." He looked up. "Or burn the boat down."

"Rest your oars!" cried the captain.

The men stopped their work. The leveled sweeps dripped into the river, which was picking up speed. All eyes focused ahead. Sam hurried to the bow.

"Watch while we marry," cried Frenchy happily. "Alleghen' wed Monongahela. Which you think the boy, which the girl? Anyhow, union makes Ohio River."

Both currents churned angrily. At the moment they came together, Sam felt a stomach-swooning drop, a fierce rise, a bigger, faster drop, and a huge spank of hull against water. Whoa—even a river wagon this big could jostle and bounce.

Then he felt something take hold of them.

"Earth's big power, rivers. You feel?" He smiled like a comrade at arms. He held up both biceps and flexed them.

Sam looked intently at the current. He hadn't imagined it, this power, this elemental energy.

"It take you forward or it take you under." Frenchy made a diving motion with his right hand, rolled his eyes, and closed them.

The river slammed the hull on one side, the bow heaved sideways, and Sam fell down to one knee.

Frenchy laughed and bounced on his sailor's legs.

Sam got up and grinned at Frenchy. Then he looked into the wild waves. He looked ahead, westward.

"Oh where does ze river carry us?" cried Frenchy melodically.

"To the west? To money? To trouble? To love? To life? To death? O, to ze boatman it is all ze same." He sang merrily—

"Den dance de boatman dance,
O dance de boatmen dance,
Dance all night till broad daylight,
Go home wiz ze gals in de morning."

The river sang back in an unknown language, boiling and gurgling and whooshing, but gave no answer to Frenchy's question.

THE CAPTAIN ESTABLISHED a routine immediately. The men slept on the open deck and rose at first light to Grumble's breakfast of a gruel made with cornmeal and salt pork, which Frenchy called *sagamité* and claimed was the only breakfast a boatman could do a day's work on. They washed it down with the first of three "fillees" of whiskey the captain issued every day. (Sam drank one and sold two for a dime.) After they heaved the boat into the strongest part of the current, the men were at their leisure, except for the steersman and the lookout. The four deckhands took turns on lookout. The captain and Frenchy split the day on the tiller; most of the time all but steersman and lookout were idle. They lunched (more cornmeal gruel), lounged, told stories, and played cards. The games might have been exciting, but the captain forbade Grumble to play, not wanting fights among his crewmen.

The profanity was prodigious. Sam heard all sorts of words he didn't know. Even more, he heard them used in wild style, so that they tickled him and made his ears smoke at the same time. He hesitated to use them, but something in him wanted to try everything new, at least once.

He liked the boat and the days of floating except for one thing. The crew spat tobacco everywhere. Captain Stuart, who abstained, cursed at them continually—"You damn Kentucks, spit overboard."

The Kentucks (that seemed to be what American flatboatmen were called, no matter where they came from) made a point of ignoring him. Not in a bad spirit—with big grins. But the chaw made the boat a sticky mess.

"You can' do not'ing wiz Kaintocks," said Frenchy.

"Damn joskins," said Grumble, looking at a gob on his shoe sole.

Sam had figured out that a "joskin" was a country bumpkin.

Sudden troubles would rouse everyone to hard work—row out of bends or out of eddies, do crossings, and especially make landings. When the lookout saw they were headed for a snag, he would sing loudly, "There's a big rock in the river." The melody sent the crew to the sweeps. The steersman would yell, "Push her out, push her out!" and turn the bow the way he wanted to go. All four hands would double-muscle the boat off the snag, to one side or the other. When an eddy caught them, they'd crawfish out in a like way.

The constant issue was running aground. When that happened, they loaded as much cargo as they could into the skiff to float the boat higher; or dug out a deeper channel by hand; or just pushed like hell. Frenchy said some captains waited for a little rise in the river, but Stuart had no patience for that.

Sam understood. He didn't want to wait to find his life, wherever it was.

He pitched in on all this work, trying to show the cap'n he would make a worthy hand.

An entertaining distraction during a typical day's float was a steamboat coming upstream, and a fine blast on the tin horn of each craft. Stuart, though, cursed the steamboats in his beard as they passed, and said they were taking his business. They'd put the keelboats mostly out of business already. Though steamboats couldn't compete with flatboats for moving freight downstream cheaply, they had the passenger traffic and the upstream freight.

Sometimes another flatboat would come up on them while they were run aground, or tied up. Usually the boat drifted on by, the crews howling at each other like wolves or Indians for fun. Ned, a wiry Kaintock with a sly wit, liked to yell out something like, "I am an Ohio River snapping turkle. I have the teeth of an alligator, the claws of a bear, and the devil's tail. By God I can whip *any man* on your boat." Plus his curse words. Replies came back in kind. Though Sam mostly couldn't make out the actual words, he didn't need to.

As the boat passed by people on the banks, the Kentucks would cry out greetings, sassy sayings, and offers of king-sized love to any woman in view. At night sometimes settlers would come down to the boat. The crew liked the visits, because the hands wanted women to dance with, any women. Sam looked through the settlers' eyes and saw what they saw in the boatman's life—leisure, pleasure, fiddling, dancing, good talk, and fun. They didn't see the hard work of sweeping, crossing, avoiding snags, landing. They missed the endless meals of corn gruel, didn't suspect the Scotch-Irish itch, as what you got from lice was called. No wonder the young sons of farmers along the way hated their work in the fields, and dreamed of escaping to the freedom of the rivers.

Sam loved the river, hardships and all.

The hard part was the drunkenness. Besides their three fillees a day, two giant brothers, Elijah and Micajah, tapped a ship's keg of corn whiskey and drank at will. Sam suspected the captain knew it, but also knew he was powerless to stop it. The fourth sweep man, with the giant brothers and Ned, was Lam. Somehow he was never sober, and once pitched into the river when he was supposed to be on lookout. He nearly drowned.

And the threat of violence. Elijah and Micajah were talkative and silent, respectively. The only times they both talked was to brag about the brawls they'd won. Both kept their thumb-nails oiled and trimmed sharp as a hawk's claw. Sam asked Elijah why. He answered, "I like to feel fur a feller's eye-strings and make him tell the news."

Somehow Stuart kept this rough crew working for a common goal, getting the boat downstream, delivering goods, picking up goods, buying merchandise for sale at a higher price downstream.

"You're a Scots trader," said Grumble, "and a good one."

"Not truly a Scot," said Stuart. "Took the name of the trader I worked for."

Grumble raised an eyebrow that said he wanted the rest of the story, but Stuart stopped there.

"You have the Scottish urge to build an empire, though."

"I damn well do."

A couple of hours before sunset Frenchy would say what a good tie-up spot would be for the night. The captain would check the river bible, Cramer's *Ohio and Mississippi Navigator*, but Frenchy's mind held the river even better than the book.

Landing was a job. Basically, two hands rowed a skiff to shore above the camping spot and hitched off a two-hundred-foot line snubbed on the capstan. The line swung the boat into the eddy, which brought her slowly up and toward shore. Finally they secured her with another taut line.

The crew liked to eat immediately on landing and while away the evenings lazily. What Sam wanted, though, was to feed himself from Grumble's kettle earlier and spend the late afternoons wandering the woods. The first two days it was Pennsylvania on both sides and the sorts of forest Sam was used to. The next ten days or so Ohio was river right, Virginia river left. Hills on both sides hid woodlands that rolled and climbed and stretched away for hundreds of miles north and south, and were a hunter's dream. Sam brought back as much of the flesh of turkeys, deer, and squirrels as the men could eat. The hunting divided itself between Sam and the giant brothers. Elijah had a shotgun and brought down ducks, geese, pigeons, and doves; but he troubled only with what he could shoot from the boat. Micajah got inspired to string fixed lines with hooks into the water and catch catfish, perch, and buffalo fish. One night the two brothers used the skiff and gigged a huge turtle that

Grumble turned into good soup. Sam thought he was far outdoing them in providing meat. Once, though, so many passenger pigeons flew over the boat that they blotted out the sun, and Elijah felled a dozen.

Sam would come back to camp about dark, seldom empty-handed, and join in the relaxation time. It was an odd little group for fun. The giant brothers, Elijah and Micajah, stayed around the sand box and helped themselves to the coffee pot and whiskey keg and seldom spoke. Sam was too shy to talk, and even slept on the bank, away from the others. Since Captain Stuart held himself apart, this made four of eight silent. Lam, a Kentucky man, constantly got card games started and always lost money. Ned, the wiry Pittsburgher, often begged to have a dance, even with other men as partners. Sam often asked himself, looking at these men, What do they want? What do they care about? What's their hunger? It must be more than lots of whiskey and an occasional woman. But he could never tell what it was. He went to sleep every night nursing his own hunger. He didn't know what he yearned for either.

An evening's entertainment usually turned out to be Frenchy, telling stories of his years as a Canadian boatman and a *hivemant*, a man who went into the vasty Canadian wilderness and stayed the winter. His stories were fun, and Sam remembered lots of them for years. One evening the cap'n pitched in with a story, with himself as the hero:

"One evening, just dark, I was hurrying to camp along a deer trail, within smelling distance of the river. Wasn't so late, I would never been careless and not noticed that big shadow on a low branch of a tree reached right across the path. By the time I saw the panther, he was in midair, leaping right at my face, them big claws reaching for my neck and his mouth wide open for my head. Wasn't nothing I could do. I jammed my whole arm down that panther's mouth and gullet, clear to where I grabbed his tail. I jerked as hard as I could and turned that critter inside out. Then he was leaping back onto the branch. He sat there, looking confused, with his innards showing, and his whiskers sticking out between his teeth. I walked calm-like away."

All this was Sam's first chance to soak himself in the comradeship of men, with their ways and their talk not softened for women. He thought seldom of Katherine, or of Owen's lies and betrayals. He got to hunt day after day, without interruption, alone, learning and seeing. He got to spend day after day lounging on the deck of a boat, enjoying the restless, relentless motion of the river and the warmth of the sun. He got to see new country every day, hour after hour, bend after bend. Living like this was his dream. At least part if it—he was always hungry for something more.

He stood on the bow, looking downstream. The river glinted in the westering sun, and the river narrowed and funneled its vast, subsurface energy into a nearly silent rush of water. The rush bore hundreds of boats and thousands of men and ton upon ton of freight implacably westward, westward, westward.

Pull, pull, pull, river. But where?

Something crouched ahead somewhere, over a horizon, or beyond the turn of a year. He wanted to get there and face it.

TWILIGHT. STILL EVENING air. A nameless creek melding quietly into the Ohio. Blue shadows from the great trees on the west bank. A shimmery light you wished would last forever.

Grumble bustled around gathering kindling for his sand box. Men tramped around the woods, gathering firewood. Sam stood on the edge of the clearing listening to the hush, and looking at the last light caught gently on thousands of soft leaves stirring in the faint breeze.

"Get me two all-nighters!" Grumble grumped at Sam. A minute

ago it was directed at the entire crew, "Leave off the kindling, you weaklings, I need some stout limbs!"

"You no are captain," Frenchy sang saucily.

Grumble drew himself up. "More important! I am the COOK!" They went through this little charade almost every night. When Grumble roared, even the captain and pilot collected wood.

"He ees lucky none of us kook good," said Frenchy, catching up with Sam from behind. "We cut him up for ze pot."

Sam mumbled something, feeling awkward. He wished he knew how to talk to the others. Everyone liked the little Frenchy—he was small, lithe, and funny.

In the half darkness the captain stood up with a limb right in front of them. It was thick as his muscly calf. He stepped to the base of a big oak.

The light shivered right in front of Sam's eyes.

THUNK!

An arrow pinned the limb fast against the oak trunk.

Frenchy dove for the nearest bush.

Sam lickey-splitted to a small tree and peeked back. He fished desperately for his knife.

Frenchy peered around, his flintlock pistol cocked. Sam would have killed for a pistol.

Captain Stuart stood calmly by the arrow and inspected it. "Very funny, Ten." The captain said, "Show yourself." Though his voice was all confidence, he was touching the top of his cap again.

A man slipped out of some bushes not ten feet behind Sam. An Indian, wearing white-man clothing. He set down his bow and arrow, reached into his hunting pouch, brought out a lucifer, and scratched it. The spurt of flame lit his face eerily against the trees and shadows. The face in the flame was doing everything it could not to laugh.

"You want to eat?" Stuart was scratching the top of his cap hard now.

"White man kill Shawnee game, no food, go hungry, demand you feed."

Now Sly Stuart couldn't help laughing. "Drop the clown act and let's eat."

Another Indian, thick as the trunk of a big tree, stepped out from behind bushes, bow raised and arrow nocked.

Sam tried to shrink.

"Very funny," repeated Captain Stuart.

EVERYONE LOUNGED ON barrels, crates, the deck, whatever was handy. Ten collected squirrels from his companion and handed five to Grumble. "Poor Injun contribute to fine white-man pot," he grunted.

"Would you cut the dumb redskin act?" said Stuart irritably. His manner was different, like suddenly he wasn't the man in charge.

That only made Ten grin bigger.

"Scrawny things hardly worth skinning out," complained Grumble.

"Nice taste next to the deer meat," Ten answered in almost unaccented English, "a little peppery." His companion, the tree trunk Indian, knelt and helped Grumble do the skinning.

Soon they sat down on the deck on either side of Sam, just like they had a right. His feet twitched a little—he'd never been so close to Indians, except for Hannibal. He'd forgotten the name of the big man on his right. He said, "What's your name again?"

"Eleven."

Sam chuckled. "Really, what's your name?"

"In English it's Eleven. In Shawnee it's . . ." and he spoke a long, incomprehensible word. "White people can't say that." He pointed to his companion. "I'm his cousin, and he's piss-ant compared to me, so I had to be more than Ten." His accent was thicker than Ten's.

Sam stuck out his hand, and Eleven shook it.

Grumble made bowls out of cups for the visitors and served everyone without distinction. The stew was soon down to the last scrapings.

Captain Stuart addressed the company at large. "There's a story in this." The style of leader and empire builder was completely gone now. "Fact is, I know Ten a lot better than I know most anyone. He's my brother. Half-brother the white way, brother the Shawnee way. In truth, brother."

Sam felt tipped into another world.

"You're the family secret," put in Ten.

Captain Stuart tried to make a silly face at him.

"I am nine years older than this little bug, thirty. Ten's family raised me."

"Wasted effort," said Ten, grinning.

The captain looked at Ten like, You going to let me tell this story or not?

"Only they were my family too. This scalawag who keeps interrupting, his uncle is Tenskwatawa. You know about him?" This to Sam, who shook his head no. "Shawnee man of medicine. Prophet, the whites called him. You heard of Tecumseh?"

"Name on the stern of the boat," Sam said. He'd heard reports of a big Shawnee troublemaker, but hadn't had the courage to ask why Captain Stuart named the boat after him.

"Great man, great leader. He and Tenskwatawa were brothers."

"Goddamn treacherous red Injun," stuck in Elijah. The giant brother was wearing his perpetual glower. Sam didn't know which was worse, his silences or his words.

"That's the last thing Tecumseh was, treacherous," the captain said evenly. Yet there was something smoldering in him that Sam couldn't figure out. "Tecumseh's word was accepted on both sides of all the troubles. He was passionately Shawnee, but also an educated man, read and wrote English. Taught me and Ten our first English." He lost a moment to the past. "We lost a great man at the Battle of the Thames."

Elijah made a half-smothered grunt.

"Ten's uncle, Tenskwatawa, he's my uncle too, he had a great idea. Shawnee should go back to their old ways, own property in common, and put down all their white ways, especially booze. Tenskwatawa had been a crazy drunk, he had a vision and reformed. Quit drinking completely."

"Pass the jug," said Ten with a broad grin. As it passed, Eleven swigged deep. The captain cast him a sardonic eye.

But then Elijah grabbed the jug away from Eleven. The giant drank deep, walked to Lam, waited for him to drink, took the jug to Ned, and last to Frenchy. He glared at the captain all the while. Ten and Eleven stared at the ground, acting like it meant nothing. Elijah finished the jug and threw it into the river.

The captain jerked his head at Grumble, and the trickster slid into the hold.

The captain took the moment to fill his corncob pipe, not deigning to address Elijah. "Even then the Shawnee had gone way white, their dress, farming, drinking, everything. And they were losing their lands to white settlers and clever treaties made up by Old William Henry Harrison, calls himself a general. Tenskwatawa and Tecumseh, his older brother, they started a new town for Indians to live this new way of the Prophet. Up there at the mouth of the Tippecanoe River, called it Prophetstown."

Grumble came back with another jug and handed it to Ten, who swigged and passed it to Eleven, who swigged and passed it on.

"Pretty quick Harrison hears about this new Shawnee prophet. He scoffs and tells the Indians, 'If Tenskwatawa is such a prophet, let him make the sun stand still, and the moon change its course.' Spring of eighteen aught six, this was. When Tenskwatawa heard Harrison's challenge, he predicted a total eclipse of the sun. It happened on June 16. Indians from hundreds of miles around come to Prophetstown then, followed Tenskwatawa's new way. Harrison damn near choked on crow feathers." The captain laughed, a good, strong haw-haw, with maybe an edge of bitterness.

"My uncle probably got word of the eclipse from somebody's almanac," Ten said lightly. "You white men are easy to fool. You assume nobody but you speaks English."

"I don't speak it," said Eleven.

"Me neither," said Ten.

"I *wouldn't* speak it," said Eleven.

The captain used two sticks to pluck a coal from the fire and dropped it into his pipe bowl. A couple of good draws and he was smoking. "Then Tecumseh, he took to spreading the Prophet's beliefs, and calling on Indians to rise up and throw the white man out. 'No more fighting among tribes,' he preached. 'All red men join together and keep the whites out of our lands.' He knew it could be done, if the Indians stuck together. He fronted that old fraud Harrison over and over and made him back down."

Stuart drew deep on his pipe, blew smoke into the night sky, and watched it disappear. "Eighteen and eleven, Tecumseh went to the South to get the Indians there to join his campaign. While he was gone, Harrison takes advantage and runs a surprise attack on Prophetstown.

"Well, even surprised at dawn, the Indians sure enough took it to the Harrison men at first. Sent a special team to kill old Harrison. In the confusion—a battle is nothing but confusion—another officer got Harrison's gray mount, and the man we killed, the Indians killed, was the wrong one. Tenskwatawa didn't fight, just sat on a hill and made medicine for his warriors."

Stuart drew in a big breath, like he was trying to drink all the sky, and let it out. "When we missed on Harrison, he rallied his men and threw us back, threw the Indians back. Tenskwatawa's men, they lost confidence in the medicine he was making. Before long it was over."

"Ain't ever over," said Ten.

Stuart threw him an impatient glance. "I was fighting next to Ten's father when he died. He bent over to help a wounded man and . . . Can't talk about it even yet."

Another attempt to drink the sky.

"The soldiers burned the village right down to the ground, with everything we owned, all the food we had stored. Tenskwatawa lost his reputation. Went to live in Canada, still up there."

"I saw my uncle when I was working in Canada," said Ten. "He's in exile. You know what, though? I took my English name, Ten, in his honor."

Stuart puffed his pipe and blew smoke into the sky, like the story had worn him out.

Finally Sam broke in with, "What about Tecumseh's plan for all the Indians to fight the whites?"

"Tecumseh lined his warriors up with the British in the War of 1812, fifteen hundred of them I heard, helped capture Detroit. Later the British retreated from Detroit, Tecumseh with them, and old Harrison got on their tails and made the British and Indians fight on the Thames when they was outnumbered near three to one. Tecumseh went under that day."

Stuart took the pipe from his mouth and slowly tapped the ashes out on his boot sole.

"But I left out what I was gonna tell, didn't I? Being kin to Ten. I fought at Prophetstown that day."

"Oughta be shot for a traitor," interrupted Elijah.

"It's ignorant asses like you make this country hard to live in," the captain said sharply. "Let's see, finish the story. I lived at Prophetstown from the start-up. My folks come up to the Mad River in Ohio from Kentucky in 1793. This was where Tecumseh and Tenskwatawa was born, Old Piqua, they called it, good place to live, some big springs. The Shawnee burned our cabin down and killed my folks for pushing into their country. That was the year after Mad Anthony Wayne whipped the Indians and put a stop to the fighting. I was a baby. I don't remember any of that, don't remember my white parents at all. Shawnees, Tenskwatawa's sister, she took me in and treated me like her own son.

"We went to Prophetstown with Tenskwatawa and Tecumseh

right at the start-up, eighteen aught eight it was. Young Ten, here, he was six or seven when we got there, making me about seventeen. Indians from all over joined up with us, thousands of them. But it all come to naught. Harrison killed the town."

He cocked his head back and looked at the moon, or the stars, or the dark gaps between them. Maybe somewhere out there were the faces of the relatives and friends he saw die that day at Prophetstown.

"After we lost the battle, my mother told me the Shawnee way was done. I should go back to the people I came from, she said. Went to work for an Indian trader, as I could speak Shawnee. He improved my English, taught me to be a white man. I'll always be grateful to him, and I took his name, Stuart. Went into flatboating with him. He owned them and I ran them as long as he lived, until last August. This is my first trip on my own." He smiled at Ten. "And now I only see my brother when he ambushes me along the river."

"Too easy," Ten said. "One day I take your scalp."

The captain flipped off the cap he always wore. He was bald from the ears up. Everyone hooted.

Ten said something fast in Shawnee, and Stuart chuckled.

"What'd he say?" asked Sam.

"Said I better not forget my Shawnee."

"We still gonna make all you whites hightail it out of this country," said Ten. "You're gonna think your boots are on fire." He raised his fist, and Eleven whooped. They were grinning.

"That time's gone," the captain said seriously to Ten.

"Time is a circle, brother, the way our people tell it. Everything comes back."

"Not in our lifetimes, or even our grandchildren's. Bi-i-ig circle."

Sam sat hunched over by his miserable thoughts. He glanced sneakily at Ten on his left and Eleven on his right. He'd broken bread with them. They seemed to be good fellows—Sam really liked Ten. Now he tried to squeeze himself smaller and not be seen, so uncomfortable were his thoughts. At last he heaved breath in and out and addressed the captain. "So you were a Shawnee twelve years. Now you're a white man. Your brother is an Indian. How does that work?"

"In this country," said the captain, his eyes gone remote again, "you are what you look like."

Sam snorted and fumed and tried to unjangle his thoughts. He slid his eyes sideways at Ten, then straightened up and looked Ten straight in the eye. "You're an Indian. You speak good English. Can you get a job? Do people accept you?"

Ten spoke in a tone of plain, simple truth. "In this country you are your color."

Sam gnawed on that.

When the fire was down to coals, the captain said he was headed for bed. The rest of the men rolled their blankets anywhere on the deck.

As Stuart walked off, Elijah said, "Goddamn Injun lover."

Captain Stuart called back, "You just come at me, Elijah. The world needs less white men like you."

Sam looked at Ten and Eleven. They didn't seem excitable about Elijah's attitude.

Elijah fumed off somewhere with his blankets. Micajah and another crewman trundled after him.

Sam's eyes followed Elijah and the others into the darkness. "Maybe," he said to Ten and Eleven, "we better bunk down together tonight. On shore."

Chapter Six

SAM STOOD WITH the sweep cocked and eyed Cincinnati. High, wooded hills cupped the town. Already ten thousand people, according to Captain Stuart, with a handful of rival newspapers and considerable pretension to respectability.

The town was built above a high, sloping bank, one group of buildings on a kind of terrace above the high bank, then a gravelly hill and above it more buildings. Sam looked across at Ten and Eleven and grinned.

Ten and his tree-trunk cousin stood beside Sam and Ned on the roof of the hold, all four holding their sweeps ready to plunge. Ten sang out a little ditty in French, and Frenchy sang back, like a chorus. Ten said he'd been a canoe man two years up in Canada, where he learned French, canoe man's songs, and he said with a wink, French girls' kisses.

Elijah and Micajah skiffed to what the captain called the Public Landing and got the long line tied to a piling on the sloping bank. On command the sweep men put to, and for the hundredth time Sam was surprised at how heavy the boat was, and how cumbersome. Step by step he forced his body forward and the sweep backward, forcing the bow into the eddy near the shore. The two currents sucked noisily at the hull, and the huge boat bounced like a stick on a wind-tossed pond.

The craft steadied as she grunted into the eddy. One more wide sweep and the upstream current had her in tow, pulling her slowly up the face of the riverfront. "Rest your oars!"

The Cincinnati riverfront was a hubbub. Two other flatboats were tied up, one steamboat, one keelboat, all moored to rough pilings.

Sam looked at Ten excitedly. Captain Stuart had said he could go into town overnight, Grumble too, the first time in a town since they'd been on the river. The men talked about looking forward to having a woman, which made Sam feel strange, since Katherine was still big in his mind. Grumble had promised Sam some fun in the taverns.

"Hard to larboard," said the captain, and swung the tiller. "Sweep right!" The bow of the big craft swung toward a big space just downstream of one flatboat and nosed toward the shore. Sam walked his sweep straight toward Cincinnati. He was excited.

"Frenchy!" shouted the captain. At the bow Frenchy began heaving on the thick line. Lam and Ned ran to help. The giants watched from where she was tightly hitched. Lam and Ned held the line on the capstan until Frenchy made fast to the snubbing post. Sam looked curiously at the hitches, only half able to believe the captain would trust the safety of the boat to these ties, no matter how thick the hawser was.

Everyone started rolling barrels to the bow. The captain had moved the barrels and crates so that Cincinnati's freight was ready to hand. The men worked quickly, eager to start their night on the town. Barrels got off-loaded, crates put onto platforms with wheels, rolled to the bow, and run down thick planks to shore. Frenchy went to let merchants know their shipments had arrived.

The riverfront was a clamor of colors, sounds, and motion, people bustling everywhere, straw bosses hollering to crews, men hoisting freight into carts, draught animals neighing and heehawing and mooing, everything and everyone going in every direction at once.

"Sam, Ten, Eleven," called the captain, "get this freight up higher." Since the barrels were hard to roll up the angled surface, they spent fifteen minutes pack-muling barrels up the incline in their arms.

When the work ended, the captain paid the hands in cash as they stepped ashore the last time. Sam noticed that the deckhands got five dollars a week for crew work. The captain probably gave Frenchy a lot more. Grumble, Ten, and Eleven walked off empty-handed. When Sam's turn came, the captain said, "Son, leave that rifle. The business folks here will appreciate it."

"I'd worry about it, sir."

"This craft will be guarded at all times. It will be safe."

Sam put it in the hold and started off, but the captain called him back.

"Here's four bucks. I fired Lam. You're hired at four dollars a week. Be back here to load at noon tomorrow." He smiled big at Sam.

"Hot damn." The feel of the dollars was good, first ones he'd ever earned. Getting to be a river man felt even better.

"Let's roll, lad," called Grumble, "let's have some sport."

Sam looked at him. Ten and Eleven waited.

Sam knew he'd have to say it. "You want me to be your shill?"

"Earn a dollar or two, boy."

Sam kicked a pebble before he looked up at Grumble. "I'd rather do something else." He cocked an eye at Ten.

"You got religion or something?" queried Grumble.

"Just want to stay clear of trouble."

"The trouble's the fun." Grumble turned his eyes to Eleven. "How about you? We play cards, you lose. You act the dumb Indian. Then they play and lose. Every five coins I earn, you get one."

"I got no problem taking white people's money," said Eleven.

As they walked off, Grumble called back, "Come to Yeatman's Tavern later, we'll have some fun."

Sam looked at Ten expectantly. "Where to?"

"I'll be your Indian guide, white boy," said Ten.

THEY AMBLED ALONG the riverfront street, which looked unsavory. They passed taverns and shops with crudely lettered signs. "You read?" asked Sam.

"No," said Ten.

"Me neither."

"I've learned to tell some words by the way they look. That one says BLACKSMITH." Sam watched the smith hammering a red-glowing piece of iron on the anvil. He studied the shape of the word above the door. He supposed he could learn the words he really needed that way. *Tavern, livery, mill,* though, you could easily tell what they were by the workings. He had a yearning to know how to read words, lots of them.

They sauntered. "Where we going?"

"I feel the juice flowing in me. Let's go to Annabelle's," said Ten.

From the outside the house was the poshest place Sam had ever seen. In Pittsburgh a lawyer or doctor would have lived in such a domicile, and the paint might not have looked so fresh. Inside, the parlor was horsehair divans, overstuffed chairs, a settee with brocade fabric, crown molding near the ceiling, a big hooked rug, an upright piano, two vases with pussy willows and dried flowers, candle sconces on the walls—Sam could hardly say what all.

"I like it here," said Ten, "because Annabelle welcomes all comers with money. Believe it or not, there's more prejudice in some of the cheap houses."

Sam wasn't listening. His eyes and mind were on Annabelle and the women she was introducing.

"This is Lily," Annabelle said in an extravagant way, her voice full of melody, her hands lively with gesture. Lily was voluptuous, and dazzlingly shown off by a low-cut gown that looked way big-city to Sam. She smiled, lowered her head, turned it, and looked sidelong at the two visitors in a come-hither way. She was in her late twenties, Sam guessed, and thoroughly a woman of the world.

"And this is Janie." Janie was dressed in a simple white cotton shift. She stood and did something that almost looked like a curtsey. She didn't lift her eyes to the two men at all. She was thin, almost wasted, and had an air like she was afraid of everybody and everything. Sam put her at about sixteen, and felt a pang for her.

Lucia was a ripe-looking black woman with big breasts and butt, decked out fancily. She went right up to Ten, and said, "Oh, I'm glad to see you again," and took his hand and rubbed herself against him.

Rhondalynn, the fourth woman, wasn't dolled up, but wore a dress with plain, fitted bodice and full skirt, hooked at the neck and wrists—she might have been any respectable housewife in town. Her sultry style, though, undid that impression—she undid the neck hook like she was hot, then the wrist hooks. She danced a few steps to imaginary music. She was playing a part and enjoying every minute of it. She made Sam edgy, though. Rhondalynn was about seventeen or eighteen and . . . The long, curly, brown tresses, the big, brown eyes, the coltish figure—she looked nearly a twin sister to Katherine.

"Annabelle, let's have a dance tune," said Lucia.

Annabelle struck up a slow waltz on the upright piano, and Lucia strutted out with Ten. Sam quickly judged that Ten didn't know how to dance, any more than he did himself, but he had fun doing a few turns and brushing up against Lucia.

Sam backed into a corner, uncertain. Immediately Rhondalynn was upon him. "Would you like a drink?" She took his hand and led him to a highboy where several crystal decanters of amber fluid glistened. Sam had never seen such elegant glassware before. Rhondalynn poured a drink in a fancy-looking goblet and handed it to Sam, then the same for herself. "It's cognac," she said, "the finest French cognac. And, honey, it's a dime for each one."

Sam fumbled two dimes out of his hunting pouch and dropped them into the dish half full of dimes next to the decanters. Then his first taste of the liquor, which looked like whiskey, took away his consciousness of the price. Fire! He blinked several times at Rhondalynn, and his eyes watered.

"Aren't you sweet?" she said. "I could take to a young stud like you."

He coughed, covered it by tossing the whole drink down, and felt like gases must be exploding out his ears.

Ten and Lucia headed upstairs holding hands. Ten threw an encouraging smile back at Sam.

"Want another drink, honey?"

"I'm good," Sam rasped out.

Annabelle switched to a livelier tune, and Rhondalynn stepped into a dance. After a few steps she smiled all warm at Sam and held her hands out. He shook his head no, jostling his thoughts. The illusion of Katherine living as a whore was driving him crazy. But the picture of what they did that day in the woods—that was driving him crazier.

Finally Rhondalynn stopped dancing and walked over to the liquor. She looked coquettishly at Sam. He backed into a corner.

Suddenly Janie was in front of him, and now she looked up and met his eye. Then back down. "Would you like to sit with me?" He did, on a padded bench like a church pew.

She glanced up shyly, and down, and seemed unsure of herself. He knew just how she felt. "I like you," she said. She put her hand on his. They sat. Eyes up, eyes down, eyes accidentally catching each other and darting away. She had the same feelings he did, Sam could see.

But wild thoughts popped up like jack-o'-lanterns in his mind. Pictures of her doing what he knew she did (though he didn't feel sure about that). Pictures of someone putting a curse on her that made her work in a house like this. Pictures of himself abducting her into the night, to a better life. He looked at her and then turned his head away fast to keep from locking eyes. He listened to her delicate breath catch, and finally ease out. He felt a pang of liking for her. Then wild thoughts stampeded out of the dark and trampled him, and he couldn't stop them.

He was embarrassed for her. He was mortified for himself.

After a while she turned, lifted her face, and brushed his cheek with her lips. "Would you like to come upstairs with me?"

He would. He nodded.

She led him by the hand up the steep, narrow stairs.

THE ROOM WAS tiny—there was no place to sit but the bed. Sam stood. With a hand Janie drew him down beside her. He couldn't look at her. This was humiliating.

She laid her head on his shoulder. He ignored it. She stroked his hand. He just sat there.

Finally she said, "I need a dollar."

He dropped dimes all over the floor in his rush to give them to her.

She waited patiently for him to pick them up, then brushed his cheek with her lips again and said, "I'm not wearing anything under this shift."

Sam heard her words of abasement and looked into her pathetic eyes and blurted out, "I'm just so sorry for you."

For a fleeting moment Sam thought he saw a wild amusement in her face. But no, he saw, she was demure. "Want to talk?"

He nodded yes.

* * *

TEN WAS PRACTICALLY skipping as they walked down the road in the crisp night air. "Damn, was that fun. That Lucia, she's hot. She's . . ."

He looked at his friend, tromping dully along. "Who'd you go up with?"

"Janie."

"How was she?"

"I just feel so bad for a girl in a spot like that."

"What?"

"I mean, how did she get there? Where's her family? Why isn't someone taking care of her?"

"What are you talking about?"

"I asked her but she wouldn't say."

"Sa-a-am?!"

"Don't you think about things like that?"

"Sam, what happened up there?"

"We talked."

"Just talked?"

"Yeah."

"You give her a dollar?"

"Yeah."

"To talk?"

"What's wrong with that?"

"Sam, she's a whore."

"She's a sixteen-year-old girl that's lost her way."

"She's a whore. And if she's sixteen, it's one long sixteen. Been there three years I know of."

"She looks sixteen."

"Last year she looked like a New Orleans floozy, wore a bright sash and a full skirt and swung it around a lot."

"What!?"

"She hadn't discovered her pathetic act yet. This suits her better."

"I don't think it's right to talk this way about her."

"Didn't you want to do anything with her?"

"Not really."

"Did you want any of those women?"

Sam walked a few steps before he let the words out. "I guess I wanted Rhondalynn."

"Why'd you pick Janie?"

"Felt so bad for her."

They walked through the darkness in silence.

"What is it you're not telling me?"

"Rhondalynn reminds me of my girlfriend. I wanted to jump on her and go."

THEY DANGLED THEIR legs off the end of the dock near the steamboat. With the swish of the river half-covering his voice, Sam spilled out the whole story. His resentment of his brother, his attraction to Katherine. Their hour of passion in his special Eden. "The very next day they announced their betrothal."

"Betrayal by betrothal," quipped Ten.

Sam tried not to hear the flippant tone.

"Katherine was the snake in your Eden."

On came his story. How he ran off. Owen's lying warrant for his arrest, which cried out for revenge. What a good time he had floating down river, except maybe for dreaming about Katherine sometimes. Then tonight Rhondalynn set off a waterfall of feelings in him.

"Let's go back," said Ten. "Let's go back and you frig Rhondalynn."

"No way," said Sam.

They dangled and kicked their legs in silence.

"Yeah, we got to go back," said Ten.

"No way in hell," Sam said louder.

Silence.

"What do you want to do, then?"

"Eat."

"Yeah, let's eat. Yeah, let's do that, let's eat."

THE QUEEN CITY Tavern was hopping. In the jumble of tables, conversations, card games, shouts, entreaties, mugs, glasses, and bodies, it took several minutes to find Grumble and Eleven. By good luck they were eating.

"Chicken and dumplings!" cried Grumble. "Go to it!" Sam wondered what chicken and dumplings was.

"A dime!" Eleven put in enthusiastically.

They ladled bowls full, cut bread off the loaf and buttered it, and paid the counter man. Sam wondered how long his four dollars would last in Cincinnati.

They joined their friends at the barrel and dug in. Sam liked the taste, thick, creamy and a little sweet. Chicken was good after all that deer meat.

"Make any money?" Ten asked.

Eleven grinned.

"A bit," said Grumble.

"I got ninety-five cents," said Eleven. "Most money I ever made in an hour."

"Show me how it's done," urged Ten.

Grumble did it without a word. First he shuffled an entire deck with a dexterousness even Sam had never seen. Then he showed an ace in his palm, turned his hand over and back and it was gone, over and back and it was there again. Then he reached over and plucked the same card from under the flap of Sam's hunting pouch. He cocked an eye at Ten.

"I get it."

Now Grumble drew out the gentleman, lady, and boy with a hoop of hearts. He demonstrated his ultra-dexterous shuffle, then in moments his arthritic shuffle. Both times he turned over the card Ten picked as the boy with a hoop. Once it was the old man, once the lady.

"I get it," said Ten.

"Really?"

"For sure."

"For fun and profit. Actually, I have more larceny up my sleeve. Who will be my fellow trickster this time?"

"Me," put in Eleven.

Grumble waited.

"Better be Sam," said Ten. "He's gonna need the money."

"I do not," said Sam.

"Yeah, you do. Annabelle's."

"Annabelle's," crowed Grumble. "Waltzing the mollishers." Grumble talk for whores. "I'm sure you boys like that. Actually, I could use all three of you. One to be the star of the show. He will get the most money."

"Sam's the man," said Ten.

"Not me," said Sam.

"You'll need that money before the cock crows," Ten said with a grin.

"No I won't," said Sam.

"Let's just pretend you will," said Ten.

SAM COMPLAINED ALL the way through rehearsal, but they saw he was taking to the idea. Afterwards Grumble said they needed a tavern where none of them had been seen. Amber's Grog Shop looked fine, especially because it was crowded.

Sam, Ten, and Eleven went in first, Sam using his new walk. He crimped his right foot sharply inward, painfully lifted and set down the whole leg stiff-kneed. In fact, it did hurt, in this awkward position. He followed Ten and Eleven doggedly, not looking at anyone because he didn't want to be pitied. They got mugs of ale and found places at a trestle table toward the back of the shop. Sam wondered if the men already seated would object to Indians, but they said nothing. Maybe the "civilized" clothing made the difference.

Grumble slipped in quietly, moving like a man who didn't want to be noticed. He made his way obsequiously to the counter, paid for his mug, and retired to a nearby wall, as though afraid to intrude on any drinkers by sitting down.

Soon Sam went for a second mug. Every step said, This hurts but I'm not giving in, and I'm too proud to accept help. The counter man refilled his mug without a word, and Sam started back to his table.

As he neared Grumble, the cherub fixed his eyes on Sam with a look of great compassion. He started to reach out, but hesitated. Started to speak but stopped himself. Made an anguished face and restrained himself by clasping his hands around his mug in front of his chest.

Sam gave him a supremely disgusted look.

This was more than Grumble could bear. "Excuse me, I beg your pardon most humbly, but I . . . No, I dare not."

"Spit it out, old man."

Grumble lowered his head, shook it, and murmured soundless words. His manner said, Certainly I am a pitiful old man, and deserving of the contempt of this young fellow who bears his affliction so nobly.

"I said spit it out."

Grumble's face jerked up into Sam's, and his eyes glistened with unshed tears. "I'm sorry, it's intrusive of me, unforgivable really, but I . . ."

Sam looked around at nearby drinkers and got their amused sympathy.

"But what? Exactly what?"

"Your affliction is so grievous, it hurts me to see you, when I know I can help. But I mustn't, truly, I mustn't."

"Help?" Sam said loudly and sarcastically. He lifted his deformed leg up, hoisted it further with both hands, and plopped it on the table so all could see the twisted foot. "God gave me this. What could you do about it? Are you more powerful than almighty God?" He turned and shared a laugh with the men watching, more and more of them.

"I have no power at all, actually," said Grumble meekly.

"Damned right you don't," Sam lashed at him.

"But I am a vessel."

"A vassal, he says," Sam called to the crowd. "Fancy word for a low-life."

Men hooted.

"I claim no status, indeed have no status, but . . ."

"But what?" Said loudly and harshly.

Grumble answered hesitantly, tremulously. "I have a gift." He continued in the tone of a sorrowful admission. "It so pains me to see such suffering. I could help you."

"Help me?! I been all the way to Philadelphia with this leg. The most uppity doctors in this nation have looked and shook their heads and despaired, I tell you despaired, of their helplessness in the face of this leg." He drew a deep breath and rose to his crowning statement. *"Go as God made you. It is not for man to contend against what God has done.* That's what them doctors said."

This struck the crowd silent.

Grumble wrung his hands. Clearly he did not want to pursue the matter any further, but . . . At last he went on in a voice as soft as a child's. "Indeed. Just so. I agree. My gift is . . . My gift is to call forth the power of Holy Spirit and heal. I have the healing hands."

"Healing hands?" roared Sam. "Healing hands, my ass. You are an impostor. You are a quack. You're one that pretends to help and in fact tortures me more!" With these last three words his voice rose into a cry of anguish.

"I beg you," said Grumble, looking around nervously at the crowd. "Let us go somewhere private. Let us go somewhere . . ."

Now his voice, though still soft, moved confidently. "I will lay healing hands upon you, sir. I know I can."

"Healing hands?!" The words were accusation. "If you make such a claim, if you offend us with this arrogance, show us. Show *here* what you can do." Now he shouted out. "Heal the lame!"

"Show us," called Ten from the rear.

"Make him PROVE IT!" yelled Eleven.

Other men took up the cry. "Show us!" "Prove it."

Some of the men in front stood up, like they wouldn't let Grumble leave until he backed up his words, and would thrash him thoroughly when he didn't.

Grumble looked at the aroused crowd fearfully. He stuttered, "All right. All right. I will . . ."

Now his movements took on authority. "Make room, please. He will lay here where all can see."

A half dozen men moved their drinks to clear the way. Grumble nodded to Sam, and he stretched out full length on the table, right in the sloshed-over beer, and closed his eyes.

"I need silence," Grumble said at large, in a voice of assurance. "Utter silence."

He lifted his face to the heavens and moved his lips in silent prayer. His face grew radiant. His body swelled with power. No man in the room heard his words, but every one of them would have sworn to their eloquence, their power, their glowing beauty.

Then Grumble turned to the prostrate form of the poor sufferer. He held his hands in silence over Sam's hip, but did not touch him. Over his knee, without touching. Over the ankle.

Then, for a moment, he withdrew into himself, head down. Suddenly he thrust his hands high, as though to call down some power higher than man. He brought those hands to Sam's sad, inward-turned foot.

The room was a hush. Men didn't breathe.

Grumble reached out with a single forefinger, paused dramatically, and eased Sam's foot straight. Nothing more. Exactly that, and all of that.

Sam opened his eyes and regarded his right foot. Everyone could see the wonder in his face. For the first time in his life it was straight.

He pushed himself to the end of the table and let his legs dangle toward the floor. First he put weight on the left foot. Then a little weight on the right. He stood, weight equal between the feet, right foot still straight.

Murmurs began, and swelled.

Sam stepped forward on the left foot, then on his right. He threw the entire crowd a triumphant grin. Two more steps. Four. He ran a few steps and leaped into the air. He danced.

Uproar. A hundred men sang out their acclaim.

Sam sank to the floor and wept.

Grumble stood above him quietly, eyes down, beaming. He helped Sam up.

Sam waved his arms for silence. He took both of Grumble's hands in his. "What is your name, healer?"

"Ada. Ada Gleason."

"Thank you, Ada. I can never thank you enough."

There were tears in the crowd, and recommitments to religion, and new conversions.

"Thank the Holy Spirit," said Grumble. "I am only a vessel for his power."

Sam shook both of Grumble's hands vigorously. "You've changed my life."

"God go with you."

"I must do something in return."

"I want nothing."

Sam was getting agitated now. "What can I do? Anything. I have to do something."

"Pay the doctor," called Ten.

A dozen voices echoed, "He's a *real* doctor. Pay him."

Sam's hand dived into his pouch and came out with coins. "Here's a dollar. I'm a poor man, but take it, please. You've changed my life. You've saved my life."

"I couldn't. No. I can't. No, thank you . . ." Grumble was backing away.

Sam grabbed him by one elbow and thrust the coins into his hand.

"Take this or I'll never feel all right about this gift. I'll never truly feel the joy of walking, and running, and dancing."

Grumble took it.

"Thank you," said Sam, bowing.

"You're very welcome," said Grumble.

And men charged forward. The first wanted help with his lumbago, it bothered him something terrible, he was a wood splitter and could hardly work sometimes. He only had a few coins, but . . .

Grumble touched the back sacramentally and predicted that it would get better and better over the months.

The second man was suffering from rheumatism in his hands. He was a clockmaker and some days couldn't do the fine work. And could he offer two dollars for the generous help?

The third man seemed to get sick every winter, like consumption, it knocked him down for two or three weeks, and he sure would like to get through a winter in health. It was worth these coins to him . . .

THE TAKE WAS enough that Grumble gave Sam three dollars—nearly a week's wage!—and Ten and Eleven fifty cents apiece.

"Good money for little work," said Ten.

Grumble looked at Sam and said, "Think it beats working for a living?"

Though Sam supposed it did, he only smiled.

Grumble switched to a jocular tone. "All right, Ten, what's this about Sam and Annabelle's?"

"He needs to go back, that's all."

Sam was grateful to Ten for not spilling the beans.

"Sam?" Grumble went on, sweeping all before him.

"Girl there reminds me of my . . . girlfriend," mumbled Sam.

Grumble appraised the situation with study of Sam's face and half a century of experience.

"Go upstairs with her?"

Sam clinched up and jerked his head back and forth for no.

Grumble and Ten grabbed his arms at the same moment and marched toward the brothel.

"I wouldn't mind seeing Lucia myself," said Eleven from behind.

The parlor looked exactly the same as this afternoon, except that the fiery Lucia was missing. A mousy-looking man of about sixty, maybe a farmer, sat uncomfortably on a chesterfield, straw hat in his nervous hands. Annabelle welcomed them with the same effusiveness and introduced everyone. Sam looked at Janie to see if she was smirking at him, but she was playing her role, demure, and perhaps damaged. Sam smiled at her. Now that he'd acted a part, he admired the way she did hers.

He looked last at Rhondalynn. He couldn't tell if she was smirking or smiling lasciviously. He decided he didn't care.

Lucia came down the stairs, trailed by a black man as narrow and hard as a cedar fencepost. She went straight to Eleven. "You come for me, honey?"

"Believe so," said Eleven, drawing out the words and looking at her with sex in his eyes.

"Excuse me," she said properly to the fencepost.

He nodded and went darkly out the front door without a word. "Lucia's on fire tonight," she exclaimed of herself, and led Eleven gaily upstairs.

"Back already, Ten? Had some luck at cards?" broached Annabelle.

"Something like that. Annabelle, I need to introduce my friend here to his girlfriend."

Annabelle was much amused. "Girlfriend?"

Ten waited. "Go ahead," said Sam.

"Rhondalynn is a dead ringer for the girl he left behind, Katherine."

Annabelle's eyes lit up, and she got every detail Ten had to give. While they chatted, Sam eyed Rhondalynn standing against the lace curtains, eyeing him and smiling slyly. Finally Annabelle waved her over. "Katherine," she began, "you have spoken so often of Sam, the man who left you behind. I did not know this was the fellow."

She threw Sam her sexiest smile. "I have missed you, lover."

Sam gawked at her moon-eyed.

"Go to it, lad," said Annabelle. "Our Katherine hasn't had a good loving since you left."

All right! Sam decided. He would play a part too, the debonair man about town. He offered Rhondalynn his arm. "Shall we have a drink?"

At the highboy Rhondalynn was quick with the pour, Sam quick with the coins. Hadn't he just earned three dollars?

"I'm so glad you've come, Sam," she said.

"You haunt my dreams, Katherine." On they chatted and flirted. Sam projected the exact memories of Katherine taking her clothes off, one by one, on the face and form of this new, enthusiastic Katherine. The more he looked at her body, the more Katherine smiled.

Finally she led him to the staircase, gently pulling his hand. Sam was grinning broadly, but something didn't feel right.

"Go to it, lad," cried Annabelle. The madam sang to the old spiritual tune,

"Rock-a her soul in the bosom of Annabelle's
"Rock-a her soul in the bosom of Annabelle's"

He reached up two stairs, grabbed her by the waist, swung her off her feet, held her to his chest, and kissed her passionately. She responded in kind, and more.

"Go, Sam," cried Ten. "Cut your wolf loose."

They dashed up the stairs howling.

Chapter Seven

EVERYONE SHOWED UP bleary to load new cargo about midday. Captain Stuart hired Ten and Eleven at two dollars a week each to be the boat hunters on the double hop on to Louisville and Evansville. Then the two Shawnees were going to go visit their families on the Wabash.

"I don't feel right about taking your job," Ten told Sam.

"I'm a crewman now. Besides, we can hunt together."

"Good." He stretched his shoulders like they were bothering him. "Damn, but I'm eager to be home."

"Where's home?"

"My folks live in a little village on the Wabash, north of Vincennes."

"What's Vincennes?"

"Old French trading post on the Wabash River. Indiana–Illinois state line. Eleven and I try to go back for the bread dance. Big ceremony for us."

"I bet the captain wishes he could go," observed Sam.

"Sly can go if he wants to," said Ten.

"He's got a business to run," protested Sam.

"Yeah, part of him is white."

"You forgotten money's important?"

"In the Shawnee world, family counts for more." Yet this was said lightly. Sam decided not to make anything of it.

On the late afternoon of the sixth day beyond Cincinnati, Frenchy brought the *Tecumseh* hard river left, and there, stretched serenely out in a nice little harbor at the mouth of Bear Grass Creek, was the waterfront of Louisville, Kentucky. It was the last place you could moor above the Great Falls of the Ohio. Even from here you could hear the roar of the falls below, and Sam tried not to think about them.

He was used to all the boats now, the many men working, the hustle and bustle, the routine of unloading lots of crates and barrels.

One sight, though, set him back—an enormous Negro working at a cart. He had a shaven head and a big gold earring. He wore no shirt, and his arm and back muscles bulged powerfully. The fellow was issuing sharp, clear instructions to white men doing the loading. Sam watched gape-mouthed. He'd never seen a Negro except at long distance, and hadn't imagined one with the air of authority and vitality this one had.

"*Le negre*, he's something, huh?" This was Ten in Sam's ear.

Sam figured out who he meant and blurted out, "Who is that?"

"Jean-Jacques. Don't know his last name. He's from Montréal. His family, they own a drayage business."

Sam gaped at Ten. He'd never heard of blacks owning businesses.

"Close your mouth, you don't catch flies," said Ten, and headed back for another load. Sam followed, and shouldered weight until he was about to collapse. He noticed Ten and Eleven never slowed down, and was envious.

Louisville taught Sam that the port life of a river man was repetitious. Most of the crew rampaged first to the taverns, then to the whorehouses, then back and forth. Sam wondered if Elijah took his hostility to bed, and decided he wouldn't want to be the whore who found out. Frenchy stood watch. Sly Stuart disappeared to . . . no one knew where. The town boasted a theater, but none of them wanted to spend a whole dollar on it.

Sam went with Ten, Eleven, and Grumble to a tavern, where the cherub perpetrated his cons on the willing. Ten and Eleven wanted to have a couple of drinks, see the town, have a couple of drinks, visit the brothel, etc. Sam went with them, but he felt like he did when he waited for his mother to finish shopping. He tapped a foot, cast his eyes around for he didn't know what, and yearned for life to begin. And begin and begin.

Later he would remember only two events from Louisville. One was in a tavern where a low class of ladies of the night did their horizontal work. Jean-Jacques walked right up to the table, sat down, and clanked his tankard on the wood in disgust. Ten and Eleven greeted him and introduced Sam. The big colored man rumbled to Ten and Eleven, "I'd be glad to see you, but I'm too disgusted." He had a big, resonant, bass voice, and his English was French-accented and formal. Sam couldn't believe Negroes talked that way.

"What's going on?" Ten asked the black man.

"You know Marylou?"

Ten and Eleven said they didn't.

"The one Negress they got here. She ran off. They won't let me touch any of the white women. You can't neither." He regarded Sam. "Your friend got all the skirt here to himself."

Sam couldn't help himself. He asked the big man, "Is this color?"

Jean-Jacques gave him an ironic dazzle of smile, teeth gleaming as brightly as his shaved head and earring. "You raised upside down in the bottom of the outhouse? What isn't color around here?" His easy tone took the edge off the words.

"Whores won't . . . ?"

Jean-Jacques laughed, a big, musical sound. "That's why they had the Negress. Some whorehouses even have Indian women." He regarded Sam bluntly. "What are you thinking, boy?"

"I never heard the term 'Negress' before."

"You heard 'Negro'?"

"Hardly ever."

"Nothing but 'Nigger'?"

"Yeah."

"You best know," he said, "I am in French *le Negre*, in English a Negro. I am a free man of color, and I don't take kindly to 'nigger.' " The words were spoken politely and the tone reasonably friendly, but menace lurked.

"Sorry," said Sam.

"No offense," said Jean-Jacques. "It's just that your education has been lacking."

WHEN THE SUN rose, Captain Stuart stomped onto the deck, acting edgy. "Let's go, Frenchy." They said they were going to scout the Falls of the Ohio. The odd thing was, Frenchy came back alone. The rest of the crew showed up at midafternoon to load and launch. Still no Captain Stuart. Sam didn't dare ask. Frenchy supervised the loading of the new cargo and didn't say a word about the captain. With the usual pack-mule work, Sam hardly noticed the three constables until they were tramping around the deck.

"Where is Captain Silas Stuart?" shouted the head cop. He was a big, blustering fellow. Sam wondered why police always took an approach of, "I'll huff and I'll puff and I'll blow your house down."

Everyone just looked at him. No one knew, unless . . . Frenchy? Ten?

The constable barked at Frenchy, "I have a warrant for the arrest of Abigail McKenna, a woman who habituates a dancing and gambling hall, also known as Sally Sling. She's suspected of being with Captain Silas Stuart of the *Tecumseh*. Where are they?"

Frenchy answered with a most eloquent Gallic shrug.

"I know, you swallow your English in front of authorities."

Frenchy shrugged again.

The constables marched around the deck, peering at every man. Elijah gave them a withering grimace, and for once Sam was glad Elijah was on his side.

"I want to check the hold," the head man said, and stomped in without asking permission. A minute later he came back into the sunlight blinking.

"What are your sailing orders?" Still barking at Frenchy.

"I'm ze captain's brother," said Ten in a phony French lilt.

From the look on the constable's face, he'd believe that one when his mother was his father.

"We sail when we are loaded."

"Bound for?"

"New Orleans."

"Without Captain Stuart?" asked the constable mockingly.

"Wit' or wit'out."

"The captain is abandoning his vessel?"

"Why you no ask him?"

"Oh, I will," said the constable. "When I find him."

The constables kept stomping around and waving their warrant.

The crew got the freight loaded.

Frenchy went to the hawser in front and untied. "We depart now," he told the constables.

They smirked at him.

"Positions!" he cried.

Every man but Grumble took up a work spot, Frenchy on the tiller, Ned at lookout, the others on the sweeps. Frenchy gave the constables a questioning look. They looked back complacently. "Pull larboard and starboard!" Frenchy shouted, like nothing special was doing. On one sweep Sam, Ten, and Eleven looked at each other.

"The man said pull," growled Elijah. They did.

The constables had to jump into the shallows to make shore. Frenchy gave them a nice wave.

The eddy took hold of the massive craft and floated it gently upstream. "Pull!" hollered Frenchy. The eddy kept easing the boat upstream.

When the stern nudged into the current, Frenchy cried "Larboard!" and swung the tiller to bring the bow downstream.

Sam always liked this moment, when the river grabbed hold of the tons and tons of the *Tecumseh* and began to carry them along. When they were fully into the current, Frenchy brought them around and cried, "Rest your oars."

Sitting on the hold, Sam asked Ten, "What the hell is going on?" Sam was starting to cuss like the others.

"You got me."

Eleven shrugged his shoulders. Nobody seemed to know anything.

"Be ready!" Frenchy sang out. Already the rumble of the falls was getting louder.

Frenchy took them to river right, near the Indiana shore. The *Tecumseh* immediately began to buck and roll. At the first downward plunge Sam fell, and nearly rolled off the hold onto the deck. "Starboard!" screamed Frenchy. His voice sounded like a squeak in the great roar. The boat plunged straight toward a huge tree that was hung across some boulders, its crown thrusting far into the channel. The current bobbed the crown up and down like the head of a drowning man.

The leafless branches gave the right side a loud scraping, but the *Tecumseh* cleared it. Just as Sam relaxed, Frenchy yelled "Push starboard, PULL larboard!"

Sam saw a row of boulders like shark's teeth. The boat must dive to the left or crash on the rocks. He pulled until he thought his shoulders would pop.

They ran by the teeth at thrilling speed. "Ready to PULL starboard!" The last tooth, Sam saw, was big as a two-story house.

"Pull starboard!"

As if by magic the boat slowed, the water still boiling around it. Sam heard a huge sucking noise on the stern. They eased forward, and the bow swung left.

"Push both sides!"

And so it went for the entire two and a half miles, the longest ten minutes of Sam's life. Sometimes the roar of the water was huge, louder than any steamboat engine Sam had ever heard, like somebody rattling rocks in a bucket when your head's inside the bucket. Several times the bow rose out the water and smacked down with a great SLAP! The pilot called out a lot of orders, and once Elijah and Micajah yelled at each other like they were wrangling. But mostly the ride was wild and fast and exciting—maybe, Sam thought, like riding a seventy-five-foot-long horse at a gallop. He didn't let himself think about what happened if you came off.

Finally they shooshed out into slow water at the bottom. "Scary!" shouted Ten.

"Wild," said Eleven.

Sam stretched out on the hold, exhausted.

"We put in at Clarksville," called Frenchy.

"Where's that?" Sam asked Ten without opening his eyes.

"Few minutes."

Sam put the missing captain, the falls, everything past out of his mind and felt the motion of the boat on the current. Evansville was next, yes, then Cape Girardeau, Chickasaw Bluffs (with Fort Pickering atop, said the captain), some other Mississippi ports, and finally the great seaport of New Orleans—he knew about all that. But what he liked was the feeling of the enormous river picking them up and carrying them off somewhere with a power far beyond their will or strength to control. They had choices—further left, further right, get into eddy sometimes, stop for the night. But the big energy, the will was the river's. People said the earth circled the sun once a year, an even more massive movement caused by some invisible force more powerful than any man could imagine. It shaped people's lives, but no one could feel it. Nor could they feel the sailing through the immensity of space. Why didn't people feel the wind of space in their hair?

Well, never mind, Sam was glad he could feel the energy of the river in his butt.

"PULL STARBOARD!"

Sam jumped up, alarmed. What was going on?

A village nestled on the Indiana side. They went through the usual maneuvers like they were going to land. And there came a skiff with Captain Stuart as a passenger.

Captain Stuart, and . . . a lady?

Sam ran and helped. Yes, a lady. Sam gave her a hand. A real lady she looked, too, not like any he'd known, housewives and mothers and store clerks and, well, whores. She wore a light green, full-skirted traveling outfit with a jacket and dark green hat, and held an umbrella of the palest peach in one hand. The way the umbrella gleamed in the sunlight was enchanting.

"Thank you kindly," she said to Sam, her voice Southern, soft, gracious. Her face was the most beautiful he'd ever seen. Not paying attention, he bumped the umbrella, and it knocked her hat off. He caught it and handed it to her. "Thank you, sir," she said, the first time he'd ever been called that. Then he gawked. Her lovely young face was topped by a great pile of henna-colored hair.

The crew was gathering around now. Frenchy had even tied the tiller and come amidships, grinning slyly.

"Sorry I had to leave you boys on your own for the falls, but as you see I had a duty to perform for a lady. Abigail, this is the crew of the *Tecumseh.*" He ran through the name of every man. Some held their hats in their hand and acted deferential. Several eyed her sharply. "Men, this is Abigail Price."

Not McKenna, Sam noticed. The men mumbled, "How do you do." Miss Abigail responded, "I'm delighted to be aboard, gentlemen, and very much looking forward to the journey."

"Sam, will you and Ten bring along Miss Abigail's bags?" asked the captain. They were a big trunk and a sizable carpet bag. This was aside from the small ladies' bags she dangled from each wrist. As they jumped into the skiff for her things, Miss Abigail paraded to the lean-to at the back of the hold, Captain Stuart in tow. The trunk was sizable but uncommonly light, the bag uncommonly heavy.

They skidded the luggage along the deck to the rear and left it near the lean-to without going around the corner. Miss Abigail appeared suddenly, "Oh, I need that carpet bag," she said, lifted it with surprising strength, and disappeared back behind the hutch wall.

Sam looked at Ten with some embarrassment. The lean-to had one modestly proportioned bed. Well, maybe Captain Stuart was letting the lady have it. They stepped quietly back toward the front. Ten quipped, "I guess I'm wondering just who she really is and what crime she's wanted for."

* * *

THEY TIED UP well before dark at a good camping place and built a big fire in the sand box. After a good supper of stew and biscuits, Miss Abigail said, "Would anyone care to dance?"

Grumble already had the fiddle out, and he cut a lively tune, "The Flowers of Edinburgh." The captain squired Miss Abigail in some turns. Frenchy got out a mouth harp and pitched in a harmony beneath Grumble's melody. Ten and Eleven began to dance as well, which embarrassed Sam, and put a scowl on Elijah's face.

Miss Abigail looked across at Sam. "Come," she cried, holding her arms out to him, "let's dance."

He crimped toward her but mumbled, "I don't know how."

"Oh, I know enough for both of us," said Miss Abigail.

"About a lot things," said Elijah from somewhere. But Sam ignored him, and off they danced.

At the end of the tune Sam thanked Miss Abigail for the dance.

"Oh, you must call me Abby," she said.

Sam nodded yes.

"I heard she was called Sally," said Elijah. A couple of the men laughed. Sam could see she heard the remark and was miffed by it.

Abigail boldly took the hand of Ned, one of the men laughing, and twirled him into a dance. "Did you put a Price upon your own head?" Ned asked her, smiling.

"I am amused by your wit," she said, "but not your curiosity." They danced, and Ned shut his mouth.

In the middle of the tune Elijah came forward to cut in on Ned. Miss Abigail threw Captain Stuart a stricken look, and he stepped forward to rescue her.

"What's wrong?" said Elijah with a sneer. "You been in a lot of men's arms afore."

Miss Abigail stopped dancing and looked at him equably. The music stopped. She opened the little bag that hung from her wrist, withdrew a small case, and took out a cigar smaller than her little finger, wrapped in white paper instead of tobacco. At her glance Captain Stuart lit it with a lucifer. It was all as much as to say, 'I am not like other women.'

"Elijah," she said, "you knew me as Sally Sling. Some of you others did too." She blew smoke to the night sky. "I danced with men, played the piano, and played cards with them."

"And done more'n that, I heard." This was Micajah.

She looked boldly back at him. Just when Sam was afraid she'd blush, she threw out a smile bright as a full moon. "What I did, or didn't do, is no one's business but my own."

"Did you do it horizontal?" Micajah again.

"You'll keep a civil tongue," cried Captain Stuart.

Abby silenced him with a hand. "No man can say that against me. The truth is, I fell in love with a gambler, some of you know Donnell, and got swept into a hard life."

"Donnell looking for you?" This was Elijah.

Her smile turned spicy. "Well, he won't catch up. Here's everything you need to know. I was one sort of woman. Now I'm making a new start."

"Good for you, Abby," put in the captain.

Miss Abigail looked into all the men's eyes, one after one. Sam saw a mouth or two start to open. But no one denied her. Elijah backed away further.

"This is America," she said, "where people can make themselves what they want to be. And," she concluded, "You may all call me Abby. Which is my *real* name."

"I bet," said Elijah behind Sam.

"I liked Sally Sling better," said Micajah.

"You liked losing money to her," came Elijah.

The men chuckled at this.

Just then Grumble struck up the fiddle. Captain Stuart led Abby out in a lively strut. She threw her head back and laughed musical notes that whirled merrily from star to star.

* * *

ABBY TURNED OUT to be the fun of the float to Evansville. At night she shared the shaded rear of the hold with the captain, which disturbed Sam. During the day she relaxed in a shaded part of the hold, or sometimes lounged on deck under her parasol, read a book, and smoked.

"I never saw a woman smoke a cigar," Sam said to Grumble.

"They call them cigarettes," he answered. "I heard the women in New Orleans and Natchez smoke them."

The first two days Sam kept an eye on Abby. She had her ways, some of them not modest. For instance, she spent a lot of time sewing on her corset, without taking care to be discreet about it.

It was in the evening she sparkled. Either they had music and danced or they played cards. Abby loved to deal cards, just like she did in the dance hall—brag, all fours, sledge, twenty-one—men's gambling games, not lady stuff.

Of course, Grumble had to play now. "Remember the bargain," Stuart proclaimed.

"If I win even a dime, I'll give it back," said Grumble in a meek, righteous voice. And since the stakes weren't real, he called for a try at the new game of poker, so everyone could learn. "Also, the deal changes with every hand," he told Abby. "That way we two professionals won't have an advantage."

The captain threw him a dubious look, but the men brought kegs for chairs, and a table of red maple for delivery downstream. At first it was Abby, Grumble, the giant brothers, and Ned. Sam, Captain Stuart, Ten, and Eleven watched to learn the game. After an hour the giants quit, losing. The Indians slipped in. Halfway through the evening, when Grumble had several dollars tucked away, Abby suddenly fixed him with her eyes and said, "I don't see how you're doing it."

Grumble smiled. "The lady thinks I'm cheating."

Every spine around the table stiffened. If a man said that in a gambling hall, the accuser or accused would have been dead in a jiffy. But Abby was very much a lady, and her eyes were merry.

"Why would I do that?" he went on.

"You like to win so much, even when you don't get to keep the money, you cheat."

Grumble shrugged his shoulders. If he'd had wings, they would have spread in an innocent gesture, 'Who, me?'

She eyed him shrewdly. "I'm damned if I can figure out how, and I know every trick in the book."

More innocence.

"I can't see any marks on these cards. I'd spot dealing off the bottom or dealing the second card or a reflecting ring instantly. You know the tricks, too. So what are you doing?"

"Dancing with the great goddess Luck."

Abby tossed out a peal of laughter. It was a good laugh, open, free, yet feminine.

She took out a cigarette. "All right," she said, "Just in case, let's switch decks." She brought a brand-new box of fifty-two cards out of the little cloth bag she wore dangling from her wrist.

"Whatever your ladyship wishes."

Over the next two hours Grumble proceeded to take the money of all players, Abby included.

"Enough," Captain Stuart said.

Grumble carefully counted out coins until each man had the stakes he started with, one dollar. When it came Abby's turn, though, she declined. "I wouldn't think of it," she said brightly. "I have my professional pride."

Grumble smiled and put the coins away.

Several evenings went by before they got into another game. "Twenty-one," she exclaimed.

"A game with just one dealer," Grumble said with a cocked eyebrow. "Isn't that an unfair advantage?"

"Then you deal." With this she whipped out another new pack and grinned broadly. From the same bag she took twenty thin half dimes and arranged them in a line. "Come on, gentlemen, let's all start with one dollar."

For two hours neither Grumble nor Abby won nor lost. Micajah gained a few half dimes, Elijah and Sam lost a few, and the others broke even.

Suddenly, Abby said, "Let's play against each other, just the two of us."

Grumble pursed his lips and nodded yes.

"Ten dollars each on the table."

Grumble eyed her and then counted out the coins.

"Here's your own medicine back," Abby said. "You get to deal. I'll never touch the cards. I'm going to cheat, and you'll never know how."

Grumble's face lit up, and then went carefully neutral.

Everyone else crowded around.

The game didn't look uneven at first. Abby won some and lost some. Only Grumble put his hands on the cards, dealing them and picking them up. Abby didn't even cut.

Soon, though, people noticed that Abby had a way of sitting on the lousy score of twelve, or fourteen when that looked unwise. Yet Grumble had to draw by rule, and busted every time. She doubled aggressively on pairs of face cards or tens. But twice she didn't, and improbably instead took insurance against twenty-one. Both times the insurance paid off.

"You act like you know what I'm holding," he observed in an appraising way.

"Don't second-card me again."

In half an hour Grumble's ten dollars turned into five. "I don't get it," Grumble said. "Does anyone have any idea what she's doing?"

Every head shook no.

He picked up the deck to deal again. "Leave the deck flat and deal," she said.

"I wasn't going to bottom-card you anyhow."

She made no comment.

Before long Grumble was down to nine half dimes. "The deck is new. It can't be marked. You're not touching the cards. What's going on?"

"Wouldn't you like to know?" Abby was greatly amused.

He pushed the rest of the half dimes over to her. "It's no fun getting whipped and whipped," he said.

She scooped up the coins and put the twenty dollars happily into her wrist bag. "Let's see," she said with a quirky smile, "shiny new pack, you're right, couldn't be marked. You're wearing nothing that would let me see a down card. You're dealing, so I can't give myself the card I need. So how did I pluck you clean as a headless chicken?"

Grumble looked at the deck, at Abby, at the empty space where he'd done battle and lost. He looked inside himself. He studied Abby, and then the empty space again. At length he said, with great seriousness, "I'll give you a hundred dollars to show me what you did."

Sam heard several gasps. It was more than half a year's wages for most men.

"No deal," she said quickly, and stood up to leave.

Grumble stared at her, humiliated.

The captain offered her his arm, and they waltzed off to bed.

Chapter Eight

"EVANSVILLE'S NOT AS big a town as Louisville," said Captain Stuart. They were standing at the bow, and Sam was on watch. "In fact, from Louisville all the way southwest and on south, fewer and fewer people."

"The country sure looks good," Sam said.

The morning sun was behind them, and their shadows jumped and jounced on the little waves ahead.

"Once we join into the Mississippi, we won't see any population to speak of until the Chickasaw Bluffs, on the Tennessee side.

Then nothing more, to speak of, before the plantation country of Louisiana."

"I like wild country."

"You got something against people?"

"Nope. Just the way they tear things up."

Stuart shrugged. The Indian life he wanted had been taken away long ago. Now he didn't think about how the world was going. He just concentrated on what he wanted to do. He wanted to go and go and trade and trade and go and go some more. Odd, how motion itself seemed to anchor his soul, and aloneness kept company with his spirit.

He looked across at the farms on the right bank, the first signs of Evansville just beyond. "I have to land her," he said, and headed for the stern.

Evansville looked not only a lot smaller but a lot more primitive. A lot of buildings were mostly raw, unpainted lumber. Some were half finished. As the *Tecumseh* eased into the eddy, Sam could see that only one other boat was moored, a flatboat. Evansville seemed to be an infant port. One long street stretched behind the waterfront, apparently the business district, with houses on the streets behind. Regardless, a town was always fun.

As soon as they had the unloading done, Elijah, Micajah, and Ned took their wages and headed off carousing. Captain Stuart, Abby, Sam, Grumble, Ten, and Eleven looked at each other. Frenchy was in charge of the ship for the first watch. "Come on, Captain," said Abby, "show us how to have a good time in a new town."

They crossed the corduroyed landing. Beyond it the waterfront street was deep, sticky mud. The good times started, apparently, after you got inside somewhere. Captain Stuart picked Abby up and carried her, to her little whoop of delight. Sam slipped out of his Jefferson boots and got his feet muddy. Beneath the overhangs of the shops, where the earth was packed, the captain set Abby down. Looked like there wasn't a low-class area and a high-class area in this town. Two hotels, one with apparent pretensions and one without, kept company with several taverns, a livery, a blacksmith, a mercantile, and other shops on the main street.

"Tell you what," said Abby, "I'll treat everyone to a sit-down dinner at the hotel." She nodded at the fancy-looking one.

"Great!" put in Captain Stuart.

"Mmmm," said Ten.

The captain raised an eyebrow at his brother.

"Place like that's not going to let me and Eleven in."

"Nonsense!" said Abby.

He chuckled. "They *won't* let us in."

"Ten, the owner is a friend. He'll accept any party I bring."

"And resent you for making his customers mix with redskins."

Eleven actually pitched in. "That's no joke, Sly."

"You are my brother, I . . ."

Ten said, "I'm not trying to barge into any fancy white-man place tonight. I just don't feel like it."

"Me neither."

"If you don't go, I won't either." From Sam. Everyone gawked at him.

"I won't either." This was Abby.

Everyone looked at each other, uncertain.

"Then let's all go to a tavern and have a cheery time." Abby again.

WHEN SUPPER WAS over, Abby said to Grumble, "I think you and I will have such fun as a team."

"Did you bring one of your new decks?"

"Sure."

"Will you tell me its secret?"

"Not a chance."

Grumble bit his lower lip for a moment. "Well, let's see what fun we can have."

"That's my fellow. You go to that tavern one door to the west. If it doesn't look good, come back quick and tell us. If it does, put together a poker game. I'll make an entrance soon."

Grumble tiddled off.

"Grumble."

He turned back.

"When I lick my lips, raise and keep raising."

Five minutes later Sam and his Shawnee friends went to the other tavern, got a table near Grumble's, and bought mugs of ale.

After a judicious interval came Abby and Captain Stuart, with the air of patricians slumming. They surveyed the room and Abby chose Grumble's table. "My gentleman here is embarrassed, but I like to play poker a little. May I join you?"

"Sure," said a big lout in an exaggerated way. He had Kentucky speech.

"You betcha," said his friend, who was missing half his teeth.

"Women, they's bad luck," said Grumble. Apparently he was doing backwoods English for this stunt.

"Oh, ease off, why don't you?" said the last player, dressed as a gentleman but evidently two sheets to the wind.

Captain Stuart seated Abby and brought a chair up for himself. "Deal me out," he said.

The way it looked to Sam and his friends, the gamblers had a great deal of fun. The three strangers seemed tickled pink at the idea of a woman gambling, and to judge by their leers wished it was strip poker. Sam and the two Shawnees drank a few rounds, pretending to pay no attention. They got nothing but Abby's gay laughter from the poker table, and an occasional glimpse of growing stacks of coins in front of Abby and Grumble. Sometimes Grumble would grouse loudly about having to play with a woman. Captain Stuart looked grumpy for real, not pretend.

Sam smiled to himself. Grumble was probably sitting there still trying to study out how Abby was rigging the game, and not coming close. That was a hoot.

After more than an hour Abby suddenly gave a big, artificial laugh, scooped up her coins, radiated a smile at the whole table, and stood. Quickly the captain rose with her. No one else did. Grumble looked more cross than usual. Passing him, she leaned down and whispered something in his ear.

"You . . ." Grumble looked into Stuart's face and squelched the word "bitch" almost audibly. Sam was impressed with his performance. Abby and Stuart paraded out.

The game broke up. Grumble sat alone for a moment before collecting his winnings, sauntering over to Sam, Ten, and Eleven's table, sitting, and riffling his deck noisily. "How about a game?"

They shook their heads no.

"Time to say so long," said Ten.

"Good-bye?" from Sam.

"This is where we split off for Vincennes."

Sam felt a pang. He knew they were leaving the *Tecumseh* at Evansville, but . . . "I didn't realize you were leaving tonight."

"We'll feel better when we're out of this town," said Eleven. "Its heart doesn't warm to Indians."

"I want to walk with them a few minutes," said Stuart. He looked at Abby. "Then I'll come back to the room."

"Sly is treating me to a night at the hotel, a setting suitable for a lady," she told them.

"So long."

"Good-bye, Ten," said Abby. "Eleven."

"Don't say 'good-bye,'" Ten said. "Shawnees only use that word at funerals."

"What do we say?" asked Sam.

"*Paselo, wisheketoowe*," said Eleven.

"What does it mean, exactly?"

"'Be careful, and be very strong,'" said Ten. "Then you walk away and say nothing more."

"You can just say *paselo* for short," said Eleven. "We do."

Sam started to speak, but Ten interrupted. "Why don't we shake hands first?"

They did. Abby offered hers too. Ten kissed Abby's hand with style, and Eleven followed suit with a big grin.

Sam hesitated, and swallowed the lump in his throat before he spoke. *"Paselo."*

"Paselo," Ten and Eleven echoed.

The three Shawnees walked west down the main street, Captain Stuart in the middle.

SAM, ABBY, AND Grumble put their arms around each other and swayed the other direction, toward the hotel. It was a warm spring night, even after midnight, and light from the taverns and two hotels spilled into the street, just enough to take the edge off the darkness. All three were a little giddy, Sam from ale and the other two from winning a battle of wits. They came to an intersecting street. Even in the dark it looked muddy.

"Lad, you be the lady's Sir Walter Raleigh," said Grumble.

"What?"

"Put your shirt down for Abby to step on."

Abby giggled.

"The devil with that," said Sam, "but I'll pick you up."

Quick as a flash he did, and staggered into the mud.

Abby laughed with delight.

"This is not so deep," Sam grunted out.

Came a voice—"Give us the bitch."

They stopped dead still.

"Give us the bitch and you can go."

Abby slipped out of Sam's arms.

"I know that voice," Abby said.

"Step out where we can see you," said Sam.

Three of them stepped out. Elijah, Micajah, and Ned. Elijah held the shotgun in their direction.

"Clear out," said Elijah with a jerk of his head. "We don't want you."

"Just the woman," said Micajah.

"And the money she's carrying," said Ned.

"What money I have is on board," said Abby.

"No, it ain't," said Elijah. "We went through everything. It ain't there."

"And we saw you sew them gold pieces into your corset," said Ned.

"You want my . . . corset?"

Sam caught a hint of the theatrical in her tone. He didn't think the robbers did.

"If you're lucky, we won't take what's under it," said Elijah.

"But we might," said Micajah, "if you make it hard."

They came closer. Micajah and Ned held wicked-looking knives. Elijah carried the shotgun and had a knife tucked into his belt. "Get gone," he said, "unless you want what she's got coming."

"I'm not going anywhere," said Sam. He wished to hell he had a weapon. He waited but Grumble didn't speak up. "Grumble . . . ," he said with menace.

"I choose to stay with my friends," said the trickster.

"Hmmpf!" said Elijah. "What an army! A woman, an old fart, and a kid."

"Unarmed," sneered Ned.

"This is gonna be fun," said Elijah.

They stalked forward.

Sam looked desperately up and down the waterfront street. At this hour it was empty.

"Wait!" cried Abby. She hesitated. Tremulously, she went on. "I'll give you what you want."

Elijah laughed.

"I will. You may have my corset. I'll strip right here in the street. You may have it."

"I'll take that little wrist sack, and the big one too," Elijah growled.

"All right. First, I want you to make sure I'm not deceiving you. I sewed my gold pieces onto the stays of my corset, all six stays. Come up, you can feel them."

She held her arms high.

Elijah grinned, hesitated, and then lumbered right up and stuck his face inches from hers.

She glared at him, commanding his hands to touch.

First he took the wrist bags and hung them from the arm that held the shotgun. Then he began to feel the stays one-handed.

"You think Elijah's groping something more than gold pieces?" said Micajah.

"The gold would settle my lust," said Ned.

"Gold is what it is," said Elijah with a leer. His fingers seemed to cant a coin sideways.

"Satisfied?"

"It's coins."

"Everybody steady now. No one get excited. I'm going to unhook my dress."

Abby's hand went slowly to the back of her neck. Her fingers grasped something. Like a snake it darted under Elijah's chin.

Elijah screamed, but the scream was drowned in a gurgle.

He crumpled, blood gushing his neck and chest.

Abby was holding a short, crimson knife.

Micajah bellowed and charged.

Abby grabbed Elijah's shotgun in midair.

Grumble's hand swooped to his boot, and he lunged at Ned with a knife.

Sam crashed into Micajah from the side.

An elbow cracked his skull.

Abby tried to point the shotgun, but it went off into the air.

Micajah drove Abby backwards. She tossed the gun away and gouged at his eyes.

Sam got his hands on Micajah's throat. The big man roared to his feet. Abby backed off. Micajah picked Sam up under the arms and flung him backwards into the street.

Pain shot down his arms and legs. His back sank into the cold mud.

Micajah landed on him full weight.

Sam tried to roll, but mammoth weight held him down. Huge arms squeezed him to the giant's chest.

Teeth bit his nose, and he screamed.

He wiggled violently, but the arms squeezed more fiercely.

He heard an explosion, maybe a shot.

He couldn't suck breath in.

He closed his eyes and heaved his chest with all his might and got nothing.

The world darkened around the edges.

Suddenly the pressure eased.

Sam breathed. Then he looked.

Abby held a lady gun, small as a man's palm, to Micajah's temple.

"Let Sam go. Get up peaceably. Then run. One sneaky move and the second barrel goes into your brain."

The air tasted like honey to Sam.

Micajah stood up. Abby went right with him, barrel to head.

Sam saw there was no second barrel on the little gun.

Footsteps slapped in mud, and then grew fainter.

"Ned's run off. You better get going," said Abby. She pushed his shoulder, and he turned.

"You killed my brother."

"The pair of you dead would make a good night."

Micajah stretched himself upward, his eyes wild with hatred.

Abby pushed the barrel so hard his head tilted. "Go!"

He ran.

"Help me with Grumble, quick. He's hurt."

Grumble's face was cut, and his chest looked badly cut. His shirt was drenched with blood. They sat him up.

"Help," he said.

Sam saw that his friend was about to die. Tears ran down his face.

"Help me get him up!"

As they struggled to lift him, a voice called out. "What's going on?"

Damn it, thought Sam.

"Who's there? Abby? Sam? What's going on?"

Sly Stuart ran up and holding his lantern, lighted. He knelt next to Grumble.

"What happened?"

Abby told him. That's how Sam found out she shot Ned with the lady gun first. "But I hit him in the collarbone, damn it!"

Sam told how she intimidated Micajah into running. "You scared the life out of me, Abby. That gun doesn't have a second barrel."

"Micajah didn't know that, did he?"

The captain opened Grumble's shirt and looked at the wound. "I can't tell if it penetrated to the lung," he said. "Hold that lantern close." Sam did. "Still can't see a damn thing."

He inspected Elijah. A brief look was all he needed.

Sam looked closely at Elijah. All that flesh, bone, and muscle, still. It gave him the dreads. He looked at the eyes. He had never looked closely into dead eyes before. His mind was struck dumb, but his body ran chills all up and down.

Sly Stuart looked around. The streets were empty. "This is some town, where guns fire and the constables don't come." He turned to Abby. "Elijah, Micajah, and Ned did this?"

"They wanted my money."

"And maybe her body," added Sam.

Abby stooped over Grumble. "Let's get him out of here."

"And ourselves," said Sam.

"Help," rasped Grumble.

Stuart and Sam lifted Grumble.

"Won't the constables come to the boat tomorrow?" protested Abby.

"Don't think so." Stuart smiled grimly. "That crew won't go to the police about this night's work."

"A body on the main street."

"Won't be the first time."

Sam plucked Elijah's shotgun out of the mud. "What'll we do with this?" he asked.

"Keep it," Abby said. "You earned it." She picked up her wrist bags.

Grumble coughed.

They bent over him. At that moment blood gushed from his mouth and ran down his chin and neck.

All three of his friends gasped. Everyone on the frontier knew that was a fatal sign, blood from the lung.

AT GRUMBLE'S FEEBLE request Abby got materials from his trunk and made a poultice. She treated the tooth cuts on Sam's nose, and then poulticed Grumble's chest. It was pointless, but she humored him.

They agreed to take turns sitting with him, and to call the others when the end came.

At dawn he was still alive.

"Hard to believe," Abby murmured to herself.

Frenchy was on watch. Sly and Sam were sleeping, and Sam needed it badly. Abby was holding Grumble while he departed from the earth.

"Not going to make it, huh?" His eyes opened, and the lids trembled a little.

She pursed her mouth. She couldn't lie to him, not now. "No, you're not." She wept openly. "Grumble, you and Sam saved my life. And I can't do one thing for you."

"Then would you oblige me with a favor?"

She blinked back tears. "Of course."

"Tell me the trick you ran on me. No one else has fooled me, not for twenty, thirty years."

She looked at his big, sad, clown face. Her heart broke. "Of course."

She took a big breath and let the story run. "My ex-husband Donnell had the idea. He went all the way to Baltimore to have the cards manufactured. The company engraved fifty-two different plates to print them. The backs, that is, the backs of the cards."

"The *backs?*"

"Yes. The cards are marked. Not by me and Donnell. By the printer. All those curlicues on the backs of the cards, every one is slightly different. It was very expensive, four thousand dollars. Unique cards. We kept the engraving plates.

"It didn't really take a lot of effort to memorize them, all fifty-two." She looked into his sad, weakening eyes. "I knew every card you had. Every face-down card. You were playing just like you had both cards face up. I even knew what you were going to get next."

Grumble's eyes twinkled, and he laughed. He actually laughed. Then he coughed. Abby clutched him to her chest.

At that moment Sam stepped up, his face pale. He knelt next to the half-reclining Grumble. "Don't die, friend, don't die."

Grumble shook his head. He blinked his eyes, as though to clear his vision. Then, slowly, he pushed his upper body erect. "Don't worry," he said, "I won't." He looked sheepish and delighted at once, like a kid who's gotten away with something. "No, no need to worry. Truth is, the knife scraped the ribs, but it didn't come anywhere near my lung."

He labored to his feet and swayed.

Both Abby and Sam grabbed him by his arms. He sat on a keg. "Perhaps I should take it easy. I did lose some blood."

"But we all saw blood come out of your mouth," wailed Abby. "It came from the lung. It's . . ."

He brushed all that away. "Believe me," he said, "I'm fine. You might give me something to eat and drink. I've been thirsty and ravenous all night, but my little ruse wouldn't let me tell you."

Abby caught on. She glared at him. "And exactly what, Mr. Grumble, am I supposed to say about your deception? How you tricked me out of, out of . . ."

"I think," replied Grumble, "you should congratulate me on the greatest performance of my life."

"IS CAPTAIN STUART awake? Grumble went on. "He'd enjoy this."

Sam disappeared and came back with Sly Stuart. He looked down at Grumble fondly. "Because of you, I didn't get to use the hotel room I paid for. What do you have to say for yourself?"

Grumble began, "I am an actor. You may call me a flimflam man, which is accurate, but it doesn't capture the full reality. I can become what people want or fear and make them believe it. I can be their friend, their confidante, their doctor, their pastor. I have been a Boston Brahmin, a John Bull, a Southern plantation owner, a Tennessee backwoodsman, a land speculator, and much more. I have even been a woman. My trunk is full of costumes, and legal-looking papers that help make me believable. I play my little game with people, do my little act, and I take away the symbols of victory, their coins.

"Joskins are easy marks for sport, too easy. I prefer the city man who thinks well of himself. I'm glad to say I have never polished iron with my eyebrows. You straight folk would call it spending time in prison.

"Sometimes, true enough, one of my playmates takes exception to my performance and gets violent. One of my recourses is this."

He stepped over to the trunk, opened the heavy lid, reached in, and held up a small . . .

"This capsule," he said, "is made of sheep gut. It amuses me that condoms are made of the same material."

Sam blushed violently, but Abby took the remark in stride.

"In it is blood, usually pig's blood, easy to get when they're slaughtering."

He paraded it in front of their eyes. "I always have one on my person. Violent men like to strike for the chest area. If they draw my blood, which offends me deeply, I put this little capsule between my teeth. At the strategic moment I bite down, and—magic!—blood pours from my mouth. Sometimes I can even ask for a priest and get one."

Abby laughed. Then she actually applauded. "Brother, you got me."

"Perhaps we're even now."

"I guess so." She looked at Sly Stuart and Sam. "He took me in."

"My dying wish, I fear, was to know the secret of her decks of cards."

"I told him. But, forget it, I'm not telling anyone else."

"Amazing," said Stuart. "But I wouldn't trade lives with you."

"In fact," responded Grumble, "you should not kid yourself. You and I are a lot alike. We live between worlds, and quite alone."

CAPTAIN STUART WENT off to hire a new crew for the *Tecumseh*. "I hope I don't get interrogated about Elijah." He scratched the top of his cap. "Oh, well, if I do, the hands just didn't come back this morning. I don't know a thing about it. Looking for a new crew."

He stuck his head back in the hold, where they had cleared a kind of living space among the kegs. "Oh. You three. Stay on board. Don't want you seen in town."

"By the constables?" Sam asked.

"The constables, Ned and Micajah, anyone. I'll bring food."

Lazy day. Nothing to do. Sam relieved Frenchy on watch. Sunny spring-coming-soon afternoon, the kind that makes you want to ease your bones and your mind and, if you're not careful, doze.

In the shade of the hold Grumble and Abby played chess. Grumble kept a board and pieces in his trunk. It was the only game they could think of where one couldn't try to out-cheat the other.

Captain Stuart's footsteps on deck woke Sam. "Damn it, some security we've got," the captain snapped.

"I'm really sorry."

"Back in a minute."

He came back with Frenchy and relieved Sam of watch duty. Oddly, Frenchy never seemed to mind watch, and regularly took duty when the crew went ashore to carouse.

As they ducked into the shade, Stuart said to everyone, "I haven't found a single crewman. This isn't a boat-building town, like Pittsburgh or Cincinnati."

Abby said, "Just as well. Grumble needs to recuperate. He's weaker than he thinks."

"Then how, milady, did I come to outwit you at chess?"

"Only two games to one. Dancing with Lady Luck, I guess."

They all laughed.

"Tomorrow I'm going to see a couple of farm boys who might want to go downriver. If they go, the livery hand will too. Meanwhile, we're stuck." Being fixed in one place, unable to go, go, go, that felt to Sly Stuart like a terrible fate.

He opened his package and spread the food out on kegs. "From the hotel," he said. Roast beef, roasted potatoes, carrots, and onions, gravy, a loaf of bread.

Grumble said, "Food to give the blood vigor," and dug in enthusiastically. They ate every bite, and wiped the heavy butcher's paper clean with the bread. They topped it off with another pot of the coffee from the pot that had been filling and emptying all day.

Everyone looked at each other like, What now?

"Abby," began Grumble, "you returned my service to you with a great favor of your own."

"Under false pretenses."

"Nevertheless. Our friend Sam also risked his life to save yours. He could have accepted the invitation to walk away, but stayed and fought for you. A friend has the right to know whose life he saved."

"Naw," said Sam. "You did the same. Nobody would walk off on a friend."

"You might be surprised," said Grumble.

"What did you have in mind?"

"Our young friend idealizes you a bit."

"I do not."

"Worthy of admiration as you are, Abby, you might tell him the true story of your life. Reality is such an antidote, telling it an act of friendship"

"Oh my, oh my."

"Tell it, Abby." This was the captain. "I want to hear too."

"Are you really prepared for this?" She reclasped her hennaed hair and plunged on.

"Natchez, Mississippi. Oh, do I remember Natchez. Part French, part Spanish, all mongrel—Natchez, first capital of Mississippi Territory. My flying fanny.

"My mother came up from Biloxi to live with her brother, Father Sean McKenna. Don't know what happened to my father. I never knew him, and Mother never talked about where he went. I don't know my father's name. She even went back to her maiden name, and gave it to me too.

"Mother kept house and Father McKenna raised me strict. Naturally, I went wild against both of them. Natchez had a neighborhood there under the hill where you could go wilder than probably any place on this continent. When I got to be sweet sixteen, I'd plenty been kissed. What was I doing to do? Clear choice, looked to me. Die of righteousness and respectability or live the way people did under the hill. I grabbed the wildest guy I knew and ran off to New Orleans with him."

She looked at Sam mischievously. He was tongue-tied.

"Benny's last name was whatever was convenient that day. I'm not sure I ever did find out the real one. He came from New Orleans and smelled of big city and daring ways and good times. He had big-money ideas. Of course, all those came to nothing. But his love for me, that came to something. He put something in my oven, gave me a big belly."

Grumble pantomimed the belly. Sam didn't think he was funny.

"In the end that also came to nothing—not my design, I assure you. You never get beyond some things the Church teaches you. I had a miscarriage." Her eyes closed and she lost herself in her own past, or her own interior, for a moment. "Sometimes I think losing that baby was the worst thing ever happened to me, and I've never been the same since." She waited and then popped her eyes open. "Sometimes I just think, that's life.

"I lost Benny. Uncle Sean always said God gives us blessings. Behind his back I called them goodies. Benny leaving me, that was a goody. That man was so scared of the very small thing in my belly. He took all our money, all our everything. Maybe he took my baby with him too. After he left, I didn't care about anything, neither the baby or myself. When I lost the baby, I damn near lost myself. Laid alone in our room, weak, bleeding, pathetic. The landlady found me like that when she came to evict me for not paying. She saved my life.

"Actually, turned out Benny was just the first of a line of gentlemen to say a come-hither hello now and a relieved good-bye later."

Sam snuck a good look at Stuart—how did he take her talking casually about her many lovers? His face was neutral.

"Back to that bad time. Where next for a girl like me? Penniless, destitute, and still weak from losing blood. So what do I do? Fall for another man, or at least throw in with him. Turned out that one wasn't interested in me or even my body—he'd just noticed how other men looked at my body."

She eye-leveled Sam until she was sure he understood.

"I kept some of the money he made off me and real quick ran off on him, just like Benny did on me.

"Ran to another one—how much choice did I have? Donnell was different. He was fun. He was savvy, he had big ideas, and he knew how to make them come true. He made good money dealing every kind of card game, and before long he got one of his big ideas—turning me into a gambler too. After I started dealing, he showed me the tricks, all the ways to cheat with a smile, all the ways to pluck the feathers off a pigeon. Something about it just feathered into my brain and made a perfect fit—I have a memory for cards and a knack for games. I think a little risk is, you know, good sport. And I have a way with gamblers, who are after all men."

She made silly eyes at all three of them.

"Soon we started romancing an idea—owning our own place, a dance hall, drinking parlor, and gambling palace in one. We saved every penny we could and went up the Ohio on a steamboat, looking for likely towns. Louisville was the first city we came to, though I always did wish we'd checked out St. Louis.

"Anyhow, Louisville it was. We had money, but we didn't have any connections. And actually, we didn't have enough money. So Donnell dealt in a place where he'd meet the main men of the town, at least those who drank and gambled. Wasn't long before he jawed the owner into letting me deal too. A new idea, it was in Louisville in those days, a female gambler—went down hard with the owner. Soon he began to see . . . A good-looking woman with some class and sass, a lady dealing cards and entertaining the customers, enticing but not available. It went over quite well, and that owner was never one bit sorry.

"Before long Donnell had our new partner all picked out. Beau Planxty was a gay blade if ever there was one, about forty, and good-looking till the devil may never care. Also, he had a piece of this and a piece of that business all over the state of Kentucky."

She sighed and looked coyly at Sam. He was all ears.

"He looked like trouble to me. Beau liked me way too well. But Donnell was scheming every angle. He pointed me at Beau like a shot arrow, and I penetrated right to that man's heart. Well, what little heart he had. Right quick, with Donnell's encouragement, he set to seducing me. Beau spent many an hour at my faro bank, and I spent many an hour at his home, upstairs. For a while I had to remind him to keep his hands polite in public. But Donnell didn't care—the way he saw it, we gained by both transactions, public and private. He was never that keen on what we did in the bed anyway."

Sam just couldn't get used to a lady talking like that.

"Pretty soon Beau bought a good building for our business and let us run the show, half shares to each. He gave us the money to make the place look classy, the way I wanted it, and to make me look very, very classy. That clothing I bought—every woman wants to wear the latest fashions from Paris, and the money I spent turned a profit. So I thought I had it made—mistress to a rich man, wife (well, common-law) to one getting rich, and half owner of one of the few kinds of business that always make money, rain or shine. We were set to conquer the world.

"Shortly after we opened the palace, we spent our capital on Donnell's next big idea. It was pure genius. That was the trick with the cards. I told Grumble, and neither of you need to know." She raised her eyebrows at Sam and Stuart. "To rig up this scheme, he had to make a trip to Baltimore, so off he went, and he came back with our pigeon bait, which was to make our fortune, in a manner of speaking.

"While he was gone, I ran the palace just fine by myself, even discovered I had a head for business. Got a good man to manage the bar, order the food and drink, hire and fire the staff. Had gamblers who didn't cheat the house out of its cut, or not too much. Learned to do the books myself, and well. And got a reputation as the faro queen of Louisville. The secret to making men lose their money at gambling is to give them a good time while they're doing it. The way I see it, women are much better at doing that than men. Some witty conversation, a bit of flirting, and a show of cleavage will take a dealer a long, long way.

"By the time Donnell got back, I had the business in good shape. The customers were happy, and Beau was happy with his profits every week. He was extra happy with getting into my, well, every nook and cranny every night while Donnell was gone. Myself, I liked the whole kit and caboodle.

"Donnell's ambition kept getting bigger. I hadn't moved forward with his plans to build rooms upstairs, where our dance hall girls could take a man for a few minutes' pleasure. He got that going, then turned the running of the girls over to me. I wasn't thrilled but didn't really mind."

What hasn't this woman done? Sam wondered.

"That winter he got our house built. It was perfect, right behind the palace but facing another street, a house with some style to it, handsomely appointed—I have an eye for fine clothes and fine furnishings, as well as a taste for good-looking men."

Why did she have to say everything right out?

"His next plan threw me for a loop at first. When the mayor came in for a drink, Donnell pointed me at him. About the third time he came in, Donnell whispered to me, "Entertain him at home." We all knew what those were soft words for. I did it, of course. Almost any adventure tickles my fancy. I also did the same before long for the banker, and the man who owned the theater and two hotels. Soon I was doing it for gentlemen of means who traveled through Louisville. I even did the dance with an occasional boat captain, if he caught my fancy." She winked at Captain Stuart.

"I wasn't a whore, though, because the pleasuring came without charge. I did, unknown to Donnell, accept gifts of money and jewelry, some of them quite generous.

"Through all this my common-law husband never got dissatisfied with me. It was me got dissatisfied with him. He should have cared what his wife was up to.

"That's when I started stealing from us. I did it to get even with Donnell, pure and simple. At first. After a while I pictured bigger things."

Sam looked sideways at Grumble. He was smiling, thoroughly satisfied.

"Donnell took the receipts every night and put them in the safe, with notes that showed what the bar took in, what the girls earned, and what we got off the tables. Every week I entered it all in the ledger, put a lot of the money in our bedroom safe, and deposited the rest in the bank. However, when it comes to depositing money, whether in a safe or a bank, there's many a slip twixt the cup and the lip. I had a hidey hole Donnell knew nothing about.

"I was twenty-two when we started the business in Louisville, Donnell was thirty-one. Within four years he and I were well-to-do, and I was nearly as well off on my own. Instead of half to Beau and half to us, it was ten percent off Beau's, plus ten percent off ours, for me. A tidy twenty percent.

"Then I began to figure. How many years until I had enough money to pull the plug, go somewhere else, and do the same business in another town, without the encumbrance of a Donnell? And no more Beaus, unless I wanted? How many years?

"I never worried about Donnell finding out—I worried about Beau. So for those years, believe me, I entertained him at our house and his house, wherever and whenever he wanted, and set my cap to keep him very happy. Still, he was damned smart, and I was far from the only woman available to him. It would never do if he found out what he was really paying for each romp around the bed."

Worse and worse, thought Sam with a sinking heart.

"In the end he did find out. And took great exception. Which is why I am here, sooner than I planned, running to St. Louis. My guess is Donnell has run to New Orleans, or is at the bottom of the Mississippi River feeding catfish."

"Who has the special cards?" asked Grumble.

Abby smiled spicily at him. "The question ought to be, Who has the plates to print more? Well, Mr. Grumble, I hope to heaven you know me well enough by now to figure that one out."

She smiled perkily at them all. "Any questions?"

"One," said Grumble. "You've trusted us, and know we won't rob you. How are you carrying the money?"

She nodded. "Well, as you almost saw for yourselves, a lot of gold coins are sewn into my corset." She corrected herself. "My two corsets." She hesitated. "The rest, actually the large majority, is in bank drafts and letters of credit, which are sewn into my underskirts."

"I want to know where you got the knife you stabbed Elijah with," said Sam.

She sparkled at that idea. She bent forward so they could see, put her hand back to the top hook of her dress in back, drew a knife from a sewn-in sheath, and handed it to Sam. It was tiny, the length of an emery board.

She took it and slid it back into the sheath.

"And that is as far as you may inquire into a lady's private matters."

* * *

THE THREE TALKED all day. When Sam took watch for Frenchy, all three sat at the bow. They shared ideas. They made plans, and sealed them with solemn agreement.

Suddenly Abby said to Grumble, "I know about you."

He raised an eyebrow at her.

"We have something in common. You were educated by Catholics."

"I was raised in Baltimore, the home of the first bishop in the United States. Bishop Carroll, among other good deeds, arranged for the education of orphans. How did you know?"

"Uncle Sean taught me to speak properly, and was hell on bad grammar. Your speech is still very correct, and formal."

"Thank you, milady."

"We have both overcome our backgrounds."

Grumble almost laughed but recomposed his face to somberness. "I fear I would be a great disappointment to the bishop, later archbishop, had he not gone on to his reward."

Late in the day Sly Stuart came back with food for supper, and everyone gathered on the lazy board. Sam noticed that the captain was keeping a pistol handy.

"I found three men," he said.

"Experienced?" asked Frenchy.

"Not a bit," said Stuart. He chuckled. "Sam, you are now my most experienced deckhand."

Sam couldn't meet the captain's eyes.

"Tell him," said Abby.

"I'm getting off at Cape Girardeau," Sam said.

"What do you mean?"

Abby explained it. They'd talked all day, the friends. They wanted to stick together. After the tussle with Elijah, Micajah, and Ned, they felt like partners.

"We're taking the first steamboat upriver together," Abby said. "St. Louis is where I've always wanted to go."

"It's as good a town as any other for me," said Grumble.

Sam didn't need to say anything.

"Steamboats are expensive."

"I have plenty of money," Abby answered. "These men saved my life."

Stuart looked back and forth between their faces. Sam couldn't tell what he saw. "Men," said the captain, "would you leave the lady and me alone a moment?"

They joined Frenchy on the bow. The sun was down, and dark could bring trouble.

From there everyone could see the captain gesticulating. Even in the way he held back they could see his urgency. And in her composure they could see that Abby declined.

"Now," said Frenchy, "this turns out hard."

Sam felt sad. Maybe it wasn't right. But for him New Orleans was the old world, St. Louis the new. As new as he himself was.

In a few minutes Abby came forward. Stuart went immediately to his lean-to, lit a lantern, and started reading.

"He actually asked me to marry him," she said. "I didn't think he would."

They looked downstream. The last of the day's light lay melancholy on the water.

"It's too bad," she went on. "He's a good man." These words seemed meant for herself. She shook her head. "The size of that loneliness. I could never fill it. No woman can."

When the captain's lantern went out, Abby made her way to the captain's small hutch.

Sam was glad.

Chapter Nine

"LET'S WALK," SAID Abby.

"Don't you want to get settled?" They were standing in the lobby of Plantation House, a hotel that looked very grand to Sam. Abby's bags had just been sent upstairs.

"I'm too excited," she said. "Come on."

St. Louis was every kind of new sight and sound. Even the street names were French. "Look," cried Sam, pointing. "What does it mean?"

Grumble read aloud from the signs painted on the corner of the building, " 'Rue de l'Eglise' and 'Rue Quicapou.' "

"Church Street and . . . Kickapoo Street?" said Abby.

"Perhaps."

"Charming," replied Abby wryly.

"Do you speak French?"

"You can't grow up in Natchez and live in New Orleans without picking up some."

"Especially words of love," teased Grumble.

She slapped his fanny.

They walked to the top of the bluff that overlooked the river. Twenty feet below stretched a huge expanse of flat rock butting against the bluff on one side and disappearing into the river on the other. Steamboats and keelboats galore crowded in, and all sorts of Negroes speaking French while loading and unloading. A uniformed black had taken them to Plantation House in the hotel carriage, his only English apparently the words "Plantation House." Abby had determined from Captain Koch, the steamboat captain, that it was St. Louis's finest. He would be glad to show Miss Price something of the town, he allowed, pulling at his gray muttonchop whiskers.

She couldn't impose on him that way, she said coyly.

Now she said to her friends, "I want to see everything."

Everything was impressive, for a remote frontier outpost. On the levee sat Market House, an imposing brick affair with a wooden gabled roof, farmers brought their wagons and carts to one wall and sold whatever they had. The grand houses of French families fronted Rue Royale, most of them stores on the first floor and residences above—the houses of Auguste Chouteau, the founder and patriarch of the city; of Pierre Chouteau, Auguste's nephew; of Sylvestre Labbadie and Charles Gratiot. "All great traders in furs," set Abby, who had pumped the steamboat captain very well. "Furs are what will make St. Louis rich."

Sam was tantalized by the compound owned by William Clark—office, dram shop, blacksmith and gunsmith shops, factory house, stables, and council house. Anything of the great Western explorer's would grip Sam, but Abby said the council house held a museum of Indian artifacts from the expedition to the Pacific Coast.

"I'd kill to see that," said Sam.

He was also fascinated by San Carlos, the fort with tower and barracks.

Along the riverfront were taverns where poor men ate, drank, rutted, gambled, and slept. The section with more pretensions sat another street back from the river.

"I want to go to the Green Tree Tavern and have lunch," Abby announced. "I'll treat." Evidently she'd put together a plan of operation from her talks with Captain Koch.

The people seemed to be mostly French-speaking, whether Canadian boatmen, shop clerks, traders and their employees, or Negroes. "How do you tell if a Negro is slave or free?" asked Sam.

"No idea," said Grumble.

He was eyeing everything curiously, probably sizing up his prospects, thought Sam, scouting out marks and suckers.

From the faces on the streets and the signs on the shops and offices, a quarter or third of the population was American. "Captain Koch said there's every sort of American here, not only Kentucky boatmen but mechanics, traders, doctors, lawyers, merchants, and more coming every day. Even gamblers."

"Oh dear," said Grumble.

She brought them to a stop in front of the Green Tree. It didn't look like the sort of tavern where Grumble and Sam usually stayed at all—a big, handsome frame building with a swinging sign in front. She perked up and made a grand entrance, which several gentlemen noticed. With her silk dress of the faintest, most shimmery blue, plus a tasteful hat and dainty parasol, both in lustrous ivory, she made an impression. Sam felt awkward trailing in behind her in the buckskin shirt and homespun trousers.

The lunch was good enough. Sam hardly noticed. He did notice the people, almost all French of an educated class, and he wondered whether he had manners enough to be there. Later he remembered only one tall, elegant-looking man who stopped by their table on his way out.

"Excuse me for being so bold, but I notice you are speaking English. Are you American, then?" He was beaming at Abby like Sam and Grumble weren't there.

She offered her left hand, and he bent over it, might have kissed it, for all Sam could see. "Abigail McKenna," she said smoothly. "My family is from Natchez."

"Pierre Chouteau," said the man, inclining his head in a small bow. Sam thought he glanced at her ring finger.

"I'm pleased to meet you."

"*Enchanté*, Mam'selle. But Natchez is an ancient and admirable French settlement," he went on, "the very first capital of Mississippi Territory. You must speak French as well."

"*Un petit peu,*" Abby answered. "A little," she said to Sam.

"With an attractive accent," said Chouteau.

"I'm afraid my French went the way of the family fortune," she said.

Sam looked questioningly at Grumble, who gave the tiniest shake of a head.

"And your companions are Americans?"

Abby introduced Grumble first, then Sam. Sam remembered his manners and stood up to shake hands. After all, Chouteau was the name of one of the fancy houses on Rue Royale, and of the town's founder.

"You are new to the city," said Chouteau to Abby.

"Yes, I'm staying at Plantation House. I'm thinking of making St. Louis my home, and starting a business. Is St. Louis a good prospect, M. Chouteau?"

"Yes, certainly. Because we are Americans now, we are growing swiftly. I am a man of business, Miss McKenna. If I can be of any assistance, do not hesitate to call on me." He bowed deeply to her, stood erect, held her eyes for too long a moment, and paraded out.

"A very proper gentleman," said Grumble.

"Smart, too, I'd guess," said Abby. "They say the Chouteaus are the hub that turns the wheel."

"He's attracted to you," said Grumble.

"Let's see," she said, "whether he chances by the Plantation House dining room this evening."

SAM AND GRUMBLE wandered the waterfront looking for a tavern as quarters. "We must avoid pretension," said Grumble.

"We need to find something cheap," returned Sam.

The Blue Stallion seemed a good enough place, cheap food, drink, and lots of men sleeping on the floor. Sam and Grumble spent extra coins for a room with an actual lock, to protect Grumble's trunk and Sam's rifle and shotgun. Grumble paid the difference. They had to share a single, narrow bed.

Sam spent supper wondering whether Abby was flirting with M. Pierre Chouteau. Grumble was running his three-card monte trick nearby, but Sam didn't feel like getting involved tonight, not even for a few dimes. He was staring into his mug and sorting out his future, or the future he didn't have. He was in St. Louis, where he'd wanted to be. He was running out of money. He didn't want a regular job, and didn't want to make his living by his wits, as Grumble suggested. Maybe he would hire on as a flatboat man, but he didn't feel keen about that, and the town was full of hands much more experienced than he was. He was just beginning to feel sorry for himself when a man sat down without invitation.

A man of indeterminate age, anywhere between middle-aged, thirty, and old like Grumble, maybe fifty. A long, expressionless face that had spent a lot of time in the wind and sun. Frontiersman but not boatman—not the red shirt and boatman's cap but shirt of hide, shooting pouch over the shoulder, rifle in hand, eyes an enigmatic gray. "Mind if we set?" said the older.

Sam hadn't noticed the other man until that moment. A younger frontiersman, round face, wild hair, and a look that was distracted, maybe far away in another place or time.

Sam shook his head. He minded, but in a place like this you couldn't take a table for yourself.

"You look lost."

"Sam Morgan, Pennsylvania." He stuck out a hand.

That steered the conversation away from the mental state Sam was in, lost or found. His companions were James Evans and a young fellow named Spoon, Tennessee and Kentucky.

"What are you doing in St. Louis?" Sam asked routinely.

"We came downriver after two seasons of hunting beaver."

Fur men. Sam's interest lit. "Where you been?"

"Sioux country," said James. "Hired out to Berthold, Pratte, and Chouteau, working from Fort Kiowa."

Those French families again, thought Sam, and Chouteau everywhere.

"This child ain't going back there." This was Spoon. "I'm not. Got to stop talking that foolish way." Sam tried to catch his eyes, but the man looked away quickly, like a skittish deer.

"Wal, hoss, this child cottons to it. And he knows poor bull from fat cow."

"Talk educated, James. You are. At least I have an excuse."

"My friend is weary of Indian country, but I'm going again. With Chouteau's outfit, day after tomorrow.

"All right, I'll try to think to talk educated, though this beaver has gotten mighty snug in the blankets with mountain talk." He chuckled at himself. "We've been working the lower Missouri," said James. "Sometimes those of us with Chouteau been hunting and trading as far up as Kiowa, even clear up to the Mandan villages. General Ashley aims to go all the way to the Shining Mountains, or near enough to see them." He hesitated, and finally said with a hint of approval, "That's Indian country."

"I fear for your soul, James." The older man just kept gazing at Sam with a half smile.

"My friend has got religion scared back into him," said James, and his gray eyes twinkled.

"You mock, just you mock," said Spoon. "But you won't come back, not from Indian country. And if you do, you won't be no white man no longer."

James didn't act interested in whatever Spoon thought.

"Tell me about the country," Sam prompted.

"Far as I've been, a vast, vast prairie, sky in every direction. No mountains, no trees except for right along the rivers and cricks. Grass, godawmighty worlds of grass in every direction, far as the sky is wide. And feeding on the grass, buffalo."

He shifted in his chair, as though to bring himself back into the present, into the tavern. "Your mind can't picture the buffalo unless you've seen them. Herds wander in thick as forests. Sometimes it looks like you could walk from the Missouri River to the Shining Mountains on their backs and never set foot on the earth. Best eatin' in the world."

He looked Sam full in the face and held his eyes. "I want to see the Shining Mountains again, and wander all over them."

"Mountain fever," said Spoon.

"That's it!" said James with a laugh. He pointed to his head. "This child's still got the mountain fever."

"More like it's got you."

James gave Spoon a look that said, 'You're no fun at all.'

Sam decided to say something sympathetic-sounding. "I've been flatboating. There's long, boring times in that."

"Same upriver," said James.

"The very same," said Spoon. "Nothing to do all winter long."

"We tell stories," said James.

"Get drunk and rut with women," said Spoon.

"A hoss has to, Spoon, or get his"—here he made a face at Spoon—"member frostbit."

"Not funny. I done plenty of rutting, whiskey too. I pray I don't burn in hell for it."

"I went to hell to get it," said James playfully, "and this child came back *confused*."

"He's about to tell a story. It's really another man's. He tells it like it happened to him. And it's blasphemy, making fun of what should be serious."

"A little fun doesn't mean we're not serious, Spoon."

"You ain't." Spoon sounded peevish.

"I went to hell and came back. That's the story. Like I said, in the winter there's not much to do but tell stories. The stories get, wal, they are *some*."

"Tell it," Sam said.

"Spoon, why don't you get us more beer, three of them, and wipe that stomach-achey look off your face."

Spoon headed for the makeshift bar.

"I was on the Cannonball River and got some Rees on my tail, so I cached. Sudden-like I remembered, I'd one time hid a jug there, and right quick I found it. 'Hurraw fur the mountains,' I cried. Down went the awerdenty—that means likker—and on I rode."

"Soon the country began to looked scorched and even burned. My mule wanted to turn back, but I kicked her forward.

"Before long the mule won't go at all, but stands a-tremblin' in place. As I gets off, a kind-lookin', smallish old gentleman, with a black coat and britches an' a bright, cute face an' gold spectacles, walks up an' presses my hand softly—

" 'Mr. Evans. How do you do, my dear friend? I have long expected you. You cannot imagine the pleasure it gives me to greet you in my home.'

"With this he offers a cigar. When I lipped it, the old gentleman reached out and touched his finger to the end—it smoked like fire had been set to it.

" 'Wagh! The devil!' screams I, drawin' back.

" 'The same,' chimed in he, biting off the little end of his'n—'the same, sir.'

" 'Hell! This ain't the holler tree for this coon—I'll be makin' medicine.' So I offers my cigar to the sky an' to the earth, like Injun.

Spoon came back with three mugs just then. "This is blasphemy, this Injun religion," he said. "Or heresy."

"Oh, go bark up a tree, Spoon. You don't know what way the stick floats.

"Let's see, I don't recollect all of the story from here on. The old gentleman gives me a tour of the place, and brags genteel-like on the clever furnishings. But it is all smell of brimstone, screeching hellcats, howling dogs, and mortals being tortured. This child even sees Cadet Chouteau, the fur dealer, coals a-burning his flesh forever, which give me a smile.

"Right then, two big, yellow snakes come slithering forward, hissing and flashing their fangs. To show the devil something, I jumps on one of them snakes and rides it, hooting and hollering. A lot of devils joins in, at first like it's fun, and then like they're gonna get me.

"I jumped off and broke fur timber. Lookin' back, the whole cavyard of hell was comin' at me, an' devils on devils, nothing but devils. About thirty-five of the infernal dogs an' slimy snakes come a top of me—mashin' and a-tearin' me, and bit big pieces out of me, an' bit an' bit again, an' scratched an' gouged.

"When I was most give out, I heered the Pawnee skulp yell, and in charged some of the best boys in the mountains. They slayed the devils right an' left an' set them runnin' like goats. I was so weak fightin' I fainted away.

"When I come to, we was on the Cannonball, just whar I found my liquor, an' my companyeros was slappin' thar wet hats in my face to bring me to.

" 'Evans, what on airth have ye bin doin' hyar? You was a-kickin' an' tearin' up the grass and yellin' like yer ha'r was taken.'

" 'The devils from hell was after me,' says I mighty gruff.

"They tried to git me outen the notion, but I swar, I saw a heap more of the all-fired place than I want to agin. An' if that ain't fact, I don't know fat cow from poor bull."

Sam kept himself from laughing out loud, thinking of his manners.

"*That*," said Spoon, "makes fun of real religion. People *will* go to hell from carrying on that way."

"There are some differences between us, Spoon," James observed equably.

"I wish I could go with you," Sam said to James.

"Another fool," crabbed Spoon.

"Chouteau signed on the men for this boat a couple of weeks back," James said. "Besides, it's a hard life for a young man. I was about your age when I first went up the river."

"When was that?"

"I was a Lewis and Clark man."

Sam felt a shiver along his spine. He couldn't get any words out of his mouth.

James laughed. "It didn't seem like such an all-fired deal until that Biddle book came out. Then we were heroes for a little while."

Still heroes to Sam.

"What's Captain Clark like?"

"It's General Clark, or Governor, depending. I'm sure he's fine. We're not companyeros like we used to be. Superintendent of Indian Affairs is a big job." It was said without resentment.

"What was the most exciting part?" Sam asked.

"Seeing the Pacific Ocean, I think. We could hardly believe that." He mused. "Hardly believe it." He yawned. "It's late, though, and I have an early morning. Start loading the keelboat at dawn."

"I thank God I'm not going," said Spoon.

James said to Sam, "Why don't you come see us off day after tomorrow? The levee. We won't cast off before midmorning."

Sam said he would.

Spoon leaned into Sam's face, his eyes wild and his breath bad. "If you go to them mountains," he said, "you'll turn into a heathen."

THAT MORNING GRUMBLE had an announcement. A message had come from Abby to their digs early, delivered by the hotel's uniformed "boy."

Grumble waved the note in front of Sam's face, though he knew Sam couldn't read. "It's a surprise for you, and you're going to love it. We meet her at the Plantation House restaurant a little before ten." He folded the note and tucked it away.

Presumably, the surprise wasn't supposed to be M. Chouteau, who was seated at the table with Abby. Grumble stopped Sam at the entrance, and they watched the pair for a moment. "In estrus," said Grumble.

"What's estrus?" asked Sam.

"What in a dog you would call heat."

Sam blushed.

"We could say the same of M. Chouteau, except that the word isn't applied to males."

They made their way between tables. M. Chouteau stood when he saw them. "Splendid!" he said. "Would you like a coffee?"

"Cadet," Abby put in, "we might be late." She was looking at a small watch pinned to her bodice, an item Sam hadn't seen before. He was wondering what "kahday" meant.

Chouteau led the way out of the hotel, and they walked wherever they were going. The city hadn't had rain recently, and the streets were dry and firm. Chouteau was expansive, pointing out every sight, which they'd mostly seen, flinging his arms this way and that. His air of power made him seem a tall man, and he was handsomely turned out. Abby was full of giggles and exclamations like, "Cadet, that's fascinating," "Cadet, that's funny," and "Cadet, you're silly."

When Chouteau stepped aside to speak with a gentleman, Sam asked Abby softly, "What's kah-day mean?"

"It's a family name for M. Chouteau, because his father is also Pierre. Like calling a young man 'Junior.' "

"Stick to Monsieur Chouteau," put in Grumble.

"The French are odd," said Sam tartly.

Where they ended up was the Clark compound, the council house. Sam hardly dared hope. Chouteau rapped lightly on a door, and a tall, stout man, red hair shot through with gray, opened it. "Your excellency," began Chouteau, "may I introduce Miss Abigail McKenna?" The red-headed man inclined his hand courteously. "Abby, Governor William Clark."

She curtsied.

"Mr. Grumble of Baltimore. I'm sorry, I don't know your Christian name."

"I go by Grumble alone," said Grumble, and shook the Governor's hand. "Honored, your excellency."

"Mr. Sam Morgan of Morgantown, Pennsylvania, near Pittsburgh."

Sam shook the hand but was unable to get himself to mumble, 'Your excellency.'

"Delighted to meet you all," said Clark. "M. Chouteau said you might like to see my Indian collection."

"Very much," Sam blurted out.

Clark chuckled and held the door open for them.

He escorted them around the large room, which had a big space set aside in the center, perhaps for meetings. Sam's mind whirled with pieces of this and that. "Your excellency," why do they call him that? I thought he was General Clark. Maybe he got to be a governor later. "Your excellency!" What are we, John Bulls?

He was awed at the treasures he was seeing. Bows and arrows of various sizes and shapes—Clark attached a tribe to each one, but Sam didn't recognize most of the names. Arrowheads. Spearheads. Bows and arrows.

"This bow is of Osage orange," said Clark. "The Osage and other Indians make exceptional bows from this wood. It's very good for the purpose."

Sam had never shot a bow and arrow. Now he yearned to.

"For the more civilized it makes a good hedge," said M. Chouteau with a piquant smile.

"This headdress," Clark went on, "is made of the head hide of the buffalo, which is especially thick. The horns are still on, you see."

Sam loved that.

"It's the Indian's idea of power," said Chouteau. "You wear the head of a buffalo, and the fighting horns, you will fight fiercely. Rather primitive."

"This headdress is eagle feathers." It was a bonnet plus a long tail of feathers. "To get each of these feathers, a man has to perform a coup. Strike an enemy. The greatest coup is to touch him with your hand."

"Not shoot him?" asked Sam.

"No. The worth of a coup depends on the danger to the warrior, not the damage to his enemy. So you see the man who wore this bonnet performed many acts of courage."

"They have their quaint notions," put in Chouteau. Abby beamed a smile at him like he was the cleverest, wittiest man on earth. Sam wished he would shut up.

Clark showed them a war club, then a knife with a blade of obsidian, a glassy substance found occasionally in the Rocky Mountains, said Clark, incredibly sharp.

"This skin sack hung from a tripod. The Indians use them to cook in. It's the stomach of a buffalo. The squaw puts in ingredients and water, like a stew, and then drops in stones she's heated in the fire."

There was beadwork, lots of beadwork. The Indians loved

beads almost above all treasures except tobacco. "You can't go into a village without tobacco and beads as gifts," Clark said.

"This is a war shirt." It was nicely decorated with beads, and hair hung from the underside of the sleeves. "What's this?" asked Sam suspiciously, fingering it.

"Those are scalps," Clark said, keeping his eyes away from Abby. Sam jerked his hand back.

"These dresses are ornamented with elk teeth and quillwork." Clark pointed at each. "Squaws make this by soaking porcupine quills and dyeing them."

"Barbaric," said Abby, "but handsome."

"Barbaric," agreed Chouteau.

Sam would have looked forever, but soon Clark ended the tour with an invitation to coffee. They adjourned to his office.

"Miss McKenna, do you mind if we indulge in a cigar?" Clark was already drawing them out of a humidor.

"Not at all. I believe I'll join you."

Clark pulled back the cigar he was extending to Chouteau and offered it to Abby. "No," she said, "those are a little overwhelming. I have my own." She drew the little case from her wrist bag and pulled out a cigarette.

Sam expected Clark to register shock, but the great man looked tickled.

Sam declined—too great a risk of coughing.

Grumble took the cigar offered and fell into the ritual of cutting the end and accepting a light from Clark's lucifer.

"Miss McKenna, what brings a lady to rough-hewn St. Louis?"

"Business, your excellency. I want to start a business."

Sam was sure Abby would embarrass them all by volunteering that it would be a gambling hall and booze den, plus women, but she only smiled prettily.

"Cadet has kindly offered to show me some buildings for lease," she said.

Clark nodded approvingly. Sam could see him take in "Cadet"

and the circumstances and comprehend everything. New liaison for the junior empire builder.

"Mr. Grumble?"

"I live by my wits, your excellency."

"Which is to say you're a gambler?"

Grumble was openly delighted. "Yes, your excellency. Also an itinerant musician and other things. I hope that doesn't lessen my welcome."

"In St. Louis we have no pretensions," said Clark.

Somehow Sam was surprised when Clark directed the conversation to him. "Morgantown, Mr. Morgan. Did your family found the town?"

"It's not much of a town, sir." He grimaced at himself. "Your excellency." Clark smiled broadly. "My father started a mill there."

"Your family's still there?"

"My brother, sisters, and mother." He wanted to mention his brother's crimes against him, but didn't.

"And what brings you to remote St. Louis?"

Sam thought a moment and decided to let it out. "I'm following my wild hair, sir."

Clark gave him a decidedly odd look.

"I was frustrated at home, country getting too settled, and . . . I met a man, an Indian, told me to follow my wild hairs, wherever they take me."

M. Chouteau chuckled wickedly, but Clark grew serious.

"And who was this Indian?"

"Hannibal MacKye, a Shawnee."

Clark laughed, a good, free, loud laugh. "I know Hannibal MacKye very well. A lot of people on the Missouri River do."

"How's that?"

"Oh, he wanders about in his way, does a little trading. If he took an interest in you, you have something to you." Clark laughed again. "Just like him to give such advice. Well, follow it, young man, follow it. The spirit of adventure, yes, it took Captain Lewis and me to the far waters of the Pacific and then to . . . advantages we'd never thought of."

"Yes, sir." Sam felt meek.

Chouteau leapt into the pause. "Tell me, Clark, what do you hear of my competitors?"

Clark understood the question perfectly, because he launched enthusiastically into the doings of fur traders in St. Louis in this March of 1823. Sam heard about Chouteau's outfit, known as the French Fur Company, about the doings of the Columbia Fur Company, led by Mr. McKenzie, a name spoken with wariness, and about the Missouri Fur Company, owned by men Sam had never heard of. Finally, Ashley-Henry, the largest outfit, was also headed far onto the upper Missouri. "A hundred and fifty men," said Clark. "Impressive."

"Or foolhardy," noted Chouteau.

"Are you interested, Miss McKenna, Mr. Morgan?" Clark rose heavily and pointed to a huge map on the wall. "Here's St. Louis. Here across the state of Missouri is Fort Osage, which has engaged M. Chouteau and myself a good deal."

"It's a private enterprise now," said Chouteau with apparent satisfaction.

"Yes, mmm. This is Fort Atkinson, the westernmost of all our military outposts. This river, the Platte, is the traditional distinction between the upper and lower Missouri. Above there you see Fort Recovery, a post of Missouri Fur"—Sam could see it was on a huge loop of the river, like a belly button sticking far out. "To here the trade is secure. But, see, above the mouth of the Grand River, are the Arikaree villages."

"Those Indians will be the ruin of someone," said Chouteau.

"Yes. And further above, the Mandan villages, where Governor Lewis and our party spent the winter. The French, excuse me, M. Chouteau, the Canadians, have traded here, but Americans very little."

"Now Mr. Morgan, already at this point we stand as far from St.

Louis as your Pittsburgh is. And look what a vast country the Missouri drains above here." He pointed—"the mouth of the Yellowstone, the mouth of the Musselshell, the Great Falls, and the Three Forks, where the Missouri begins. A great, unlimited trapping country, all on this side of the mountains. American territory."

"Closed to Americans by the Blackfeet," said Chouteau.

"Perhaps. Governor Lewis and I had no significant difficulties with the Blackfeet, but later Major Henry did."

"A good country to lose your young scalp in, Mr. Morgan," said Chouteau with a wolfish smile. "Or I am mistaken that you show more than a casual interest in the fur country?"

Sam didn't know what to say.

Clark rose. "I have another appointment, sorry."

"Thank you for seeing us, Excellency," said Abby.

"You're very welcome." He seemed to throw a fatherly glint toward Abby. Suddenly he turned to Sam. "Mr. Morgan, would you be interested in becoming a fur man?"

"More than interested, sir."

"If you'll give us a moment," he said to the others.

Clark pointed again to the huge map. "What catches your fancy? Chouteau outfit to the Sioux country? Missouri Fur all the way to the Three Forks? Dangerous, of course. I couldn't help you with Mr. McKenzie's firm. What about Ashley-Henry?"

Sam thought of James Evans and his admiring remark, "That's Indian country."

"Ashley-Henry would be my choice, sir."

Clark grinned. "General Ashley will be hiring men for two boats soon. To join the first two at the mouth of the Yellowstone."

Sam held his heart in his hand. "I'd love to go with the Ashley men, sir."

"I'll put in a word with Ashley for you. Go to see him day after tomorrow." Clark chuckled. "Anything for a protégé of Hannibal MacKye."

* * *

SAM GOT HIS spot on an Ashley-Henry keelboat to head up the Missouri easily, but he didn't meet Ashley because the general was away on business. The expedition leader, Daniel Patterson, signed Sam up. "We may be absent from the settlements as much as three years," Patterson warned sternly. Sternness and stiffness seemed to be his way.

Sam noted silently that the men of the Lewis and Clark expedition were gone for three years, and was happy. The terms? Hell, Sam couldn't tell. The deal was, he was to work as a hunter on the way upriver. Once there he would help build the fort, and defend it against Indians if necessary. In the autumn and spring Sam would be part of a brigade sent out to trap and hunt the beaver. In return, the company would furnish him with powder, lead, and other necessities, and he would get to keep half the furs he took.

"I see you have a rifle. What bore?"

"Thirty-six."

"Too light for the mountains. Go see the gunsmiths Lakonen and Hawken, they'll make you a decent trade."

This irked Sam—by God, he would keep his father's rifle. But Patterson went on without noticing. "The Three Forks of the Missouri are possessed of a wealth not surpassed by the mines of Peru," Patterson said. He spoke flatly, like he didn't think wealth was any fun. He was a strange duck.

Sam didn't know whether he'd come back rich or poor. He told himself, "It's my wild hair."

"We leave within a couple of weeks. Check in with this office every few days."

Yes by God, SIR! Sam thought flippantly. But he just grinned and took his leave.

"FIFTY-CALIBER, THAT'S the ticket for the mountains," said Jacob Hawken. "Better yet fifty-four. Those buffalo need a kick.

Not to mention griz. Have you heard about the griz?" Hawken looked at Sam with crazed eyes.

Sam didn't answer, since it was always good to hear more.

"*Ursus horribilis,*" Hawken growled. "The largest flesh-eater known to man. Mind your hair."

What a funny expression, Sam thought. He supposed it meant, 'Watch out or you'll lose your scalp.'

"Let me see that Pennsylvania of yours."

"I don't want to let it go. It was my father's rifle."

"A Pennsylvania won't do for the mountains. I've made many fine Pennsylvanias myself, but you need a fifty caliber. Or heavier."

"Could you bore out my thirty-six to fifty?"

"Short of dollars, are you? Why don't you trade me the thirty-six and that shotgun for a brand-new fifty?"

"Is this barrel thick enough to stand boring out?" He handed the Pennsylvania to Hawken.

The gunsmith took it and inspected the thick, octagonal barrel. "I guess so," he said. "Jacob Schmidt of Lancaster, a good gunsmith." He set it on his workbench with other projects. "A dollar and a half. Pick it up a week from today."

"One more thing, sir."

Hawken gave him a stern look.

"I want my father's name engraved on the stock."

Hawken picked up the rifle again. "What's his name?"

"He called himself The Celt."

"All right."

"And a circle around it made of Celtic love knots." Lew Morgan had worn a belt of Celtic love knots, made of cord by his wife. "How much for that?"

When Hawken told him, Sam pondered. "How about if I have a small circle and just the word 'Celt'?"

"Sure. One week today. Don't come until afternoon."

* * *

SAM HAD NO time to be bored—he got swept up in Abby's whirlwind.

Immediately she saw her first problem was cash. St. Louis had no bank to honor her bank drafts and letters of credit. Since the town was short of currency, the merchants issued a kind of paper money. The warehouses gave out receipts called deerskin notes—worth one deerskin, five deerskins, etc. The taverns gave out similar receipts; even a bakery gave them out—good for one loaf, good for two loaves . . . People used this paper in place of legal tender—what choice did they have?

But Abby had to pay workers and buy materials.

Cadet came to the rescue by trading her deerskin notes for her bank paperwork. She had enough to buy a good building, but she wanted to lease. She'd spend her savings on renovating, decorating, and operating capital. She hired Grumble to be her major factotum and Sam to be her man of all errands.

The right location, she thought, was a Chouteau building that housed a tavern and a small shop. She and Cadet convinced the lessee of the tavern on Rue d'Eglise that, since his wife had died, he ought to be in New Orleans with the rest of his family. Chouteau evicted the renter of the shop and leased the whole to Abby.

Immediately she hit on a name for her tavern, and a theme. Pirates' Cove, she would call it, because pirates led by Jean Lafitte had fought heroically to save New Orleans from the British eight years ago. She got a dressmaker started on pirate outfits for her servers, and pirates' bawds dresses for her girls. She required every sort of nautical knickknack as decoration, hawsers, fishing nets, and the like, and enlisted Captain Koch to spend a judicious amount and bring what he could find on his next return—the round trip to New Orleans took ten days or less.

The building needed refurbishing. Her carpenters quickly cut a wide door that connected the tavern and former store, and next to it installed a big double fireplace that served both. A blacksmith built cookstoves for the two rooms, designed to stand in the fireplace. Then she instructed the carpenters to change the upstairs of the former tavern, once a storeroom, into a series of small bedrooms and bought real beds—no tick mattresses on the floor for her girls. The small room over the one-time shop she converted into an apartment for herself. "Until I have time to pick out a house," she said.

Meanwhile, she lived at the hotel and installed Grumble and Sam in the unfurnished apartment. They got free rent for watch-dogging.

Grumble agreed to be Abby's pianist, but he made her promise to hire someone else for two nights a week, Saturday night so he could play the fiddle with piano backing and Sunday night so he could have a day to run his repertory of tricks at another tavern. "I don't know if I'll make a good employee," he fussed to Abby. "I'm used to being on my own."

"You're the only one I can trust," she said. After a while she promised to give him time to make two steamboat trips to New Orleans each year, taking advantage of marks each way. "And if you work for me for two years," she said, "I'll go partners with you on your own tavern."

Grumble liked that.

"At your age," she added, "you should stop wandering and get some security."

He didn't like that.

She set herself the goal of opening in ten more days, ready or not, but she didn't seem to drive anyone hard. She progressed by charm, flirtation, and fun.

Sam knew right away that she was giving M. Chouteau more than charm, much more. But that was her way, and she was his friend. With Grumble and Abby, whether it seemed hard or easy, he'd made more room in his mind for friends to be different from the way he was brought up.

He ran whatever errand she asked, lent a hand wherever she wanted. She ran him from daylight to dark and paid him five dollars a week. He thought maybe he could save enough to buy beaver traps. And he would trade the shotgun to Hawken for a pistol. The one he picked out was fifty caliber, so he could use the same lead balls the rifle used.

SAM PIVOTED ON the balls of his feet, looking over the heads of the opening-night crowd from his perch on the stairway landing. The house was full—people ate, drank, gambled, and danced merrily. Abby's opening was a success. William Clark was in attendance. The governor of the new state of Missouri, whose name Sam didn't get, was there. Two or three men of each of the prominent French families had turned out—Pratte, Labbadie, Gratiot, Laclede, and a couple of branches of the Chouteaus. Abby had persuaded M. Chouteau that a grand opening night was essential, and her lover had responded well.

Sam hoped he wasn't going to have to do anything. His job was to stand somewhere conspicuous, holding the fine new side by side Abby provided, and keep an eye out for trouble. If patrons took to fighting, he was to fire one barrel at the opposite wall, well over everyone's heads. The birdshot wouldn't hurt the wall much, or people either, except at very close range. "Don't get eager beaver," she said. "If you see trouble starting, go to Mr. Jim first. He'll handle it."

Mr. Jim was one of the two bartenders, the bulky one. Sam didn't know why he was called Mister.

"There's only a chance in a hundred you'll need to use that thing."

Sam's hands rested on the muzzle of the side by side. He felt self-conscious in the fancy new cotton shirt Abby had bought him, which was pleated in front and had sleeves that puffed from dropped sleeve to wrist. "Very handsome," Grumble commented.

Grumble was at the piano, decked out in one of the new pirate outfits, dashing out "Johnny Has Gone for a Soldier" and other dance tunes.

Abby was dealing at one of the tables. She'd told Sam she intended to do a lot of losing on opening night. Her laughter carried all the way across the room to Sam. She liked playing games with men, all kinds of games.

M. Chouteau was the ringleader of the French billiards players just below Sam. Abby had paid a fortune for the mahogany table with polished slate bed, expropriated from Plantation House with money and charm. Sam had a good view. The game was played with three balls, one white and two red. Apparently you scored by hitting your ball with the long cue and making it bounce off both other balls. If you missed, you lost your turn. The French elegants strutted when they played well. To Sam this was the thing that made civilization a bore.

All of a sudden things weren't boring. A woman made a grand entrance. Except for Abby and the dance hostesses, she was the only woman in the room, and boldly unescorted. Begowned and bejeweled, she drew the eyes of every man in the house. Grumble stopped playing the dance tune. Everyone got quiet. Slowly, grandly, she paraded toward the billiards tables. Grumble launched into a siren song from a Rossini opera. When she arrived, she wrapped her arms around M. Chouteau, kissed him on the cheek, and threw her head back. She sent out a squeal of phony laughing.

Abruptly, Grumble started ripping out a lively, polka-like dance tune, a schottische.

Mr. Jim materialized at Sam's side. "Madame Hélène," he said quietly. "A local widow. She was M. Chouteau's mistress until Abby came to town."

Though the widow looked a little older than M. Chouteau, she was splendidly preserved—a huge abundance of blonde hair, a long, elegant neck, beautifully shaped shoulders revealed by her off-the-shoulder gown.

"Isn't she a little out of bounds?"

Jim grinned. "Right where she means to be."

Madame Hélène was all over M. Chouteau, arm around him, the other hand stroking his. He turned his back on her, bent over the table for a shot, and nearly poked her with the butt end of the cue.

His shot missed everything.

She did not take the hint, but draped herself on him again.

M. Chouteau's opponent, M. Bernard Pratte, scored twice in a row. With an ironic eyebrow cocked, he said to Chouteau, "Two in one."

"Ought we do something?" Sam asked.

"Wouldn't want to be rude to a lady, would we?" Mr. Jim was not quite chuckling out loud.

M. Chouteau detached himself from the lady, said something to her quietly, and took a step away.

"But, chéri," Hélène said theatrically, followed by something fast in French.

Chouteau stepped to the table to shoot. As he began, she touched the elbow of his shooting arm.

Chouteau whirled, his face furious.

She stepped forward, threw her arms around his neck, and kissed him full and long on the mouth.

At that moment Abby came up. "What is it you want, Madame?"

She turned her head to Abby but kept Chouteau in her arms. He looked frozen there. "I think I already have it. Cadet, aren't you going to introduce me to your new . . . friend?"

Abby spoke up. "Abigail McKenna, owner of this establishment. Are you looking for work? I do have positions for women."

"My, my, I think the lady's calling me a whore. Cadet, will you not defend my honor?"

Chouteau bristled but held his tongue.

"Madame," said Abby, dead level serious now, "for your own sake you'd best go."

One of the billiards players walked up to Hélène and grasped her elbow lightly. "That's M. Labbadie, her late husband's brother," said Mr. Jim to Sam.

Hélène responded by turning more fully into Chouteau. She touched her necklace and then held her wrists, heavy with bracelets. "Look at these fabulous jewels Cadet gave me. *Pauvre petite*, you have none."

Abby looked up at the stairway landing and gave Mr. Jim a tiny, come-here jerk of her head.

"Hélène," said Labbadie softly.

But she just tossed off another cartload of French.

Abby answered back in French somewhat hesitantly, but the warning in her tone was clear.

"Oh, chéri, that gutter accent, how do you stand it, especially in *amour*?"

The crowd laughed. Sam realized Grumble had stopped playing, and everyone was watching the two women.

Mr. Jim arrived, and Abby whispered into his ear.

Mr. Jim marched straight to Madame Hélène and grabbed one arm firmly. "Madame, you're leaving."

"Cadet!" cried Hélène.

"Take your hands off her," said her brother-in-law, stepping up close.

Mr. Jim calmly took his hand off her arm, reached into her mass of blonde hair, and snatched her wig off.

Abby hooted.

Underneath Hélène was half bald. The sparse, thin, scraggly hair she did have was a drab brown.

She slapped Mr. Jim.

With an open hand he knocked her to the floor.

The place erupted.

M. Labbadie hit Mr. Jim with a fist that reflected gold cuff links.

Jim punched him in the stomach and doubled him over.

Abby grabbed Chouteau before he could get into the fray and pulled him back.

All the billiards players leapt at Jim, cues raised as clubs.

The nearby Kentucks laid into the billiards players.

Hélène snatched her blonde wig off the ground and ran up the stairs past Sam, bawling. He watched her open the door on one of the whore bedrooms and then notice the door to the outside exit. She dived into the night.

Watching her go, Abby and Mr. Jim took a moment to wink at each other.

In a far corner one poker player, a loser, hit the table's big winner.

A rodent-like man attacked his faro dealer.

Men in every corner jumped into the brawl. "Is this a private fight," yelled one, "or can anyone join in?"

The dance girls quailed against the walls.

Tables were overturned, chairs broken when they crashed onto someone's back or when someone crashed into them.

It was a fine old time.

Abby gave Sam the signal.

He lifted the side by side and discharged one barrel into the plank wall opposite.

The room dropped into a hush. Men froze like they were carved into the side of a building.

"There's another barrel," hollered Sam, swinging the shotgun over their heads.

"Enough!" cried Abby. "The drinks are on the house!"

Grumble struck up a dance as loud as he could.

Men rushed to the bar.

Mr. Jim got back behind it and started serving customers. A cut in one eyebrow was bleeding down his face, but his grin was natty.

Abby smiled up at Sam. He reloaded, just in case.

SAM FELT BEREFT.

He also felt very tired. He was leaning against a brick wall of Market House looking down onto the waterfront. His comrades were loading the *Yellow Stone Packet* and the *Rocky Mountains*. He didn't want to stir.

Last night, after Abby's opening, they'd stayed up most of the way to dawn, partying. First himself, Grumble, Abby, and Chouteau. Then just Sam and Grumble. He had said good-bye to his friends. He was going into Indian country, which was twice as big and twice as lonely as the frontier he was leaving behind. The only friends he had, he was leaving behind.

"Follow your wild hair," he whispered to himself. He pushed himself off the brick and wandered toward the boat.

"Morgan," snapped Daniel Patterson, "you're late."

Just then a smallish, slender man walked up, bearing an air of authority. "Captain Patterson, we have three leaking whiskey kegs. Get the cooper."

"General Ashley," said Patterson, "this is one of our hunters, Sam Morgan of Pennsylvania."

General Ashley? Sam had expected something more.

"Sam, this is General William Ashley."

Ashley offered his hand. "Glad you're signed on with us. Good luck. Captain Patterson, have you. . . ."

They turned and hurried off to bark instructions here and there. Sam watched them go and felt a pang. He'd met Hannibal MacKye, Sly Stuart, Grumble, and Abby, and he was going to follow these men?

For two hours he helped load trade goods for the Indians. Ten thousand dollars' worth, Patterson had emphasized. Sam was tired, and his back hurt. Ashley, though, was bustling, bustling, bustling, preparing the *Packet* and *Rocky Mountains* to sail.

Ashley wasn't going. "Captain" Daniel Patterson would be in charge. Sam wondered why men in private businesses got called by military titles, and he didn't quite understand how the general got other men to do the work and make money for him. Did his soldiers do his fighting too? "Morgan, look sharp there." It was Patterson barking again.

This wasn't what Sam was looking for.

A friendly hand touched his shoulder. Grumble. He turned to Patterson and addressed him respectfully, asking for a moment to take leave. Patterson gave a grudging nod.

Grumble put an arm around Sam's shoulder and led him aside. "I know you don't have much time, and we said our good-byes well last night. But I have something more for you. You could call it brotherly advice. Note! Brother, not fatherly."

Sam looked into his eyes.

"Sam, you've got a hunger. For what I don't know. But I do know this. No one else can guide you. Not your father, not your brother, not Hannibal MacKye, not me. My one bit of advice is, Do your own hunting."

He reached out and hugged Sam. "May fortune smile on you."

"Good luck to you too."

The cherub spun gracefully on a heel and walked away.

"I'll be back," Sam called after him. "I'll be back."

Grumble waved without turning.

Sam looked at the keelboats and his rough companions and the charging river, and pictured tens of thousands of Indians in a country unimaginably vast and thought, 'Maybe I won't.'

Part Two

INDIAN COUNTRY

Chapter Ten

SAM THOUGHT HE heard a sound. Maybe. Sort of. He didn't know.

All his nerves strained. He heard nothing. Sounds of the river, but that was always so. The Missouri was forever lapping-swishing-gurgling its way to the Mississippi. And after some time on watch—by the Big Dipper it was nearing midnight—his nerves got jumpy.

Did he hear a paddle?

He was on lookout, and desperate not to foul up. They were

only a few miles below the Ree villages. The old hands of the fur trade agreed that the Rees were bad Injuns. You could never tell whether they were going to be friendly or hostile. Everyone was edgy—which would it be?

Lookout was more listening than watching. Ashley usually anchored the two keelboats, *The Yellow Stone Packet* and the smaller *Rocky Mountains*, in the middle of the deepest channel and strongest current, so enemies would have to use boats to come at them. Lookouts were always posted. But what could you see in the darkness? The nearest town was maybe five hundred miles back, the nearest trading post a couple of hundred. Where was light to see by? Moonlight? Starlight? Not much on a night like this, though the moon lit the clouds from behind.

Sam saw shapes in the blackness, but didn't know whether they were real or phantasmagoric. He peered into the darkness from the bow of *The Rocky Mountains* and imagined he saw the silhouettes of tens of thousands of Indians out there in the darkness.

If the Rees came, they would use dugout canoes. They would float silently. They would put a man or two on board as quietly as possible and try to find the lookout before he could holler out, and kill him.

Sam would see their shadowy shapes, wouldn't he? Wouldn't he?

He sharpened his ears. He sorted out every sound and decided none was a paddle dipping, or being lifted from the water. Hoped none was.

General Ashley said Indians were not to be treated as enemies. How could ninety men on two keelboats fight hordes of angry Indians? Without the U.S. Army closer than Fort Atkinson, hundreds of miles downriver and getting further every day? Without a white man between the Missouri and California? Most of these ninety men had grown up on the frontier. If they hadn't fought Indians, their fathers had, or grandfathers. And their blood told them Indians were the enemy. So did jiggers in their skin when they approached a village. Besides, that's what Sam was posted for, to listen for Indians, because they might attack.

Klip-PINK!

His toenails curled. That was the sound of a paddle—he was sure of it. He padded softly to larboard, where the sound seemed to originate, and peered into the darkness. Something moved.

No, it was a trick of his eyes. He saw lots of shapes in the blackness, figments of his imagination, of his fear.

He walked amidships along the cleated deck, where the crewmen planted their poles, staring into the darkness.

Nothing. Pointless. Hopeless.

KLUNK!

He ran to starboard, where this sound came from.

S-S-SCRAPE!

No doubt about it now. That was the sound of wood banging the hull.

He opened his mouth to bellow, but his voice got caught.

"Help me!"

Someone speaking English?

"Help me!"

An American voice in the darkness. He hurried forward and saw a shadow against the hull.

"Give me a hand up!"

Sam ran to the sound.

His eyes read a human shape, reaching for the deck.

"Who are you?" Sam cried.

"A man who needs a hand," the voice came back calmly.

Sam ran forward. As he got there, a bag of gear flopped onto the deck, and two hands reached up. Sam took the hands, but one was full of rope and the other full of rifle. Sam grabbed the stranger's wrists and heaved him onto the deck, rope, rifle, and all.

Someone came forward with a lantern. A dozen men were stirring from their blankets on the deck.

The pull of the rope banged a dugout canoe against the hull.

"Thanks."

The man who spoke was a tall, slender white fellow with a serious face. He stuck out a hand to Sam. "Jedediah Smith."

"Sam Morgan."

"I might be James Clyman," said the man with the lantern, "if I knew why the hell you're mucking about in the middle of the night a thousand miles from anywhere."

"Bringing an express to General Ashley," Smith said.

Everyone absorbed what that meant as Smith confirmed. "I've come down from Fort Henry."

All the way from the junction of the Missouri and the Yellowstone, evidently alone. Sam was speechless.

"The General is on the other boat," said Clyman.

"It will keep until daylight. I could use some food and some sleep." He picked up his bag of belongings and saw Sam looking at it oddly.

"Possible sack, we call it," said Smith. "Everything I own in there."

"I'll hitch your canoe at the stern," said Sam.

DIDN'T MATTER TO Sam whether the physical miles from St. Louis were a thousand miles or not, and they damn near were. He knew he was further than that from the world he knew. Two months into Indian country, a world into alien territory.

First, it had been far, far harder work than he'd imagined keelboating could be. The hands moved the boats upstream against the spring current mostly by poling. The edges of the decks were cleated; the men planted their long poles in the bottom and walked downstream, pushing the boat the other way. Get to the stern and pull your pole and walk back to the bow and start again. It was muscle-popping work.

Much of the time, though, poling wasn't enough. Then the men went ashore with a long rope called a cordel and heaved the boat upriver by main might. Or they tied the cordel to a tree, stood on the deck, and hauled that rope on board.

Poling or cordeling, they heaved a lot of weight up the river—goods to trade to the Indians for safe passage, for horses, and for furs. They carried a sort of mercantile store west—blankets, pots and pans, kettles, needles, awls, calico cloth, wool strouding in red and in blue, guns, powder, lead, tomahawks, knives, coffee, sugar, lots more, and most of all tobacco, the so-called sacred plant needed to start any discussion with Indians. You couldn't do business with Indians unless you had this merchandise. But the men griped about the weight.

Fortunately, Sam was spared most of this brute labor. Signed on as a hunter, he spent his days walking the shore with his rifle, The Celt, in search of deer, turkey, or whatever else was available. He had a partner in this work, the lank, slow-spoken Virginian named Clyman. As Sam was maybe the youngest crewman, Clyman was the oldest, in his thirties. Well, maybe that crusty old Hugh Glass was the oldest. Anyway, Sam liked Clyman, liked the country, and loved the hunting.

But it wasn't the glories of the landscape in spring that enchanted Sam, not exactly. It was the sense of himself as a man with feet on the earth and eyes on the horizon. He couldn't have said what this meant to him, nor did he try for the words. But he felt small changes within himself. He was going somewhere inside.

In three weeks they passed Fort Osage, an outpost of Missouri Fur Company, with its tame Indians, not much different from what Sam saw back in the settlements. In another three they came to Fort Atkinson, the last outpost, military or otherwise, of the

United States. Beyond this point adventurers were on their own, for life or death. White men had pushed beyond. But some people didn't think they came back as white men.

Beyond this point they were also in a world Sam didn't know. They visited a Sioux village above Atkinson, to give gifts, trade for furs, and get the news. Sam wanted to eat what he saw with his eyes. Here were human beings living in a way he had never imagined, and somehow it worked for them. Yes, somehow it did. His curiosity was frustrated, for the hands weren't allowed to roam the village on their own, and their visit was short.

Three more weeks, with short stops and a couple of fur trade posts, brought them where they were now, just below the Ree villages. Which according to all report meant their lives were at stake.

SMITH HAD TO answer a lot of questions when he woke up, but they were friendly, even admiring. How did you do it? Travel all the way from the Yellowstone, maybe three hundred miles away, alone? How did you avoid the Indians? Every man jack of them knew that, no matter how they might declare friendship, warriors would be tempted by a white man traveling alone. How did you find us in the dark? What's your message for the General?

Smith didn't mention doing it alone. He said he traveled at night in his canoe and cached in brush cover by day. The hard part, he said, was not the Indians but avoiding the whole trees sweeping down the river in high water—they careened downstream, popping up anywhere. Find you? Luck. He saw the keelboats from several miles above. Before starting out each night, he used the twilight to climb to a high point and look downstream as far as he could. This past night he'd seen where the boats were, and then saw them as rectangles blacker than the darkness.

The message?

"That's for General Ashley's ears."

Soon, though, it was known to every man on both boats. Henry wanted Ashley to trade whatever was necessary for lots of horses and bring them. Traveling to the Indian villages to trade, hunting the beaver, all this required mobility, which meant horses. The price of a horse in Missouri was doubled when you got to the villages of the Sioux, and doubled again up where Henry was. The firm needed horses.

Someone yelled, "We'll get them from the Rees."

Edgy, crackling laughter everywhere.

Sometimes the Rees were cordial. Two months ago in March, though, they beat and robbed hirelings from Cedar Fort. Not long after, they got nervy and attacked the fort itself. The mountain men—that's what the fur men were calling themselves—fought the attack off, killing two Rees and wounding several others. One of those killed was the son of Grey Eyes, a principal chief.

Plenty of reason to approach the villages with sharp eyes and ears.

SAM GAPED AT the two villages there on the right bank, less than a quarter mile apart on a big horseshoe bend in the river. The earthen lodges were surrounded by pickets, new ones.

"They're ready for an attack," said Diah Smith.

"They won't get one from us," answered Ashley. He was glassing the lower village with binoculars. "I think there's a ditch just inside the pickets."

"Probably expecting trouble from us or from the Sioux," said Smith.

Sam didn't say much in this crowd, but he liked to be near Ashley and hear what was going on. Ashley had said any friend of Hannibal MacKye was a friend of his, and he stuck to it.

Anchors were being set in midstream.

"If they trade us horses, where shall we hold them?" asked Smith.

"On the far bank," said Ashley.

Smith shook his head. "I've seen Indians over there already." The ground was high and broken, with lots of good places to hide.

"On that bar then." A wide sand bar bordered the bank below the villages.

"No really good place," said Smith.

"We'll have to move the land party away fast, then. Sam, bring me Mr. Rose."

Sam took the small skiff, dropped down to the other keelboat, and called out for Rose.

Edward Rose was a dark-skinned man, by his claim a mulatto, sired by a white man and birthed by a Cherokee-Negro woman. He looked scary—his face was much scarred, and his nose had been bitten off, he said in a fight. He'd been in Indian country a long time, and said he'd lived with both the Rees and the Crows. Not that he said much. Most of the men didn't trust him. But he was invaluable to Ashley, because he knew the country and spoke both Crow and Ree.

"We need horses to travel in Crow country. We'll send a party from here on horseback. That's if the Rees will trade horses. Will you guide them?"

Rose nodded yes.

"What route will you take?"

"Drop down to Cheyenne River, follow west."

That river was about seventy miles back down the Missouri. They talked a little about practicalities. Rose wanted to know how many men. Ashley said it depended on how many horses they could get. Rose said a party of at least twenty was needed for safety. Ashley answered that he was thinking even bigger.

"Smith, will you command the party?"

"Sir?"

"You're the most experienced man here. These *voyageurs* are good hired men to run boats, not traders and trappers."

"I'd be honored, sir."

This Jedediah Smith always seemed a little formal.

"How do you see this, Rose?"

"The Rees are dangerous. Always. The Sioux maybe troublesome. Once a hoss gets to Crow country, he's safe. To them I'm a big man." He said it matter of factly, not like a boast, but Sam wondered.

Just then two Indian men, chiefs from their dress, came down the bank to the sand bar, making signs.

"Sam," said Ashley, "get the skiff. We'll go parley on the beach."

IN HALF AN hour they were back on board, with Grey Eyes in tow. Chief Little Soldier had declined to visit the boat. To Ashley's surprise and delight, Grey Eyes agreed to come, alone. Rowing them out to the *Packet,* Sam wondered why he didn't act angry about the death of his son, and why Grey Eyes wasn't worried about his own safety.

They sat on the lazy board, normally the pilot's spot. Ashley gave Grey Eyes several big twists of tobacco, a beautiful six-point light blue blanket, and some red cloth. He had coffee served.

At length Ashley began. "We had nothing to do with the fight at the Cedar Fort. Nothing. I can't be responsible for what every white man in the country does."

Rose translated, and the chief's eyes said he understood.

"I promise that the Great White Father will investigate. If the white men deserve punishment, he will punish them. In the meantime, we'd like to trade with your people."

Grey Eyes told Rose that the Rees had to consider this matter in council. His expression gave nothing away.

Sam rowed Grey Eyes and Rose back to the beach. The morning sun lit the chief's face but shrouded his deep-set eyes in shadow. Sam couldn't help wondering.

They all wondered. Ninety men on two keelboats lounged in the sun and wondered whether the Rees would be friendly and trade with them, or rain death down on them. Every man measured the distance from the pickets to the boats with his eye.

THAT AFTERNOON GREY Eyes came back to the beach. Sam rowed Ashley and Rose in to talk to him. Grey Eyes motioned them to sit. Sam couldn't help looking up at the pickets, to see if any Rees with arms lurked there. He saw no one.

"We have good hearts toward you," Grey Eyes said. "We will trade."

Or that was how Rose translated the chief's words from his own language. Sam had wondered downriver, at the Sioux camps, how much the two peoples misunderstood each other because of translations. Did Grey Eyes really speak of hearts, for instance, or use another expression? When Ashley spoke of the Great White Father, what words did Rose use in Ree? Sam figured the idea of a distant white man being his father, well, that would be absurd to Grey Eyes. It was absurd to Sam.

Ashley said how glad he was to be able to trade with his friends the Rees. He would especially like to trade for forty to fifty horses—he planned to send about forty men west by land. Rose flicked his eyes sideways at Ashley but said nothing. Sam suspected he didn't like the Rees knowing their plans.

Grey Eyes answered with a suggestion that Ashley pitch his tent on this beach in the morning for trading. The Rees would bring the horses then.

Ashley nodded and looked at Rose. The interpreter made some statements in the Ree language, apparently compliments, assurances, and protestations of good faith.

Grey Eyes stood, turned, and left without another word.

"I've never been so relieved in my life," said Ashley.

"You damn well should be," Rose said. "It shines to wake up alive."

* * *

ASHLEY DECIDED NOT to trade from a tent on the beach. He had Sam and two *voyageurs* ferry trade goods in with the two skiffs, the small boat rowed by one man and the big one by two. That way most of his trade goods stayed on the boats at any given time. The Rees would not be able to swoop down and make a bonanza in one raid.

In return Ashley wanted horses and buffalo robes. His great aim was beaver pelts, which the men of the fur business called "plews" from a French word. Most of the thick hide was not germane to Ashley—he had no use for the whole, or for the thick guard hairs that kept the beaver warm in cold mountain streams. He wanted the beaver's underfur, which made the finest felt known, and fine felt made fine hats. Frontiersmen wanted beaver hats. Gentlemen and ladies in the great cities of the East wanted them. The monied, the aristocracy, even the crowned heads of Europe wanted them. Beaver was a fortune. But the Rees were too far downriver to have beaver skins.

John Jacob Astor had made his fortune in the trade. Pierre Chouteau and the other entrepreneurs of St. Louis were in mid-stride making theirs. Now Ashley intended to make his by journeying to the most prolific beaver country left on this fertile continent, the Rocky Mountains. It was risky not only for the trappers and traders, who might lose their hair, but for the owner of the company. Last spring, for instance, one of Ashley's keelboats sank, and he lost ten thousand dollars in trade goods. Trapping parties got robbed—sometimes they lost everything and got left helpless on the prairie. A man who outfitted fur brigades could lose a fortune as quickly as he could make one.

All day long Ashley bargained. To the Indians went cotton cloth, three- or four- or six-point blankets (the points indicating that it was worth that many beaver plews), metal tools, and other bounty of an industrial society. Ashley gave them everything that was customary in the fur trade but high-quality guns and whiskey. Whiskey was too dangerous, right at the moment. The Sioux didn't want the Rees to have good guns. Neither did the mountain men. Instead Ashley traded them the cheap, inaccurate *fusils*.

In return he got nineteen horses and more than two hundred buffalo robes. A good day's work.

Until one chief insisted on trading for the good American guns. Ashley refused. The chief got loud and belligerent. In a few minutes Ashley had himself, his men, and his merchandise back on the keelboats, and double watches posted. All was safe except for those nineteen horses and the Kentucks on the beach who guarded them.

As everyone else was packing to leave the beach, Ashley told Diah Smith, "We ought to move these horses to the other side." He glanced up at the logs picketing the downstream village, and Sam knew he was thinking of the guns that might stick over them.

"Not enough time," Smith said. "I'll take charge of them for tonight and move them in the morning."

Sam could hardly believe his ears—he wouldn't have camped on this beach, right below the pickets, for a moment.

"I'll need men."

On the *Packet* and then the *Rocky Mountains*, Ashley asked for volunteers for the beach detail. Nearly a score of the American backwoodsmen stepped forward. Not a single *voyageur* came forward—not one Pierre, Jacques, René, or Yves. Sam felt humiliated for them. After a deep breath, he stepped forward himself.

"No," Ashley shook his head, "I want you with me." Sam suspected Ashley of protecting him, and he felt mixed about that.

Sam and a huge *voyageur* took the big skiff and rowed the Kentucks to the beach. Sam couldn't keep his eyes off his fellow oarsman, who was contaminated by his countrymen.

As the Kentucks splashed through the shallow water onto the shore, Sam looked at them with an odd longing. Diah Smith gave him a thin smile. "Don't worry. Probably nothing will happen tonight." Men were already gathering driftwood for a bonfire. They would be all eyes and all ears all night. Sam looked up at the pickets and wondered what dawn would bring.

THE NIGHT WAS perfectly quiet, except for one thing Sam thought was incredible. Several men took the small skiff without asking and went into the villages. A huge French-Canadian, Gideon, rowed them in. When he brought the skiff back, he came to the bow and sat next to Sam on watch. He offered a hand. "Gideon Poor Boy."

Sam shook the hand "Sam Morgan."

"Ze Americans call me Poor Boy. Real name Dubois." He let out a deep chuckle. He was a barrel-chested man sporting a big, silky black beard with streaks of silver in it. "Some men, zey want ze woman big-big, no?"

Sam felt like he had to answer. "I guess."

"Ze cock, it is divining rod. You hold it in front of you, it lead you to trouble." Gideon laughed. He looked around the boat. Men were sitting up everywhere, talking. "No man sleeps tonight."

Sam didn't answer.

Gideon got out his small white clay pipe, filled it, and lit it.

"You think French are coward, no? Coward because we do not go to beach, be ready to fight?"

"Yeah."

Gideon chuckled. "Different men, they are brave for different things. Zese men, they run rapids that would make ze Kaintocks get out and walk. I swear it."

This didn't impress Sam much.

"Some things we don't like. Don't like ride horse so much, don't like shooting war."

He fished out a second clay pipe and filled it. "Here," he said, handing it to Sam. "Enjoy."

Sam took the pipe and thought what the hell. Gideon lit it for him.

"I am not French, *exactement*, you know? I am Jew."

"Jew?" Sam had never even seen a Jew, as far as he knew.

"*Oui*. My father, he is Montreal Jew. My mother, she is Cree."

"Indian?"

"*Oui*. My father, he give me name." He pronounced it the English way, GI-dee-on, the first syllable as in GI-dee-up.

"I thought you were called zhee-day-on."

"I like the way Americans say it. Whatever, it means 'strong in battle.' So I must be brave."

"What kind of man was your father?"

"A fur trader. I am *hivernant*. Understand?"

Sam shook his head no. He drew the smoke into his mouth and puffed it out. Tasted pretty good.

"A winter man. I spend two winters in the *interieur*. The *voyageurs*, they are most *engagé*, hired men who paddle the canoes to Fort William on Lac Superieur in spring, carry things trade to Indians. Then summer, paddle back to Montreal, carry furs back. *Compris*?"

Sam nodded. He blew smoke at the moon, and wondered if he could learn to blow smoke rings.

"Some men, they are *choisi*—chose?—to stay the winter at the forts, among the Indians. These men become—how you say?—very tough. Strong against cold. Make long snowshoe trips in bad, bad weather. Sometimes carry a message, maybe, from one fort to another. Very, very tough."

Gideon tapped the ashes out of his pipe into the river and put it away. "You like that pipe?"

"Yeah."

"You keep. Ashley, he issue you some tobacco." Gideon chuckled. "And charge you mountain price."

Gideon refilled his own pipe. "Once I saw two men, Chouinard and Robles, brag big about how very brave. One man tell a story how much courage he has, other man tells a bigger one. Chouinard tops Robles story, Robles tops Chouinard.

"Not long they get angry. 'We fight,' says Chouinard, 'see who is more man.'

"All men listening say, 'No, no, not fair.' Chouinard is greatly small, Robles greatly big.

"But Chouinard, he insist. They make ready. Throw off blankets and pouches that get in the way. Set rifles and pistols aside, but not knives. Make big circle of men watching, fighters must stay in circle. Every man fears Chouinard will get hurt, we all like him.

"Then *personne* holler out, 'Grizzly!' *Vraiment*, a grizzly now walks right in camp, sniffs for food.

"Robles, he say, 'Man who fight the grizzly bravest, he win.'

"Chouinard, he shout, 'Yes!'

"Each man, he take up rifle. Robles, he aim. But Chouinard, he walk in line of fire, toward grizzly. He hold his ramrod in the air. Someone say, 'He going to conduct bear music.' Is very funny.

"Chouinard walk straight on, closer and closer to grizzly. Bear, he don't know what to think. Man seem very, very crazy. Bear sniff in every direction, try understand what happens.

"Chouinard, he just walk forward.

"Bear, finally, he stand up hind legs. He twice tall as Chouinard. He roar. Me, I near piss pants, even so far away.

"Chouinard, he walk straight forward, like walking into bear's arms, walking into mouth of death. He no stop, he get close, I bet he smell bear's breath. Then he reach out and tap bear on head with ramrod."

Gideon gave a peculiar smile. "Oh, t'ink on zat. He count coup on grizzly bear standing up, ready to fight. Then he turn and walk away calm.

"Grizzly, he don't know what to think. This is crazy man. He get down all fours. He look around. He wander off.

"We all laugh, shout, clap Chouinard on back. Every man say Chouinard bravest man in camp, even Robles say. Count coup on grizzly bear!"

THE DAWN BROUGHT rain, thunder, lightning, and howling wind. Ashley had Sam skiff him to the beach, and they nearly got swept downriver. Diah Smith and the others on the beach were all agreed that the horses couldn't be moved in this weather. Doubtful they'd even go into the water, and if they did, they'd go wild and some would be lost.

Ashley went back to the boats grim.

He waited for the weather to break. And waited. And waited.

Late in the afternoon the wind calmed and the rain eased.

A Ree chief, Bear, sent out an invitation for Ashley to join him in his lodge. Several men thought the general should ignore it, but Ashley said he couldn't let Bear think the white chief was afraid. Sam rowed him and Rose, the interpreter, to the beach.

Smith came up. "Now's the time to move these horses."

Ashley answered, "Wait until I get back. Chief Bear wants to talk to me."

Smith accepted these instructions, even curtly delivered as they were, with only a mild look.

Sam was glad someone followed orders. Most of the crew, he guessed, both Frenchy and Kentuck, were strictly every man for himself. A fight would be a chaos. Sam supposed that Ashley, as a military man, hated that.

"Wait here for us, Sam," said the general. He and Rose made their way up toward the lower village.

Sam sat down on a log and tried his new pipe. Jim Clyman sat down next to him. Clyman's job was party clerk, since he was older and more experienced and had some education.

"I don't like it here," said Jim. He was tall and lanky. A sunken place on one side of his mouth suggested he'd done some fighting somewhere. His gray-blue eyes saw everything and gave back nothing.

"I admire you volunteers," Sam said.

Clyman gave an odd smile. "You're young and still see heroes around you."

"Maybe I should."

"Heroes are usually involuntary," said Clyman. He looked around his companions with some amusement. "We're quite a crew, recruited from the grog shops of St. Louis, and other sinks of degradation."

"I came out of those myself," said Sam.

"As I recall, you came out sober. You didn't put in enough time to get ruined. Most of these men don't think much of being sober. Those that can remember it."

Sam was starting to feel testy. "I look up to these men."

Gently, Clyman got out a knife. "Some you should. Diah Smith, Tom Fitzpatrick, Tom Eddie, Bill Sublette, maybe old Glass." He started whittling on a piece of driftwood. "Jack Larrisson, Jim Davis, Reed Gibson are not bad men."

"That's half the men on this beach."

Clyman chuckled. "The rest, I'd say, well, Falstaff's battalion was genteel in comparison."

Tom Eddie and Hugh Glass came up. Glass was a dour fellow, had never even spoken to Sam, and paid little attention to what anyone said to him, leaders included.

"What you going on about, Clyman," said Eddie, "using my name? Who the hell is Falstaff? Where you off at when you oughta be right here?"

"A story by William Shakespeare," said Clyman, unruffled. He followed with a short account of who Falstaff was, what his drinking companions were like, and how they nearly spoilt Prince Hal.

"Sounds to me like they were having the fun." Eddie was a man who liked fun and would take any dare, like diving off the boat's cabin or swimming through a wild rapid.

"Who was this Shakespeare?" asked Sam.

"Wrote plays, stories for actors on the stage. Want to hear one?"

"Sure," said Sam.

"If it ain't too foofuraw," said Glass.

"Romeo and Juliet," began Clyman, "were young lovers."

"Too foofuraw already," put in Glass, "them names. Was one of them a man?"

"We'll call him Eddie," said Clyman, "and the girl will be Velva Mae."

"Better."

"They were important families there in Italy, and I'm a gone beaver if those families didn't hate each other. Eddie and Velva Mae, though, one look and they were goners, you know how that feels. Just teenagers, but they were bit bad by love.

"Romeo—"

"Eddie," corrected Eddie.

"One night, even knowing her folks couldn't stand him, Eddie climbed up to the balcony outside Velva Mae's bedroom—"

"Balcony?" objected Glass. "More foofuraw."

This time Clyman quelled him with a glance. "And they made big eyes at each other. Velva Mae gave a big speech—"

Glass groaned—

"Eddie, Eddie, wherefore art thou Eddie? What's in a name? A rose, if we called it something else, it would smell just as sweet."

"Did Eddie mount her?" Glass wanted to know.

Clyman nodded gravely. "They loved each other good. Then they asked the priest to help them get married and escape together."

"I don't hold with no priests," put in Glass.

"The priest done his best. He got a sleep potion would make

Velva Mae seem just like dead. Then, after they put her in the crypt, she could run off with Eddie, and no one the wiser."

"That's clever," said Eddie.

"It went bad, though. Eddie didn't get the message, so he didn't know what way the stick floated. When he saw Velva Mae looking dead, he got all sad and put his knife into his own lights. 'Fore long Velva Mae, she wakes up, sees Eddie all bloody and gone from this world, so she runs the knife into her own heart. Fell right across his body, like they was together forever."

"Like they was doing the deed," said Glass.

"It's a good story," said Eddie, "but the ending's dumb. Why you want to tell them kind of stories?" With that he and Glass stalked off.

"I liked it," said Sam. "You glad you can read and write?"

"Yes. When it comes to writing, though, I have no respect for a man who can only spell a word one way."

Sam wasn't exactly sure what that meant. "I wish I could read and write."

ASHLEY CAME BACK from Bear's lodge cussing. He snapped at Smith to sit down with him a minute. "I don't know what's going on," he said. "Bear showed us every courtesy, acted like we were friends. The conversation got maybe a little too friendly. This other chief, Little Soldier, told us right out that the Rees are going to attack us. Or, if they don't attack before the boats leave, they'll hit the land party after."

Smith asked Rose, "What do you make of it?"

Rose shrugged. "I can't tell. My guess is, Little Soldier doesn't want trouble, for whatever reason. He's warning us honestly, maybe. Maybe he thinks that if we know, we'll take precautions so trouble never gets off the ground."

Smith held Rose's eyes for a moment. A lot of the men didn't trust Rose, who was colored himself—hadn't he even lived with these red niggers? Smith raised an eyebrow at Ashley.

"I don't trust Little Soldier, or any Ree," Ashley grumped. "Likely as not he wants us to move the horses across the river to get them further away from the boats. Then they can fight the shore party without having to fight all of us. It would probably be over before we got there."

Smith said softly, "It's your call, General."

Ashley looked at Rose, at Smith, even at Sam. He was not a man, Sam guessed, to overanalyze beforehand or second-guess himself afterward. "We'll hold them here. Our chance is better patching things up with the Rees than running from them."

Smith just nodded.

THAT CHANCE STAYED good, maybe, until the wee hours of the morning.

Rose came tearing down the bank yelling. "Aaron Stephens is killed! Aaron Stephens is killed!"

Jedediah was up and alert immediately.

Ninety feet away on the *Packet*, the general bounded out of bed.

Sam rolled out of his blankets.

In a couple of minutes five dozen men on the boats were at arms, and the beach party was too.

Sam went after Rose in the small skiff.

The interpreter didn't have much to say. Like some other men, and Rose himself, Stephens had gone to the village looking for a woman.

"Hot blood and no sense," said Ashley, not caring if Rose was offended.

Rose went on evenly. He didn't know how the trouble started, just that Stephens ended up dead. Rose wasn't a man to add words where none was needed.

"We've got to talk to Smith," said Ashley.

When Sam, Rose, and the general landed, the beach party was already in a raging debate. One said, "We've got to move the horses right now."

"Not in this dark," judged another.

"I'm staying here."

"We're safer where we are."

"They can shoot right down on us! From behind the pickets!"

"We'll fort the horses."

"I ain't gonna give them the satisfaction of tucking tail and running."

There were as many opinions as there were men.

Clyman and Fitzpatrick walked up to Smith, Ashley, Rose, and Sam at the big fire. Clyman eyed the general questioningly.

"What do you think, Mr. Clyman?"

"Don't matter what I think, General. This outfit doesn't have military discipline."

"Or any other kind," added Fitzpatrick. He was a banty Irishman. Though the Irish were known for blarney, Fitzpatrick was realistic and sensible as could be.

"General," said Smith, "Every man's gonna do what he wants to do. I'm afraid there's no sense giving them orders."

Jack Larrisson walked up to the fire. "General, the men want Aaron's body. We got to have it. Decent burial."

Somehow "decent burial" rang hollow, coming from this crew.

Ashley said, "I'll attend to it, Mr. Larrisson." Larrisson waited for something more but finally stalked off.

"Mr. Rose, are you willing to carry the message to the Ree?"

Without a word, the interpreter walked up the bank and toward the pickets.

"Mr. Smith," said Ashley, "do whatever you think is best. Tell all the men—do what you think is best. If that means coming back to the boats, do it. I mean that. To hell with the horses."

In the distance came Rose's voice, calling to the Rees behind the pickets. Ashley, Smith, Fitz, Clyman, Sam—they all stood and looked at each other. There was nothing to say or do. They looked bleakly into the darkness. Sam wondered if every man's scalp prickled, like his did.

Finally Rose came back. The general looked questioningly at him. "We'll see," Rose said. "I'll stay here."

"Let's go."

On the black river Sam couldn't see the general's face. Finally the man blew breath out and said to no one in particular, "Doesn't matter what Stephens did or didn't do. All skirt-chasing stories end the same."

THE REE VILLAGES were aflame with noise. More than one man on the beach said, "Indians are working themselves up."

First light came as a murky gray behind clouds. The men on the beach fidgeted. Some muttered about getting off this beach. Others agreed—they sure as hell didn't want to wait around.

Just then a voice came from the pickets. Suddenly the fifty yards to those pickets seemed way too little.

On the second or third try Rose understood what was being said. A Ree wanted to return the body of Stephens. Without hesitating, Rose walked up the bank.

Diah Smith blew his breath out. He guessed the interpreter was counting on his friendships among the Rees to spare his hide.

From the pickets Rose called back that Stephens's eyes had been put out, his head cut off, and his body otherwise mutilated.

As though the word "mutilated" was a signal, a fusillade came from the Rees.

The horses fell, whinnying and spouting blood. The men on the beach dived behind their carcasses.

Jedediah Smith put his face in the sand behind a slain animal and said a silent prayer for the soul of Edward Rose, a brave man.

Horses screamed. The ones still on their feet, not already flat and bleeding into the sand, sprinted around wildly, their eyes crazy with fear and pain.

Sand gouted up everywhere, flying from horses' hoofs and from lead balls tearing up the beach.

Jedediah Smith peeked his head up far enough to take stock. The hardest part was getting the mind clear enough to look and see what was happening. In just seconds most of his horses were dead or wounded. About half his men were the same. The living crouched behind dying horseflesh. Lead flew through the air like leaves in a high wind. Diah thought grimly that Ashley had traded the Rees this lead just two days ago.

The men near Diah, those left alive, bellowed for rescue by the boats.

Smith rested his rifle on his horse's neck, waited for a head to appear above the picket, and squeezed off a shot. Shooting up at assailants hidden behind pickets was pointless. Maybe any action was pointless. He began the slow, awkward business of reloading.

The situation was simple. Either Ashley would take them off this beach with one of the boats, or no man would get off alive.

ON THE *PACKET* William Ashley was screaming at his *voyageurs*. "Weigh anchor! Put in to the beach! Weigh anchor! Put in to the beach!" He stared at them and tried it again, even louder. "Weigh anchor! Put in to the beach!"

His two pilots, the men who did the poling, every man Jacques of them looked back glumly. Some of them shrugged. None of them moved.

The occasional shot thwacked into the hold of the boat, or chipped the wood of a cleat. The *voyageurs* gathered behind the hold.

Before he was hoarse, Ashley caught on. His Frenchmen simply were not going to go onto that beach, into fire. End of story.

"Sam! Row me to the other boat!"

Sam did. A few pieces of lead gurgled into the water around the skiff. But Sam was thinking of the French-Canadians. They were a disgrace.

Ashley hollered the same words for longer at the *voyageurs* of the other keelboat. The result was the same. Except these boatmen wore expressions that said, 'Our commander has gone insane. No reason we should act the same way.'

Finally the general relented. "I want volunteers to take the skiffs to the beach and bring those men back," he cried in a level tone.

Sam and Gideon stepped forward at the same time.

"Sam, take the small skiff." Sam darted for the boat.

"I need one more volunteer." The big skiff took two oarsmen, and would hold up to twenty passengers.

Another Frenchman stepped out.

Sam was halfway to the beach when he saw the second skiff get started. Kah-LUP! Kah-LUP! The sounds of lead balls plunking into the water got way too regular. He kept his back to the beach and pulled.

As he brought the boat onto the sand, Sam started yelling, "Let's go! Let's get out of here!"

A ball thunked into the gunwale next to him. He jumped out of the boat and crouched in the water behind it. "Come on! Let's get out!"

Not a man on the beach moved. Some lay tight behind dead horses. Some sprawled in the open, their bodies spattered with blood.

"Let's get out of here! Now!"

"Go to hell!" someone answered. A couple of other voices echoed viler profanities and blasphemies. "The goddamn rowboat ain't no help!"

Sam couldn't tell if they were angry because the big keelboats hadn't come or frozen with fear to their corners of shelter.

Wood chips from the gunwales flew into Sam's eyes. He ducked his head in the water and washed off.

The big skiff beached next to him. *"Allons-nous-en! Allons-*

nous-en!" bellowed Gideon. They wouldn't have paid him any attention had he spoken English. Which he promptly did. "Let's get the sheet out of here!"

Several men crept to their feet and staggered toward the skiffs, all bleeding. Some fell, shot again. Four made it to the boats. Gideon herded them into the big skiff and immediately set out for the keelboats.

Sam peered over the gunwale. No other Americans were coming. A big gang of Rees were, though. They'd reached the upriver end of the beach and were advancing steadily.

"Let's get out of here!" Sam screamed. "They're coming on foot."

He saw Diah Smith and Jim Clyman, each behind a prone horse, turn their rifles upstream. Not a single man came to Sam's rowboat.

His heart somersaulted into his mouth.

Sam jumped into the empty skiff and rowed like hell. With his back where he was headed, he had to face the beach, face the enemies who were shooting at him, face his companions who were about to die, and he didn't want to witness one damn bit of it.

THE BIG SKIFF got to the *Packet* and unloaded wounded men. Immediately, Gideon started for the beach again. A bullet hit the other oarsman, and he toppled into the water. Gideon snatched his own oar out of its lock and tried to use it as a paddle. When he saw that wouldn't work, he dived into the river. The skiff floated downstream, empty.

Sam pulled into the shadow of the *Packet*, tied off, and watched. Before the Rees got too close, men began to jump up like birds flushed from cover and run for the water. First one, then another, then two, and at last three at once. Some ran strongly, some clutched wounds, some hobbled. By miracle every man got to the water and started swimming for the keelboats. Within ten yards, though, two or three sank and never came up.

Sam held on tight, but pointlessly, to the rope that anchored him to the deck.

The keelboat began to float downriver—the *voyageurs* had weighed anchor. Sam saw a crewman on the other keelboat cut the cable to its anchor. Even as the Kentucks were swimming out, the keelboats were sliding away.

Two men ran headlong for the river. Sam recognized one of them as Clyman.

Jedediah Smith was the last man left on the beach. Sam saw his muzzleloader belch black smoke.

He would need close to a minute to reload. Knowing, the Rees stood up and ran toward him.

Diah Smith sprinted downstream and made a flat dive into the water, rifle in one hand.

THE KEELBOATS FLOATED downstream, but Clyman got swept even faster than the crafts. Sam saw him go below even the lower boat, *The Rocky Mountains*. Tom Eddie grabbed a pole and stuck it out. The Ree fire, though, was now hitting the keelboats, and Eddie had to stay behind a box, so the pole didn't reach Clyman.

Sam went after him.

Clyman knew he had to swim across the river. He thought his chances were poor, and the way he was weighted down, next to zero.

He jerked at the rifle in his belt. The damned lock caught in his belt.

He went under.

After a long while, he came back up, sputtering for breath. The lock was still caught, and the rifle felt more awkward than before. He twisted it hard, the lock cleared the belt, and he dropped the rifle.

A couple of strokes let him know he was still heavy. He unbuckled the belt and let it sink, with his pistols.

He worked his shooting pouch off his shoulder and dropped it.

When he felt how heavy his buckskin shirt had gotten with water, he slipped out of one sleeve.

He sank.

When he flailed back to the surface, Clyman heard Sam Morgan crying, "Hold on, I'll help you."

With a few strokes the rowboat was close.

Clyman was so exhausted he couldn't pull himself on board. Sam had to heave him up. Clyman flopped into the bottom of the boat and breathed.

Sam pivoted the rowboat to see the situation.

Fire bit his left shin, and he screamed.

Both men lay in the bottom of the rowboat, which went adrift in the swift current.

Clyman saw the blood on Sam's pant leg and understood. He slipped his shirt back on, took the oars and rowed for the far shore.

When he beached the boat, Clyman said, "I'm going up the bank to see if they're after us."

He saw several Rees most of the way across the river, swimming straight toward him.

"Sam, they're coming fast."

"Save yourself! I can't run!"

Clyman looked back at the swimmers. He thought, Maybe I can row out and brain them with an oar. But there were too many and they were too close.

Sam crawled up to where Clyman was.

Clyman looked around for a hiding place. Nothing but scanty brush.

"Run, Clyman. If you escape, write my family at Morgantown, Pennsylvania, and tell them what happened to me."

Clyman ran.

Sam crawled into the brush.

The Rees took out after Clyman.

He sprinted for open prairie.

Soon Clyman looked back. Three Rees were coming for him, one out to the left, one out to the right, and the third directly toward him. They wore nothing but belts holding knives and tomahawks, and carried bows and arrows.

Clyman ran for his life.

The ground was smooth and level, with no places to hide. He had a lead of maybe a hundred and fifty yards. He could see high ground maybe three miles off. He headed for that.

He ran. He just ran. There was freedom in running, even exhilaration. He felt the sun on his body, the earth beneath his feet. He ran forever.

His side hurt. Breath burned his throat.

He ran.

He looked back.

He still had his lead.

He ran, and after a long while the rising ground looked closer. It was still a long way. He might never get there, and the earth there might still be too smooth and perfect to give him a hiding place.

His job was only to run. He did.

He felt his heart flop about in his chest madly.

He slowed. He turned his head.

The man in the center was gaining on him.

He ran.

Now the land began to roll. For the first time he topped a little rise and dropped out of sight.

He saw a little rain-washed hole, as wide as his body, maybe three feet long and two feet deep. He dived into it. The prairie grasses rose about a foot high on either side.

He silenced his breath.

His main pursuer passed about fifty yards away.

He waited.

His left-hand pursuer passed.

He waited.

Much later, the right-hand pursuer went by.

Something like hope welled in his heart.

He trotted off to the right.

A glance told him the Rees had dropped into some low ground and were out of sight.

He hit sloping ground the other way and plunged ahead.

Soon the slope became a ravine.

Later he climbed out and mounted a ridge.

About a quarter mile away stood the three Rees.

James Clyman spread both his arms and bowed low to them.

SAM WAITED TO die. He lay flat on his back and looked up at the wide, wide sky. He hated this, the waiting. Why didn't they come and kill him decently? I don't care what they do after, he told himself.

He was in a rage that they didn't get it over with. He whispered, "It'll stop my damn leg from hurting."

The leg kept throbbing like hell.

Soon his breathing eased.

He looked around what little he could.

He turned onto his right side. No Indians.

Painfully, he pushed himself onto his left side. No Indians.

But so what? The brush blocked his view as much as it blocked theirs.

He slipped onto his back again, rigid and determined.

He waited.

Nothing happened.

Nothing.

Carefully, gingerly, he rolled onto each side again. He seemed to be alone. He pushed onto his belly and forced his head up.

Alone.

Feeling like a fool, he started crawling. In a few feet he was at the edge of the brush. He lay very still and looked. No Rees on the beach. No Rees in the water. No Rees across the river—he'd been swept a ways downstream. No Kentucks or *voyageurs* in sight. No boats on the river.

He might have been alone on a desert island.

He held his heart with his ribs.

The keelboats had drifted downstream, getting away from the villages for safety. However many men had died on that beach, most of the whites were on the boats and had survived.

If he floated downstream. . . .

He got to his knees and looked around in every direction. Evidently, the Rees had ignored him to chase Clyman. Unbelievable. He wondered if Jim was alive.

Right now it didn't matter. He had a job to do.

He crawled back to the rowboat. He refused to think about luck or no luck. He thought of the rowboat and floating to wherever the keelboats were. If he had to row, he would find a way.

He took stock. He had his rifle, The Celt, and the pistol and knife in his belt. He couldn't walk a step. The nearest fort was about two hundred and fifty miles downriver. The boats were his only hope.

The eddy immediately took him upstream. He had to row. It was awkward, pulling the oars on one leg, and it hurt like hell. He set the other leg in the boat bottom, a useless thing, but somehow it shot with pain every stroke. He forced the boat into the current and floated downstream. He rested his oars. If he just steered a little and stayed in the current, he would find the keelboats.

WHEN CLYMAN CONSIDERED his circumstances, he didn't feel so feisty.

He had dumped his rifles, his pistols, even his knives in the river.

No telling where the boats were. They picked up anchor and floated down. They might go all the way to Fort Kiowa, which he guessed to be three hundred miles south.

He walked to some high ground and looked around. Though he

knew the river lay west and south of him, he was out of sight of everything. No boats, no Indians chasing him, no villages, no white men—no one.

He needed a drink. Which meant the river. He could see timber along the bank. He could drink, hide, and rest.

As he scooped up his second double handful of water, the keelboats floated right in front of him.

The men hailed him as quickly as he shouted at them.

The small skiff was launched to get him.

The *small* skiff?

Was Sam . . . ?

Chapter Eleven

SAM WAS GLAD to see Clyman standing over him. It took his mind off what the surgeon, Fleming, was doing to his leg, and off the pain that would have made him scream, except for the stick Fleming made him bite down on.

"I gave up on you," said Clyman.

Sam took the stick out and looked at his friend. "Did you give up on Rose too? He's here."

When the attack started with Rose at the pickets, everyone gave him up for lost.

"Praise be."

"The ball broke the little bone in your shin," said Fleming. He stopped probing and put a poultice on the wound.

"What's the total situation?" Clyman asked.

"We left ten bodies on that beach," said Sam to Clyman.

"Plus Aaron Stephens."

"Three more went down in the river," said Fleming. He'd already cut away the lower leg of Sam's hide pants. Now he bandaged the wound with cotton cloth. He picked up two boards he'd scrounged somewhere. "Hold these for me while I tie, will you?"

Clyman held the boards tight against the front and back of Sam's leg. As the surgeon bound them to the leg with hide thongs, the young man put the stick back in his mouth and wheezed big breaths.

"How many wounded?" Clyman asked.

"Eleven wounded," said Fleming, "three or four of them mortally, I think."

"They made clowns of us."

Sam giggled, maybe hysterically.

Fleming finished and raised up. "Put no weight on this leg for at least six weeks."

Sam jerked the stick out. "Six weeks?"

Fleming nodded. "That's *no* weight. Sit, lie, or use crutches without touching the foot to the ground. If you ignore me, you'll break it again."

"How long before I'm back to normal?"

"Two months, at least. The pain will tell you." Fleming stood up.

"Want me to get a green deer hide?" asked Clyman. "Wrap it around the leg? When it shrinks, it will hold the bone tighter."

"Sure, why not?" said the doc.

Sam noticed that his tone meant, Guess it won't hurt. Doctors felt the same snotty way about wards and protections made with herbs, though everybody knew they worked.

"You want the hide?" This was to Sam.

"Hot damn, bring it on."

"Young man, you don't appreciate how lucky you are. Think about having a Ree spear through your chest." Fleming walked off, probably to see to other patients.

Clyman squatted next to Sam, and they traded survival stories. To Sam Clyman's sounded heroic, while his own sounded like dumb luck.

When Clyman was finished, Sam said, "You decoyed them off me."

"Not on purpose," said Clyman, and laughed. "It worked out good. Worked out great."

They looked long at each other.

Sam felt different inside. He couldn't have said how.

THEY FLOATED ON down to an island. Ashley thought an island would be easier to defend if the Rees showed up again. The men dug holes to bury Reed Gibson and John Gardner. Then they stood around leaning on their shovels, looking at each other somberly, feeling like something was left out.

Jedediah Smith stepped forward, a Bible in his hand. Most of the men, not knowing him well, squirmed or backed away. He looked around at them, and without a word bowed his head and began to pray. He appealed to the God whose sternness all of them had just witnessed; he declared that they all needed, in this moment, to believe in His compassion. As he prayed, men looked in wonder at their companion. Bible stuff was for kids and women. If these men thought about it at all, they joked about it. But now they saw idealism and perhaps nobility. Though they feared his God, they felt admiration and respect for Diah Smith.

When Jedediah said "Amen," Gideon surprised them all. He floated out a tune from his fiddle—Sam didn't even know Gideon was a fiddler. It sounded like an ancient melody, handed down for a hundred generations in a haunting minor mode, drenched in melancholy. It spoke of the sorrows of the Israelites of over thousands of years, the heartache of mothers, father, brothers, sisters, of one feeling common to all human beings, grief at the loss of a loved one to death. Yet as it languished in sorrow, it spoke in the same moment of motion, of the pulse of life that carries all human beings on.

When the last of Gideon's tones drifted away on the evening breeze, men stood silent, their hearts stirred.

Then they put the bodies in the graves, and left only a log as a memorial—otherwise Indians might disturb their friends' rest.

Sam couldn't sleep that night—his broken leg throbbed. He laid on the deck of the *Packet* and stared at the stars and listened to General Ashley. The stars stayed maddeningly still, and the general paced maddeningly all night.

IT WAS THE general's bark that awoke Sam at dawn.

Turned out Ashley was bound and determined to take these keelboats upriver and get his hunters into the field to find beaver. He lined the men up on the deck of the *Packet*. Apparently he'd worried up a plan during the long darkness. "First we will picket the larboard side of the two keelboats," he said, meaning the side that faced the villages. "That's for protection against their fire. Then we will pass by the villages at night. They'll never know we're there."

It didn't fly with the *voyageurs* for a moment. Sam could see that in their faces. He'd expected they might be stubborn and sullen. Instead they were panicked.

Gideon spoke up for them. "General, I don't think these men will go to the Rees again for any reason."

After some bickering, Ashley asked for commitments. "I'm going to send to Major Henry to reinforcements. How many men are willing to stay with me until help comes?"

All the Kentucks volunteered, even the injured ones. Except for Gideon, the French-Canadians didn't—forty-three of them wanted out now.

Ashley asked directly. "What will happen if I order them to stay?"

Gideon answered with seeming casualness, "They will desert."

The general considered. Sam read the look of his face as desperation. Maybe he thought his whole enterprise was going to go under right here. He said, "I want two volunteers. You will go overland to Major Henry and let him know we need reinforcements."

Without hesitation Diah Smith stepped forward. Sam studied the face of the man he considered very admirable and a little odd. Why did he take every risk? To get in good with the general? Because he thought it was his duty? Because, under the mask of quiet dignity, he liked danger and difficulty?

Gideon stepped out next to Smith. Sam thought maybe he was making a statement on behalf of all the French-Canadians.

"We'll talk in a minute," Ashley told them.

He assigned the *Packet*, the bigger of the boats, to the French-Canadians. They would take his trade goods back to Fort Kiowa and give them the news. Then they would float down to Fort Atkinson and tell Colonel Leavenworth of the defeat here.

He talked briefly with Smith and Gideon. Smith showed the general the maps he'd been making of the fur country in his notebooks. Diah understood navigation instruments and cartography. He showed the general how he and Gideon could go up the Grand River, strike the Yellowstone, and follow it down to Fort Henry.

Gideon left them to talk it over. He would do what had to be done, just that, however it needed to be done.

The pair left immediately. Since all the horses had been killed, they had to go on foot.

The big keelboat pushed downstream. No Kentuck was sorry the forty-three *voyageurs* left. Sam wondered if the general would be able to get the furs he needed without them. Sometimes he talked nervously about his creditors.

Ashley built some fortifications for *The Rocky Mountains*. He said he'd float slowly down to the mouth of the Cheyenne River, just in case any other men escaped alive. There everyone would await Major Henry.

The high point of Sam's day was when Clyman brought him two crutches, fresh cut from saplings on the island. Very quickly, though, he found out he didn't have the energy to clomp around, and motion started the bleeding again. He collapsed on his blankets exhausted and stared at his bloody leg.

He thought about it, and that evening he asked James Clyman. Clyman had been a surveyor in earlier years, and had the habit of saying exactly what he saw without blarney. "Jim, is Fleming telling me the truth? Will this leg heal up? Will I be able to walk?"

"Depends," said Clyman. "I've seen them go red and pussy and make a crip, or worse. I've seen people limp for good. And I've seen them walk like it never got broke."

That was not what Sam wanted to hear. He spent another night watching the stars and listening to the general pace.

"HELLO THE BOAT! Hello the boat!"

The men looked toward the west bank. There a human figure was waving at them wildly. It spoke English, which was all they needed to know. The general dispatched a rowboat.

Four days after the defeat they'd found a survivor.

It turned out to be Jack Larrisson, naked as the day he came into the world. And badly sun-blistered, skin puffed up all over him, and in some places hanging in sheets.

Fleming put him in the shadow of the hold. He had a bullet wound in both thighs—the ball passed through one leg and lodged in the other. Fleming took the ball out and rubbed fat on the blisters.

Clyman helped Sam over to Larrisson so they could hear his

story. He got wounded on the beach, hobbled into the water, and was swept downstream. His hide clothing felt so heavy he stripped it all off. Quite to his surprise, he washed up alive on a bar a half mile or so downstream. He didn't know where the boats were, and he could barely walk. He found a log and floated downriver holding to it, looking for the boats. Then he gave up on finding them. . . .

Soon Larrisson passed unconscious. Fleming poured some meat broth into his throat, and he drank without waking up. Sometimes he raved. He developed a fever—Fleming gave him willow bark for it and predicted he'd come out of all this good as new.

THE NEXT MORNING Sam didn't wake up, not really. His forehead was burning. When Fleming checked his wound, he saw a big circle of red around it, and yellow pus. "Going foul," Clyman said.

Fleming gave Sam willow bark, and asked Clyman to put cloths dipped in river water on his forehead regularly. When Fleming wasn't looking, Clyman took the bandage off and exposed the wound to the air. Different people had different opinions about these things.

The Kentucks anchored the boat at an island off the mouth of the Cheyenne River. Men went ashore to hunt only occasionally—they were still worried about Rees. Supplies ran short. So did tempers.

In three or four days Larrisson was up and around, hobbling but cheerful.

Sam spent every day in half delirium. His wound kept suppurating.

FAR DOWNRIVER COLONEL Henry Leavenworth, in command of Fort Atkinson, was outraged at the news brought by Ashley's *voyageurs*, and declared that the Rees must be punished. Indian agent Benjamin O'Fallon agreed completely. "The problem is," he said to Leavenworth, "the tribes of the Upper Missouri have no respect at all for American military prowess. They need to be taught a lesson."

O'Fallon was also incensed at the forty-three *voyageurs* who deserted Ashley. His sense of national pride was aggrieved. Leavenworth was mounting a great expedition against the Rees, he told them, and needed boatmen. "This is your opportunity," he told the assembled men, "to revenge the death of your friends, and bury the bones of your brave comrades whose spirits have pursued you downriver, shedding tears in your tracks."

Either O'Fallon's exhortation or Leavenworth's offer of wages persuaded twenty of the French-Canadians to go back. Twenty-three decided it wasn't their fight, much less their national pride. Men of the wilderness, they would make canoes or dugouts, or simply walk wherever they wanted to go, two hundred fifty miles from the nearest fort.

Joshua Pilcher, head of the Missouri Fur Company, was equally eager to teach the Rees some respect, and keep the Upper Missouri open to mountain men. He was in with whatever Leavenworth would do. O'Fallon sent an express to Ashley, telling him help was on the way and promising an end to the Rees' intolerable behavior.

Leavenworth headed upriver with three keelboats full of supplies and artillery, and two hundred and thirty officers and infantrymen, most of them advancing by land.

Pilcher got word from upriver that his men on the High Missouri, above even Fort Henry, had suffered two massacres, and their year was a disaster. His firm was in trouble. All he could do was put together forty or fifty mountain men and follow Leavenworth.

ASHLEY AWOKE IN the wee hours of the morning. He twisted in his buffalo robes and looked up at the Big Dipper. About four o'clock. He was long used to telling the time in the dark hours of the night by the Big Dipper's rotation around the North Star. In his year and more in the fur trade he had worried and worried.

He slipped out of the robes on the pallet he kept for himself. He had his own sleeping spot with some small accommodations, like a lantern and a washbasin—he believed in hierarchy, which meant keeping himself apart from the men. But they were his constant concern.

He padded quietly around the deck, checking on several of them by moonlight. All were out of danger, he thought. He spent a minute or two listening to young Morgan's breathing. It seemed steady, easy, deep. Infections carried men away in wars more often than the wounds themselves. Sam's youth had saved him. It was not a card he could play forever.

He went to the bow, took off his Jefferson boots, lowered himself into the ankle-deep water, and splashed to the riverbank. They were still camped on the island at the Cheyenne River, and the men slept on the boat. Every night Ashley had trouble sleeping. Every morning these last ten days he kept a dawn vigil. At this hour he would have to walk first, walk back and forth and worry. If he did that on shore, at least he wouldn't keep the men awake.

This felt like a war, this fur-trading. For now. He hated that. As a military man he knew enough of war to despise it. He didn't want to plunder the land, he wanted to trade. Naturally, he wanted fortune—fortune was the will-o'-the-wisp that drew big men to big risks. But he wanted to earn fortune, not steal it.

Once at a party Cadet Chouteau had challenged him in the Frenchman's usual superior tone about this matter. "What do we do to the Indians, hmmm? We take the riches of their lands, the beaver, and give them trifles and trinkets in return. Hardly a course that does us honor. We are not creatures to admire, we capitalists."

Ashley made a retort to Chouteau with a confidence that he recognized as peculiarly American. He did not see his enterprise that way, not at all. The fur trader took to the Indians wealth that was almost unimaginable to them—cooking pots, knives, axes, awls, blankets, cloth, guns and ammunition, all the bounty of an industrial civilization. In return he took the skin of an animal the Indians had no use for, the beaver. "We take little, we leave much," he said.

At that moment he noticed that most of the guests, nearly all French old-timers in St. Louis, had stopped to listen curiously to the ambitious American upbraid the young and arrogant Frenchman.

So he plunged on in style. "We also leave something that is not material," Ashley announced. "Something for the mind. The greater civilization shows the lesser the heights of possibility. The conversion of earthen ore into metal, which results in cooking in pots instead of buffalo stomachs; in metal awls instead of sharpened bones; in rifles instead of arrows. Blankets and cloths instead of the hides of beasts. Altogether we bring to them the idea of advancement, of progress itself. Having seen it, they want it. They bestir themselves in small ways even now, to the attainment of a greatness they see they lack. This is a high gift, a boon without charge."

Chouteau took the pause to reply, "That is, my dear Ashley, if our trappers make white men of the Indians. And what if it turns out the other way, we become savages?"

There was a titter of nervous laughter in the room. Everyone had seen the rough men who came back from Indian country.

Someone in the back said, *"Bien sur, ces Americains sont tout naifs."* "Oh, these Americans are all so naïve."

Now Ashley paced the bank feverishly. Regardless of any debates, he didn't like fighting Indians instead of trading with them. So now he shook an imaginary finger at himself. He lusted to show those damned Rees. He wanted to boat past their villages, fortified, and glare at them defiantly. Or sneak by them at night and let them discover in embarrassment, later, how he had bested them. Or he wanted to fight them straight out and give them a whipping. If Leavenworth came with troops, that's what he would do. He would attack the villages straight on and let them feel the might and majesty of the United States. They would learn that white men were not to be trifled with. If they were penitent afterwards, he would sign a peace treaty with them, knowing what they did not—that it was infinitely to their benefit. If they were unrepentant, he would burn their villages.

He walked this bank night after night, keeping this vigil, his imagination filled with gunpowder and blood. War was ugly, but it was necessary.

He noticed the sky glowed with the first light before sunrise. He walked swiftly to the upstream end of the island. He would keep watch, as every day. If they came, he thought they would come at dawn.

The trouble with all this inner debate was that he knew it was childish. He knew what he needed—a good fall hunt. The word Smith had brought from Henry was not encouraging. Because of their immobility, Henry's men had not gotten much beaver in their first season. Twenty packs, a thousand hides. For a hundred and fifty men that was a miserable showing. The year's income was less than what two minutes had cost him on the way up, when the keelboat sank and took ten thousand dollars in trade goods to the bottom. Aside from that, Henry had tried to make progress in establishing good relations with the Indians on the high Missouri and reaped a bitter harvest. The Blackfeet attacked his party on Smith's River, above the Great Falls of the Missouri, killing four and driving the rest from the country. Henry had decided to abandon the fur-rich Blackfoot territory and hunt in the country of the Crows, who welcomed the mountain men.

A year of retreat after retreat, loss after loss.

He looked upstream, squinting, hoping to see something in the thin light.

Now the Missouri River was closed to whites, so he couldn't even get another party to the high Missouri.

Ashley had spent a lot of capital and gotten nothing for it, or less than nothing—in huge regions he was the enemy.

This fall and winter his creditors would press him. He needed to get some men into the villages to trade for furs, and into the creeks to trap beaver. He had to show a few nuggets of the vast wealth of the mountains. Or he would be just another man with a big dream, a beseeching smile, and empty pockets.

A good fall hunt, yes. But he wanted to punish those Rees.

Ashley looked upstream hard, not knowing what stirred him, hope or fear. Sometimes he didn't like being General William Ashley.

An hour later shouts startled him out of a reverie.

Men on the keelboat were crying out. Voices floated down from upstream—in English. Ashley stood and stared.

Movement on the water. He lifted his telescope.

Canoes. Filled with white men.

He forced himself to put down the telescope and wait.

Someone hallooed the boat. He threw up the telescope. Andrew Henry cupped hands around his mouth. Jedediah Smith was waving.

Smith and the French-Canadian had gotten through alive.

Everything was saved. Maybe.

A stout heart experienced a moment of softness.

The canoes paddled up to the *Rocky Mountains*, and lines were grabbed and held by eager hands. Fifty men, blooded hands every one and well-armed, jumped on board. The stranded men of the keelboat welcomed them like water after a long drought.

The thirty Kentucks begged to hear the story of the adventure of Diah Smith and Gideon—four hundred miles traveled on foot through dangerous country with not a scratch! Came back with rescuers, and all this in about four weeks! What a feat! They pounded the two on the back, exclaimed things like "You boys are some!" Smith wore a quiet smile that said, 'All in a day's work.' Gideon beamed like a conqueror.

FROM THE DAY he shook off his fever, Sam felt his immobility painfully. He couldn't hunt, he couldn't jump in the river and cool off, he couldn't go for a walk to stretch his body out. He could do nothing but crutch to the water pail for a drink, crutch into the shade or into the sun, or crutch to a different group of men to talk to. It was slow, it was awkward, it was humiliating.

He gave Diah Smith and Gideon awkward, crutch-bound bear hugs, and was glad to see them as any man, in fact exhilarated. But it also hurt. Diah and Gideon walked four hundred miles and paddled several hundred more and got to be heroes. While he, Sam, hunkered over his wound. Sam wanted to do big things, too. He could taste it like brass and blood in his mouth.

Now things were going to get a lot worse. Right after Henry and his men arrived, Ashley ordered the keelboat dropped down to the Teton River. Maybe there they could find the Sioux, he said, and trade for some horses. Which meant men would be heading out to Crow country for the fall hunt. And meant that Sam would be left behind.

His leg was far from mended. As they were floating down to the Teton, another forty miles, Sam asked the surgeon Fleming if he could try putting weight, just a little, on his leg. All he got in return was a stare-down. It was worse than being called stupid.

He didn't try it. All right, weeks to go, he would wait. He wondered where the fur brigades would be then, and whether he would have to go downriver with General Ashley, and spend the winter in St. Louis. He wanted to spend it in a Crow lodge.

Within several days a letter changed everything, like a wave of the hand from God.

Ashley got an express from Benjamin O'Fallon, the Indian agent. Ashley read it out loud to all the men. Colonel Leavenworth was marching north with infantrymen and artillery—six-pound Howitzers! The men cheered. Joshua Pilcher of the Missouri Fur Company was coming along with forty or fifty mountain men. They hoped to recruit several hundred Sioux warriors as light cavalry. Men applauded. The Sioux had been fighting the Rees for years. They would take this chance to deal them a mortal blow.

Ashley concluded with ringing words from O'Fallon—the combined forces of Leavenworth, Ashley, Pilcher, and the Sioux would put an end to "the repeated and most shocking outrages" of the Rees forever.

Leavenworth had left on June 22, so he had already been en route for a couple of weeks. Two more weeks and he might be here. And then, by God, things would be set right. The mountain men shouted to the skies.

Sam shouted too. More than wanting vengeance, he was hugely relieved. Two weeks or more before Leavenworth got here. A hundred miles to boat upstream to the villages. A battle to fight. Two hundred miles back downriver to Fort Kiowa, where the trade goods waited. A month at least. Sam surely would be walking again by then. Maybe he could go on the fall hunt. He felt good, damned good.

Until Ashley spit on his polish. "Sam, I'm sending some men to Fort Kiowa to try to trade for some horses. You'd best stay down there until after the campaign."

Then Sam looked it in the face. A canoe trip of several days, being constantly lifted into and out of the canoe like he was a baby or an old man, a fort where he didn't know anyone, and a month of sitting around doing nothing, this time alone.

He was disgusted.

Chapter Twelve

SAM WOULD HAVE been more disgusted if he had known it would be most of July and all of August before the Ashley men showed up again, and almost into September before they could trade for enough horses to start for Crow country. The likely sources for horses, the Sioux, weren't around Fort Kiowa but well to the west, hunting. It seemed the marching of armies and brigades up and down the Missouri, both red and white, had driven the game away from the river, to where sanity prevailed.

A certain madness instead had held the day in the campaign against the Rees. Leavenworth's infantry and artillery did at length get up to the villages, in the company of over a hundred mountain men commanded by General Ashley, Major Henry, and Joshua Pilcher, and six or seven hundred light cavalrymen—the Sioux. This great force, which they called the Missouri Legion, had met the enemy and produced a fiasco.

Sam wanted to hear every morsel of what happened, but the men who fought the battles wanted only to forget them. The first day the Sioux rode ahead and got into a good skirmish in front of the lower village. When the white army appeared, the Rees ran for the village. Very well, everyone thought. The bear is in his den, and we will shoot him.

The next day the army fired their six-pounders at both villages, with no apparent effect. At least the artillery fire did not force the Rees to come out and fight. Bored, the Sioux went off to steal corn, beans, pumpkins, and the like from the Ree fields. Leavenworth asked his officers about a direct assault on the villages, and was informed that the picketing and the ditch behind the pickets made it risky. Pilcher brought up the news that the Sioux had lost all interest and were wandering away.

Now Leavenworth saw some Sioux parleying with the Rees near the village and went up. The Rees begged for mercy, especially for the women and children, who were suffering from the artillery. The troublemaker Grey Eyes was now dead—the tribe wanted peace.

They proceeded to formal terms. Leavenworth demanded that Ashley's property be returned to him, the river be opened to Americans to travel. The Rees were to promise agreeable behavior henceforth, and Leavenworth was to be given five hostages as a show of good faith.

The Rees agreed, pleading only that the Sioux had stolen all the horses, so Ashley's twenty couldn't be replaced. Later it turned out that the Rees were willing to produce nothing of what Ashley had traded for the horses, except for a few fusils and buffalo robes.

Now Leavenworth balked. Then Edward Rose, always willing

to dare anything, went into the village and came back with a report that the Rees were getting ready to evacuate during the night. To keep them from running, Leavenworth capitulated—he said they didn't have to make good on what was taken from Ashley.

Pilcher was infuriated. Most of the mountain men were enraged. Leavenworth's own officers were steaming.

The next morning it turned out that the Rees had snuck past Leavenworth's sentries during the night and were gone, gone, gone.

Had they been taught a lesson? Maybe. That they could taunt the American bear and get away with it.

Was the Missouri now open navigation?

No fur trader would risk finding out.

RIGHT NOW ALL that felt long past. A dozen and a half men stood in a clump, packing their horses. Sam had no idea how to throw a diamond hitch, as the guide called it. He had to do it three times before the guide, Mathews, approved. Sort of a bossy guy, Mathews.

The first brigade to be captained by Jedediah Smith was assembled and ready to head for the country of the Crows. Sam looked around at his companions. He was glad he was in. So was Clyman, the grave, slow-spoken Virginian. Bill Sublette, a gaunt, iron-faced Kentuckian. Irish Tom Fitzpatrick, small but sinewy and smart. Tom Eddie, a daredevil. Edward Rose, a brave man with the blood of three races. Also Arthur Black, Branch, Stone, and a handful whose names Sam couldn't remember yet.

He looked at Diah—most of the men called him 'Captain Smith' now—and wondered how he felt about being the leader. Sam had thought maybe Ashley would hold back with Diah, who was in his middle twenties, and choose Clyman, in his thirties. But Jim himself said, "Hey, who better?" Diah had taken expresses from and to

Henry up at the Yellowstone. He'd been the last man off that beach at the Ree villages. He was smart and he had nerve.

For nearly a month they'd tried to trade for horses and failed. These horses were borrowed from Fort Kiowa and had to be returned. The guide, Mathews, would help them find the Sioux, then bring the horses back.

Meanwhile, they walked. The horses were to carry supplies and trade goods, not riders. Diah advised Sam to carry his possible sack, not leave it on the packhorse, in case Indians ran the horses off.

Sam did.

They set out on foot. Embarrassing.

Sam wasn't sorry, though. He could barely ride a horse.

Only Mathews rode, a king among peasants.

The first several days were a nightmare. They walked all day across a high, rolling plain and finally dropped down into the valley of White River. Mathews warned them about the water. It looked white and gooey, and tasted sweetish. If they drank too much, Mathews said, they'd get the pukes and the runs.

They'd been almost without water all day. The next morning nearly every man was sick. Sublette, the gaunt Kentuckian, was the sickest. Tom Eddie made a lot of fun of him, the sort Sam would never tell his mother or sisters.

After a day and a half following the stream, they did a dry cutoff, avoiding a big bend in the river. Twenty-four hours dry, then a water hole, Mathews said, then another fifteen miles to the river. Being underprovisioned, they had little way to carry water. They trudged, thirsty, the horses uneasy.

They made a miserable dry camp.

At midday the expected water hole was dry. Dry beyond dry. So dry it wasn't worth digging to try to find water.

They trudged.

Mathews rode ahead. Sublette drawled at Fitzpatrick, "You know where that bastard went?"

"He doesn't want to watch our lips split and our skin peel and our eyeballs go dry in their sockets and refuse to turn," said the Irishman.

"Don't make no difference where he's gone," said Eddie. "All the water in this desert is burnt up."

Sam still wished he knew where Mathews was.

The party straggled. Men spread out right and left, hunting water. Sam thought they might not ever get together again. Diah walked at the rear to keep an eye on everyone, but how could he?

The horses fought the lead ropes. The party was nearing breakdown.

From ahead and to the right, a rifle shot.

Sam veered that way. Slowly, hope dawned in everyone—all the men hobbled that way.

Sam topped a rise and saw Jim Clyman and his horse, both standing withers deep in a water hole.

Sam's horse tore the lead rope out of his hand, galloped for the water, and made a tidal wave jumping in. Sam did the same.

Every horse broke free and outran his human being. Most men jumped in whooping. Tall Sublette walked up to the water and fell in stiff as a plank. Tom Eddie found the energy to take several quick steps and do a somersault into the water. Fitzpatrick stepped in quietly, with dignity. Every man, as soon as his throat was lubricated, shouted for joy.

They counted up. Actually, four of their number were missing. Mathews was presumably somewhere ahead, maybe at the river. Diah and two others—who knows?

Soon Diah struggled over the rise, alone. He baptized himself and said the two others had collapsed. He'd buried them in sand up to their necks, to keep the wind from parching them completely, and promised to carry water back if he found any.

Every man was thinking, I've had all I can take. I wouldn't go back, at least not today. Before long Diah took a horse and some water and rode back. After dark he came in with the two men.

Sam thought, He's odd about religion, but I'd follow him anywhere.

WAITING FOR THEM at the river, Mathews acted faintly amused at what they'd gone through.

Here the whitish, sticky water had turned into a bright, clear stream on a gravel bed among pine-tufted hills. Better yet, they soon came on an encampment of Sioux, a subtribe the Kentucks called Bob Rulys. That made Gideon sniff, and he explained to Sam that they were the Bois Brulés, or Burnt Wood Sioux.

Sam was fascinated by the camp. Though they'd seen villages on the way up the river, he hadn't had a chance almost to live in one, as he did now. Diah Smith wanted to take time to exchange trade goods for a lot of horses. Sam filled his eyes and ears and mind with the way Indians were, not what he'd heard all his life, and not what they were as a broken people.

First the village held a council in a big tipi and gave the white men an opportunity to say why they'd come to the country of the Lakotas. Diah explained that they were hunting furs, especially beaver hides, that they wanted to be friends with the Bois Brulés. We have some presents for you, he told them, and we want to trade for some horses. Mathews handed the man who seemed to be the chief the gifts of tobacco and beads and other small items, and he seemed to accept them with courtesy. Diah went on, Mathews converting all this into sign language. The Indians listened politely, without interrupting even once, or asking any questions.

First Sam noticed that these Indians weren't a bit pathetic or bedraggled-looking, unlike most of the Indians he saw in towns back East. They were handsomely dressed in a barbaric sort of way, their clothes ornamented beautifully and suitably. In fact, Sam felt like he was in rags compared to them, the plains and the hard work having been hard on the little clothing he owned. The women were attractive, and particularly modest, the young ones not meeting the eyes of the older women, or of any men, certainly not the strangers. They didn't act a bit whorish, which is what the men back home often said when their women weren't listening.

When the Indians began to speak, any man in the main circle was apparently allowed to put in his opinion. They did it in a mannerly way, everyone waiting for others to finish speaking, never disputing with anyone. Sam had a sense of particular respect for the elders. Young men, women, didn't offer opinions.

Sam felt a longing to understand their language and really know what was going on. He thought Mathews was a ruffian who probably didn't understand much about any people.

At the end the man who sat directly behind the fire and acted like the leader seemed to sum up what had been said, balance some of it out with other points, answer some questions and objections, and finally to welcome the whites to the Bois Brulé country. The meeting adjourned, and the mountain men made their camp near the village.

While Diah made his bargains for horses over the next several days, Sam wandered the village and observed. He looked for their ways of doing things before they had trade goods. He watched squaws drop hot rocks into buffalo stomachs to heat stew. He saw them soften and dye porcupine quills, then apply them to hide—an older form of decoration than beadwork, and they certainly did love beads. They scraped the fat off elk and buffalo hides and started the hard work of tanning and softening the hides. They sewed shirts, breechclouts, and dresses with buffalo sinew as thread, and sewed elk teeth onto their dresses in beautiful patterns. They made buffalo hoofs into rattles for small children, and fashioned dolls out of pieces of hide. They folded rawhide into big envelopes for storing things, and painted them with geometrical shapes. Sam thought their life had a primitive beauty.

The children were curious about Sam, and followed him everywhere. The women, though, mostly ignored him, or talked to him gently with their eyes cast down. Maybe some Indian women were wantons, but not these Sioux.

Among the men Sam really saw bows and arrows work for the first time. A warrior could get half a dozen arrows in the air before the first one landed, and they teased Sam about the time he needed to reload his rifle, which was about a minute. Their accuracy was remarkable. Yet every one of them, Sam knew, would have traded high for a rifle like his.

They had remarkable knives of their own making, with handles fashioned from the jaws of bears, antlers, or antelope horns, and blades of flint or obsidian. Still, they liked the metal butcher knives they traded for.

Sam thought their dress was practical—mostly they wore nothing but breechclouts and moccasins. But he thought his companions would tease him if he gave up his pants and boots for this light gear.

The Tennessean Stone got a little testy over Sam and Gideon "gawking" at how the Bob Rulys did things. "I learned all I need to know about Indians on the beach at the Ree villages," Stone said.

Clyman walked up at that moment. Sam couldn't help thinking of Captain Stuart, Ten, and Eleven. "I've known Indians that were more honorable than the white folks they were with," he told Stone.

Stone just spat tobacco between his feet and walked off.

Sam said quietly, "I saw it the other way at the Ree villages."

Gideon, the half-Indian, said, "What do you think, Clyman?"

Clyman said in his measured way, "It's easy to make a savage of a civilized man, but impossible to make a civilized man of a savage in one generation."

After Clyman walked on, Sam thought of his retort. "I don't know how you can tell the difference sometimes."

Gideon laughed long and hearty.

"I gotta admit it confuses me too," said Sam. "I don't know whether they're good people or rotten."

"Why waste a fine evening on such a question?" Gideon insisted they sit by the river and smoke their white clay pipes.

In the end Diah Smith was ready to move before Sam was. Diah sent Mathews back to Fort Kiowa with the borrowed horses, and gave every man of the brigade one animal to ride and another to carry equipment. Edward Rose would guide the brigade on west to Crow country.

"Good riddance," Fitzpatrick said at Mathews's back.

"Amen, brother," said Sublette.

BEFORE LONG THEY rode into the Badlands and found out what travelers learned to their grief before and since. They were repelled by the steepness of the country, the unbroken barrenness of the gray soil, and the way gullies cut this way and that and every way, with never a foot of level ground to ride on. Then it rained, and the gray soil ("remarkably adhesive," Clyman would later write dryly in his memoir) clumped on the horses' feet and made them clumsy. "The whole of this region" Clyman would record, "is moving to the Missouri River as fast as rain and thawing snow can carry it."

Beyond the Badlands rose the Black Hills. Pine-covered mountains, big, grassy meadows, cool, refreshing air, even hazelnuts and plums, a paradise for man and beast. They felt like staying for weeks, but Crow country and the beaver hunt called.

The country west of the Hills was rugged, full of cedar and prickly pear instead of grass. Maybe a little desperate, Diah sent Rose ahead to find the Crow Indians, get fresh horses, and come back.

Five days later they were riding through a brushy bottom, walking single file, leading their horses. Smith was in front. Suddenly, about halfway down their line, a big grizzly rambled out of the brush.

Men went for their rifles, but getting powder into the pan, aiming, and firing took precious seconds.

Running back, Diah Smith charged out of the thicket and right into the bear's face.

Griz grabbed Diah in a hug. Both of them went sprawling onto the ground. The bear took a swipe at Diah's middle. Luckily, the big, sharp claws hit his shot pouch.

Griz took Diah's head in his mouth. Diah jerked it out, but the head emerged bloody.

Men wanted to shoot, but all were afraid of hitting Diah.

Somehow, beneath the bear, Diah got off a pistol shot.

Arthur Black ran close, knelt, and shot upward into the flurry of motion that was the bear.

Suddenly, Griz stopped and looked at Black, as though asking, 'What the hell are you doing?'

As suddenly as it came, the bear bolted into the shrubbery. Men fired, but none could say he hit.

The men ran to Diah's bloody body. "What are we going to do?" someone said. They looked at each other. Not a man knew anything about medicine, or mending wounds, not even Fitzpatrick.

"Do something."

"Stop that bleeding!" someone put in.

"Why don't you?" said someone else.

Clyman knelt down by Smith. "What's best?" he asked his captain.

"Send one or two men for water," answered Smith steadily. "Meanwhile sew up the wounds around my head." He told Clyman where in his pack were the needle, thread, and scissors. Sam brought them. And then Sam saw, really saw. The head was a bloody, bloody mess. How could the captain be talking? How could he be alive? How could he be clear and sensible when everyone else was useless?

Clyman checked Smith's chest. Though the bear claws had scratched his hunting pouch instead of ripping him open, some ribs were broken.

Big scrapes of tooth marks slashed from his left eye to the crown of the head, and from the right ear to the crown. The ear was torn from the head to the outer edge. White bone gleamed where the teeth had raked.

Clyman cut Smith's hair off with the scissors. He sewed the raw edges of scalp together. Smith lay silent.

Finally, Clyman said, "There's nothing I can do about the ear."

"Oh," Smith said, "you must. Stitch it together some way, however you can."

The amount of blood on Smith's head and face, on his shirt, on Clyman, and on the ground made Sam sick.

Clyman held the two parts of the ear with one hand and laced them together with the other. It was crude. Clyman considered and said, "Best I can do."

Smith got up on his horse and the brigade rode down to the creek, about a mile away. There they erected their only tent and put him in it.

That night men sat around the same fire but apart from each other, each one in his own thoughts. Which were bloody. Which were less about the captain than what would happen to them without him.

In a crisis he had acted like a man. Most of them were half in awe of him. And they weren't happy about how they behaved.

WHILE THE CAPTAIN recuperated, the men explored the country. It seemed safe enough, now that they were far from the Rees and close to the Crows. Sam, Gideon, and Clyman rode through what looked like a fine quarry of slate. Clyman commented, "Here or at some place like it Moses must have visited, and got the stones the Ten Commandments was inscribed on."

Further west Rose and Sam rode into a grove of trees whose wood seemed to have turned to something very hard. Sam dismounted and picked some up. "What is it?" he asked Rose.

"Strike your steel to it," said Rose, meaning the D-shaped piece of steel he struck against his flints to make spark.

The wood actually sparked.

"Stone. It's stone." He held it high. It took the shape of a little limb.

Rose got down beside him, picked some up, inspected it, dropped it, and picked some other pieces up. "I seen a whole forest of it once, a putrefied forest."

"A what?"

"A putrefied forest. Sure as my rifle's got hind sights, and she shoots center. I was up in the Yellowstone country, and if it wasn't cold about that time I wouldn't say so. The snow was about fifty foot deep, and the buffler lay dead on the ground like bees after a beein'. Not whar we was, though, for there was no buffler, nor any meat, and me and my band had been livin' on our moccasins for six weeks. One day we crossed a canyon and over a divide and got into a prairie that was green grass, and green trees, and green leaves on the trees, and birds singing in the green leaves, and all this in February, wagh! Our animals was like to die when they seen the green grass, and we all sung out, 'Hurrah for summer doin's.'

" 'Here goes for meat,' says I, and jest ups old Ginger at one of them singing birds, and down come the critter elegant. Its damn head comes spinning away from the body, but never stops singing, and when I takes up the meat, I finds it stone!

" 'Here's damp powder and no fire to dry it,' I says quite scared.

" 'Fire be dogged,' says old Rube, 'here's a hoss as'll make firewood.' Schr-u-k goes the axe agin' the tree, and out comes a bit of the blade as big as my hand. We looks at the animals, and there they stood shaking over the grass, which I'm doggone if it wasn't stone, too. Young Anderson comes, up, and he'd been clerkin', so he knowed something. He looks and looks and scrapes the tree with his butcher knife and snaps the grass like pipe stems, and breaks the leaves a-popping like Californy shells.

" 'What's all this, boy?' I asks.

" 'Putrefactions,' says he, 'putrefactions or I'm a nigger.' "

" 'Putrefactions'?" says Sam. "Why, did the leaves and the trees and the grass stink?"

"Stink, Sam, would a skunk stink if he was froze to stone? No, I didn't know what putrefactions was, and young Anderson's version didn't shine, not in my eyes, so I chips a piece out of a tree and puts it in my trap sack and carries it safe to Atkinson. Well, a doctor fella comes along the next spring. I shows him the piece I chipped out of the tree, and he called it a putrefaction too. And so, Sam, if that wasn't a putrefied prairie, what was it? For this hoss doesn't know, and he knows fat cow from poor bull, anyhow."

IN TEN DAYS or two weeks the captain was healed up and the brigade ready to ride. (No longer tuned to the ways of the settlements, the men didn't count the days.) They rode west, into the country of the Powder River, with the Big Horn Mountains high on the sunset horizon. They were sliding from Sioux and Cheyenne country into Crow country, and it was a region of the most plentiful game any of them had ever seen.

Though the season was getting late, sometimes they stopped to trap the swift, cold mountain streams coming down from the Big Horns. Sam learned how to set his traps in this kind of water. You spotted beaver sign, chewed trees, slides, dams, or lodges. You slipped into the creek well away from where you wanted to set the trap to keep the man smell away and waded to the place you'd picked out. You set the trap on the bottom, and anchored the ring on its chain with a limb several feet away. You attached a float stick, so that if the critter dragged your trap off you could find it, and him. Between the jaws of the trap you stuck a slender wand, its end first dipped into your "beaver medicine," castoreum, a glandular secretion of the beaver. That would bring the curious beaver to find out what stranger was invading its territory. When it stood up to smell the medicine, SNAP!

He loved the work. He and Gideon worked as a pair, riding up the creek to set a dozen traps, returning to take their beaver and skin them. They got comfortable with each other. Each man knew what the other would do, and usually what he would say. Each knew the other would protect his back, fight Indians for him if need be. They shared their catch half and half. Sam said to himself that Gideon was a real, true friend, a partner. Then he had to chuckle. A French-Jew-Indian partner. A year ago he hadn't known any of those three.

In camp they cleaned the hides and stretched them on hoops made of willow limbs. When these dried, they were collected into packs, borne by the horses.

The many streams, good water to drink, deer and elk a-plenty, good companions, no enemies—it felt like an idyllic wilderness life to Sam.

That was why he could not have been more surprised, late one afternoon, to see an outfit of white men riding toward camp. Captain Smith welcomed them—that was your obligation with white men, even competitors. One leaned down from his mount, said, "Hello, little fella," and gave a twisty smile.

Sam looked up into the big, lumpy face of Micajah.

"Glad to see you," said the giant. The big face didn't match the words.

"Sorry I can't say the same," Sam answered.

Sam went straight to Captain Smith, but had to stand by quietly while Diah, Fitzpatrick, and Sublette greeted the two leaders of the Missouri Fur expedition, Charlie Keemle and Bill Gordon. The captain introduced them to Sam with, "They fought against the Rees with us."

From what Sam had heard, that was no recommendation.

In the end Sam had to speak up in front of Fitzpatrick and Sublette. "One of their men robs women, and is damn near a murderer."

Diah said, "Tell us the whole story."

Gideon heard that and walked over, his grave expression saying he wanted to hear too.

Sam told it as dry and straight as he could, Abby, Grumble, and him, the call out of the darkness, the weapons, the threats and intimidation, Abby's trick that killed Elijah, how they fought off and outwitted Micajah and Ned. He left out Grumble's near-death act afterward, but said firmly he thought Micajah would try to take revenge for his brother's death.

Diah considered for a while, running his eyes around the meadows and piney hills while he thought. Finally he said to the others, "What do you think?"

"This is the mountains. There's no law," said Sublette.

Everybody chewed on this.

"If he acts up, we'll take care of it," said Fitzpatrick. "Until he does, we can't."

"Something to be said," Gideon put in, "for past is past when you come to mountains."

Sam eyed Gideon unhappily.

"I don't see what I can do," said Diah. "He's their man, not ours. Nor would I take action if I could. Let everyone have a second chance, I say. We judge them by what they do here, not what they were there. It's the right thing."

The five of them eyed each other uneasily.

"I believe you, though. Best be careful."

"Should I tell the other men?"

"Sure," Gideon said. "Not that they haven't heard worse, and maybe done as bad."

"The bottom line is, I think he's carrying a grudge."

Diah said, "I wouldn't go anywhere by myself."

"Me neither," said Gideon. Then he roared out a laugh. "When you head for the bushes, take your ass wipe in one hand and your pistol, loaded, in the other."

Sam did.

He also kept an eye on Micajah all the time—he knew where the man was riding in the line, where he threw his blankets, what fire he sat by and where. Sam didn't wander off into the woods if he didn't know where Micajah was. When he and Gideon went off trapping, they made sure they chose a creek well away from the direction Micajah went.

He wondered how long this would go on. Keemle and Gordon said their outfit was going right where Captain Smith's was. Had got on their trail on purpose. Meant to trade with the same Crows they did and spend the winter in the same Crow village they did. In short, they meant to compete for the Crow trade, and not give Ashley a free hand.

Sam sure couldn't see spending the whole winter in a village with Micajah.

After about a week Micajah suddenly plopped down next to Sam at the evening fire. Though the sun was long gone behind the Big Horns, in the twilight Sam could see his smile, and it didn't look mean. Just then Gideon sat down on the other side of Micajah, which pleased Sam.

"I own I've been a little tickled by the way you avoid me," Micajah began, "but you don't have to. I'm sorry for what we done back in Evansville. It wasn't right. I wouldn't do it again."

Sam just gawked at him. Micajah looked sincere.

"I know it was a trouble to you. It was to me too. I lost my brother. That set me down so hard I've quit drinking. Quit flat. You watch, you'll see."

He seemed to wait for a response from Sam, but none came.

"Anyhow, altogether, I apologize." With that Micajah clapped Sam on the knee just like they were friends, stood his great bulk up, and walked away.

"He mean it, you think?" This was to Gideon.

"Looked like it. Let's watch, see if he's still boozing."

The next evening Edward Rose rode into camp with fifteen or sixteen Crow men. They said their greetings and quickly set up their own camp, with rope corrals for their horses. They had good-looking animals, and extras for the Ashley party.

Three outfits were moving together now, noted Sam, all about the same size.

Soon, though, the Crows left some horses to relieve the Ashley men's broken-down ones and headed home. Held back by tired, overworked horses, the mountain men were too slow for the Indians. Rose guided the Smith and Keemle-Gordon brigades across the Big Horn Mountains, which were turning wintry, across the Little Horns, and up the Wind River to the village.

Downstream from camp several riders met them, the men who'd brought the fresh horseflesh. They traded some words with Rose, and Sam gathered that the guide would put camp across the river.

Eager, Sam was trotting his pony alongside Rose—he had a fair seat on a horse by now, and intended to get good. "How big is this village?" he asked.

They could see several giant circles of buffalo-hide tipis, each representing a family.

The guide drew his sleeve across his mouth. "Don't know this winter. Most winters maybe several hundred lodges."

"Look at the size of that horse herd," Sam exclaimed. "Must be hundreds." The animals were against the foothills on the southwest side, and Sam could see young men around them, probably guards.

Rose smiled wryly. "That will be just one herd. There's more horses than people. These are Crows. As horsemen, they are *some*."

The circles of lodges were all on the west side of the river, between the cottonwoods along the water and the foothills. Rose led the brigades splashing through the shallow stream to the other side. A creek rolled in from the north.

As they rode by the first circle, children ran out to see the strangers. Several teenagers rode their horses up fast and fell in alongside, grinning madly. Dogs barked wildly and dashed beneath the horses' feet.

Sam filled his eyes. "I can't believe it," he said.

"You ain't gonna believe it," said Rose. "These ain't no tame Indians creeping around the edges of your towns. These is *real* Indians, and we're in *their* home."

Chapter Thirteen

IT WAS A NEW world. It felt to Sam almost like he was living in a land of Bible stories, or tales of romantic style in far country and a remote time.

The circles of tipis stretched on a flat along the river for about a mile. Every one of these circles, it seemed, was a big group of relatives, each with an older man who was by common consent the leader. Each tipi was a family, parents, children, sometimes a grandparent. How many lodges altogether Sam never counted. The young, single men lived in brush shelters out of the circle, to themselves.

Immediately behind the camp rose gorgeous red cliffs, and beyond those foothills and then high mountains with eternal snows; opposite loomed barren hills that looked like mud turned to stone in hoodoo shapes. Snow didn't seem to stick long in this high mountain valley, so the feed for the horses was good all winter long, and the game was plenty.

Soon another trapping brigade rode in, led by Captain Weber and sent by Major Henry to join the Smith outfit. That made three camps of mountain men, about fifty altogether.

It seemed like the fur trade was counting big-time on the Crows. There were lots of good reasons. The Crows were friendly, and various other Indians had proven themselves distinctly unfriendly. Crow beaver also had a reputation. Since the Crows lived in mountain country, not on the plains, the fur grew longer and thicker against the alpine cold. Also, the Crow women prepared the hides better, scraping and rubbing them until they were more pliable. Last, beyond Crow country was reported to lie the greatest beaver country of all, on a river the Crows called the Siskadee.

Sam spent the first day perched on top of a big boulder, just watching the Crows. The men were tall and handsome. Sam could see they liked to tease each other and play pranks—they were a people of laughter. The men seemed to have no tasks but to protect the village against enemies and hunt, or get ready to do those things. All the domestic work was done by women.

Sam saw infants tied onto horses in their cradleboards. Maybe they were getting used to the motion of the animal. Children who looked no more than four or five years old were riding, mounted alone.

Everything was beautifully done. Climbing up on the boulder next to Sam, Gideon said, "Those are the biggest, best-looking lodges I've ever seen. And look at the clothes. Other tribes trade high for Crow robes, shirts, and breechclouts—the women really put a lot of work into them."

Sam just watched. He was feeling that pang again, what came

from feeling left out because he didn't know a language. He longed to know just what these people were saying to each other, and what they would say to him if they could do more than smile when he passed. He wanted to know several Indian languages, like Rose did. He also wanted to learn to read. He hated being shut out of words, which were how people told you about themselves.

"You hear about the women?"

Sam raised both eyebrows at him.

"You know the Crows fight all other Indians—Sioux, Cheyenne, Blackfeet, Snake, all the tribes around them. But *formidable*, they like white men. Best part is, *bien sur*, Crow women like white men very much. They are not like Sioux, they love the coupling, they talk naughty, they are maybe kind of wild."

Sam pretended not to be interested.

"Here, this is what Rose told me. Rose, he knows. He say the Crows have ceremonies, they use single woman known sure as virtuous. Guess what? Have trouble sometimes do ceremonies. No young woman known for that." Gideon haw-hawed.

Right then Rose walked up. "Be ready in the morning," he said. "Buffalo hunt. *Big* buffalo hunt. It's gonna shine."

WALKING AND RIDING west, Sam had gotten damn little experience of buffalo. True, they saw bands here and there, once a huge band with bulls and cows thick as trees in a forest. But they didn't have the horseflesh for the job—none but packhorses at first, and then mounts half-gaunted by hard travel and poor grass. Also, the brigade had no way to transport fresh meat, and not enough time to stop for several days and dry the flesh. Thus cramped, they hunted on foot for single animals and took only what they could eat in that camp. Sam didn't get to do even that, because his leg ached and he made a point of resting it.

So today, fully healed, Sam was raring to go. An entire tribe hunting a big herd of the beasts. Gideon said it was the best fun in the world.

Most of the red hunters and all the white men rode down the valley to a place where it narrowed. The young Crows with the swiftest horses rode upstream and gathered out of sight of the far side of a big herd. Sam had no idea how many animals were in the herd—thousands, it looked like—how could any man, by looking, know the number of such a multitude?

Sam and Gideon sat their horses next to a score of Indian hunters, rifles ready. Sublette and Fitzpatrick were ready in front of them, Diah a little off by himself.

"Cows only," Gideon said quietly. "The bulls are tough and stringy."

The swift-mounted young men rode toward the buffalo, then spread out across the valley until the beasts saw them and bolted.

Pell-mell they came, and now they seemed immense to Sam, the bulls blonde on the front and top, brown on the tail and underbelly, as tall as a man at the hump and nearly twice that long. In the early morning, after a light dusting of snow, the entire running herd kicked up a powdery, white halo.

"Place your ball just above the brisket," said Gideon. "That's the only place. They're hard to kill. It's like shooting trees."

Sam breathed the cold air into his lungs, and it felt intoxicating.

Closer the herd roared.

"Best stay on the edge of the herd," said Gideon. "If your mare goes down and you're in the middle, you'll get trampled."

Caution was the furthest thing from Sam's mind. He was headlong for the kill.

Up the valley Indian riders began to fall in with the herd from both sides, young men and old, stripped to breechclouts even in the late-autumn air. They rode without reins, both hands on bows and arrows, guiding the horses with their knees alone. Sometimes a bull would charge a horse and try to gore it, but the horses dodged nimbly. The riders were superb horsemen, keeping their balance and their seats no matter what jump or cut the horse made. Eventually, the rider would nudge the horse close alongside a galloping cow, plunge a couple of arrows into her chest, or even through the chest, and ride on for the next shot.

The mountain men and the Crows around Sam sprinted forward, and Sam spurred into the midst of the buffalo.

He could not believe the chaos. Dirt flew into his face, even big clods. The cloud of snow nearly blinded him. The stampede made an incredible noise, like putting your head inside the biggest steam engine in the world. His mare ran, she skittered sideways, she jumped over gullies. A bull hipped her hard, and she nearly lost her footing but got it back.

Sam tried to get The Celt into shooting position and then saw he'd lost his priming. At full speed he poured priming powder into the pan and was amazed that he got it in. He reined the mare toward a cow that didn't seem too fast. Just as he brought the gun level, a bull charged from behind the cow, the mare crow-hopped twenty feet sideways, and Sam was on the ground.

By miracle he wasn't stomped and gored immediately. Since he was nearly outside the herd, he hot-footed it for the nearest rocks and scrambled up.

His mare was gone, and he didn't know when he'd find her.

Surprisingly, he still had The Celt in his hand.

The captain came riding hard along the herd edge and shot into a side of a running cow. Sam watched astonished as Diah dumped powder into his muzzle at full gallop, spit a lead ball out of his mouth into the barrel, whacked the rifle butt on his saddle, ignored ramming the ball home, maneuvered alongside another cow, and shot again.

That horsemanship would have defied belief, except that Crow riders were doing more amazing things all around.

The first cow Diah shot rumbled to a stop. Blood streamed from her mouth, and her tongue stuck out. Her eyes rolled, bloodshot and glazed with death. Yet she refused to go down. She widened her legs and braced herself, swaying from side to side. She stomped. She lifted her head to an indifferent sky and bellowed for help. Suddenly she lurched and teetered. Purple blood gouted from her mouth and nose. She rolled from side to side like a ship in big seas. Gradually, she stiffened, convulsed, and crumpled onto her knees.

Sam exhaled like a whale spouting.

Suddenly he had to get in on it. He rushed forward, The Celt in hand. He was mad to shoot a buffalo, and right now. He was only a dozen steps from the outside of the herd, which seemed to run faster and faster, blindly plummeting to its unknown fate. Maybe if he followed one with its sights as it came toward him. . . .

That was a nice cow there, on the outside, nothing between him and her . . . He squeezed the trigger.

The Celt exploded and Sam got knocked tail over teacups. He sailed one direction, The Celt another. A dark creature blotted out the sky for an instant and was gone. His left shoulder screamed in pain.

Someone rode between him and the herd. Micajah of all people, protecting him, maybe saving his life.

Gideon trotted up leading the mare. "Damn, we almost lose you."

"Thanks!" Sam shouted at Micajah. The giant waved and rode off into the hunt.

Sam grabbed The Celt with his right hand and the reins with his left. The left protested violently. He swung onto the mare with his right alone.

"What happened to me?"

"As you fired, a bull jumped right over you."

Sam rubbed his shoulder, which hurt like hell. "Kicked me too, I think."

"You're damn lucky he decided to jump."

Sam looked back toward the cow. She was just then staggering around in a daze. "I got her!" he yelled.

"She'll need more killing than that."

Sam tried to shoot her again, but his shoulder hurt so much he couldn't hold up The Celt's barrel.

Gideon rode up close and finished her with a head shot. She knelt unwillingly, and her head sagged onto her forefeet.

Sam got out his knife to start butchering, and realized he didn't have the faintest idea what to do.

"I want to get one more," Gideon yelled, and rode off.

Three Crow women, maybe a mother and two teenage daughters, ran up and made shooing motions. With pantomime the mother indicated that they would butcher out the cow.

Sam motioned that he wanted to help.

The mother spoke to the daughters and they ran along to the next downed animal. One girl, Sam noticed, was about fifteen years old, and very beautiful. She wore moccasins with blue beads and light blue leggings from the tops of her moccasins up under her skirt, and looked like she was running on a piece of sky.

The mother had a wide face with a vertical, straight-line cut on the outside edge of her left eye, cheekbone to forehead. She looked at Sam like she didn't know what to do with him. Sam realized this must be women's work, but he didn't care—he wanted to learn.

Motioning for him to hold the mouth open, she cut out the tongue first. Then she made a cut the entire length of the spine and peeled back the hide on both sides, like a tablecloth laid on the ground. Slowly, sometimes signaling for help, she took off the boss, a sort of hump on the back of the neck; then the hump and hump ribs, the meat on the big extensions of the vertebrae; then the fleece, the long double strip of flesh on either side on the spine, and the thick layer of fat on top of it; then the belly fat.

That done, Cut-Eye and Sam rolled the beast onto one side. She opened the belly and took the liver and kidneys. She slithered the shiny guts out. Then she cut out a thigh bone and used it to break some smaller bones for marrow.

Cut-Eye looked up with a broad grin. She looked like she'd been in a whirlwind of blood. Hell, Sam thought, maybe I look the same. She ran off to join her daughters at the other animal. He looked for the girl who ran on sky, but she was bending out of sight behind the beast.

Sam stood there. So this was his first buffalo. He had a suspicion the meat wasn't his, or not all of it. What was he supposed to do now? What was he supposed to feel?

He knelt and looked into the cow's eyes. Nothing there. Not life, not a hint of life, not even the memory of life. Sam breathed in and out slowly. Life was made the way it was.

The herd was gone down the valley. He caught his mare, mounted, and rode slowly behind. The morning was quiet. Arms with knives raised and fell all over the valley floor. Everything felt empty.

Gideon rode back the other way.

"What do we do now?"

Gideon grinned fiercely. "Rub your belly and dream of gorging yourself. You like the hunt?"

Sam remembered the giddy exhilaration of the chase, the blinding moment of the kill, the sadness of life turned into emptiness. "Damn right," he concluded, "It shines."

THAT NIGHT THE fur-man camps were full of meat and feasting. Tongue, roasted under coals. Hump ribs, spitted above flames. Gideon and other Frenchies took sections of gut, turned them inside out, stuffed them with chopped meat and herbs, and roasted them like gigantic sausages. Gideon offered Sam a slice. "Wonderful," he exclaimed, though he could hardly believe it.

"Boudins," said Gideon.

Every man ate all he wanted, and hugely overate. They'd been hungry sometimes on the long ride from the Missouri, and knew to eat big when they could.

The Crows, though, didn't eat big. Half of them, it seemed like, stayed out all night with the fresh meat. "Keeping the wolves and coyotes off," someone said.

"How many buffalo do you think we killed altogether?" Sam asked.

The big man considered. "The Crow hunters near us, maybe twenty of them, they kill I see kill thirty or forty. So . . . way up in the hundreds?"

Incredible.

The next day the village was a hubbub of meat-making. The women cut the buffalo meat into long, slender strips and laid the strips on racks of cottonwood branches head high, so the dogs couldn't get it. They built low, smoky fires beneath the racks.

Sam walked around camp, gawking. This was meat for the whole winter, at least. "How will they save it?" Sam asked Gideon and Clyman.

"Those strips," Gideon said, "they make *charqui*."

"Jerked meat," Clyman pronounced it.

"Much of the *charqui*, they make pemmican. Permit me to show."

In a few minutes they found a woman willing to trade a hide sack of pemmican for some vermilion. Gideon pulled back the edges of the sack and sliced some off. It looked like fine-shredded meat mixed with fat.

"They pound the meat fine against a stone. Pour on fat so hot is liquid. Stuff." He made a motion of putting the meat into the casing. "Sew up sack."

Sam pointed to something else in the mixture. "What are those?"

"Wild cherries," Gideon said. "Best pemmican, it have berries. Try."

It tasted . . . not bad.

"You can roast, fry, put in stew, whatever you like. Last forever.

The women of my people, they make the best pemmican, trade it to Northwest Company for good, good price."

Soon Cut-Eye brought Sam a deer hide full of jerked meat and pemmican. When he thought how much work she did, and how little he did, it seemed like a bargain.

ALL THAT MEAT-MAKING used up the local firewood, so everyone moved camp again, farther down Wind River. Some of the mountain men built brush shelters. Several, looking down their noses at the shelters, put together rough lean-tos or cabins. Gideon and Sam were considering when Edward Rose said, "Why not trade for a lodge cover? Make a tipi. It's better."

"Good idea," said Sam. "Why don't you come in with us?" Privately, Sam was thinking he could learn the Crow language from Rose.

Rose and Gideon looked at him in mild surprise. "I have a woman," said Rose, "in the village." Meaning he was housed for the winter. Everyone had noticed the Crows treated Rose like a hero, and trusted his word.

"Where can we get one?"

Rose gave Sam a sly smile. "I think Needle would trade you one."

"Needle?"

"The woman with the cut eye." Rose indicated the cut with a finger.

"Oh, yeah." Which meant he'd get to see Girl Walking on Sky some more.

Except that her name, it turned out, was Meadowlark. Her sister was named Turnip. They had two older brothers who weren't home at the moment, Rose said.

Through Rose, Sam and Gideon struck a deal for a small lodge cover for a kettle, some beads, tobacco, and vermilion. Sam noticed

Gideon carried the vermilion in his shot pouch. As they walked away with the cover, he asked why. "Willing women," Gideon said with a sly smile. "I keep it handy."

Sam shook his head.

"Why you not like?" Gideon asked pointedly.

"What kind of woman would sell herself for a little color to put on her part?"

"They don't sell themselves," Rose said. "Crow women love to fornicate. A gift or two, such is a natural part of courting." Gideon gave Sam a wink.

The cover was old buffalo robes, hair scraped off and stitched together. Rose went with them to cut poles for the lodge, saplings of lodgepole pine. When it came time to rig it, though, he begged off. "Women's work. They'd lose respect for me."

So Gideon set to rigging it.

That was when Needle and her daughters turned up, merriment in their eyes. Sam tried to do what Gideon said while watching Meadowlark from a corner of his eye. They tied three poles together and raised them into a tripod. They fit other poles into the crotches. Gideon stomped around a bit, trying to remember how it went. "Among the Blackfeet my squaw, she done this," he said.

"I didn't know you'd been married."

"Country wife and city wife," said Gideon.

Sam decided not to ask.

They raised the lodge cover into place, tied onto the end of a pole, and stretched it around the framework. Staking it down, they felt quite proud of themselves until they saw how it sagged in big folds.

The Crow women were giggling. Sam looked toward them, unable to think of even the simplest of his few words of Crow. Please, he signed. Meadowlark wouldn't look at him, but Needle came forward brassily, and both daughters followed their mother. They took the cover down, rearranged the poles, put up the cover so it was taut, tied the whole rig down to the earth, fixed the ear flaps and showed Sam how to adjust them, and dug a center fire. Sam took in everything with hungry eyes.

Then the women laughed and ran off.

From a distance Jedediah said, "It looks good."

Sam hadn't realized the captain, Fitzpatrick, and Sublette were watching. He grinned at them and used an expression he'd heard from Gideon. "When in Rome . . ."

"I wouldn't push that one too far," Jedediah answered. "Let's get a fire going."

They built an inside fire and an outside fire and soon were eating warmed-up buffalo stew inside.

Other mountain men checked out their tipi. Most said nothing. A couple sniffed like they didn't approve. Tom Eddie mumbled, "Going native."

Gideon didn't let that one pass. "My people, they always been native," he said in a cadence that mocked Eddie. This was in fact true only of his mother's people.

"That's why I'll never be sure about you," said Eddie.

Micajah grinned and said he didn't see the point in a tipi without a woman. "Plenty of room," he said. "Get two women."

"Ten," replied Gideon, taking Sam off the spot. "One a night."

Sam and Micajah laughed, but Sam's laugh wasn't easy.

OVER THE NEXT few weeks Sam learned what a winter camp was like. Three mountain man camps, separate. Circle after circle of tipis. No trapping in the winter. Occasional hunting, on fine days, but on the flat, not in the mountains, where the snow got deep.

Games of every kind. With whites and Indians together, shooting rifles and pistols, shooting bows and arrows; throwing spears, throwing tomahawks; foot races and horse races; tobogganing on lashed buffalo ribs; kicking the ball games, dart-throwing games. Among the whites, endless card games.

Also making things. The Crow men, expert in their craft, made weapons. The women made clothing and domestic articles—buffalo robes for blankets and for trade, spoons, ladles, dolls, needles of bone, thread of sinew, hide suitcases, and much, much more. The mountain men studied these crafts from the Crows—the utility items, the weapons, everything. Doing it, though, they felt like fools while they bumbled along, and most decided to trade a few beads for something instead of making it themselves. Some whites said stubbornly that studying on Indian crafts was foolishness, aping the backward methods of a savage people.

Sam pressed himself to learn. He felt sure that knowing was better than not knowing, and that applied to almost anything. Still, he felt uncomfortable with the teasing of his comrades, and sometimes wondered if he was disloyal to his own race.

On Christmas Eve—Captain Smith kept a careful journal and told them when Christmas and New Year's came—the brigade captains broke out kegs of whiskey to celebrate. Sam drank one cup and traded off the rest of his allotment. The brew was raw alcohol mixed with creek water, tobacco, and spices each captain believed in, good to give the mind a whirl, but to Sam acid on the tongue.

Micajah announced that the occasion was enough for him to break his rule against liquor. "Hell," he said, "I don't have to worry out here. A coon cain't be a bad drunk when there ain't hardly any whiskey nohow." Sam went back to his lodge, nervous. He sat in front in the sunshine and used his mold to make fifty-caliber balls for his rifle and pistol.

At midday a big crowd assembled in the Missouri Fur camp, with some shooting and lots of cheering. Sam went to see. Micajah and a buddy from the Missouri Fur camp, Iz, had drawn the crowd. Iz, a short, skinny Kentuck with a body like a knotty tree, stood legs astraddle facing Micajah, a queer grin on his face. Also, Sam saw now, a tin cup on his head.

Micajah leveled his rifle, steadied, and blew out a cloud of black smoke and a huge BLAM!

Also blew the tin cup off of Iz's head.

The queer grin turned to a big laugh. The men rushed forward and embraced each other.

Sidling up to Sam, Gideon said, "They started out filling the cups with whiskey. Now it's water."

The two grabbed their jug, took big swigs, and lined up again. This time the tin cup was on Micajah's huge head.

BLAM! Iz barely even came to steady, but the shot was dead-eye—the cup sailed clear into the crowd. The watchers erupted in cheers, Crows as well as mountain men. That fellow was a marksman.

Again the ceremonial swig of whiskey.

They lined up. Here came the queer grin. Sam thought he'd be nervous too, damn nervous.

Smith, Fitzpatrick, and Sublette joined Sam and Gideon.

As the shooters walked back to their places, Sam said, "Where's this going to end?"

"Not until one of them decides he's too drunk to shoot," said Gideon.

Diah answered, "We know when that will be."

"Want to make stop?" said Gideon.

Smith nodded.

Gideon strode straight through the cleared spot toward Micajah. When he got close, they made an impressive brace, probably the two biggest men in camp, though Micajah was bulkier. "Whoo-oop!" said Gideon. "Look at me!" He posed in front of Micajah. "I am the old, original ball of flame from Red River, with the roar of a lion and the meanness of a wolverine! Take a look! They call me Sudden Death, though I prefer to be known as Hell Beast of the North! I was sired by a hurricane, dam'd by an earthquake, half-brother to the cholera, and related to the smallpox on the mother's side! Micajah, lay low and hold your breath, for I am about to turn myself a-loose!"

Micajah set down his rifle, and his eyes gleamed. "Sich big

words." Even in the winter cold, he stripped off his coat and shirt, laid his pistol, knife, and shot pouch on them, and began to bounce up and down on his feet. He wavered a little, and Sam could see he was tipsy.

Suddenly Diah Smith stepped between them. "None of this fighting until one quits." He looked back and forth between them. "How about falls?"

"That's chicken droppings," said Micajah.

"*Mon ami*, he is try protect you." Gideon's grin was something to behold.

"Chicken droppings."

"Falls!" yelled Fitzpatrick and Sublette from the back of the crowd.

"Falls!" echoed Sam.

"Falls then," said Diah loudly to the circle of watchers. "Best of three falls. Any way you can get the other man down." He turned back to the combatants. "Any way at all. I'll call it."

"Who will bet?" called Gideon to the crowd. "Who will bet against me?" He circled and called in a singsong voice, "I am bet this knife." He pulled his butcher knife out of his belt and held it high. With Rose translating, he bet the knife against two pairs of beaded moccasins, then made bets for tins of vermilion, and put up one of his two pistols for robes to use as blankets.

"I bet you pistol against pistol," Micajah called in a taunting tone. *Pistol* came out *pishtol*—Micajah was drunk.

Gideon turned and eyed him hard. Suddenly he smiled, shrugged, and said, "Sure," as though it was no moment to him.

"Rifle against rifle," Micajah went on.

But Gideon turned his back to make a bet with a comely woman.

"You wanna fight or flirt?" growled Micajah.

Gideon smiled at the woman and answered, "I prefer flirt." But he turned to Micajah, stripped off his shirt and gear, and walked toward the other big man.

Micajah charged, head angled for a butt.

With amazing agility Gideon dived into Micajah's legs. Micajah went topsy-turvy through the air and landed on his back. Gideon rolled and came up on his feet.

The crowd roared.

Micajah lay flat on his back, heaving for air.

"One," said Gideon.

"Fall against Micajah," said the captain coolly.

When Micajah got his breath, he asked Diah, "Didn't he go down too?"

"You didn't knock him down," said the captain. "On with it."

Sam loved it. It was like watching a buffalo bull fight a mountain lion.

This time Micajah approached slowly in a crouch, arms out. Gideon just stood at the ready. From six or eight feet Micajah lunged.

Gideon dodged, but Micajah somehow changed direction. He caught one calf in a huge paw. From his knees he seized the foot and twisted it hard. Gideon hollered, spun to keep the ankle from breaking, and flopped on his face.

Micajah jumped up, snorting.

"Fall against Gideon," said Diah.

Gideon eased to his feet and limped around on the twisted ankle.

Suddenly Micajah walked forward with a broad smile. "I think I messed up your ankle. Didn't mean to," he said. "Let's call it off." He stuck out his paw for a shake.

Gideon reached for it, and as the fingers of the hands neared, Micajah grabbed for his upper arm.

Gideon was ready—he spun fast all the way around and sprang onto Micajah's back. Micajah stumbled forward. Gideon tried to trip him. Both men flailed. Micajah bucked like a wild horse, but Gideon stayed on. Finally Micajah tried to throw himself over backward. Gideon jumped clear and dragged Micajah onto his back.

"Fall and match to Gideon," cried Diah. Most of the Kentucks cheered. The Crow women mouthed their high trills.

Gideon went straight to Micajah's gear and took the pistol. When he held it up toward Micajah, who was getting up, Micajah looked like he was about to boil. "That was your bet," said Diah.

Gideon walked up to Micajah holding the pistol out in both hands. "I was very lucky," he said. "You had too much to drink. I can no take advantage."

Micajah hesitated. He fumed. He thought. Finally, he said, "Naw, you won her fair and square. But I tell you what. Tomorrow we compete shooting and I'll get her back."

Gideon looked delighted. "Good. Tomorrow. Good."

Sam knew there was no way Gideon would win that contest.

Gideon came up to him. "Collect the winnings, will you? One buffalo robe is yours to sleep on."

"Good idea to go easy with Micajah."

"Idea more than good. He's as strong as he look and much more quick. Unless his head is full of liquor, I can no whip him. Make friend, not enemy."

With that he stepped over to the comely woman, the last he'd bet with. She was smiling lustily. "Sam, I collect from this one in person. Don't come back to the lodge for maybe one hour, hmmm?"

ABOVE ALL, WINTER was a time for telling stories.

One morning Edward Rose came to Sam and Gideon's lodge with an invitation. Would Sam and Gideon like to have supper tonight with him, his woman, and the Gray Hawk family? The family of Needle and her daughters, Rose explained.

They accepted eagerly. Sam wondered if Rose knew he had eyes for Meadowlark.

Good. They would eat and then Gray Hawk would tell a story. The Crows loved stories, and Gray Hawk was a well-known raconteur.

The supper, unfortunately, couldn't have been more chaste, without even a chance to flirt. Rose, Sam, and Gideon sat by the center fire with Gray Hawk and his older sons, Blue Medicine Horse and Flat Dog. Magpie, Rose's woman, sat in back with the girl Sam wanted to see, her mother Needle, her sister Turnip, their little brother, and Magpie's children. Sam never even caught her eye.

The conversation drove Sam crazy. Rose spoke Crow with Gray Hawk and Blue Medicine Horse, and signed most of what the two Crows said to Sam and Gideon. But, beyond pleasantries, they spoke only to Rose. Sam just sat there wondering what the hell was going on. Maybe he should put himself to school in the Crow tongue.

Finally Rose invited Gray Hawk to tell a story.

"Winter is the time for people to tell stories," Gray Hawk agreed, "after the first frost and until thunder is heard in the mountains. And they should be told at night. This is because the morning star comes only in the winter, and the stars come out at night." But then the invited speaker turned the invitation back. "First, why don't you tell us a story? We hear you are very funny."

Apparently this was what Rose was waiting for.

"When I was a very young man," he began, speaking first in Crow and then in English. He looked around at his audience Several Crows piped up—"*E!*" Later Sam figured out this meant, "Go on, go on."

"When I was a very young man, I went on the mountain." He explained to Sam and Gideon that this was a way of saying, 'I sought a vision to guide my life.'

"I didn't prepare properly, though. I didn't ask the guidance of a medicine man or other older man, I just went."

The Crows made sounds that sounded like a giggly version of, 'Oh-oh.'

"A grizzly bear came to me and gave me a sacred song. I will sing it for you."

Awē̓raxkēta bāwasa'cīwa

Immediately all the Crows began to laugh loudly.

Bacū'ca daxē'tsixēre
Tsēt' ācu tsi'cikyāta Tsēt ācu tsicikyāta
Awaku'saat ērusak'
Īs ara'papēi awakōwate barappēkyāta

The laughter got louder, and people pounded their own legs, or each other's backs, in hilarity.

Ciwicī'kyātawe
Mi'cgy iaxba'sūrake ōpī'rake haha huhu haha huhu.

People were holding their faces laughing. Tears squeezed between their fingers.

Sam had never felt more left out in his life.

"Is song sing for child sleep," said Blue Medicine Horse to Sam and Gideon. Sam looked at the young man in surprise. "Story silly—I run, fall hurt leg, the wearer the wolf mask, his face itches, he wants be like dogs, they smoke after eat. You sing a child to sleep with this."

"Yeah, it's a lullaby. What's funny," said Rose, "is that I pretend it's a sacred song my animal guide gave me in a vision quest."

"E!" cried female Crow voices—go on with the story.

He did. "The bear, he promised I would do great things on the warpath, as long as I never ate bear meat.

"Soon I went out alone against the Sioux nation. I cut a thousand horses out of their pony herds"—now people began to laugh again. "They sent five hundred men against me. The first one, he came from the east with his face painted red. I killed him with my rifle. The second one, he came from the south with his face painted yellow—I killed him with one shot from my pistol. The third one came from the west and his face was painted black. I killed him with my tomahawk. The fourth one came from the north, his face painted white. I killed him with my knife."

Rose accompanied each of these murders with preposterous, exaggerated pantomimes—his audience was screaming with hilarity.

"E! E!"

His next foes he killed in creative ways. He drew his breath in mightily and knocked one into the river with a single huff. Another he strangled with his own hair. A third he pretended to kiss and drowned with a gush of water from his mouth. Another one, he slipped the fellow's moccasins off, put them back on the wrong way, and the fellow found himself running away. And so on, and so on. He came back home in triumph, and every woman wanted him.

The women screeched at this.

Nothing had made the Crows laugh, though, as much as the lullaby doing the work of a sacred song.

Sam looked at Blue Medicine Horse curiously. "You speak English?"

"Little. Rose, he teach." The fellow was perhaps a little older than Sam and had a noble-looking face, like he should be a leader. Sam liked him.

Rose said, "Now you must honor us with a story, Gray Hawk."

Gray Hawk told three stories. The one Sam remembered best was the last, about the first time he saw white people. Rose translated:

"Several other boys and me went hunting beaver. Off by myself, I found a beaver lodge. Wanting to see the inside, I dived underneath and then crawled up a tunnel into the home. It was dark in there, and tight. I was tired. I slept a little, or maybe I fainted, I'm not sure.

"When I woke up, it was still very dark in there, but now I could hear my companions somewhere far off—they were singing a death song for me.

"Then I realized I could see something. A man and woman were sitting by a pool in the forest. They were white! That scared me—I had never seen such people.

"With great effort I struggled back to the daylight and went immediately to the pool of water I saw. There I beat a hole in the ground with my war club and sat down to watch it. Before long I saw the nose of an old male beaver poke up. I grabbed him and dragged him out. Two female beavers followed the old man out, and they were mine too.

"These beavers, they were the white people I saw sitting by the pool. I know that because beavers and whites are the craftiest people on earth, and must belong to the same species."

After this story, Sam realized some women and children in the back had gone to sleep. Gideon stood, like it was time to go home. Sam thanked his host, and then made a point of thanking Blue Medicine Horse. Maybe he could make a friend.

The next morning Sam asked Rose about Gray Hawk's story. Rose didn't seem to find anything odd about it.

"But it's different from the way we tell stories."

"How?"

Sam thought. "The story goes forward like ours, sort of, but it also drifts sideways, like a dream."

Rose laughed. "You got a lot to learn about Crow stories. They are big storytellers."

Sam blurted, "You've got to teach me Crow!"

Rose cocked an eyebrow at him and shook his head. "What you got to trade?" he asked. When Sam hesitated, thinking how poor he was, Rose walked away.

SAM EASED QUIETLY down the slope. Moving silently was much easier here than in the forests. Pine needles didn't crackle, and there were no leaf-bearing trees except right by the creeks and the river.

He was hunting. He didn't expect to see elk or deer, really, within a few hundred yards of camp. But winter camp was tedious sometimes, and he had to do something. He hadn't gone into this brushy draw before.

He came on a scene he thought he shouldn't see. Two men, Blue Medicine Horse and a gray hair, came out of a low hut perfectly naked. The gray hair crossed the clearing and hung his head down in weariness. Blue Medicine Horse nearly stumbled toward a boulder to sit. Both men looked bleary and exhausted.

Sam needed a moment to understand. The sweat lodge. They were holding a sweat lodge. He was sure he shouldn't go near the sweat lodges, and never had. He hadn't known one was in this draw.

Then he really saw the coyote. It was slinking toward the two men, trembling, agitated. It would quiver and kind of jump sideways, not at all the way a coyote would slip up. It was slobbering.

Sam threw his rifle to his shoulder and fired.

The coyote tumbled straight into the clearing.

Both Crows began to shout angrily.

Sam wanted to run off, but he made himself walk forward.

The gray-hair ran up to the coyote. Sam poked at it with his rifle and pointed the muzzle at the slobber.

"Understand," said Blue Medicine Horse. "Understand. Thank you. Sam, thank you."

The gray hair said a lot of words Sam didn't understand, but they sounded friendly, plenty friendly.

"Sam," said Blue Medicine Horse, "wait here, you please, wait here. We must . . ."

The gray hair went back into the low, dome-like hut covered with buffalo robes. Blue Horse took a forked stick and, one at a time, in a ritualistic manner, picked up hot stones with it and put them in the lodge. Before long he ducked into the lodge, stuck his head out and held up a finger toward Sam, and closed the last robe behind him.

Sam sat. He yearned to have an idea, any idea, what they were doing, but he didn't. They sang a long song, or it was more like a chant. By turns they each said a lot of words, like praying. Sam could hear water being poured on the hot rocks almost continuously, and steam hissing up.

Finally the robe door opened, steam vented out, and Blue Medicine Horse's head followed. He looked dizzy from the heat. Both of them came out, smiled at Sam, and sat, resting, like they were dazed.

When they got dressed, they took Sam into camp and paraded him around, crying out to everyone. People came out to look at Sam. Rose came rushing up.

"What are they saying?" Sam asked.

"My boy," Rose said with a big grin, "you're a hero."

GRAY HAWK ANNOUNCED he was going to have a fine supper cooked in Sam's honor.

Gray Hawk intended to make this gesture in front of Sam's friends too—Gideon, Diah, Clyman, Fitzpatrick, Sublette, Rose and his family, all were invited, and anyone else Sam wanted.

He decided not to share the meal any more widely.

They all smoked the beautiful, long pipe Gray Hawk brought out, with proper offerings to each of the four directions, the sky, and the earth. The ceremony was solemn.

They ate with plenty of laughter, and Sam had to admit the stew was tasty.

Rose said that if this was other Indians on special occasions, they'd be eating dog. Only the Crows did not consider dog a delicacy. Then he had a lot of fun in English with the notion of eating dog. "Oh, poor Fido," he cried in lachrymose tones, "such a sad fate. Oh noble beast, man's best friend, brought down so low." He elaborated this theme, making quite a comic performance.

Sam couldn't help laughing and was glad the Crows didn't understand English.

Every time Needle ladled stew from the pot, Rose would say, "Down, boy, down! Down!"

The hearts of the two races seemed good that night.

After supper Gray Hawk said he wanted to give Sam something big for saving the life of his son. He had heard of something Sam wanted. Gray Hawk would make it possible. Rose would teach Sam the Crow language. Gray Hawk would give Rose two horses for his efforts.

Blue Medicine Horse pitched in that he wanted to work with Sam and Rose, so he could learn more English while Sam learned Crow.

Sam said that sounded like a kit and caboodle of fun.

Every day from then on, all morning, Sam and Blue Medicine Horse sat in front of Rose's lodge, and the mulatto taught one English and the other Crow. The two young men helped each other, modeling pronunciation, correcting idiom. Then they wandered the camp together, Blue Medicine Horse speaking English, Sam faltering along in Crow. At the same time they both practiced the signs for what they were saying. In a week they were fast friends.

After a couple of weeks Blue Medicine Horse suggested that Sam help him make some new arrows, and so learn how. Near the top of the tipi he had some shafts of willow, cut, peeled, and hung to dry. Medicine Horse said you took big ones, for the smaller would get too thin when they were scraped straight. He showed Sam how to use a deer shoulder blade with a hole drilled in it to scrape the shafts to one common diameter, and a piece of basalt with a groove worn in it to take the knots off and rub it smooth. Then came the part that required a lot of patience. You heated the shaft, rubbed oil on it to make it supple, and used a bone with a hole in it as a lever to straighten it slowly—you had to hold it a long time while it cooled. At the end of the afternoon they had some fine shafts, and Medicine Horse put his mark on them, like signing something you wrote.

Sam was amazed at the patience, concentration, and delicate skill needed to make a good arrow shaft.

Medicine Horse had already traded for a bunch of points, so that was time they wouldn't have to spend. He had hawk feathers for the fletching. You spent a lot of hours splitting the quill and scraping the shafts thin. For today they built a low fire and set rawhide to simmering. By tomorrow it would turn gluey, and they could attach three feathers to each shaft. That would leave only one job, lashing on the points. Medicine Horse showed Sam how you would split the end of the shaft, lash that, insert the point and lash that, and then daub glue on all the lashing.

A fine and demanding craft, worth learning.

The next day, with Rose's amused help, the two young men had an unlikely conversation in the way of getting to understand each other. Blue Medicine Horse told Sam for the first time that the Crows find white people very odd, and why.

"Odd," said Sam, taken aback.

"Yes."

"What's odd about us?"

Blue Medicine thought, and then spoke carefully. "You live without women. Why don't you have families? If you do, where are they, and why are you so far from them for such a long time? Why don't you want to be with them?"

Rose was much amused.

Medicine Horse waited, but Sam just said, "Go on."

"What do you care about the skins of the beaver, which are not good for much? They're not like deerskin, which you can wear, or buffalo robes, which keep you warm."

Medicine Horse waited, but Sam just prompted him again—"Go on."

Rose said some words which Sam understood as reassuring Medicine Horse—"It's all right to speak."

"Why are the white men willing to give so scarce an object as a blanket, or even a rifle, for something as common as beaver skins, which every creek is full of? Where did the white men get so many, many of these objects, which no one else has ever seen, and no one has the medicine to make?" Blue Medicine Horse concluded, "Altogether white people are very peculiar. But it's all right. We are willing to be good hosts, and show you around this country, which you don't know, and show you basic things like what plants can be eaten, how to hunt with bow and arrow, what water is good to drink and what not." He smiled at Sam, pleased with his people's generosity. "But we wonder why you don't know these things."

"Tell him," said Sam to Rose, "that I take his questions seriously and will think them over and answer every one. This will take some time."

But in truth, Sam didn't think he could answer some things.

That night Blue Medicine Horse came to Sam's tipi to eat and share a social smoke. Something was bothering Sam. He knew he wasn't being completely honest with his new friend. Finally he drawled out, and signed, "You know why I'm keen to learn Crow?"

Blue Medicine Horse looked at him curiously. "Maybe not."

"I want to speak to your sister Meadowlark," Sam said. "I want to ask her to be my woman." He let it sit there like a lump.

Blue Medicine Horse gave him a very sympathetic look. "Cannot be."

Sam gave him a sharp look. "Why?"

"Hard to explain. You come to Rose with me now."

They found the guide sitting behind his center fire, smoking.

"Tell him."

Sam did.

Rose shook his head. "Can't happen, can't happen." He chuckled. "Here's the story. Meadowlark wants to be one of the two girls who leads the dancers in the goose egg dance, and them girls, they gotta be virgins." He grinned.

Sam looked crestfallen.

"Everybody knows it, she's talked about it for months."

"It is a beautiful dance," said Blue Medicine Horse. "The songs are beautiful. At the end the young men, they come to the circle and kiss the girl dancers."

Rose nodded but then said to Blue Medicine Horse. "Come back later, will ye? I want to talk to Sam jest the two of us."

They waited for the young Crow to leave. Sam felt humiliated in his friend's eyes.

"You don't need to know about that dance, not especial. But if I see things right, you haven't figured how these things go among the Crows."

It was a question. "I guess not."

"Women, they're supposed to be faithful, but not really. Very few of 'em are, and everybody winks at it. So, normal-like, you and Meadowlark could make all the whooptedo you wanted to. But you picked one of the only two women in this camp you can't have, the virgins for the goose egg dance. That's the way that stick floats, and it ain't gonna switch and float upstream."

Rose waited, but Sam was too unhappy to say anything.

"Speaking of it, looks like you haven't figured it for men neither."

Sam looked at him, waiting.

"For men it ain't that way at all. A beaver's supposed to dip in everywhere he can. If you don't, they think you're peculiar, or lacking in some way. Way they see it, a buffalo bull mounts one cow in the herd, he don't quit and hang around her. He goes right on and tries to mount 'em all. If he has any spunk."

Sam made a face.

"What's the matter?"

"Meadowlark would think bad of me."

"The opposite," said Rose. "Take this child's word, the very opposite."

Right then Sam made up his mind to show he had plenty of spunk.

* * *

THEY PASSED THE winter nights not only with storytelling but with music and dancing, sometimes in the Kentuck style, sometimes the Canuck, sometimes both. Isaac Culbertson, a wiry little man with beard up to his cheekbones and a hand of the Missouri Fur outfit, sawed the fiddle the American way in that camp. Gideon liked to sit in front of his and Sam's lodge and play French-Canadian tunes and draw a crowd to kick up their hooves.

On New Year's Eve Gideon strolled over to the Missouri Fur camp with his fiddle—the party would be here. All the captains broke out the whiskey jugs, and the mountain men set out to have a shining time—booze and fiddling and dancing and women!

Since everyone wanted to dance, here came no slow ballads or songs of woe. Isaac purled out several tunes in the new Virginia reel form, a popular dance with two lines of facing couples. Another favorite was the old-time reel, a lively dance from the Scottish highlands; also the schottische, a round dance like a polka; and a jig, a vigorous dance in triple time with lots of jumping. In camps on the way upriver, the men had danced with each other, some taking the female part half-willingly. But now they'd taught a few young, single Crow women this sport, and those were very popular women.

Gideon's songs were also tunes to shake a leg to, similar to country dance tunes, and no one cared that the original words were Frenchy—Gideon made those rhythms bubble and froth.

Sam had noticed that mountain men and Crow men often walked into the dark during and after these dances, looking amorous. New Year's Eve—now's the time, he told himself.

He had even learned, in the earlier dances, which leg to shake and when and in what direction, at least sometimes.

He stood with Diah, Fitz, and Sublette, watching. Customarily, the captain never danced, and Fitz and Sublette hardly ever stopped. The fiddlers stood near the bonfire in the center, and couples frolicked all around. Sam wondered how the devil he would get started.

He decided to watch Fitz and Sublette. Crow women—many of them only girls, really—stood outside the circle and danced along to the music standing in place. Fitz poured himself a tin cup of whiskey out of a handy jug, tossed some down, strutted right up to a shy-looking young woman, and offered her the cup. She beamed at him, emptied the cup in one swig, and handed it back to him. He flung the cup in Sam's direction and led the young lady into the dance.

Sam decided he needed a cup to get started.

Halfway through the cup he thought he noticed a nearby woman looking at him. As soon as he looked back, though, she cast her eyes down. Hmmm.

He had noticed her around one of the lodge circles. She was short and round, but always full of fun. Tonight she was very well turned out. He found her appealing, and couldn't help imagining certain activities.

Though Sam saw the result, he didn't know how much the woman had done to look her best. Her dress was sheepskin, tanned a light *café au lait*. The bottom of the skirt, just below her knees, had a fringe, and bells were tied to the thongs to make a happy sound when she danced. The waist was held in by a wide belt she'd beaded herself in her favorite colors, which were called in the Indian trade Crow blue, Cheyenne pink, and greasy green. The bodice showed off a featherburst of porcupine quillwork she'd done over many hours. She'd tied ermine tails to the fringe of the cape on her shoulders. Her hair was rubbed glossy with a blend of oils and herbs she made herself, and brushed with many, many strokes by her sisters. Vermilion shined in the center part of her hair. She'd also rouged her lips. She even wore a perfume, a mélange she learned from her mother and made with grasses, herbs, flower petals, and wild mint. Altogether she might have spent a good deal more time on her presentation than a young lady of the settlements who had a date for a country dance.

When the cute young white man finally brought her a cup, she downed it quickly and gave him a big smile. Clumsily, he told her his name in the Crow language, a gesture she found endearing. She told him her name was Yellow Leaf and let him take her hand, an awkward, new custom she'd learned, and lead her out among the dancers.

Even she, it turned out, had learned these dances as well as he, and they pranced their way through some turns almost nimbly, laughing when they made mistakes. He wasn't a bad fellow, this white boy.

Then he took her hand again, led her back to the whiskey jug, and offered more. She drank—she liked whiskey, or rather the whirly effect on her mind. Then with a quite unbelievable embarrassment, the young fellow offered a handsome piece of red strouding. She looked at him teasingly. It was a nice gift. She threw it over her shoulders as a shawl, and this time took his hand. She led him out of the dance circle and toward his own camp. She knew very well which lodge he lived in. In the darkness away from the fire, she turned, stroked his hair, and kissed him. "Your white hair is beautiful," she said. She ducked through the low door ahead of him and immediately embraced him. She intended to have a very good time for an hour or so, and was glad to take him along for the ride.

MUCH LATER THAT night Sam stood near Yellow Leaf listening to the music. Though she smiled at him from time to time, and acted like she sure liked him, she accepted other trappers' cups when they were offered, and danced with quite a few men. He couldn't help wondering if she would spend the whole night in the lodge of some one of them. He moved away quietly, because he didn't want to see.

A schottische ended, and it was Gideon's turn to offer a song.

He strolled around the fire head down, apparently thinking. Finally, he planted his feet wide and declared, "This song, it's a wedding song belong . . . it is of the Jews of the old country and the old ways. Is a *gasn-nign* people use to march from one house to another—for the ceremony, it take seven days!" He looked around the circle of dancers merrily, "Dance who will, and parade where you will!"

It was a slow, ceremonious tune in a minor mode, three-beat. It hinted of the mysteries of the Near East, and moved with the emphatic rhythms and yet the silkiness of a belly dancer, erotic and stately in the same breath. Sam had never heard such music, and was deeply affected.

When the song ended, Gideon sat down by the fire with his fiddle, his head down, his mind and spirit perhaps lost in ancestral memories.

Isaac didn't strike up a new tune. It didn't feel right, everyone sensed it.

And then the mulatto Edward Rose stepped into the circle. "This is a song of my mother's people," he said simply, and no more. He began to sing an old, old plaint of the slaves.

Nobody knows the trouble I've seen
Nobody knows my sorrow

After these few bars he started dancing around the circle, a head-down shuffle, and yet in the bounce of his legs and the suppleness of his body, there was a hint of strut, and pulsating life.

Nobody knows the trouble I've seen
Glory Hallelujah!

He made them ring out bold against each other, the troubles and the glory.

Sometimes I'm up, sometimes I'm down, O yes, Lord!
Sometimes I'm almost to the ground, O yes Lord!

There was joy in that down, joy on the ground, and vitality.

He danced around the circle and sang it all again, more mournful.

Nobody knows the trouble I've seen
Nobody knows my sorrow

Now he howled it like a wolf.

Nobody knows the trouble I've seen
Glory Hallelujah!

He shouted the last hallelujah to the black heavens and the infinite stars.

Then, suddenly, he stopped. He looked at the assembled crowd of mountain men and Crows, like he was realizing for the first time who they were. He began to chuckle. The chuckle came out like the rumble of a big river and grew loud like a waterfall and finally geysered out into a huge haw-haw-haw. He bent over and slapped his knees.

He looked up at everyone. "Happy New Year!" he said gravely. "Happy New Year to every one of you. Though it ain't no new year for the slaves, all the way across the American South. Nothing new about it."

Sam had never heard him mention the Negroes before.

Rose dropped his head and shook it, but when he raised his face to all it was smiling broadly. "I didn't mean to spoil the party. Here, I got another song, a party song."

I got a shoe, you got a shoe
All God's children got shoes

It was a kind of stomp, and both fiddlers caught on right quick and bucked up the dancing rhythm.

When I get to heaven gonna put on my shoes
Gonna tromp all over God's heaven
Heaven, heaven

The whole audience began to do the stomp.

Everybody talkin' 'bout heaven ain't' a-goin' there
Heaven, heaven
Gonna tromp all over God's heaven.

Rose led the stomp like a pied piper.

I got a shoe, you got a shoe
All God's children got shoes . . .

SAM SPENT JANUARY courting Meadowlark. In the early darkness of the winter evening he went to the circle where her family's lodge was and stood outside until she came. Then they would stand together with his blanket wrapped around their shoulders, their sides touching. The blanket was a handsome Witney Sam had signed for with the company, sky blue with a black stripe at each end. He chose it to match the leggings and beaded moccasins of Meadowlark. (Signing for things, he was getting a good bit of debt against the wages Ashley owed him.) Unfortunately, from Sam's point of view, their sides were all that ever touched. Certainly her lips never raised to his, nor did her hand find his, even in the privacy of the blanket. And Sam felt obliged to respect her desire to walk at the head of that ceremony (whatever the *hell* it was for) as a virgin. Forbidden to touch, they watched the evening stars. Sometimes Meadowlark told him stories of the star people, and what they had done long, long ago, before the memories of the grandfathers of the oldest men. Sometimes she told him stories of the doings of her people, especially great fights they had with the Sioux or Snake or the Blackfeet. Though she was no storyteller, the stories had a ring of fairy tale, true stories in their way, but more than fact, and beyond true. Sam talked of his family, the father he loved, the mother he felt sorry for, the sisters he wanted to see again, the older brother he resented, the younger brother who died, Coy, and whose company Sam sometimes longed for. Sometimes he spoke of his dreams, and then his tones took on the gong and clamor of heraldry. It was these stories she loved best, and sometimes she pitched in and elaborated them further— "And maybe then raven sees bear run down the tree, and raven will tell. . . ." He hoped she was falling in love with the hero he wanted to be. He was long since in love with her.

Though brim full of romance, he also wanted sexual play. The dances seemed to come about once a week and he found it then. Meadowlark, maybe knowing, never appeared at any of the dances.

Gideon, and another man or two, got what Sam wished he had, a kind of regular girlfriend. Gideon's young woman, Sapling, made him a *gage d'amour* as a token of her love, a small, heart-shaped bag, ornamented with beads, made to wear around the neck and hold a clay pipe and a little tobacco. Sam was ripe with envy.

He and Gideon developed other forms of play. The two of them and Micajah started a shooting game on the ice of the river. They'd throw a piece of log on the ice and shoot at it with their pistols, driving it farther away with each shot. When all but one man missed, he was the winner; if no one hit at a certain distance, they shot until someone did. None of them were as good with their pistols as their rifles, but Micajah was the best of the three.

One day when they were walking back to camp from the river, Sam said to Micajah, "I'll be damned if I don't think you've turned into a friend."

Micajah gave him a merry look and said, "Let's prove it by shooting the cup off each others' heads."

"Nobody's shooting at me if they're boozing," answered Sam.

Micajah clapped him on the back and haw-hawed and allowed, "Don't blame you."

Gideon showed Sam how to make snowshoes by lashing long, stiff pine boughs to his moccasins, and the two went elk hunting in the foothills with Blue Medicine Horse. Blue Horse's mother acted very grateful for the fresh meat in the middle of winter, and so did Meadowlark.

It seemed to Sam that Gideon was the good older brother he'd never had, and Blue Medicine Horse the good friend. He just wished Meadowlark would be the woman.

Instead she stirred up feelings that bothered him. He went to Jedediah to talk it over.

Captain Smith, Tom Fitzpatrick, and Bill Sublette were sharing a lean-to they'd built against a huge boulder. The log walls kept some of the wind out, and the boulder held some heat from their fires into the night.

Since it was late, the fire down to embers, Diah, Bill, and Fitz sat deep in their blankets against the cold. They helloed Sam and told him to have a seat. Three pipes stuck out from blanket-shrouded heads.

Sam sat, tried to act deliberate by taking time to get his pipe going, and blurted out, "I'm in love with Meadowlark, damn it."

"Sorry to hear that," quipped Fitz.

"What a pain in the ass," said Bill with a wolfish grin.

Diah just waited.

"I want her to be my woman. You know what's she waiting for."

"And maybe waiting for a young man she fancies as well," said Fitz.

"Someone handsome," teased Bill.

After a silence, Diah put in, "Do you have a woman back home?"

"I've all-the-way forgot about her," said Sam.

"That doesn't sound good."

"Well, she married my brother."

A stricken look Sam had never seen before flashed across the captain's face.

"An experience every man should have," quipped Fitz.

"What'll I do?" Sam looked at Diah mournfully.

"Well," said Diah, "fornication is out of the question."

"Not out of any questions I'd ask," put in Bill.

"Nor Sam either," said Fitz quietly.

Diah ignored them. "Marriage? Are you ready to commit to spend the rest of your life with the Crow people? I don't think so."

"Not when there's so many good-looking Sioux women," said Bill with a chuckle.

Diah frowned at his friend, though he was used to this banter.

"Do you want to raise your children without the blessings of a Christian church?"

Sam couldn't answer that one. Actually, though he thought of himself as a Christian, he'd never been in a church.

"So far from a Christian community, I think your immortal soul would be in danger."

Fitz and Bill fell silent. Talk of souls apparently silenced even their scoffing.

"Has she given you a *gage d'amour*?" asked Diah.

Sam put his hand to the empty spot at his collar bone and shook his head.

"I didn't think so," said Diah.

"I got to have her," said Sam.

"Her sister is probably available," said Bill, a glint in his eye.

Sam blushed.

"Where will we be after the spring hunt?"

"No way to know," said Diah.

"Hope we'll be in Snake country," said Fitz.

"Beaver heaven, that's what they say." This was Bill.

Sam pondered, but it didn't seem to help. "Let's talk on something else," he said.

"What about the horses?" asked Diah.

Sam looked at him questioningly.

"Her family would expect a gift of horses, especially since you're a rich white man. Do you have four, five, or six horses to give?"

"I guess not."

Everyone was quiet for a while, smoking.

Sam got an idea. This summer, if he could do something heroic, he could get the horses. That perked him up.

"Sam," said Diah. "In a week or two, whenever the weather looks a little better, we'll be leaving for Snake country."

That night, deep in his buffalo robes, Sam dreamed about raiding the Snakes for ponies.

Chapter Fourteen

THE DEPARTURE WAS a disappointment to Sam. He wanted something, he didn't know what, maybe seeing all the trappers and Indians lined up on two sides and his brigade riding down the middle, waving; women would run out and give their sweethearts good-bye kisses, and children would cry.

Instead the outfit heard light scoffing from the Weber boys, and the Keemle-Gordon brigade too. Early February was too early in the season to move, they said. Hardly any snow here, but plenty everywhere else. Haw-haw. Neither of the other brigades would push west. Tales of beaver heaven be damned! They were in beaver heaven right here. Weber would work his way down the Wind River until it turned into the Big Horn and down that river to Henry's Fort, and would harvest plenty of plews. Keemle and Gordon would head down the Wind, across the Little Horn Mountains, across the Big Horns, across the Black Hills, and over the plains to Fort Kiowa—they had a good take from trading with these Crows. The other men wondered what burr Diah Smith had under his saddle, that he had to go casting about for a new place to trap. How did he know the Indians wouldn't be hostile? Why didn't he accept what was very, very good and be well satisfied?

By watching and listening, Sam had mostly figured that out. Captain Jedediah Smith burned with something. He was itchy partly for dollars. The Ashley-Henry firm was off to a shaky start, maybe worse than shaky. They needed a good spring hunt so the general could show the men who backed him some return. Partly, Diah was determined to do well for General Ashley, who had put confidence in a very young leader. Partly he had the desire to see what was over the next hill—Diah harbored the traveler's hunger, the lust to see what a piece of country looked like—he yearned to see the shape of the shoulder of a mountain, the way a creek wound through its valley, as much as other men yearned to see the flesh of woman. But with Jedediah Smith, Sam sensed, it was really something beyond all of that, something that turned and turned inside him and would always be churning, driving. That something, Sam was sure, would fill in the blank spaces on his map, maybe all the way from the Missouri River to the Pacific Ocean. Diah's thirst was big and it would take that much country to slake it.

From the Crows they couldn't tell about the country ahead, the pass they wanted to cross. Rose was gone on a war party, and had told the captain he didn't want to work for Ashley anymore, instead would stay with the Crows. Now the outfit had no guide. Sam and Blue Medicine Horse translated between Diah and the men who knew the country. Sam thought they were hinting that it was too early for the pass, but didn't want to be so impolite as to say so right out. Also, the captain seemed plain sure white men could do what Indians could not. The lure of adventure shone bright in Diah's eyes, and they would go, regardless.

They loaded up, this baker's dozen of men, one packhorse to each rider. Sam and Gideon abandoned their lodgepoles as too cumbersome to carry, but took the cover. The brigade mounted and rode slowly upriver, first past the circles of the Crow camp. Though Sam said good-bye to Meadowlark the night before, pledging a return for summer, now his eyes searched her circle. No Meadowlark running out to wave good-bye. No Meadowlark at all. For sure, no brass band farewell.

They rode northwest along the river toward a high pass, Union Pass, it was called. Captain Smith had a map he'd put together from the country he'd seen and what was known from the Lewis and Clark men and the Astorians and the few others who'd ventured this far. The pass was on the map, and the Crows confirmed it. Beyond that pass, they said, was Snake country, the Siskadee River, beaver heaven. Why, you didn't have to trap them, you could kill them with a stick.

The first day they made maybe fifteen miles, easy riding in snow no more than hoof deep. From the Crows and the maps Diah had figured it was thirty miles to the pass, and no telling how many miles of high country on the other side.

The second day the snow was cannon-bone deep, and they had to take it slow with the horses. After five or six miles, it was hock deep, and they got off and led the horses. The men wondered what the animals would feed on. That night a majority in camp was for turning back. The captain, though, had his mind made up to go on.

Through here the route wound between high mountain ranges. The river had long since become a narrow creek and was invisible between snowbanks. Another creek came hurtling in from the north. They floundered across. The captain gave the hand signal to stop, and every man followed his eyes. He looked at the little creek they were following. They all wondered whether it was flowing east, and was the headwaters of Wind River, or whether it flowed west. Did they tread now for the first time on the waters of the Columbia River? Were they across the Great Divide, on the Pacific side?

Sam decided to find out. He handed Gideon his reins and floundered toward the creek. He would see what way that water went. If necessary, he would stick his hand in it and feel the current. If it rolled west, he would put his lips in and taste Pacific waters.

But he couldn't get close enough. A high, soft snowbank shouldered the creek. If he went any further, the bank would cave in, and Sam would get a dunking.

He hesitated. Maybe . . .

"Sam!" came the captain's voice. "It isn't worth it."

He came back.

"So we don't know," said Clyman.

"Do we care?" asked Sublette, always ironic.

"Doesn't matter," said Fitz, looking hard at the captain.

"You're probably right," said the captain.

Diah and Fitz saw it the same way, though Diah hated it. The men were in snow over their knees, and had to lift each leg out and heave it over snow awkwardly. But the horses were worse. They didn't want to go on. Their feed was buried a couple of feet down. Tomorrow they would be shaking from cold, weakness, and hunger.

"Even if we're over the top," Fitz said, "there'll be a lot of snow. Might be days to feed. Back, it's only one day."

"We can't ruin these horses," agreed the captain. Diah might have pushed the men on, but he was mindful that the horses were worth about one hundred and twenty dollars each in this remote place, and the company had to have them for the spring hunt.

When they got back to the Crow camp the next evening, every man knew it was the right decision. The horses were done in, and beyond that. They'd need at least a week's rest on this fair-to-middling winter grass.

Diah gave himself no rest, though. The next morning he was at Sam and Gideon's lodge before they'd had breakfast, wanting to go see chief Rides Twice, wanting Sam to translate.

Sam told Diah to wait until he'd finished his coffee, and invited the captain to join him. Diah declined. The man wouldn't rest. Most of the trappers would have gladly relaxed another month among the Crows. Plenty of food, plenty of company, plenty of women, shining times. But Diah was edgy to be getting on.

Soon they gathered up Fitz, Clyman, and Sublette to visit with Rides Twice.

Now Rides Twice's politeness let him affirm effusively what they'd learned the hard way—the pass to the north was too high and too snowy in this moon.

"Ask him if there's an easier pass to the Siskadee."

Sam was wondering if he was to blame for the false start up Union Pass. Maybe if he'd understood all of what Rides Twice and the others were saying . . . Now he faltered through some Crow sentences and some signs.

Rides Twice gave an answer, but he was hesitant. He didn't understand, or wasn't sure he did.

Diah looked at Sam impatiently.

"We better get Blue Medicine Horse," said Sam.

Sam's friend was sent for. Word came back that he was out hunting.

Crow men who knew the country well were called for. While they were waiting, Clyman had an idea. He got a buffalo robe, shoveled a lot of sand onto it, and dragged it into Rides Twice's lodge.

The Crow men who came were big bellies, middle-aged men. Rides Twice was a white hair. The trappers figured they had plenty of expertise at hand.

Clyman shaped the sand with his hands to represent the Wind River Valley, the Absaroka Mountains on one side, and the Wind River Mountains opposite. He drew a line for the river, all the way down to where it made its big turn, carved its way through the Little Horns, and changed its name to the Big Horn River. Sam sounded out every name carefully, and the Crows clearly understood.

Then they got involved, and bit by bit the picture came into focus. The pass was south, beyond where the Wind River made its big turn, and well to the west. First another river, the Popo Agie, came in from the west. You went up that river, passed a spring of some kind Sam couldn't understand, and then crossed over several more divides to the south to another river, the Sweetwater. This river flowed down from a break in the mountain chain, and beyond that break, several days' ride beyond, was the Siskadee.

Diah Smith gave his hosts plenty of tobacco in thanks for the information. Before leaving, he said, "Tell your young men not to steal our horses after we leave."

Sam stumbled through this in spoken word and sign.

Rides Twice laughed genially. "I will tell them, but it will do no good. Stealing your horses, that's their fun."

"We don't expect our friends to rob us."

"Oh, we won't rob you. If the young men get your horses, come back and trade us something for them. We wouldn't really rob you, or harm you. If we did, you wouldn't come back, and then we couldn't steal your horses."

Rides Twice and all the big bellies got a good laugh out of that one.

Every night that week Sam courted Meadowlark. They stood through the late winter evening in the blue blanket he'd bought because it matched her leggings, her moccasins, and something about her spirit. They talked and talked, of his dreams and hers. They didn't kiss, they didn't hold hands. Sam told her that no matter what happened, whatever grizzly bear or high mountains got in his way, he would be back in this village next summer. And he would bring many horses.

He saw in her eyes that she knew what he meant. Her eyes said something eloquent back, but she gave him no words.

The next morning, as the brigade rode south out of camp, she did give him the send-off he yearned for. She ran out from her circles, sky-blue legs flashing, and held something up to him. The line of riders stopped.

He reached down and took . . . a *gage d'amour*.

Its heart shape was outlined in beads of Crow blue, with a thin black line, also heart-shaped, inside that. The enter was Cheyenne pink.

Solemnly, he put it around his neck. "It's beautiful," he said in the Crow language. "Thank you." With one hand he touched his heart.

Someone said softly behind, "She done carved her initials and the boy's in a tree."

Someone else shushed him.

Sam reached down and brushed her cheek with soft fingers. It was the most intimate touch that had ever passed between them.

The other men were moving on, circling around him.

He touched his heels to his pony and was off.

THIS TIME THE men of the brigade felt like they knew where they were going. Down the Wind for three and a half days, to where a decent-sized river did roll in from the west. Up that river to a big spring of black oil—now Sam knew what the Crow big bellies were trying to tell him. With confidence now they set out over a divide to the south, and on south. Eventually, they would come to the Sweetwater.

Didn't look like it was going to be easy, though. They were up high in alpine country in the first week of March. The buffalo were back down where, some of the men thought, any critter with sense would be. So they hadn't had fresh meat since leaving Wind River for higher country. They better get over this pass before it came to starving times.

SAM, CLYMAN, AND Sublette are pushing ahead, looking for meat in this frozen wasteland around the southern end of the Wind River Mountains. Sam casts evil glances at his two friends. The damn snow is deep enough, he curses to himself, and drifted enough, even its shapes fool you. Hollows are full, rises thinly crusted, and you can't tell the difference. You can in deep drifts. You fall into little creeks running under the snow. You see only one color, a white that stretches to the sky on either side. It is a kind of blindness.

Sam draws his hooded blanket coat, which the men call a capote, tighter and yet again tighter. He turns his head away from the wind that skips and plays down from regions where only wind can go, but somehow it finds his nooks and crannies, dries his lips, makes his eyes tear. When he gets the edges of his hood too close, his eyelashes freeze to it. His hands and feet, as far as he can tell, are absent without leave.

Sam rides up alongside Clyman, scanning the frozen flats and slopes for the black dots that might mean buffalo, or elk, or anything a man can eat.

The sun drops behind the peaks to the west, casting the landscape into cold, lavender shadow.

Just then they spot three buffalo standing in the open about a mile away. The frozen men look at each other. They look at the horses, who stand heads down, eyes glazed. The hunters will have to get close to their quarry—there will be no chase.

Dismounting, they slip toward the buffalo. Buffler are funny. Sometimes when you shoot, the others stand there, dumb. But sometimes if they smell you half a mile away, or see you and you look like a wolf, they stampede away scared. You can never tell about buffler.

The wind is swirling, but it's headed down this wide canyon. *Can we get close enough?*

Though the cold doesn't seem to matter as much, the ache of hunger is worse in Sam's belly. A quarter mile away they drop to hands and knees and start crawling forward. The animals are bulls. Nothing has ever felt so important.

The wind picks up, getting ready to howl. It spits the snow up in their eyes. Their lips are parched with thirst, puckered with cold. They crawl, and crawl, and crawl.

Suddenly one of the bulls fidgets, paws the earth, and stomps nervously. He's seen them.

It's too far away for a sure kill.

All three men spring up, throw down on the bulls, and let fly.

The bulls thunder off.

"That one's running queer," says Sublette.

"Maybe a broken shoulder," answers Clyman.

Sam's lips are too cold to move.

In the twilight they can't be sure about the buffalo. Time is running out.

While Sublette goes back for the horses, Sam and Clyman follow the bulls up the valley. Maybe they can pin the wounded one against that ridge about a mile away. Clyman breaks into a trot, and Sam forces himself to keep up.

The snow is crusty in most places and holds their weight. Sometimes Sam breaks through to midcalf and stumbles forward. Sometimes he pitches headlong into the snow. The wind is whistling down the canyon now. Desperate, they keep running.

The bulls have gone up along a patch of timber and veered off left, toward the ridge. The men take a chance and cut through the deep shadows of the timber. When they come out into the last of the graying light, there stands the wounded bull, in easy range.

While Sam is still gasping for breath, Clyman fires without aiming.

Mountain luck. The bull tumbles into a small gully.

When Sublette catches up, Sam and Clyman have the hide open and are cutting off meat and stuffing it down raw. The flesh tastes wonderful, the juices taste wonderful, and the warm body is kind to their frozen hands.

In the three-quarters dark they gather a little sagebrush and try to start a small fire. It's hard to get sparks from flint and steel to light the tinder. When it does light, the wind scatters the fire immediately. Over and over they try and fail. All three want some buffalo meat roasted. Instead they cut off last hunks, wrap themselves in their blankets to gnaw, and pretend they don't notice the wind and cold.

After only about an hour of the long night Sam decides the cold coming through the blankets from the snow may be even worse than the wind. He sees no choices. He huddles, painfully awake, shivering. He wiggles his fingers and toes, thinking that in the morning he may have none to wiggle. In fact, in the morning his body may be hard as an ice-covered boulder.

He watches Sublette and Clyman carefully for signs that his partners are awake. Conversation might make this wait hurt less. Nothing could make it hurt worse.

After half an eternity of watching, he calls Sublette's name, then Clyman's. The wind rips the words away, so he tries again. Nothing. He speaks again and again. Nothing. He ponders giving one of them a punch or a kick, but he can't bring himself to do that. Because he has realized that his partners have frozen to death. He's not a bit surprised. He feels superstitious about touching the bodies, though, like he might catch something, maybe that old enemy mortality.

Sam starts pumping his arms in the air, swaying his trunk, kicking his legs up and down on the snow. When he's out of breath, he rests. And rests some more, intending to go back into motion soon. Sam doesn't intend to freeze to death, not one bit of that, not a bit . . .

Damn! He almost went off to sleep. He's sure that would be fatal now—that's how his partners froze to death.

He looks up at the Big Dipper, checks its angle to the North Star, and makes up his mind to keep track of the time by the movement of the Dipper.

He pumps, sways, and kicks to a fare-thee-well. He wiggles each of his ten fingers and each of his ten toes twenty times. He grabs his nose and then his ears and wiggles them. He looks up at the Big Dipper. It hasn't moved an iota.

He goes back to wiggling, now doing each finger and toe fifty times. It's going to be a long, l-o-n-g night . . .

SAM CONSIDERS CAREFULLY whether the sky to the east is really a tad paler. It's probably his imagination. Or his hope is painting the horizon a hint lighter.

Hope is a small flame within his breast, but now it flickers. Light is never coming to this part of the world again. As it will never come back for Jim Clyman and Bill Sublette. Gone beavers. Sam is damned sorry about that. He let his partners down.

He studies the eastern sky. Probably it's just his fancy playing tricks on him.

The wind has eased off at last.

Resolutely, he faces to the west and starts pumping, swaying, and kicking once more. When he's finished with one round of that, he does his complete finger and toe-wiggling routine. Then, fixedly, he stares to the west, into the high range of snow-shrouded peaks, for as long as he can stand it. Then he turns around.

Lighter. Yes, he's sure. It's sure.

And Sam knows he's going to live.

Live, by God—LIVE!

After another eternity, this one maybe a little shorter, he stirs. He doesn't know how his muscles and bones will work this morning. Maybe they won't.

He looks over at Clyman and Sublette. He can't bury his friends. He'll take what buffalo flesh he can, bring back compañeros this afternoon to get the rest of it, and take care of them then.

He looks at the pathetic remains of the fire they tried to build last night, a few broken, charred twigs of sagebrush. In a moment he's going to have to try again. There's only the barest breeze now, he ought to be able to get one going.

"That's what did it, fellows. That damned fire, we couldn't get it. I'm sorry, damn sorry."

"What?" says a voice.

"Bill?"

"What?" A different tone this time, irritated at being waked up. Clyman.

Sam has never felt so glad to have someone irritated at him.

"I . . ." He doesn't know what to say. "Damnation, help me build a fire." He will never understand how Clyman and Sublette slept through that terrible cold and lived.

Jim grumps, "I'll gather some wood. You two get your hands warm enough to strike a spark."

But Sam can't do it, Sublette can't do it. The steel bites into their flesh and freezes. Their fingers are too numb to hold flint tight.

Clyman can't either. Over and over the three take turns trying. No luck.

Desperate, they shoot their rifles into the tinder, thinking maybe a spark . . .

No luck.

Bill rolls up in his blankets and turns his back to Sam and Clyman. "Leave me alone."

They look at Sublette's back. Bill will be dead for sure before they can ride to the brigade and get back.

Sam looks around at the bleak, alien, frozen landscape.

No, by God, I'm not ready to die. We can't stay here—we have to move. Sam stands up, takes a last look at Bill, and walks to his horse.

Clyman nods his understanding. They take the reins and swing into the saddles.

Then Clyman gets one last idea. He dismounts and kneels by the remains of last night's attempt at fire. He sorts twigs and ashes through his fingers, groping for what he cannot see.

And finds it. Warmth.

He brushes ash away. A small, red coal, no bigger than a kernel of corn.

"Goddamn hoorah!" he mutters toward Sam.

He makes the best sagebrush tinder he can. Then, glad to burn his fingers, he drops the coal into it. Sam drops to his knees and helps blow.

In moments they have a nice little blaze going.

"Bill! We got fire!" grunts Clyman.

Slowly, lethargically, Sublette rolls over and sees.

A moment later their hands and even faces are in the flames. All three breathe the smoke gladly.

In a few minutes they are riding for timber. Clyman and Sublette hunch in their saddles. For warmth, Sam walks. In two hours they reach good timber. While Sublette sleeps again, Clyman and Sam roast buffalo. Sam smiles to himself. We did it. We did it. And our meat will save the brigade.

STARVING TIMES WERE not past.

In a few days they crossed the last divide and came onto the Sweetwater, a narrow, meandering river that wandered east, but where they didn't know. Captain Smith looked at his map and said it might be one of the tributaries of the Platte River, or the Arkansas River, no telling which.

They were looking for enough water to float their furs down when summer came. Furs had to go to market. Platte or Arkansas made a devil of a difference. Several hundred miles above St. Louis where you could float them down easily, or several hundred below, so you'd have to haul them against the current.

The upper Sweetwater was still in the clutches of a high mountain winter. True, there was one sign of seasonal change to come. The south-facing slopes were sometimes bare of snow. But the game was still in the valleys far down the mountain. That told some of the men they didn't belong up here, not yet. Captain Smith was driving them to start before the time had arrived. They would never quite understand their captain. But he was some man, and they would damn well follow him.

Right now that meant hunger. They had no fresh meat at all. Soon the dried buffalo would run out. They were already hungry, almost to the point of pain.

What Sam would always remember about the Sweetwater, though, was the wind. It rose the first night they camped along that river. It swooped, it whooped, it howled, it roared—no man there had ever seen anything like it. It scooped up snow and hurled it at them. It tried to pull the hair out of their scalps and their jowls and fling it toward the settlements. It scoured flesh cold and raw.

They huddled in their blankets and robes. A couple of times during the night men couldn't stand the cold any longer and got up to make fires. Each time the wind darted among the embers devilishly, flung them into the air, and scattered them far and wide. Sometimes the huff-huff of the gale sounded like a mocking cackle. The poor fire-makers went back to bed colder than when they started.

The gale roared all that night, then all day, and most of the next night.

That "most" was critical.

Sam and Clyman, unable to bear the cold sitting, decided about midday to go for a walk to warm up. They walked fully encased in blankets and robes, and couldn't have said they were more comfortable moving than sitting. But a dull inertia kept them padding on, toward some rocks to the south.

Here they found a crevice between two boulders and tucked themselves partly out of the wind. Sometimes they talked to keep their minds off their hunger.

Suddenly Sam exclaimed something out loud, threw up The Celt, and fired. Clyman couldn't believe what happened next. A mountain sheep fell right beside them.

They started laughing and couldn't stop. Funniest thing either of them ever saw. A mountain sheep posed majestically right uphill from Sam, and when shot, the critter had the good manners to fall right at their feet.

They set to skinning it out immediately, their hands glad of the warm flesh and hot blood. They cut off pieces of the fleecy fat and ate them raw, grinning. Suddenly this journey was changed completely. This isn't a catastrophe, it's an adventure.

They hauled the meat back up the valley to the wind-whipped camp. By the time they arrived, it was again a brutal day. Several men tried to get a fire going to roast the meat, even shielding the fire from the gale with a phalanx of blankets. Nothing worked. A few ate some meat raw, but it didn't satisfy. They wrapped themselves in their blankets cold and hungry.

Until Clyman was awakened in the wee hours by the silence. The wind had lulled.

Instantly he was up, striking flint to steel, getting his tinder to flame up, feeding the fire. He started roasting sheep meat on a stick and gorging himself on it. As soon as they smelled the cooking flesh, all the men woke up and joined the feast.

The next morning the captain gave in to the reality of winter. He told the men to go downhill in various directions and find a place with plenty of firewood, some shelter, and some game. Sam and Gideon wandered four or five miles down to a canyon and found there a grove with plenty of downed wood, grass and bark for the horses to eat, and mountain sheep roaming the cliffs above. Gideon shot a sheep. They buried it in a snow drift, and went back for their companions.

After a week or so, the mountain sheep were too skittish to make easy hunting. It was time to move on. First, though, they made a big cache. Taking turns, they dug out a hole with a small entrance and a big basement. There they put lead, powder, and other essentials, and covered the hole with the sod they initially removed, making it all but invisible to thieves. Diah told them this was the place. "If we split up, we'll meet back here. If we divide into two parties, we'll find each other back here. On June first."

And now some of the men thought, for the first time, that it was useful, even in the mountains, to know the month and day, the way Captain Smith did.

Up the Sweetwater they went, and then into what they hoped was the Southern Pass. It was a wild-looking place, mountains to the north, knobby buttes and monuments to the south. If it was the pass, it was high, wide, and handsome.

South Pass was not, however, accommodating. No game. No water. They melted snow to drink. And they went hungry.

On the sixth day, four of the days with nothing at all to eat, Clyman and Sublette went ahead looking for antelope. They'd seen some the previous evening, just before dark. What they found was a buffalo lying down. They debated about how to shoot it, since the vital parts were buried in snow. They decided on the rump and the shoulder simultaneously. One, two, three—both guns exploded.

The buffalo lurched violently and did not get up.

When the men heard the shots, they came running, and topped a little ridge just as Sublette made the finishing shot to the head.

Never was butchering happier.

They traveled on in hope of finding wood for a fire, but had no luck. They ate raw meat that night, and drank melted snow. Melting enough for the horses too was slow work.

While they indulged themselves in a very primitive and partial feast, Captain Smith walked out for a look around. When he came back, he said he could see it clearly. The peaks were behind them. Ahead, downhill, was the valley of the Siskadee.

"We did it." This phrase alone was excess for Diah. "We crossed the pass. The next water we drink"—

"—if we ever find any," Fitz called out—

"—will be the waters of the western watershed, flowing to the Pacific Ocean."

The men laughed and cheered.

THE FIRST WATER they found was the Big Sandy River, frozen. The men chopped at the ice with their tomahawks until their arms would reach no farther down. "Froze to ze bottom," said Gideon miserably.

Clyman drew a pistol and shot into the bottom of the hole. Water welled up fast, plenty for man and beast.

By the time they reached the Siskadee, they were half-starved again. But the river had lots of wild geese, which they feasted on, and soon they had buffalo.

"Starving times to shining times is a short distance in this country," said Gideon.

Snow still patched the ground, but the days were pleasantly warm, the living easy.

There was beaver sign, and plenty. They were eager to reap a bounteous harvest of plews to send down to General Ashley, so he would continue to finance their mountain adventures. Captain Smith split the party in two, himself to take some of the men south along the Siskadee, and Fitzpatrick to lead the other outfit north along the river. Three sets of partners, Clyman and Sublette, Gideon and Sam, and Branch and Stone went with Fitzpatrick.

Back to the routine of trapping the wily rodent. Pick a likely-looking creek, ride upstream with Gideon in the early light. Spot beaver sign. Wade in some distance from where you want to set the trap. Set it, chained, with medicine for bait. Get the job done early, before Indians are about.

At dusk, ride the trapline again, taking your beaver and skinning them out. Set the traps somewhere new, so you can take hides again at dawn.

Make meat when you need to. Enjoy lounging in camp during the middays and the evenings. Give a name to the creek you found, and the pretty peak near its head. Observe everything, the creeks, the ridges, the mountains, the elk, deer, and buffalo, the ducks, geese, and cranes. Savor these moments. You are the first white men ever to see this country, to set foot in these creeks.

Eden, Sam said to himself, and thought of his father, and their special place. Sometimes I miss home, he admitted to himself. But Eden was here, not there, and his father was gone.

He said to Gideon as they rode down the creek toward the camp, their packhorse bearing fresh hides, "This is a perfect country."

Gideon shrugged. "If the people can learn to live with each other."

They trudged along a little.

"White men and Indians don't get along, I guess," said Sam.

"Look at me." He stuck out a bare arm that was between red and white. I do fine wiz both. And you go good with Meadowlark."

Sam chuckled. "Yeah."

"The French, we do. You Americans not so good."

Soon they came on a family of Indians camped on a creek. Shoshones, they called themselves, the tribe the whites called Snakes, from the hand sign for their band. They were a peaceable family, very shy-seeming, making the signs that meant they were hungry.

Fitz looked them over and talked it over with the others. Sam and Gideon argued for feeding them, making friends. Branch and Stone said to tell 'em to get gone and stay away—"They'll steal us blind."

"They had no luck hunting," said Clyman.

Sublette agreed, "Could happen to any of us."

So Fitz said yes. They gave the poor creatures beaver tail to eat, the one edible part of the critter. The family stayed close to the outfit for maybe a week, feeding on beaver. Sam tried to get to know them, but they were too shy.

One morning the Snakes were gone. So were the outfit's horses, all dozen or so.

"Damn it!" shouted Fitz.

Trusting, they'd let the horses graze loose overnight. Branch and Stone threw out I-told-you-so looks.

The men tried to find the damned Indians and take the horses back. But the Snakes had disappeared. How? Half a dozen people, more than a dozen horses—a crowd can't walk without leaving a track. They looked again. Across the stony ground, looking for where the party crossed onto dirt and left sign. Up the creek, down the creek, trying to find out where they left the water. No luck. Finally Fitz decided. "We're losing prime trapping time. We'll set traps and bring 'em back on foot."

A damned nuisance, and worse than a nuisance, marching up and down the creeks and taking beaver on foot. Walking to the next trapping ground. Burying your furs in a cache to get later, because you have no way to carry them. But they did it. Beaver were plenty, and the hunt was very, very good.

WHEN JUNE NEARED, Fitz said they better start walking. They had to get to the cache to meet Captain Smith by June first.

Their horse gear, their plews, their traps, and other essentials were put in a cache. When they had mounts, they would come back for it all, get the furs en route to St. Louis, and then maybe be out of time to do anything but start the fall hunt.

Sam was mindful of his promise to Meadowlark—'I'll come back next summer, regardless.' But he couldn't go to her village, not alone and on foot. Too dangerous. Also, he couldn't go in as a pauper.

That's why he was so happy when, about noon on the day they started walking, they came around a corner and saw face to face five or six Indians, mounted on the trappers' horses.

Rifles pointed quick at the Indians.

The Indians' weapons were bows and arrows, spears, and war clubs. None of those could be put into play as fast as a trigger could be pulled, and they knew it.

They dismounted and handed over the reins. The men jumped on their horses gladly. They threw hard eyes at the Indians, who were surely Snakes. They talked it over. Half a dozen horses were still missing. Branch and Stone halfway wanted to lift hair. "Then we'll never get our horses back," said Fitz.

Sam made the signs. We come in friendship. We want our horses. Take us to your village.

It was a steep mile up the mountains, a camp of maybe four score Snakes, including the ones Fitz and the fellows had fed beaver tail.

They made their own camp within easy rifle shot of the village. They talked in council to the village leader.

In another half hour they had all their horses, except one, Branch's riding mount.

Quick like a snake, Branch dived and caught a young man by the ankle and yanked him to the ground. It was one of the family they'd fed. Branch tied the fellow up, both hands and feet. Then he gave Sam a hard look. "Tell them if my horse isn't back in an hour, we'll kill him."

Sam flashed the signs to the watching crowd, though there was no way to indicate "one hour."

The horse was back in a jiffy.

Branch let the young fellow go, reluctantly, Sam thought.

While the outfit roasted meat over a common fire that night, Sam brought it up. "You treat Indians like they are only half human."

"Half human is what they are," mumbled Stone, his mouth full.

Sam raised his eyebrows but said nothing. He looked into Gideon's face, wondering what his friend thought of this.

"Pilgrim," Branch said to Sam, "I don't have to learn things all over again. My father fought 'em. My grandfather fought 'em. My great-grandfather fought 'em. They knew they were savages. It's settled. Frees my mind to think about other things."

"I don't see it that way," said Sam. "There's good and there's bad, both."

Stone said, "You forgot what happened on that beach at the Rees? You forgotten your dead friends? What kind of man are you?"

"I'll never forget," said Sam. "The Rees were bad. The Crows are good."

"Nothing good about Crows but the pussy," said Stone, laughing. Some of the others laughed too.

Sam asked, "What do you think, Clyman?"

"There's good and bad, or better and worse, but they're savages."

"Gideon?"

He shrugged. "I am half Indian, but all mountain man." He waited and asked Sam, "Why you no say what you think?"

What could he say? He doted on Meadowlark all the time. Just now he had thought of Ten, then of Hannibal. He couldn't tell them about Hannibal, he just didn't see how. "Don't know," he said.

Gideon turned and got right in his face. "You better know. I am your partner."

Sam smiled easily and said, "You, yeah, you I know about."

Gideon gave him a big clap on the back.

NO ONE WAS at the cache on the Sweetwater. Fitz figured the date now at June 5—they were late. Had Jedediah come and gone, giving up on them?

No tracks or other signs. The cache was untouched.

Where were Diah and the men who went with him?

While they waited, Fitz and Sam rode downstream a dozen or miles, checking the river. It was broad and shallow, no water to float boats, even the bullboats they would make.

Fitz looked seriously at Sam. "You up to going downstream, finding a place where you're sure it's navigable, and waiting for us?"

Sam hesitated.

"Don't play the hero. But we won't wait more than three or four more days, then we'll come along with him or without him."

"Glad to do it," said Sam. He made his voice clear and strong when he spoke.

"When you find a likely place, ride on down a way and make sure."

They didn't want to build the boats and load the furs, then have to unload the boats and go back for horses after a few miles.

"Right," said Sam.

Without further ado Fitz rode back. Sam could hardly believe how lonely the world seemed. Himself, his horse, The Celt, a pistol, what was in his possible sack—these against the world. But he was glad Fitzpatrick trusted him with this job.

He took his time wandering on down the Sweetwater. Since the moon was nearing full, he rode at night and slept during the day. No sense taking a chance on Indians, not a lone man.

In three or four nights' travel he came to a big river, rolling in from the south. Was this the Platte? Or was he on the Arkansas? He didn't know.

Either way, the river would float boats from here. He slept the day through, hidden in a clump of willows on the south side, above the joining of the rivers. At evening he decided to make his camp for the four or five days in these willows and set to cutting down enough of them to make a brush hut.

Suddenly voices. Human voices.

Too soon for Fitz and the boys.

He peered out of the willow thicket. Indians, plenty of them, just across the river. He counted twenty-two, he couldn't tell what tribe, and more horses than that. He lay down very still and watched. They started several fires. They tethered their horses. Clearly they intended to camp.

In which case Sam meant to get the hell out of there.

The ground beyond the willows was sandy and flat, with little vegetation. The moon was full. A horse couldn't sneak quietly. They would easily see him riding away, and his life expectancy would be very short.

He took stock.

Then he got The Celt and his pistol, knife and tomahawk, and his possible sack. He left his horse tied to some willows. Probably lose it, which pissed him off.

Walking backward, and as silently as his father had taught him, he eased across the sand. His tracks would look like they were going toward the river, and his horse was there.

After less than a quarter mile he backed onto a rocky ridge. He turned and climbed to a pinnacle, where he could see the Indians very well.

They lay down to sleep. Good, maybe they wouldn't see his horse, and would leave in the morning.

About midnight they got up and gathered their mounts, but two horses wandered across the river. Damn, right near Sam's horse. When the Indians went to collect the strays, they immediately sent up some whoops. Commotion about his camp. Checking of his tracks.

They mounted and rode around in all directions for maybe an hour. Then they had a talk, and all of them rode off to the north. With Sam's horse, of course.

Hell, what a fix. Fitz, come on!

In the morning Sam went exploring downstream. Right away he found a swift, whitewater canyon. He scrambled up several hundred feet of rock wall to get a better look. No boats could go through here. They'd have to start floating farther down.

Just then he saw twenty Indian men walk to the north bank of the river. Damn! Was this a powwow place or what? Again he couldn't tell what tribe. On foot. Probably a horse-raiding party—out walking, back riding. Way too many strange Indians around here to suit Sam. They built a raft of driftwood, crossed the river, and walked off to the south.

He went back to his pinnacle and waited.

And waited.

Come on, Fitz.

And waited. And waited.

On the third day he slept the entire day, didn't know why.

Bitch of a fix.

That night he considered. He said to himself, hell of a fix. This time the meaning reached deeper.

The fourth day he began to imagine what had overcome Fitz, Gideon, Clyman and Sublette, Branch and Stone. Pictures of tomahawks splitting skulls. Arrows riddling bodies. Bullets tearing up hearts, lungs, and heads. The pictures drove him wild. He ordered them to get out of his head and go away.

That night he dreamt of Indians celebrating the deaths of Diah and his men. They cut the scalps off gleefully. Tied the half-dead bodies to posts, jammed splinters into their flesh and lit them afire, built fires beneath their feet. They danced circles around his friends, waving their blood-dripping scalps on lances.

The fifth and sixth days he spent wandering around the countryside, looking for deer. He stayed within sight of the Sweetwater, so he could see his friends when they came. He forced himself to walk with a swagger he did not feel.

The seventh day he shot a deer and started drying the meat. If the noise drew Indians, too bad. Being chased was better than starving.

He checked his ammunition. Plenty of powder left, but only eleven lead balls.

On the eighth morning he began to wonder if he should go on.

Go on?! Preposterous. Where would you go?

Down the river to the settlements.

What settlements?

About six to seven hundred miles away, I think, maybe. Isn't that what the captain said?

That's if this is the Platte. A lot more if it's the Arkansas.

That's right.

You don't even know if you'll end up on the Arkansas three hundred miles below St. Louis, or at Fort Atkinson, four hundred miles above.

No, I don't.

Why would you do such a crazy thing?

Because I have only eleven balls.

And what exactly does that mean?

With eleven balls, I can shoot a critter once a week and get some food. That would give me two and a half months to walk seven hundred miles.

I can't believe you're thinking of walking seven hundred miles. Or a thousand.

If I stay here and my friends never do come, because they got killed by Indians or whatever, I won't have enough ammunition to get to the settlements.

(That stilled the arguing voice.)

I'll starve to death.

He slept the rest of the day, and all night.

On the ninth morning he began to know what he would do. But he waited, and glutted himself on deer meat.

Please, please show up.

The tenth day he did the same. Now the deer meat was mostly jerked.

Oh, God, where are you? He had to admit he was not thinking as much of the probable fate of his friends. He was racked with anxiety about his own.

On the eleventh day he knew he had to go. He just couldn't bring himself to start. To actually put one foot in front of the other and go down the river.

Once he left, his friends would never find him. Simple as that.

Part Three

THE JOURNEY

Chapter Fifteen

ON THE MORNING of the twelfth day Sam Morgan, who until now had been drawing his life in children's colored chalks, faced a reality: He was a god-awful distance from nowhere and all alone. He faced the likelihood of getting killed by Indians, and the likelihood of a thousand and one dangers of the country getting him. Faced the choice of taking action or starving to death.

He set off walking to the Missouri River. Or Mississippi River. Or wherever help might be. Wherever civilization might be.

His whole life he had thought he wanted to be alone in the wilderness. Now the yearning for company raged in him.

Those first days he walked.

He walked, and walked some more.

His flowing lifeline, his wellspring in a parched country, the river stretched ahead of him, to a horizon. And then on to a horizon he couldn't see. And then farther to a hundred more horizons beyond sight, receding forever.

Is this a joke? Am I kidding myself?

He walked for a day, two days, three. Maybe he would walk forever. Walk for twenty years and never stop walking and never find anyone, any human beings at all.

He went in a daze, in a kind of delirium. The world was a phantasm. It faded into the sagebrush plains shimmering in the summer heat. Shrub blended into demon, which blended into phantom bear, which blended into elusive ghost. To all of it Sam had the same response. Feel numb. Walk.

He saw no one, white or red. He hardly saw a critter. He walked.

In the evening he ate his deer *charqui*. He'd stuffed his possible sack full of dried meat, but every day he emptied it a little. After three days he restricted himself to one meal a day, right before sleeping.

The worst was not the hunger, or even the fear. Yes, he was damned well scared. He shook half the time. There was a world to be scared of. But the worst was the loneliness.

His ears screamed for conversation. At night he dreamed of nothing but social give and take, speak and listen, smile and laugh, duck and dip. In his dreams he went for walks with his father and talked of everything in the world. He sat with his mother at her sewing and told her what he had never said, that he was really worried about how she seemed to be retreating into a private world, and he needed her. He sat in his sisters' kitchens and laughed and played with their toddlers while the husbands finished up the day's work and Betsy and Gwen got supper ready. He had philosophical conversations with Clyman. He talked religion with Diah, and was glad to listen more than he spoke. He laughed and sang songs with Gideon. Oddly, Hannibal appeared several times, and they had long, long talks. Sam knew these dialogues were very important, but he could never remember what the two of them said, or even what they talked about.

After a while—he'd lost track of time completely—he came on a bullboat on the shore.

The sight of it roused him from his languor. Indians didn't make bullboats, only white men did. They stuck the butts of willow branches into the ground, bent them into a bowl shape, glued buffalo hides on, caulked the whole, flipped it upright, and launched a crude, unwieldy, tipsy boat which had the advantage of almost no draft.

There were white men in this country.

His heart rampaged up and down and side to side in his chest.

He checked out the area. Quickly he found that a big Indian camp had stood near the river on the north side. The signs were everywhere. Circles of stones that held down lodge covers. Sticks standing as tripods to hold cooking pots, or medicine bundles. Cold ashes. Dog dung. Bones. Horse tracks and horse dung. The scrapings where the butts of lodgepoles were dragged away. A big camp. He wished he could tell from the moccasin prints, as Rose could, what tribe they were.

He felt a stabbing pain in this chest. White men. Hell, if even the Indians were still here, he'd probably walk right into camp, just to be wrapped in the sound of human voices. And get scalped for his trouble.

He sat down in the camp and had an imaginary conversation. He explained to the principal tribesmen how he came into their country, by getting lost. How he was their friend. How sorry he was he had no presents for them. How, yes, he was going to drink their water and eat their game and not give them anything in exchange. How his friends would give them presents later. He himself would come back and bring presents.

Then the leaders talked things over among themselves. When they finished their deliberations, they told him what a fine mark he was going to make, tied to a post, for the young men to shoot arrows at. What a great competition that would be!

Sam stood up in the middle of that abandoned camp, looked around at all his imaginary companions, bloody-minded as they were, and walked down the river.

And walked.

And walked.

It was his discipline, it was his monk-like practice, it was his salvation. Walk.

He ran completely out of jerked meat. He would have to find buffalo soon. A day spent hunting, even if successful, plus a couple of days to dry the meat—that was time away from his forever walking, away from his journey of body and spirit. The time away would be welcome, in a way, and in another way not. The pattern of the walking, the rhythm of days spent marching on forever got deeply rooted in his being. The motion had an endless music for him. Besides, three or four days of hunting and drying meat was three or four days more until he got to Fort Atkinson, or an outlying farm, or an Arkansas trading post, or whatever kind of civilization he might find first.

Most nights when he lay down to sleep, he fantasized about being back in Meadowlark's camp. In these daydreams she came close and nuzzled against him, and wonderful things began to happen. Or he would fantasize about coming on a living Indian camp. Here he looked down on the camp from a rise, and seemed to see there everything vital, full of energy, charged with life. Slowly, dreamlike even in a dream, he walked straight in. The people came toward him, jabbering. The fantasy ended there, with the people talking animatedly and congregating close around him, for good or ill.

One midday of his walking-walking-walking, he saw horsemen running buffalo on the far crests of the hills across the river. At this distance he couldn't even see if they were white men or red. He heard several gunshots, but most Indians had some guns. He forced himself not to go find out who they were. They might be miles away before he could walk there anyway.

At midafternoon that day he saw a huge herd of buffalo, probably the same one, crossing the river from the south side to his side.

He looked around for the hunters. No sign of them. He climbed a hill and looked harder. Still no sign. Maybe they had the meat they wanted and were now busy with butchering.

He edged close to the great beasts, stopped now to graze. He took the time and effort to get very close for a sure shot. The cow dropped with one ball. Ten lead balls left—more than one a week for his journey, he hoped.

As fast as he could, watching every moment, he got some meat butchered out and got into a cottonwood grove along a creek, where he started a low, smokeless fire.

No one came to investigate.

Then he realized, *I hoped someone would. A friendly Indian, even. That would do a lot to ease my pain.*

He gorged on hump rib roasted on a stick over the flames. Drying meat all the while, he gorged again the next day, and the next.

Suddenly he felt an urge to look at himself, to see who he was now. He stripped off his hide shirt, his hide pants, his moccasins, everything, right down to bare skin. He regarded himself. This wasn't the body he left home with a year and a half ago. It was harder, more shaped, less a body in transition, more a man's body. It was taller, too, he supposed, though he didn't know. Mostly what he saw was that it was used. His shin bore an angry scar where the bullet ripped his skin and broke his leg. His hands and wrists were reddened and dried. But this wasn't what he wanted to know.

He knelt by a creek and looked at his reflection in a still pool. Some face. The wind and sun were starting it toward the face of a middle-aged man while he was only nineteen. His white hair seemed to him as outlandish as ever. He wanted to see more, though. He looked hard for the expression in the eyes, but the reflection wasn't clear enough. What he felt sure of, though he didn't know why, was that he would see the eyes of a stranger.

This was frustrating. He splashed the water hard with one hand and fractured the reflection.

The next morning he filled his possible sack with the dried buffalo meat and set out again. It felt almost like he had found a path, a way, like in the Bible stories his mother told. Walking, walking, walking, that's my salvation. Which might be Fort Atkinson. Unless I'm walking, walking to my death.

He didn't know how many days he walked, or how far. The sun seemed to get bigger and strong and hotter every day, like someone who kept saying the same thing insistently, day after day, louder and louder, until you paid full attention.

What did it say? Death, death, death, death? You are walking into your own grave?

Yet the oddity was that Sam had never felt more alive. All the world was here, powerfully present. The heat of the sun. The cool of the evening breeze. The stars studded bright all across the sky. The meat, dried, unsatisfying, but filling after it swelled in his belly. River water to drink—sometimes he even lay down in the river, all the way. The sandy beach or leafy loam he stretched out on at night.

Never had his life been so fully with him.

Felt not like death but life, real life.

It occurred to him, sometimes, to wonder how far he had walked, where on the captain's map he was. That seemed unreal, as the map itself was the most meager hint of the reality it represented, a pretender to a realm it didn't know. The map knew nothing of the slap of the sun, the relentless sucking of the wind, the baked earth beneath your feet, the cool, green-blue shade of cottonwoods along the river, the vistas of grasslands reaching to every horizon, north, east, south, and far, far west.

East was the direction that mattered to him.

How far? Only ten miles some days, he thought, half a day's walk. Maybe twenty-five miles other days, when he felt coltish, or was impatient of everything but walking. How far was unpredictable, barely thinkable, irrelevant to his real existence.

Where on that map? He had no idea. He didn't even know how long he'd been walking.

Civilization? An infinity away. He barely thought of it. His life was here, these plains, this wind, this throbbing sun, here and only here.

That night, though, he lay back on his sleeping place, without blankets or robes, and took note of the moon. It had been new when he started. Now it was coming around to new again.

He shifted against the hard ground, trying to get comfortable. Did that mean one month of walking? He took thought. Could the moon have circled to new once already, and now be coming round again? He pondered it. No, he didn't think so.

He tried to remember the days. He had walked a while, began to run short of meat, rationed himself to one meal a day, and finally walked a couple of days hungry. He shot a buffalo, dried meat, and walked on. No, didn't seem that could add up to two moons. Just one.

He chuckled at himself. He was figuring time the way the Indians did, by moons full and new. If he remembered, he could figure it by half moons too. An equivalent of what white folks called weeks. He liked that. Not that anything in these measurements of time mattered, except one, the seamless smear of the long days of summer, endlessly unrolling before him.

Before he went to sleep he thought, as he usually did, of Meadowlark. He had made a promise to her. Though he had meant it, he had broken his word. What was she thinking? That his word couldn't be trusted? That white men were unpredictable and unreliable?

Or did she think of him at all? Was she enamored of some new suitor? Her virginal ceremony was for summer, when all the Crows got together. Had she already performed it? Was she in someone's arms? Was she already married? Pregnant?

Why not? He had taken his sport with other women.

But he loved Meadowlark.

He longed for her.

He drifted into erotic dreams.

ONE MORNING HE woke up, in a grove of big, old cottonwoods, to a peal of bird sounds. He opened his eyes. Martins, hundreds of them, chattering, twittering, bickering, singing, making every possible bird sound, all of them exuberant.

He closed his eyes. It was fun, all this chirping. Kind of like being in a place crowded with people, in a tavern with folks you didn't know, with jabbering and prattling you couldn't follow—but it all added up to a big, fat, social babble. He loved it. It felt like company.

As he lay there with his eyes closed, the morning sun on his lids, a breeze beginning to perk up, he imagined that he was having lunch in St. Louis with Abby, Grumble, and Governor Clark. Clark was expansive this day, telling tales of his experiences in the West, poking fun at himself. Sam, Abby, and Grumble were immensely entertained. Cadet Chouteau joined them, and this time was utterly amiable. He and Clark traded stories about adventures up the river, which seem brightly populated with incidents and people, not a bit like Sam's current life. Then they both told stories about their friend Hannibal, also Sam's friend, as they acknowledged. He couldn't get the exact content of what they said about Hannibal, but it was admiring—Hannibal was a good influence everywhere he went, and a person of respect among red man and white.

Sam lay there for several hours, listening and imagining, until he woke up and realized the birds had moved on.

He did the same.

Beyond the grove, about midday, he pushed up a little rise and saw that the river looped to the south and, after ten or fifteen miles, back again. He could cut off several miles by heading straight across country. He looked carefully. He didn't like to go without water, not if he could help it. But across his shortcut, from northwest to southeast, slanted a meager line of trees, which in this country meant a stream. Halfway across, he could strike the creek and drink. He studied the line of the river to get his bearings—its fringe of green would be his landmark—and off he went.

Toward evening he came into the cottonwoods along the little creek and sat down in the shade. He would camp here tonight. Maybe if he camped in a grove, he would be wakened by birdsong again.

Then he saw his good luck. Three buffalo bulls grazed on the prairie beyond the grove. He took thought. It was about a half moon, maybe a little more, since he shot that last buffalo. He wasn't completely out of meat yet, but would be soon. Bulls were not good eating, not like cows. Usually, though, buffalo came in big herds or not at all. A few straying animals, that was a gift he shouldn't turn down.

He barely had time before dark, and the bulls might be gone in the morning. The wind now was easy and from the northwest—they hadn't caught his scent.

He slipped quietly through the trees and came to the end of the shade. Just as well not to go out and take a chance of spooking them. It was maybe a shot of a hundred steps. He considered. He didn't want to take a chance on wasting a lead ball. But it would be worse to leave cover and lose the buffalo.

He said thanks, in his mind, to his father, who taught him to shoot and left him this good Pennsylvania rifle. He rested The Celt against a bump on the trunk of a cottonwood, held his sights steady on the brisket of the biggest bull, a brute with one horn. When he was sure, he fired.

One Horn ran off. So did the others. Damn.

He ran after One Horn. All three were headed directly into the wind, which would take them across the creek upstream. . . .

He saw that the beast's gait was faltering. One Horn stopped. The other two rumbled on. Then Sam's bull stumbled awkwardly after them.

He had to take the chance. Reloading as he moved, he ran after One Horn.

The bull slowed down and stopped. Its sides were heaving. When it started to walk again, Sam fired.

The brute sank to one knee, rose, teetered to within a dozen steps of the trees, pitched forward, and flopped onto one side.

Relieved, Sam ran up to him and cut his throat open, letting the life blood spill in the dust.

The light was fading fast. He needed to get this bull butchered out, and needed a fire. He decided the fire was the more urgent need—keep the wolves and prairie wolves off the meat. The butchering could mostly wait.

He gathered wood and built a small fire near the bull. Then he opened him up and got the innards out—that would keep the meat better.

By the light of the fire he cut off some hump ribs and roasted them on his wiping stick over the flames. That would be enough butchering for tonight, when he couldn't see. He might need to stay awake and keep the fire going.

When he woke up, the fire was dead, probably even cold, from the look of it. No wolves or coyotes. He sat up. Something wasn't right.

Then he saw something queer. Dawn was breaking in the east, and there was another dawn, very red, in the northwest.

He tried to take this in. He breathed deep. The wind was warm and stifling.

What's wrong?

He heard a distant rumbling, like thunder. But the sky was cloudless. He stared to the northwest.

He coughed. Now he realized. The air was acrid with smoke.

Fire. It was a fire to the northwest. The glow was actually flame, flame from the far northwestern to the far northern horizon.

He checked the wind. Northwest to southeast, straight toward him.

Fear spasmed in Sam's gullet.

He'd heard about prairie fires, the way they raged through the dry grasses, driving the game in front of them, outrunning everything, laying waste to miles and miles of grassland. But he'd never seen one. He quaked at the thought.

On the northwestern horizon the entire earth was lit with flame, fed by the brown, midsummer stems and blades. Half the heavens, it seemed, danced in the lurid light.

He looked around. By the half moon he could see buttes to climb, above the flaming grasses, but none was within running distance, not even close.

The river. He thought about its arc. It was four or five miles away. He saw himself running among the coyotes, the wolves, the rabbits, the deer, a bear, perhaps even last night's two bulls, running, running ahead of the scorching breath toward the delicious, hide-saving wet and cool of the river.

He thought of the speed of the wind-whipped inferno. He peered into the darkness and saw only shadows. The animals must be making their tortured sprints down wind, dying out there, run down from behind.

I'd never outrun the flames.

Here comes my death.

This wild card, this completely unexpected . . .

But, said his father's voice, death is never unexpected . . .

The creek. I'll lie down in the creek.

He grabbed The Celt and jammed it under the buffalo carcass, in case he survived. He stumbled through the dark grove and plowed into the water. Damn! Ankle deep. He hadn't paid any attention when he camped last night—then the depth meant nothing to him.

He splashed up and down the stream, looking for a hole that would be deep enough. He couldn't find one. Ankle deep everywhere, or less, as far as he could tell in the half light.

He tripped and fell to his knees. That gave him an idea. He rolled in the water and got everything he could wet, deer hide and human hide.

He gazed to the northwest, trembling now. Not much time.

No, he made up his mind. He would find the deepest spot nearby in this creek and dip himself well down into it.

I will survive. I will survive. Yes, by God, I will.

He made that a solemn promise to himself.

The fire struck the creek a couple of hundred yards upstream, hitting like a clap of a huge hand. The tops of the trees erupted into flame.

The blaze catapulted toward him, leaping high in pyromaniac ecstasy. It was as if the world as he knew it was melting away, being transformed into a demonic pyre before his eyes. Geysers of fire gushed upward, and streams of flaming embers roared up to the skies. Sparks fled downwind, swirling spindrift. Torches of branches burst off trunks and raged to the ground. Strange flowers of bonfire bloomed, burst to full flower, and died.

He shook his head hard—hell, I'm getting mesmerized. He looked around desperately. My God!—nothing, nothing, nothing deep enough to save a human hide.

Done for.

He heard a mewling behind him, toward the dead bull.

Pay it no mind!

Mewling and yipping. Something was scratching at the carcass.

A coyote pup, for God's sake. Mother was probably gone downwind, trying to save herself. Pup fussing around the belly slit, like trying to get in with . . .

Wild hope shot up in him. Sweet Jesus. Maybe . . .

No, I'll be roasted whole!

Hell, it's my only chance!

He sprinted to the carcass. He slipped on the innards he'd pulled out and fell onto one knee and elbow, landing on the pup's paw. The pup squealed and started to run. He seized it. He jerked open the great slit he cut in the belly and looked into the maw.

He hesitated.

He felt for The Celt under the carcass and left the rifle there. He felt the wet hair of the upward side of his head suddenly get hot, damn hot. He grabbed it, burned his hand, and dived inside.

He realized he had the pup clutched to his breast, like he was going to nurse it. The pup pissed on him. He laughed wildly. Both of them crouched inside a dead buffalo, Sam in fetal position, cowering for safety.

He came into a darkness. . . . it was strange beyond strange. Beyond words, beyond thoughts.

Then he realized—my knees are burning. They were outside.

He rolled over, clutching the pup. The poor thing whimpered.

In seconds his back and butt were scorching, or maybe boiling.

He rolled over again.

His knees burned.

He screamed. He screamed and screamed and screamed. The pup yipped, and the yips meant terror.

Soon he wondered if he was screaming at the pain or at the darkness inside the bull. He had always heard that men should not descend to beasthood—We're expected to be something more.

I am a beast. I am a coyote. I am a buffalo.

I am become bestial, baptized in blood and slime and goo and piss.

I will rise out of this carcass reborn as a man-buffalo.

He kept very, very still. Maybe death would tiptoe by.

I am reborn. I am a man-buffalo.

Chapter Sixteen

AFTER A WHILE he noticed that, though his knees hurt terribly, the pain wasn't new. It was old. The pup hovered quietly, quivering.

He poked a hand between the great flaps of buffalo hide.

The tops of the trees were burning, but not raging.

He let the flaps close, retreated back into his buffalo-belly cave, and closed his eyes.

After a few minutes he stuck his hand out again.

The tops of the trees were smoldering. Branches on the ground were turning to embers. The fire had eaten and raged on.

He retreated a final time.

How would I live if I was a buffalo? Breathe, drink, eat, piss, shit, look for food, keep clear of enemies, mount the cows, play with the calves.

What would I be?

Just what I am.

He petted the pup. He had the impression it was asleep.

He didn't know, later, whether they had stayed in the bloody, mucous-smeared carcass for five minutes or five hours. When they came out, the ground was still alive with burning fragments. His knees felt scalded. His back felt scalded. His throat raged at him, he supposed from smoke going down. He limped to the creek, occasionally jumping off a hotfoot he gave himself, knelt in the water, and rolled in on his back. He stroked water onto the pup's fur. Holding the pup out of the creek, he rolled onto his face and chest, then flipped again onto his back. The pup fell into the stream, rolled, and lapped.

The two of them, creek and pup, taught Sam the meaning of the word *blessing*.

THE SUN ROSE on a vast desolation, burned black and ashen gray, with a thousand plumes of smoke where the earth still smoldered.

He inspected The Celt. The barrel, ramrod, lock, and trigger were fine. The butt was scorched. In fact, the brass plate was warped from the heat. Then he noticed. The plate was partly melted and discolored. Something had burned white hot right next to it, which was why his knees hurt so much. The engraved letters "Celt" were smeared, but the Celtic love knots were intact.

Sam walked out across the land carrying the pup, drawn into fascination. Everywhere scorched carcasses were strewn, rabbits, wolves, deer, and a hundred more commonplace species. Sam felt like the crows, when they came to feast, would make the landscape less lonely.

His wounds were bothersome but not terrible. Huge blisters on his knees and shins, his lower back and butt. If they didn't putrefy, he'd be fine.

He walked back to the grove, which was no camp, and set the pup down. "What am I going to do with you?" The pup was a boy, he saw. It went to the carcass and began to tear off small bits of meat with its tiny teeth. Sam smiled. Little pup was probably sucking just a moon ago.

He knelt down at the buffalo and set to work listlessly on the butchering. For once he didn't even give a damn about eating. It didn't seem right. This bull saved their lives. Still, meat was meat. That's how the pup saw it.

Sam went to work harder. He had only eight balls left, and now two mouths to feed.

The fat between hide and flesh had been softened, but the meat itself was unchanged. He cut the thick fat into small pieces and fed them to the pup by hand. All day he butchered, and fed, and then began to eat, and butchered.

That evening he said to the pup, "What are you going to do? I'm not your mother." He looked around at the vast, ashen prairie. The mother was probably a smoldering carcass out there, no longer a mother, or even a creature, just a thing.

He fed the pup by hand, and they drank from the creek side by side.

"You're my friend. I'm not gonna let you go." Somehow, in fact, he felt brotherly toward the pup. He thought of Coy, the little brother he knew too briefly.

The next morning everything had quit smoking. He broke blackened branches off trees that had once been alive, built a fire, and set to drying the buffalo meat. He probably spent five days at a job that needed three. He dawdled with the pup. He chatted with it. Told it stories about when he was a kid, stories he'd never been able to tell Owen. The pup acted attached to him, like it had lost one parent and found another. He wondered if he could train it. He supposed so. If not, it would be a nuisance, maybe even a hazard.

But he wanted the pup. Except for the pup, he found it hard to care about anything. He looked around at the world, nothing green, everything death-blasted, and he felt limp, lethargic. Except for the pup. He named it Coy. Finally, on a morning no different from any other, he shouldered his possible sack, full of all the jerked meat he could carry. He whistled at Coy.

Coy cocked his head at the odd sound.

Sam set out, and Coy trotted along.

IN TWO DAYS he saw a big river flowing in from the south. "That looks good," he told Coy, "real good." Diah Smith had said that if this was the Platte, the maps of Captain Long showed that its south fork flowed in, just as big as the north fork. His memory was that Diah sketched in the south fork about halfway between the mountains and the Missouri. Though he couldn't read the names of the rivers and mountains, Sam remembered well enough where those squiggly lines went. Still, he didn't mention any of this to Coy. No sense getting the pup's hopes up. Nor did he want to begin to think, for the sake of his own peace of mind, that they might be halfway to civilization.

AT THE FORKS he took two days of rest. He spent the time training Coy, using slivers of jerked meat. They were partners now. Coy hadn't shown the least inclination to wander, but walked within a few steps of Sam all day, and slept next to him at night, sometimes even cuddled against him.

First Sam taught the pup to sit, which was simple enough. Except that the command to sit down was "charge." Figured he'd have some fun with other fellows. "Now if he sits when I say 'charge,'" he would tell them, "how do you know, if I say 'roll over,' he won't attack?" They would get a chuckle out of that one.

Then he taught Coy to stand on his hind legs and take meat

from between Sam's fingers. Then to jump a little and get the meat. Then to jump high and get it.

This wasn't hard. He'd watched his dad train a dog but had never done it himself. Turned out a coyote learned the same way as a dog.

The last trick, for now, was to jump really high and snatch a stick from Sam's hand. Then he gave Coy some meat and a lot of head-rubbing as a reward.

Finally they started downstream. They were running short on meat. Sam thought, Coy and I could roam around forever if I had enough lead balls, but I don't.

The Indian made his own weapons, didn't need a manufacturing system to get food. The white man did. In a way, that need was Sam's last tie to civilization.

They walked and walked. They talked as they went. They played, and kicked up their heels. Coy was good company.

They had made a sort of camp on a sandy beach along the river and were playing fetch when the four Indians stood up in the bushes.

Sam stopped, fetch stick cocked to throw.

The biggest, oldest Indian motioned for him to come there. Another one grabbed his rifle where it lay across his possible sack, and the sack too.

He wished he knew what tribe they were.

Coy didn't like them. He barked, and the hair stood up on his neck. The Indians laughed.

They took Sam's pistol. They took his shot pouch. They took his knife. They took every valuable he had, except his hair.

Then they put him second in line and began to lope. Luckily, Coy kept up, whining all the while. After about a mile they came to a creek, and a sizable village spread out along the banks.

THEY LED HIM to a big lodge, evidently the council lodge. Coy didn't get to come in. Before long a white hair came and sat behind the center fire. A half dozen big bellies sat near him, and they put Sam on the white hair's left.

None of his belongings came into the lodge, and Sam figured they were goners. Without a gun he couldn't survive.

He wished to the devil he knew what tribe this was. They didn't look like Crows, so he didn't dare risk his Crow words.

"The elder," said the man on Sam's left in accented English, "is Raven. I am Third Wing, and I will . . . make his words into English for you, and yours into Pawnee."

Sam was careful not to let his face show surprise at the English. Or the shiver he felt at these people being Pawnee. Except for their cousins the Rees, they had the worst reputation on the plains.

"I am called Sam," he said. "I came to this country with my companions, the beaver hunters."

One of the men who captured Sam said something, and everyone looked at Sam with the greatest curiosity.

Raven spoke and Third Wing translated. "They want to see your coyote pup do his tricks." Third Wing was a beefy fellow with a pie face, but he had a wild gleam in his eye.

Everyone trooped outside. "I need a few bits of meat." Third Wing nodded and spoke to a woman who was watching. In moments meat appeared.

In short order Sam got Coy to sit, stand on his hind legs, and leap to his hand to grab a stick.

Exclamations. Sam could imagine what they were saying, Medicine Dog. Carefully, he kept his face grave.

Back inside they smoked a pipe, and Sam began to get a glimmer of hope. When it was done, he told Third Wing, "I come in friendship. I got separated from my friends. I'm going back to the big house on the Missouri" (he hoped they knew about the fort). "I'm sorry—normally I would have brought presents for my Pawnee friends, but the presents are with the other beaver hunters. When these men come to village, they will give you many presents on my behalf."

As Third Wing rendered this message in Pawnee, the Indians listened impassively. Then the discussion of his fate began. Third Wing, sitting right next to Sam, spoke first and at length in Pawnee, signing to Sam what he was saying. He liked Sam. Sam was his friend. He wanted Sam to be safe in this village.

None of the others signed what they said. From the tone Sam was sure they didn't like him, not one bit. They were probably discussing how to torture and kill him. Did they want to let him run for his life against all their young men (as happened to old Colter)? Did they want to tie him up and burn him nice and slow from the toenails up?

No telling. All he could do was what he'd heard was the only way to go—put on a nonchalant face, pretending that whatever they decided was all the same to Sam Morgan.

He wondered where Coy was.

Finally, the council disbanded. "Come with me," said Third Wing. The rest left without meeting Sam's eyes. For the first time Sam wondered about the peculiar name. What kind of man would be named Third Wing, and what would a third wing be for?

At Third Wing's lodge Sam got lots of stealthy glances from his wife and two small children, but they didn't say a word. He sat down next to Third Wing outside and relaxed, like he was completely unconcerned. "How did you learn English?" he asked Third Wing.

"I was raised mostly by traders," said Third Wing, his face lighting up in a twisted way. Somehow this Indian seemed to think everything was funny-peculiar.

Apparently Third Wing didn't intend to tell Sam his fate—probably too black to tell. Sam wondered about Coy's fate and looked around until he spotted the pup across the circle, tied to a lodgepole with a rawhide rope around his neck. Children were yelling words that sounded like commands, but Coy was having none of it. The pup was busy making yelps of protest at the rope and trying to bite it. Sam was damned sorry for Coy.

He cast his eyes around subtly until he identified the lodge of the young man who took his rifle and shot pouch. It was a brush hut, and the rifle hung from thongs at the back, parallel to the ground. If he got out of here, he had to get the rifle. Not just any rifle, The Celt.

He marked the brush hut in his mind—a paint horse was tied outside.

After they ate dinner, Third Wing took Sam inside and told his family to leave the two of them alone. "Now I'll explain. Tomorrow morning you'll be offered the choice of dying brave or dying quickly." Third Wing seemed to think this was curiously crazy too. "Everyone thinks you look like a real man, one with warrior spirit, so they're sure you'll choose to die brave—they're looking forward to it." Now Third Wing started a nutty cackle and cut it off. "This means the women will kill you as slowly as they can, thinking of every possible way to inflict pain. And if you're brave, you'll endure it all without protest, and for sure without begging for your life, or even the mercy of death."

Third Wing shook his head madly. Like, Gee, what a compliment, the chance to die brave. "Afterwards you'll be greatly admired."

Sam's mouth wanted to grin at this guy. His feet wanted to run like hell.

"Maybe I got a better idea," Third Wing went on. "I like you, I want to see you live. So maybe tonight, when I am supposed to be keeping you under close watch, we'll sneak out of the village."

Third Wing waited, a crazy expression on his face.

"Suits me," said Sam, keeping calm as he could.

"Not one person can know, not even my family. When we get to the river, you must go fast and leave no trail, or some of our young men will catch you."

"Thanks," Sam finally ventured.

Third Wing held up a hand, as if to say stop.

"I want something in return." Now his eyes took on a little madness. "I want your hair."

Sam gawked at him.

"Not your scalp. Your hair. I like your white hair. I want to keep it, a way to remember you."

Sam was stupefied. He couldn't speak. He felt of his hair, which hadn't been cut since he left home more than a year and a half ago and hung below his shoulders.

"Thank you," he forced himself to say. "You honor me."

Third Wing hooted and slapped his thighs.

He took his knife out of his belt and reached for Sam's long locks. Sam flinched. Suddenly his mind whooped like a calliope, and the tune was terror. *This is a cruel trick. This damn Third Wing is about to take my scalp.*

But Sam's new friend started hacking an inch or two away from the skin.

Sam slowly tamed his terror. Deliberately, he lowered his head toward Third Wing to make the cutting easier. It took a long time, and gave Sam plenty of time to get himself calm and figure out what he needed to. Sometimes it seemed like his hair was being pulled out by the roots, but in the end Third Wing got it all. He held it up proudly and admired it. Then he tied a leather thong around it and hung it from a lodgepole. Way too much like a scalp for comfort, Sam thought.

Third Wing gave a queer grin. "You lost your hair but saved your scalp."

Sam made himself speak up. "One thing," he said. He considered one last time. He'd been figuring hard. It was between his father's rifle and Coy. "I have to take the coyote pup with me."

He'd thought it through. Coy would probably be tied outside, easy to get at. The rifle would be hanging in the thief's hut. No Indian would give up a rifle willingly.

Third Wing shrugged and said, "Impossible."

"That pup is my medicine," said Sam. This was the only approach he thought might work. Unable to think of anything else to say, he repeated lamely, "The pup is my medicine."

Third Wing looked at him seriously for once.

"Better to die than go without him," Sam added.

Third Wing pondered and finally gave a delighted smile. "Then we'll steal it."

A HAND SHOOK his shoulder gently. He opened his eyes without starting and saw the big, dark hulk that must be Third Wing. It was time.

Third Wing and his woman slept at the back of the tipi, children on each side of them. Sam had been put in blankets nearer the door. The two had to be very quiet.

Third Wing knelt, cut a long slit in the lodge cover, and peered around outside. After a moment he slipped out and held the cut open for Sam. Thinking that the slit was a good trick, Sam slipped outside.

A slender quarter moon gave the camp a faint light. Tipis here and there were lit with a fire glow from inside, like lanterns. The night was evidently young.

The big man handed Sam a sack of some kind. He felt what was in it. Parched corn, felt like. Food. Sam put his hand on Third Wing's shoulder in a thank-you gesture.

Third Wing moved off quietly, and Sam did the same. No mistakes, he told himself. No trips, no noises. This is not a game. He placed each foot gingerly, surely.

Good luck. Coy was outside, still tied, sleeping.

As they approached, Sam could see several dogs stretched out asleep. *Step on one by accident and die*, he thought.

Third Wing stopped and motioned for Sam to go ahead. Must think the pup will make less noise if his master wakes him.

Sam bent and stroked Coy's head. The pup woke up and sniffed his hand. Sam felt a pang of relief at touching his friend. Coy went back to sleep.

Sam got the little patch knife out of his *gage d'amour*. The extras he kept in that flat pouch, beneath his tobacco, were a very sharp patch knife, flint, and fire steel. A mountain man survival kit.

Carefully, he cut the rope around Coy's neck. Then he picked the pup up.

Coy yelped. A dog growled. Another barked hesitantly.

The two men stood very still. The barker approached. Third Wing bent and petted it.

The dogs quieted down.

Third Wing gave Sam a wild look and slipped outside the lodge circle. Sam followed, carrying Coy.

After a score of steps they started up a little bank. They weren't headed for the creek, evidently, and not for the river either. Sam followed without a question.

They made a big circle away from the bank. Halfway through, Third Wing pointed across the creek and whispered, "Horses." Sam understood. That was where the pony herd was kept, certainly under guard. They had avoided the sentries.

They walked parallel to the creek until they came to the river.

They faced each other, and Third Wing gave Sam a kind of off-hand wave or salute.

"Wait," said Sam softly. "I want to know. Why is your name Third Wing?"

"Ask me," the Pawnee said, "next time you see me." Without another word, he disappeared back toward the village.

Sam said to himself, "He saved my life, and I'll probably never see him again." In that moment he made up his mind to come back someday.

Then he thought, We did it.

He set Coy down.

But, he thought, the hard part is still to come.

Chapter Seventeen

HE SPLASHED ALONG the edge of the river for at least an hour. In the darkness he kept stumbling and falling in above his knees. Coy followed along the bank, yipping. Poor pup couldn't figure out why Sam didn't walk on dry ground.

Sam thought about Coy's tracks along the river. But what could any Pawnee make of another set of coyote prints?

At one place a sandstone bluff shelved into the river. (Sam was amazed at how well he could see in the dark, once his eyes got used to it.) He drank deep, not knowing when he might come back to water. Then he climbed up the shelves, picking Coy up when he had to and setting the pup above him.

Luckily, the bluff turned into a ridge and meandered to the north. They walked for an hour or so on stone, no tracks. They stopped to drink out of a depression in the rock. Sam wondered how old the water was, and what creepy-crawlies were in it. Maybe from a very recent rain, maybe not. Good thing he couldn't see what he was drinking. He took a long look toward the dark line of trees to the west, where he knew the creek and the village must be. No lights at all. He hadn't been missed.

Sam decided to go on for another hour. At last he found a likely spot with shade from a single cedar. He wedged himself into a crack where he would be in shadow during the afternoon, put Coy on his lap, and slept.

When dawn came, he watched the prairie. Well across, maybe two miles and in the fringe of trees, stood the Pawnee lodges.

From time to time he saw riders along the creek and along the river, weaving in and out of the trees. One by one, three enterprising trackers even wandered out over the prairie in Sam's direction, studying the ground. Nothing to find, fellows. Sam sat quietly in his crack, ate parched corn, petted Coy, and waited.

By midmorning thirst was talking to him loud. Did he dare move around? He spent several minutes eyeballing in every direction, especially the east. No sign of any human beings. If he hunted on the east side of the ridge, and was careful, and kept watching, it might be all right.

It was Coy, after maybe an hour, who found water. When Sam got there, the pup was already lapping it up fast. It was a foot and a half across, maybe, and only saucer-deep. Sam lost his squeamishness in an instant, dropped to his knees, and slurped.

When they had drunk the saucer dry, Sam looked into Coy's eyes, thinking, We have a lot in common.

Watching hard, he eased back toward the crack. If he was spotted, he damn well needed to know it. When they topped the ridge, Sam slipped quickly into the crack and studied the prairie to the west. No sign of anyone.

Toward late afternoon Coy got interested in two ground squirrels. Not seeing Sam move, the squirrels evidently felt safe enough. Coy started to jump at them without a sound, but Sam held him. Maybe they would both profit from watching the creatures.

The squirrels came and went several times from an underground burrow, where they must live. Once in a while they chirruped. Sam couldn't guess what this meant, if anything. At first they seemed to nibble on dry grasses. Then Sam saw they were taking the seeds off the stems of these grasses. For a while they fed on these seeds—Sam saw them swallow. Later, though, they held the seeds in their cheek pouches, darted underground, and came back with empty pouches. Sam didn't know whether they were storing food for the winter or feeding their young.

After an hour or so of watching, Sam reflected that Coy was hungry and probably wouldn't eat the parched corn. While both squirrels were underground, Sam set the pup high on a rock and let him go.

Coy went immediately to the hole of the burrows and crouched down on all fours to wait. He had no hesitation about what to do.

A squirrel stuck its head out of the hole.

Coy had chosen the spot behind it.

After a moment of looking, the squirrel hopped out.

Coy was on it in a flash. The squirrel was all wriggling legs, tail, and head in Coy's jaws.

One crunch and the squirrel was still.

Sam couldn't believe how fast it all was. Coy had watched and watched and figured it out perfectly.

He tore the squirrel apart and fed. Sam didn't watch. Good that, if they were short of food, Coy knew how to get his own.

Sam got an idea. Using his patch knife, he cut off his left pant leg at midcalf. Then he cut the stove pipe of leather into long, circling strips, like peeling an apple. Had he not let his blade wander too close to the edge, he could have cut it into a single, long thong. Instead he ended up with three thongs, each of several feet.

The fact of three gave him another idea. He did the same to his right pant leg.

When he was finished with that, he tied the thongs end to end until he had three long ones. Then he braided them into a rope five or six feet long. He held it up, admired his handiwork, and made a slip knot in one end of the rope. It would work.

He turned his attention back to the village. Nothing to see, really. No active hunt for him, not that he could tell. Nevertheless he would wait another day. They might be half on their guard tonight. By tomorrow night they would assume he'd hightailed it as far as he could.

That's when he would strike.

BY THE TIME dark fell the next day, he was more thirsty than he'd thought a human being could ever be. Coy had slipped off a couple of times during the day and maybe found some water. Sam didn't want to risk it again. A coyote moving around some sandstone cliffs, that wouldn't attract attention at all.

When full dark came and he left the crack, what he had to do first was drink. Instantly, though, he realized how stiff his body was from being jackknifed in that crevice all night and all day. He stretched like he'd seen cats and dogs do.

He walked a big circle to the north. When he approached the village, he wanted to come down the creek, not up, where they might expect him. He just had to hope that the horse herd downstream was the only one. Hope, and watch very hard.

He smelled the creek a hundred yards away, before he even got to the trees. He'd often wondered how animals did that. Now he knew. For a person, you just have to be thirsty enough.

Before he slipped into the trees, he sat quietly and looked for a long time. His throat was so dry it ached. The gibbous moon gave good light. He needed to be sure. He waited until he knew he wasn't just giving in to his thirst.

At the creek Coy drank until he threw up.

Sam drank a little, laid down full length in the creek, and drank again. He couldn't afford to be sick, or to lose the water he was getting.

He padded to the edge of the trees and studied the prairie to the west. Ghostly. He couldn't help it, that's how it looked to him. Maybe nothing was moving, but it looked like anything might leap out at any moment.

He imagined a tomahawk flashing toward the skull from behind.

He rubbed the back of his head.

He jumped.

Something moved.

No, he saw now. A lump of cloud floated in front of the moon and changed the light out there slightly.

He kept looking. He felt pretty sure no horse herd grazed there. With the village maybe a mile away, he couldn't be sure a herd wouldn't yet be downstream.

He called Coy and the pup came.

It hurt him to do this. He looped the slip knot around Coy's neck, and then made another knot to keep it from opening. He tied the far end to the trunk of a sapling.

Coy sat contentedly. Sam moved away, and Coy ran at him until—WHAM!—the leash knocked him off his feet.

Coy ran at Sam twice more, then pawed at the offending place on his neck.

Sam knew it wouldn't come off, and was far too strong to break or give in to teeth.

He hated tying Coy. He trotted downstream before he could think more about it. Coy yipped and yipped and then gave a piercing, mournful croon of good-bye.

Sam kept going.

No one in the village would hear a coyote complaining a mile away, or think anything of it if they did.

A hundred yards downstream he started watching hard. Every camp put sentries out. Best to walk in the edge of the trees, he thought. Less likely to be seen, better able to see.

If he saw a sentry—*when* he saw one—he'd have to make a choice. He didn't know what he was going to do. He'd never killed a man.

He stopped still and looked around. He also thought. To head off without a weapon, without a way to hunt, that was certain death.

He refused to think any further.

He eased down the creek, every sense alert. His mind was as wide open as the night sky, the moon and stars like the trees and bushes and shapes of earth and rock.

Long time, long time. He stepped slowly, each foot placed with care. Yes, I have the patience for this, Father. Fear gives me patience.

His mind knew fear. His response was, Clear head, keep your head clear.

Time didn't change until he began to hear sounds. He listened. A horse stomping, shuddering, blowing its lips.

Herd?

He kept very still.

Then he looked downstream, looked until he saw.

Dark shapes against sky and prairie. Yes, dark, triangular shapes. Tipis. Yes, he was sure. The horse was staked fifty yards downstream, on grass but not water. A buffalo horse or a warhorse, then, too valuable to leave with the herd. Must belong to a brush hut he couldn't see, low between here and the tipis.

His heart teetered. Clear head, he instructed himself.

He got his patch knife out of his *gage d'amour*. He smiled wryly at himself. Why didn't I have my one weapon in my hand all along?

Perfectly still, he moved his eyes around the dark night. The Crows always kept a sentry to each of the four winds, east, south, west, and north. If Pawnees did the same, there should be one close to the creek, here on the north. The sentries were young warriors, seeking coups to establish themselves as men worthy of respect.

Where were the brush huts? The north and northwest, he remembered clearly.

A thin line of hope shot up in his chest. How many brush huts had he seen? Probably two young men to a hut. How many lodges? Maybe another young man on average in each lodge. A score of young men altogether, or two dozen. Maybe whatever sentry he found would be the man who stole The Celt.

He wiped that bit of foolishness away and started to tease himself when . . .

A night owl called.

Sam wished he could go invisible.

The sound was well to his left.

A night owl called back.

He jumped. The call was shockingly close, maybe twenty yards ahead.

He thought he knew what was happening. He got all of himself but one eye behind the tree, and then looked fiercely.

A dark shape got to its feet.

Way too close. My God, I almost walked up on him.

Another shape materialized from the darkness of the grove. The two stood close together. Sam thought maybe he heard soft words. A shape walked away.

The guard had changed.

He squatted behind his tree and thought like a madman. The new sentry would be rested and ready. What? . . .

He decided to observe. Different sentries had different ways, whether white or red. Some stood absolutely still. Some stood still but turned a different direction every minute or two. Some paced a little. Some sat down.

This one sat on a low boulder facing north, body erect, head looking very alert. Sam couldn't make out his face.

Sam quaked a little. Maybe the man had a rifle. That would be enough to get Sam and Coy down the river. Not going into the village would cut his risk way, way down.

His chest hurt. He couldn't do it. At least he didn't think he could. Couldn't leave The Celt.

Safety! Dad would tell you safety!

He watched. He saw no rifle silhouette. If his eyes told him truly, the dark shapes in those hands were probably tomahawk and war club, or the like.

About twenty-five steps to where he could do what he had to do.

He backed away quietly. Regardless of what he did, this wasn't the angle to start from.

He sat. His mind swayed. My God . . .

Clear head.

He insisted to himself. Clear head.

He probably sat for half an hour. Then he had a plan. He marked the spot where the sentry stood with three distinctive trees. He backed away further into the moonshadowed grove. My God, I'm going to do it.

He approached from the same direction the new sentry had come, deep within the grove, the direction of the creek. He moved one foot pad at a time, shifting weight carefully, advancing with infinite patience. He thought of the panther, as they called a mountain lion back East, the creature his father had given him as a model. One paw at a time goes down, in perfect control. The cat puts it down, but lightly, so he can pick it up again. When he's sure, he puts weight on it.

He looked often at his three trees, to be sure of them as the shapes changed with angle.

When he was directly east of the sentry, he began to move toward him. Not straight toward him. Three steps this way, two that, from tree to tree, watching all the time.

His sentry was still sitting, position unchanged. He wondered if this man's father had taught him silence and attentiveness in the woods, and the extraordinary patience of the hunter. His heart stirred a little.

No, he corrected himself, if the Pawnees are like the Sioux, it's the mother's brother who teaches hunting and war. Then he tossed this useless thought out of his mind.

He took two long breaths in slowly and let them out slowly. He would do what he had to do.

The sentry's head turned toward him.

He froze, and thought he must have turned white enough to see. He didn't breathe.

The sentry's head turned in another direction.

Then Sam realized. The man looked west for some seconds, then north, then east, then north, then west, and so on. The movement of head and torso was very regular, disciplined. He faced upstream and didn't look back toward the village. Sam wondered if he was saying something in a ritual way, maybe, timing his turns. 'It is a good day to die' several times over. He'd heard that's what warriors said.

He pursed his lips against a pang of sadness.

He circled to the left, back toward the village, on his lion pads. Twenty yards from the sentry, directly behind him on the "safe" side, he started his move straight forward. One foot at a time, test, shift weight. Repeat. He zigged this way and zagged that way, keeping trees between the two of them. If the sentry turned, Sam would look like a thick place in a tree trunk.

Soon there were two trees between him and the sentry. Then one.

His heart burst into his throat like a duck flapping up off water.

Head clear. Body steady.

He felt of the blade of the patch knife in his right hand. Very sharp.

No rifle. The man had a tomahawk, maybe, in each hand.

He stepped out from behind the last tree. Since the sentry was looking left, he stepped to the right. With the sentry's movement timed, he wouldn't be able to hesitate. Right, test, wait, shift, repeat. Forward, test, wait, shift, repeat. When sentry's head turns to center, pad left, test, wait, shift, repeat. Left again. Watch for sentry's head to change direction. Pad ahead . . .

His heart was loud enough to hear. He waited for the sentry to whirl and attack.

My God, one step and I'm within reach.

He told himself to breathe—not to breathe quietly, to breathe at all.

He resisted lunging.

One step. God, I'm going to do it.

He wanted to laugh. He wanted to let his laughter crack like thunder.

All caution to the winds.

Sam took one running step and lunged.

Left hand grabbed for mouth.

Mouth twisted free.

Right hand cut neck hard.

Left hand grabbed for mouth and went in.

Teeth crunched fingers.

A scream charged up Sam's gullet, but he sent it into his blade. He cut throat, hard and deep.

The sentry gagged. He coughed. Spasms convulsed him. He crumpled.

Sam pulled his bloody hand out of the mouth and let him fall to the ground.

Sam couldn't tell whether the hand was bloody from his own veins or the sentry's. Maybe it was all the same.

He thought maybe his fingers were broken.

A paroxysm racked Sam. He made an odd sound. He honestly couldn't tell if it was laughing or sobbing.

He looked at his bloody hand, started to wipe it off, then stopped. No, he would leave the blood, his or his enemy's. It meant something.

Quickly, he started back into the grove. Just as quickly he turned around, grabbed two tomahawks out of the dead hands and a knife from the belt. He ran lightly into the trees.

He decided to move quickly. If someone heard and came to check, he wanted The Celt in his hands before the uproar started. He walked fast to the edge of the clearing and circled toward the west, behind the brush dwellings, his eyes raging for the hut he wanted.

The damn things all looked the same.

He stopped and looked hungrily for orientation. He didn't dare walk into the main circle, for fear of disturbing some dogs.

He couldn't tell much about the lodges at night. The painting on them, what made them different—the colors were washed out in the moonlight.

Carefully, he remembered where Third Wing's lodge was, on the west side facing east. In his mind's eye he looked at the brush hut he wanted, a little north of west.

Then he looked at the north star and put it directly to his right. He studied out the shape of the circle. Its western arc, then, was right over there. Farther west was . . . And a little north of that was . . .

He could see it would be one of three huts.

Quietly, behind the arc of the brush dwellings, he circled to the west.

How was he going to know which one?

His heart fluttered. He could hardly believe it was going so well.

No uproar yet. No one had discovered the sentry's body. They hadn't heard the scuffle.

When he got close, he caught a break. He recognized the paint horse staked in front of the brush lodge. He'd forgotten about the paint. He wanted to laugh.

He stepped with care-care-care in that direction.

Damn, he wanted to laugh.

In two or three minutes he was alongside the hut. Stepping out in front of it seemed like a big moment somehow. Dangerous.

He did it.

Instantly he dropped to his knees.

The moon threw his shadow into the hut. He stared in. My God, had he woken them?

A dark shape within stirred.

Nothing happened.

Rolling over, he decided. He stayed crouched on his hands and knees, waiting.

Nothing.

He crawled forward. Then he saw. Only one dark puddle of robes was in the hut. One of the young men was away. Was he on a war party? Horse-raiding party? Was he on sentry duty?

My God, did I kill the man who stole my rifle?

He grinned. No. Too good to be true.

Forward, hand pad, knee pad, testing, careful, shifting weight.

A much worse thought came to him. Was The Celt on a war party? Horse-raiding party? Sentry duty?

Nothing to do but go forward and find out.

The paint stomped and flabbered its lips.

Sam kept very still, watching the robes.

Forward, carefully. Now, in the shadow at the top of the hut, he saw The Celt hanging, just as before.

He looked at the dark spot on the robes next to him. Surely this was the man who stole The Celt.

An urge to kill boiled up his gullet.

He let it pass. Foolishness.

He took two careful knee-steps forward and rose on his knees.

Now he could hear clearly, the deep, regular breathing of sleep. Strangely intimate, to hear the breath of a sleeping enemy. He reached up, patch knife in hand, and leaned over the sleeping figure.

With his left hand he grabbed The Celt in the middle. With his right he sliced the thong in the corner.

The Celt's barrel suddenly swung down.

My God! It didn't miss the sleeper by much.

Then, when he cut the second thong, he damn near dropped The Celt right on the sleeper.

He took two of the deepest breaths of his life, synchronizing them with the sounds of the sleeper's breaths.

Then he reached up and gingerly lifted down his shot pouch.

His eyes almost filled. Lead balls, powder, and a rifle to shoot with. Food. Life.

He slung the pouch over his right shoulder and under his left arm, as he always wore it. He dropped one of the two tomahawks as too awkward. The other stayed in his belt.

He backed up, on hand and knees. Backed up again, carefully. He burned with the desire to jump up and run, but he quelled it. Slowly and carefully.

Outside, finally, he stood up. He looked around. No visible problems.

Then he had an idea. He stepped to the stake that held the paint and pulled it.

No, I won't steal the horse. Pony tracks would be much too easy to see. But if he spends a little time in the morning hunting his horse, so much the better.

If his luck held, Sam would be long gone.

It held.

Soon he was out of the village.

Giddy, crazy feelings washed over him.

Quickly, he got to the creek and stepped in.

By God. By God. I did it.

Chapter Eighteen

HE HAD TO get moving. This was a long way from over.

He and Coy splashed up the creek less than an hour, until Sam got impatient with the slow pace. The Pawnees would eventually find where he left the creek anyway.

He drank deep. Then he lay down in the water and rolled in it. Reluctantly, looking back, he moved to the edge of the grove and looked out toward his rocky ridge, visible as a dark smudge on the land.

They went at a lope across the sandy plain. Carrying The Celt in his right hand, the rawhide rope over one shoulder, Sam was conscious of every footprint, until they got to the ridge. Here the Pawnees would expect him to turn toward the river—they knew he had no way to carry water. Therefore, glad of his wet clothes, worried about eventual thirst, he turned to the north.

Along the ridge, along the ridge, no tracks. He watched the Big Dipper—he couldn't afford to be visible when the sun came up. That was a long time off.

When the ridge melded into the plain, he turned east. Where the hell am I going? There's got to be a creek over those next low hills, or the next ones.

Again he went at a lope—distance might be his salvation. Coy kept up.

The hills were no obstacle, but the watercourse beyond was midsummer dry. His throat was so parched it hurt. The dry air coming in and out on every breath felt like sandpaper.

Across the northeast ran more low hills. He had to get across them, find water, and get a hiding place before dawn. *Otherwise I'll probably die.*

If there was no creek in the next little valley, he would have to head for the river and not stop until he got there. Moving around in the daylight, that's what he probably wouldn't survive.

THE LITTLE STREAM was manna from heaven. He smiled at himself. Small manna, an inch deep and a foot or two wide, and a blessing. He lay on his belly and drank. Coy slurped it up greedily. Sam flopped down in it.

He washed his bloody left hand. Blood was blood, and whose didn't matter. The hand was swollen, and maybe only half useful for holding The Celt's stock so he could shoot. He would have to shoot tomorrow, maybe.

He walked in the creek toward the river. He decided to hope a hiding place would work. No other chance.

In first light he saw some watercress growing in the creek, yanked it out with both hands, and stuffed it down. Coy sniffed the watercress, sat, and watched forlornly.

It was time to hide. So far he had been very, very lucky.

And got lucky again. Around the next bend another little creek flowed in, a bigger one. He stepped into it and realized the damnedest thing. This creek was flowing north. Not toward the river. In the dark he hadn't seen a low divide. Maybe this one led to another creek that went to the river. . . . To the devil with that.

He walked in the water right upstream, south, toward the river, stepped out onto thick grass that would show no tracks, and cached in some dense bushes.

Best I can do today.

Better load The Celt before I sleep.

Oh hell. When he opened the shot pouch, he saw there were only four lead balls left. He rummaged around in the bottom. Only four. The thief had practiced with the rifle.

Damn.

He thought clearly, I'm not going to make it.

He loaded The Celt. Then he reached for Coy, snuggled up to the coyote pup, and both went to sleep.

COY WOKE HIM up at midday, squirming.

What was going on? Did Coy hear something? Smell something?

He wanted desperately to leave the thicket, walk up the nearest hill, and look around. I have to see my fate coming.

He stayed put. Stayed put all the way to dark.

Then they walked back down the big creek to its junction with the little creek. There, even by moonlight, the tracks of several horses were obvious in the sand along the bank. They had tracked him this far and turned upstream.

It gave him the chills. They'd ridden close by him and Coy,

sleeping, and he hadn't heard them. If Coy had, he'd kept quiet. He scratched the coyote's ears well.

He frowned. They would be searching this creek again tomorrow.

No tracks. We have all night. All night over this divide should get us to the river. But that's what they're looking for.

He thought. This is a wide valley. Any creek a little to the north will flow into the big river. No telling whether upstream or down, but . . .

What if we went the other way?

They set out, and soon found their creek flowed into a river, and the river was headed east alongside the big river, and surely into it.

Mountain luck.

JUST ABOVE WHERE the rivers joined, in the first light of the new day, he found a patch of cattails. Thinking they'd be great cover, he slogged his way in. When he sat down in the muck, he decided to pull some tails and eat the roots. He'd seen them sliced into stews but never eaten one raw.

It was bad. He ate another one, and another. Coy watched pathetically. Sam was going to have to make a kill today or the pup would disappear on the hunt, maybe never come back.

He stretched out in the muck and went to sleep.

About midday he stirred and saw Coy feeding on a prairie dog next to him. He went back to sleep.

When he woke up again, he still felt exhausted but not sleepy.

He looked around and decided he was still alive. Sometimes life seemed charmed.

He stretched and discovered that every muscle he had ached. He went back to sleep.

As the sun set, he left the patch of cattails quietly and walked in the shallows to the big river. This could be a danger spot. He eased to the edge of the border of cottonwoods along the stream and looked out to the north. Nothing. He crossed the very wide, very shallow stream and looked out to the south. Nothing.

Not that they weren't searching for him. They just weren't looking right here right now.

Probably they weren't close enough, he guessed, to say where a shot came from, even if they heard it. In two nights' travel he was certainly more than twenty miles from the village, maybe even thirty.

Far enough from the enemy, and too close to starving times.

He sat very still in edge of the trees. Sat and watched more. His patience paid off. Across the plains, looking for a drink, came two muley does and several fawns. He held Coy and petted him—can't let the pup scare the deer off.

He would have to make sure with one shot. Couldn't shoot again. If he wasn't desperate, he wouldn't even think of using one ball on a deer.

The shot was clean.

The other deer bounded off. Take care of those fawns, he said in his mind to the remaining doe.

He trod softly to the southern verge of trees and looked out. No riders.

He splashed across the river and looked out across the more dangerous prairie to the north. Even after about ten minutes, no riders.

Coy was tearing at the doe. He opened her and gave the pup the gall bladder. He himself ate the liver raw. It was the best mouthful he'd ever tasted. He ate the heart raw too.

While he built a low fire, he skinned a front quarter and let Coy feed on it. For himself he roasted back straps on a stick, ate his fill, dozed, ate his fill again, and repeated the process twice more. Gideon claimed an *hivemant* could eat ten pounds of meat at a sitting. You learned to do it, said Gideon, to store up against the days you spent starving. Sam hadn't believed this until now.

All night he kept the fire going, ate, dozed, and ate. Coy did the same.

At dawn he cached in some bushes a quarter mile from the doe. It would be a draw for the crows, but he didn't care. If it drew Indians too, that would tell him something. Since he was slept out, he watched.

He also considered. Still too close to the village, he thought, to risk taking a couple of days to dry this meat. He had to make time, which meant leaving a lot of the deer. After some thought, he figured a way to carry a hind quarter over his shoulder on the rawhide rope. Best he could do.

Watching all day, he saw no Indians. None on the deer, none on the prairies to the north or south.

During that afternoon he did something about his moccasins. The bottoms were holey. If he had an awl and some sinew, he could sew a new sole on. But he had neither, nor rawhide for soles.

He cut off the belly of his deerskin shirt, hand-span wide and about two feet long. Using the moccasins for size, he cut soles out of the skin and stuffed them loose into the bottom of the mocs. All he could do.

At dark he moved back to the carcass. He could see where the crows had pecked. It took him only an instant to say to hell with that.

He built another small fire, roasted meat again, and consumed all he could hold. He napped a little. He went through the process twice. At about midnight, according to the Big Dipper, he gathered up The Celt and a hind quarter and said to Coy, "Let's go." He teased himself, *I am now a man of possessions.*

After traveling the rest of the night, he cached again, fed himself and Coy from the hindquarter, and slept. At midday, though, he decided he was far enough along to start traveling during the day. He could make better time, and he was for more likely to see a buffalo.

Three lead balls left. For how many weeks ahead?

The rest of the afternoon he alternated trotting and walking.

Seemed like a good way to make miles. He didn't let himself think how many miles. How many weeks, that he did wonder. Things were different now. At first he'd wandered, rudderless, across vast plains that stretched infinitely in every direction. Now he wanted to go somewhere. He smelled a life for himself somewhere ahead.

THAT NIGHT SAM held up the hindquarter, looked at it thoroughly, and in a way said good-bye to it. One more good meal on it, tonight's. He chawed. Coy made pathetic eyes at him. He cut some off for the pup. The little beast—and I am a beast, too, Sam told himself—gobbled it and made eyes for more.

Sam thought about keeping it all for himself, but that would never do. True, Coy could get his own food with tooth and claw. Sam couldn't. But Sam also couldn't eat while Coy watched, belly rumbling. Somehow their connection said no to that.

He started to cut Coy another good chunk and thought better of it. He was sharing with crows, why not his brother? Put your mouth where a crow's beak has pecked, and where your brother-friend has gnawed.

He put the whole quarter down in front of Coy. The pup flattened his belly to the ground like he was going to sneak up on it. He looked at the quarter, looked at Sam, back at the quarter. He wormed forward and began to chew. Sam smiled.

After a couple of minutes Sam reached out and took it.

Coy jumped to his front paws, bottom on the ground, feet stiffly forward.

Sam gave him a look and a grin. Then he chomped down right on the place Coy had been chewing.

Coy's expression got quizzical. Then he lay his head down on his paws and watched Sam, a look that was sidelong but persistent. Like a raven waiting for the wolves to get off the carcass, Sam thought.

When he'd had his share, he gave the quarter to Coy and went to sleep.

THE NEXT DAY he loped as much as he could. Make miles, make miles.

He cached and slept hungry.

The next day, once more, he loped every minute he could. And he could almost all the time. His legs were devouring the distance now, pushing it from in front of him to behind him. Nothing else was on his mind. He watched the next rise, looked long ahead from the top without stopping, and kicked more miles behind him. Go, go, go.

Coy kept alongside comfortably. Seemed to Sam he liked traveling that way.

Life seemed charmed again that afternoon. He came on a rivulet draining toward the river, and the banks were crowded with blackberry bushes. He ran toward them, Coy nipping at his heels.

Just then the griz roared.

Sam skidded to a stop and fell on his butt.

Griz was up on his hind legs, glaring.

If Sam and Coy were lucky, this griz was a he, and there were no cubs around.

Probably aren't, he told himself. A she-griz would have already charged them.

Griz roared again.

Sam thought. The Celt was loaded. But one shot wouldn't do the job. Was it worth it?

Sam roared back.

Griz flapped his paws in the air and roared again.

Then he dropped to all fours and loped away.

Sam Morgan, you are a fool, and a lucky fool.

He waded in. He picked with both hands and ate as fast as he could. Berry juice ran down his face and neck and onto his shirt. It ran up his arms and smeared onto the insides of his sleeves.

He ate like a wild man for, well, just a few minutes. Then he hightailed it for the river.

Odd thing was, when it came time to camp, he was hungry again.

Coy damn well wouldn't go to bed hungry. Each evening, when they cached, he left and came back with a ground squirrel, chipmunk, or prairie dog.

At the end of this third day of running and hardly eating, just berries, Sam felt weak. He would have to hunt tomorrow. He hated to. It violated his desire to go, go, go forever. But it was necessary. And at sunset he had seen buffalo in the distance. Too far for this evening, good for the morning.

The moon was full. He lay on his back and looked the old grandma in her face. His own grandmother, she'd had lots of stories about the moon. The full moon makes you crazy. It makes your plans come true. The full moon is the time to cut your hair. He just looked, and didn't come up with any words for what he saw. He knew that he was content. Like Coy, like a bluebird, like a tree, even like grass, he was well content to inhabit this spot on the earth.

When he fell asleep, he dreamed.

He walked up to a buffalo cow. She was lying on her side, like the one where he and Coy had cached themselves against the prairie fire. Somehow, though, he did not think this one was dead. She was . . . waiting. His eyes kept coming back to her belly, naked and vulnerable.

He hesitated, uncertain. Then, as though he knew when he didn't, he went up to her on the belly side, set down The Celt, and stripped all his clothes off. He stood before her, wholly naked, with his arms out and palms up, as for inspection, or in supplication.

She made no movement or gesture. He could not even see by her eyes if she was living or not.

He got down on all fours, crawled to her, and scooched up against her, back to belly, the way Coy lay with him that dawn of the great fire.

As he knew he would, though he didn't actually know, he melted into her. He, Sam Morgan, human being, backed into the being of the buffalo, his flesh uniting with her flesh, his hair hers. Inside, willingly, he stretched out into her. He reached into her front legs with his arms, into her rear legs with his own. Rump squirmed into rump. Head merged into head. He wiggled his fingers and toes, writhed his whole body, and as he did, the fibers of her muscles entered his, and vice versa. Last, he felt his heart unite with hers, unite absolutely, until they beat the same beat and pumped the same blood.

He felt the buffalo blood mingle with his and flow into lung, gut, brain, loin, and limb. He would have known that she felt his blood in the same way, except that there was no longer any she to feel such a thing. Nor was there a he. There was one being, truly one. He was something new.

He drew breath into his lungs, and the breath was buffalo breath.

He got to her feet, grand and shaggy, and looked out across the prairie and the world, poised for something great.

He woke up.

Sam looked around at the infinite night. He saw some stars between the canopies of the big cottonwoods overhead, and felt like he could see the rest, a panorama of leafy astronomy, the sky revealed utterly and simply to him, opened entirely, and it was beautiful beyond beautiful.

After a while Coy squirmed next to him and whimpered, dreaming a coyote dream, which was probably a human dream. "I am a buffalo," Sam whispered. He put his hand around the pup's belly, scooted it against his chest, and murmured, "I am Sam-alo."

He slept. No new dream came. He basked in the beauty of the old one.

* * *

When he woke at first light the next morning, he got up and got to traveling in the direction of yesterday's buffalo. They were gone. After an hour or two of looking, he moved on. It was all right. From now on the buffalo would come to him. But he did not spend what was left of his strength running. He walked and walked.

His mind stayed in his dream, but he didn't know what to do about it.

The day was elemental. He drank from the river, washed his face, wet his hide shirt, put it back on, clammy and delicious against the day's heat. He loped. He saw birds circling over something to the north, and wondered if it was meat, and if he and Coy should go there and share it with the crows and wolves. They kept loping. He watched clouds gather to the northwest and wondered if they would get a rain. It had hardly rained during his whole journey. They kept going. The next day was the same, and the next.

Three balls left. His mind turned that thought over and over. Running step, three balls left, running step, three balls left.

The buffalo will be there for me.

The next day he took a cow and fed. Coy fed as well. Sam felt like a predator.

Two balls left.

He used his hide shirt as a possible sack to carry meat, tied with the rawhide rope. He and Coy could eat on it, probably five days. He tried counting how many days the meat would last, how many he could travel hungry, how many days before starvation. . . .

The counting was too much work.

Run. Go every step possible at a lope. Walk only when essential. Run again. Make forty miles a day. Hell, make fifty.

Get there.

Odd how important Fort Atkinson was to him. He needed powder and lead. Maybe he should learn to hunt with bow and arrow, free himself entirely from provisions. Live like the Indians do.

Enough. He might try that. And he might not. It was for later.

One day he had to swim a big river. He got his powder wet—now he was the same as unarmed. He started to dry it and then thought better. He would run and run and run and dry it tonight. Before he lay down that evening, he spread both kinds of powder out on a rock. The night air would not be as hot and dry as the daytime air, but maybe eight or ten hours would dry it.

After a few bites of dry meat in the morning he was off. With dry powder.

Soon he had hunting luck again. The dream had hinted that the buffalo were his kin, and they seemed to be—they came when he called.

One ball left.

On a morning like a million others he came to another big river. He swam it, awkwardly because of The Celt in one hand. On the far bank he felt weak and decided to spend a couple of hours drying out his powder. He debated with himself about how long he could go on without eating. Earlier, he could move strongly on the days he fasted. Now he felt weak, even on the first day.

You have no cause to feel weak, he told himself. You ate yesterday.

Nevertheless he worried. Instead of trotting the rest of the day, he walked.

The next morning he felt so weak he wondered if he should hunt buffalo that day, only his second without food. His last ball.

I will run until I die, he thought, run until I die.

He looked at Coy. You will be all right, he said in his mind to his friend. You will be all right. Such is your nature.

He saw no buffalo that day.

The next morning he saw no buffalo, no deer, no nothing. Feeling unsteady, he walked.

Right away he came to a big bend in the river. It ran off to the south here. Looking ahead, he saw a well-worn trail heading straight east. On an intuition he followed the trail. Maybe it cut across a big loop in the river.

By midday he was forcing himself brutally to keep going. By midafternoon he was faltering. Once when he stumbled, he stayed where he fell and napped, or lost consciousness somehow. He woke up with no idea how long he'd been out.

He walked eastward, walked eastward, walked eastward. He could hardly hold his head up to look ahead. His feet, these he saw. But with his head down he might have walked into the middle of a war party without noticing.

A rise faced him. He dreaded it. The rise was nothing in particular, he had run strongly up slants much steeper. But today he wondered if he could walk up this little hump.

One more time, he told himself. And he did.

At the top he sat on a boulder to rest, panting. He looked around. And saw to the east the council bluffs of the Missouri River. On the bluffs perched log buildings of Fort Atkinson. Beyond, the river.

His mind swirled, and he fell.

A while later he sat up. The fort was still there.

He got to his knees. It was too much. He sat back down. He stared at the fort, he ate it with his eyes.

Then he blubbered like a baby.

After a while he laid down and napped.

Twenty minutes later, an hour, two hours—who knows?—he woke to the touch of a hand on his shoulder.

And woke looking into the face of . . .

None other than Hannibal MacKye.

Part Four

THE RETURN

Chapter Nineteen

"IT WAS NOTHING mystical," said Hannibal. "The sentry picked you up in the glasses and I came out."

Sam swigged deep on the flask. He held it out to Hannibal, but the educated Delaware held up a palm. Sam swigged again. In the flask was hot coffee with lots of sugar. "That will pick you up," Hannibal said.

Sam looked at his friend and grinned. "I suppose if you're found laying flat on the trail, you need it."

Hannibal looked into Sam's eyes curiously. "What the devil happened to your hair?"

"Lost my hair but saved my scalp."

"Sounds like a good story."

Coy crouched belly down in the dust half a dozen feet away. Seemed like he didn't know whether to protect Sam or run like hell. He watched Hannibal with sharp eyes.

Sam drained the flask. "Sorry my pup's standoffish."

"Coyote, isn't he?"

"Coyote and friend. I'm surprised he's unfriendly."

"They have their own reasons. He'll come to me when he's ready."

Sam put a hand on Hannibal's shoulder and levered himself to his feet.

Hannibal took his hand and gently drew him back down. "Take your time." He scooted around backward on his bottom and said, "Look."

Playfully, Sam rat-a-tat-tatted his heels around until he had also pivoted backward.

"Behold a great drama of a sunset," said Hannibal in a fake-operatic speaking voice. "A glow of indescribable orange fierceness tears across the sky. Across that slashes a violence of wine-colored cloud. A band of pink, peculiarly gentle, mediates between the flaming orange and the serene sky, which is a perfect, robin's egg blue." Hannibal grinned at his own silliness.

Sam beheld and said, "Looks like the prairie fire that damn near got me."

Hannibal raised his eyebrows at Sam. "Guess you've got some stories."

They watched the sunset. When it turned violet, and then purple, Sam got to his feet.

"The sentry's not going to be happy about a coyote in the fort," said Hannibal. "Officer of the day won't be either."

Sam put the rawhide rope on Coy. In the last few days he had taught the pup to walk on a leash. Together the three ambled toward the fort.

Last mile, thought Sam. He could hardly believe it. Last mile of seven hundred.

"First thing, you better eat."

TELLING THE STORIES seemed to come ahead of everything but eating. "We can get you some boots from the quartermaster tomorrow. Also some better clothes, cover those blistered spots."

Sam hardly noticed anymore that his face and neck were always red and peeling. His belly and calves too, where he'd cut off his own deerhide covering.

In line for supper he suddenly blurted, "What month is it?"

"Moon when the leaves turn yellow."

Sam glared at his friend.

Hannibal laughed. "September. Time of the change from summer to autumn."

Sam thought back. "I left Fitzpatrick and the fellows on June 1, or maybe it was June 1."

"Three months by yourself," said Hannibal.

"The first two weeks, about that by the moon, I waited for them." He wondered at it. "Two and a half months to walk those seven hundred miles." He walked his mind back a little, across that vast distance. He chilled.

"The man who came to the end of journey," asked Hannibal, "was he the same man who started out?"

"No," said Sam. He was damn sure of that much.

A soldier was offering to ladle food onto his tin plate.

Lord, I'm hungry.

"I'm pleased for you to be in our mess," said the soldier politely. "Don't intend to feed no coyote." Coy was tied well off to the side, but he'd attracted some notice, mostly incurious and unfriendly.

The mess was ship's biscuits, meat, and beans. The texture of bread seemed impossibly exotic. Sam ate three plates full before Hannibal cautioned him. Sam remembered his buffalo feasts and went back again anyway. Then he drank cup after cup of coffee, which he hadn't tasted since he left Fort Kiowa a year ago. "You've got maybe twenty pounds to put back on, looks like," observed Hannibal.

When Sam got up to piss, he and Coy walked out to look at the scene in twilight. The fort stood atop what were known as the council bluffs, and had a fine prospect. There Sam gave Coy a full helping of meat, and the pup gobbled it. Sam was proud of the beast for not making an intolerable racket while tied within smell and sight of all the food.

After dinner they lounged on the great bluffs, Coy curled up on Sam's lap. Hannibal got out his pipe, and offered Sam some tobacco. Sam lit his white clay pipe for the first time in months. He could hardly believe the brittle thing had survived all his adventures. Smoking felt good.

When he'd finished a pipe and refilled his bowl, Sam decided that what he wanted to tell Hannibal about was the prairie fire, and the buffalo.

At Sam's description of the fire itself, its maniacal raging, Hannibal said, "I've seen them. Never from downwind, though. Hardly anyone who saw one from downwind lived to tell about it. You were lucky, and you were good."

"Yeah. And Coy led me."

Hannibal raised an eyebrow at him.

"Coy led me into the buffalo belly. I wouldn't have thought of it."

Hannibal nodded and smiled with satisfaction. "I guess you owe him a lot of helpings of meat then."

After a moment, Sam asked, "What starts prairie fires?"

"No one knows. Probably lightning. Might be Indian people, though. They burn grasslands off from time to time. Believe it renews them. You know the story of the phoenix?"

"No."

"The Egyptians, you remember them from the story of Pharaoh and Moses?"

Sam nodded.

"The Egyptians believed in a bird called the phoenix, big as an eagle, all scarlet and gold. It had a song so beautiful no one who heard it could ever forget it. Only one of these birds could ever live at any one time, and they lived a thousand years. When time came for it to die, the old phoenix flew to the temple of Re, god of the sun. There it sought out the altar, and burned itself to death on the altar fire. From its ashes the new phoenix arose."

Sam nodded.

"Kind of like you, one man went to the buffalo altar, another came away."

"Yeah." Sam thought a minute. "I want to learn to read."

"Good idea."

"You read a lot."

"I told you, my father was a classics scholar. I read English, Latin, and Greek."

"What's it good for?"

"When you can't drop off, you recite verses until you bore yourself to sleep."

"What else?"

"You can insult people and they don't know it."

Sam looked at him quizzically.

"Copro cephaly," quoted Hannibal.

"What does it mean?"

"Someone's got shit where their brains should be."

Sam chuckled. Then, "Is it good for anything really?"

"It is. Lets you hold things up and look at them from different angles. Even lets you see you're like a myth, a man that went into the belly of a whale, or a buffalo, and rose from the dead."

Sam pondered. "I feel like a buffalo sometimes."

"I can see that."

"I need to tell you about my dream of being a buffalo."

"All right."

"But after I sleep."

"It's a clear night," he told Hannibal. "I'm going to sleep outside." He was worried about Coy's reception anywhere inside.

"Me too." They found a place by a cedar, under the stars but on the fort grounds.

Sam got to sleep in blankets. Half a dozen men offered him covers. They felt good, like luxury.

"YOU DIDN'T SAY how you happen to be at Fort Atkinson," Sam said.

These were the first words of the morning. They'd both been awake for a few minutes, watching the morning sky.

Hannibal yawned, then grinned. "I was waiting for you."

Sam gave him a disgusted look.

Hannibal corrected himself. "I make some money trading to the river tribes. About half the year. The rest of the time I do whatever I feel like, including go see my parents."

"What do you like?"

"Seeing people. Lending a hand where needed."

"You trade alone?"

"Yes."

"That sounds dangerous."

"People along the river know me. Red and white."

Coy stirred, shook himself, and came to lick Sam's face. Sam felt a little embarrassed about that, but it was the way they began most mornings.

"You were going to tell me about dreaming of being a buffalo."

"Back in a minute." Sam rolled out of his blankets, grabbed their tin cups, strolled into the barracks, and poured coffee from the speckled pot hanging over the fire. He was going to get all he could as long as he could.

As he told the buffalo dream, new details came out. He wasn't sure whether he was remembering more of the dream or his mind was filling the dream out more now. Didn't seem to make any difference which.

Sam began with his feeling coming up to the cow, as if he knew exactly what to do. Which was odd, because he couldn't know, yet he did.

He couldn't tell whether she was dead or alive when he came up—that was a mystery.

Spreading his arms and then getting down on all fours to approach felt humble, in a way. Backing up to her seemed at first like rejoining his mother—this stuff was embarrassing to tell—but when he went into her, like being absorbed, it wasn't mothery at all.

He expanded into the buffalo. He became more than he was, larger of dimension. It was very satisfying to fill her rump with his, and wildly exciting to melt into her head. Now the thinking, the seeing, the tasting was all one.

The uniting of heart, loin, and lung, blood and breath—especially breath—these felt . . .

Sam didn't have the words. "Mysterious," he said. "Very wonderful."

He chuckled, remembering. "I called myself 'Samalo.' "

Hannibal just looked into his coffee.

After a long moment, Sam asked, "Hannibal, why did I dream that?"

Hannibal shrugged. "The dreamer knows. Somewhere in there," he tapped Sam's head, "you know."

THE NEXT DAY convinced Sam he never wanted to work for the U.S. government.

They would give him a set of clothes to cover his hide and boots to protect his feet, they said, if he agreed to enlist in the U.S. army. Purely for the records, the officer assured him. Sam also had to go in and out of every office at the post, it seemed like, check with every officer, get every permission, and wait, wait, wait. They had to pretend Coy was a dog and belonged to Hannibal. The army wasn't about to let a mere private have a dog.

Since Hannibal wandered around with him most of the day, it wasn't too boring, and Sam got to tell a year and a half's worth of adventures. "It's all your fault," he began. "You told me to follow my wild hair."

He began with Grumble, Captain Stuart, and Abby, not failing to include Ten and Eleven. He had fun telling about the French woman who got humiliated by losing her wig in Abby's bar. About how he met Governor Clark, got referred to General Ashley, and became a mountain man, or was becoming a mountain man.

Hannibal had heard about the Ashley troubles at the Ree villages, but not how Sam got his leg broken by a ball and nearly got caught and scalped. Hannibal had not heard of Jedediah Smith, and listened with wonder to the stories of the young leader's coolness, capabilities, devout Christianity, and high ambition. He knew of Edward Rose, whom he called a good friend. Sam didn't know Rose was good friends with anybody, and couldn't help wondering if that was because they were both breeds.

"No, it's because Rose is an unusual man. Totally, fiercely what he is."

Then Hannibal laughed. "And don't look at me like that. Your thoughts are easy to read, and understandable."

Sam reminisced about the best friend he'd made, Gideon. And commented that French-Canadians seemed to get along with Indians a lot better than American mountain men did.

Sam told about starting over the Southern Pass too early and damn near freezing to death and starving to death and getting blown all the way to Missouri. About the beaver-hunting haven of the Siskadee River, and the Snakes who put them afoot. About missing Jedediah Smith at the cache, Sam scouting downriver while Fitz and the others waited, and never seeing his friends again.

He had to admit he was damn worried about them. Maybe he was the only one who came back alive.

"Sure you want to go back?" asked Hannibal.

Sam shook his head. "Not sure of anything except having a partner." He nodded at Coy.

He told about getting so crazy on the way downstream, and aching so lonely, he wanted to walk into a hostile camp. How he really did damn near get killed by the Pawnees. He didn't have to tell, again, about getting baptized in the fire, and resurrected.

Mostly, though, he spent the day standing around waiting for officers to figure out if they'd get into trouble for treating a young man decently. By the time he stood in the mess line that evening he was damn tired of human company, except for Hannibal, and almost wished he was lost in the wilds again.

THEY PULLED THEMSELVES out of the river, dripping, padded onto the sand, and flopped down naked. The Missouri gurgled by restlessly—always whirling, dervishing, roiling its way down, down, down, ever moving, that river, whooshing its way to St. Louis and an even bigger energy of water.

"You're a red and white man," Hannibal said, teasing. Sam looked down at his body. Alternating bands of color. Chest white, lower arms red, belly red, thighs white, calves and feet red.

His body needed some time off.

"Your body adjusts to it, always being outdoors. Human beings are born to it, actually."

Sam looked at Hannibal. Though his skin was all bronze, it was darker in the hands and face, where it was exposed.

"What did you learn about red and white men out there?"

Sam thought. "Strange." He recounted in order. "Ten and

Eleven became friends. The Osages were tame, kind of intimidated. The Sioux were proud, haughty. The Rees did their damnedest to kill us. The Crows befriended us, kind of gave us a home. But they'd rob you blind and laugh about it. The Snakes took the food we gave them and then stole our horses. The Pawnees, well, they were for me and against me. Most of them wanted to do me in nice and slow. One said he liked me and saved my life."

"What were the big differences you saw between the mountain men and the Crows?"

"The Crows were glad to share their women. White men wouldn't. Crow men do a hell of a lot to toughen themselves. They have *some* warrior attitude. Take blistering hot sweat baths. Go around in the winter naked to the waist. Wash off in the river even when there's ice along the edges, morning and night." Sam laughed to himself. "Come to think of it, they're a lot cleaner than we are, too."

"So how do you feel about the Indians you met?"

"Mixed up."

"How'd the men you were with feel?"

"When you travel, you ride watchful, camp with a guard, keep your horses close, and always assume that Indians are hostile. When they're not, you're grateful."

"If one rode into your camp alone, how would you treat him?"

"Invite him to sit by the fire, have coffee."

"How would Indians treat you?"

Sam laughed. "I don't mean to risk it."

"If you saw a white man being chased by Indians, what would you do?"

"Save his hide."

"If you saw an Indian being chased by white men?"

Sam got it, and it made him uncomfortable. "Watch, I guess."

"Tell me more about the attitude of the mountain men you were with."

Sam thought. "Diah Smith wants to be kind to them, but he treats them like children. Come to think of it, like unpredictable, dangerous teenagers. Fitzpatrick and Clyman?" Pause. "Mostly the same. Most of the men? Micajah? Branch and Stone? Indians are enemies. Or else they're like animals. You tolerate them. Mount their women if you can. Kill them when you need to, and don't think twice about it."

"When you know Indian people," said Hannibal, "they're not unpredictable."

Sam blinked at the sky.

"History tells us that this stuff of different people living on the same land, it doesn't work. One drives the other off. Or enslaves them."

Sam thought. "Sounds like troubled waters ahead, two peoples here."

"Three peoples."

Sam looked at him.

"Red, white, black. And the white has already enslaved the black, and is maybe killing off the red."

Sam considered his friend. "What about those who are two colors?" Or three, he thought, like Edward Rose?

"I spend a lot of time telling white people I'm a human being, just like you. Same wants, same frailties, same pleasures. Spend a lot of time saying the same to Indians."

Sam thought that maybe Hannibal had a harder row to hoe than even Ten and Eleven did.

SAM GOT UP, stood on the rock, and jumped into the river, knees to his chest, bottom first. After a few strokes out and back he beached himself some yards downstream. "That thing's swift."

He sat back down next to Hannibal. "I'll trade you a big story for a big story."

"All right."

"You first. I don't know much about you. What did you do when you got out of Dartmouth?"

"I ran away from Dartmouth, actually. I had the heebie-jeebies, wanted to get out of Latin and into the real world." He laughed. "So I joined the circus." Now his voice got dreamy. "My father took us to see John Bill Ricketts's circus in 1799 in Philadelphia. I was just a boy. When I got old enough, but still full of boy dreams, I ran away to the circus."

"I've heard of circuses, I guess they're big shows, but I don't really know anything about them."

"They started as riders doing tricks on the backs of horses, and that's still the main thing. I worked taking care of the horses first. Then they let me help train them. Finally I got to ride and do tricks myself. You ride bareback, standing up. One of the main tricks is jumping through a hoop. You're riding at a canter, circling in a ring. Your assistant holds up a big hoop at the edge of the ring—maybe it's covered with paper, or maybe it's flaming. As the horse approaches, you leap up and forward, pass through the hoop, do a somersault, and land on the horse's back."

"You're kidding."

"Not a bit. The landing is the hard part to learn. You also ride two bareback horses at once, a foot on each back."

Sam felt, as he sometimes did around Hannibal, that he was transported into the world where the big stories happened, like Bible stories, or tales of knights and fair maidens.

Hannibal went on, "But then you start doing other things to please the crowd. For instance, after Peter, that was the man who taught me the horse tricks, after he did three or four tricks, his horse would come out riderless and prance around the ring. John Bill, or whoever was running the show, would tell the audience that Peter got just got kicked by a horse and couldn't perform. Then a drunk in the audience would stand up, waving his bottle, and shout that the program was a bust.

"Indignant, John Bill would challenge the drunk to ride the horse."

"The drunk came running out of the seats, staggering. He climbed on the horse and fell off the other side, and had some more troubles, and drew a few laughs before he finally got seated.

"Then John Bill would let the bridle go, and the bareback horse began to canter. Up jumped the drunk, riding the horse standing up. The audience applauds. Right quick the drunk begins to do tricks, first somersaults, then bouncing down to the ground and sailing back onto the horse. At the same time, he throws off his shabby old clothes, and underneath—behold!—is a beautifully muscled Indian in nothing but a gorgeously beaded breechcloth—me."

Hannibal grinned. "That was fun. And I made lots of money, *lots* of money."

"Is this real?"

"Absolutely. A Brit named Philip Astley, he was a trick rider himself, started the modern circus in the 1760s. It spread all over Europe, and John Bill Ricketts opened the first American circuses in New York and Philadelphia in 1793."

"Why'd you quit?"

"The circus changed. All shows change, to suit the audiences, but I didn't like some of the new ways. We got a tiger and an elephant for people to look at. They liked that. We'd even parade the animals through the streets before a performance to draw people in.

"Then we got a dromedary, which is like a camel, and a monkey. Then, and this is where it turned, we got a huge, powerfully muscled black man, a little, shrivelled up Chinaman, and a woman who weighed three hundred pounds and had a beard."

Sam deliberately gave Hannibal a queer look.

"We would parade them through the streets, too, like they were prize animals, or freaks. John Bill paid me extra to be one of them. He lined us up like we represented God's creation culminating in white people—all in a row the chimpanzee, the black man, the Indian, the Chinaman, the fat lady, and next to them the crown of creation, John Bill himself, handsomely decked out.

"A step on the way to white folks—that was more than I could stand.

"Now it's your turn, Sam."

"I FELL IN love with a Crow woman."

"I'll be damned."

So he told Hannibal about Meadowlark, all about her. How she looked, how she sounded, how she moved. About the ceremony she was waiting to do. About how they stood in the blanket together. How he learned Crow so he could talk to her. How she gave him, on the last day, the *gage d'amour* now carefully laid on top of his new army-issue shirt. How he promised to come back and didn't.

Hannibal regarded him. It seemed like a wise look, but Sam had no idea what it meant. "What should I do?"

"Whatever you really want to."

"What?"

"Whatever you really want to."

"Been thinking about going back to Crow country. But not alone. Too dangerous, and Meadowlark doesn't want to see me a pauper, no horse, no nothing."

Hannibal smiled at him a little.

"I was thinking, those last days coming down the river, I ought to go home for a little."

"Because?"

Sam shrugged. "Something . . . I don't know." He wiggled his shoulders, like trying to get something off his back. "Unfinished."

"What else are you thinking of?"

"Going to St. Louis and working for Abby until spring, then go back upriver."

"Any other choices?"

"I can't work for Ashley when I can't find the brigade. Don't know what to do."

At that moment they saw a soldier come walking to them. When he got close, he averted his eyes, as though embarrassed by the sight of male skin. "They sent me to tell you, Morgan, your friends just arrived."

"What?"

"From upriver. Fitzpatrick and the others just got here. They came walking down the river, just like you."

Sam jumped up and skinnied into his pants.

"Sounds like you just got another choice," said Hannibal.

GIDEON GAVE HIM a king-sized bear hug, Fitzpatrick and Clyman formal handshakes. Branch and Stone were with the army surgeon, getting patched up.

Sam looked at his friends while he introduced Hannibal. "You look maybe even worse than Sam when he got here," the Delaware said. "That must be a bad walk."

Sam hoped to hell he didn't look that bad, skin about to peel off and poking through. The biggest, Gideon, who was also the biggest around, actually looked the most haggard.

That night was all stories. Diah Smith had gone downstream to look for Sam, found the sign where he camped, found all the Indian tracks, and concluded he was gone under. He went back upriver while Fitzpatrick and the others built bull boats to float the furs downstream. But they capsized in the swift, whitewater canyon and lost all but one of their rifles and all their balls. They cached the furs and started downstream for help. On the way they got stopped and robbed by the Pawnees, same ones who got Sam.

Now Sam didn't wonder at how they looked.

They had pried the brass mountings off the remaining rifle—they showed Sam and Hannibal—and bent these into balls. So they were able to kill a few buffalo on the way. Also, they had each other for company.

Sam told his stories, too. The stories were as different as each man, they saw, and in a longer view the same. Men did hard things and lived to tell about it. Every man jack of them was thrilled.

The evening ended, though, with Fitzpatrick back to business. "We got to raise the cache. You want to go back?"

That gave Sam something to think over.

IT TOOK HIM two days to decide. He didn't consult with Hannibal at all, which felt a little strange, but that's the way he wanted it.

"I'm going home for a while," he told Fitzpatrick. "Don't know how long. I think I'll be coming back as quick as I can."

"Your decision," said the Irishman. "I'll give you a letter to take to the general."

Fitzpatrick also used Ashley's credit to get Sam a pirogue. By God, Sam thought, using a river to help me go. It's been a while, feels good.

Gideon, a boat man, helped him pick out the pirogue and paddle. They tried it out, and Sam was impressed by how well a hollowed-out log moved on the water. "Travel at night until you get to Fort Osage," Gideon reminded him. "Maybe ten days. Mind your hair."

"I hope I'll see you soon." The French-Canadian bear-hugged him again.

It occurred to Sam that not long ago a lone journey of a week and a half or two weeks in Indian country would have felt like a real challenge. But not if he didn't have to walk.

At sunset Sam and Hannibal walked down to the river. The pirogue was ready to go. No baggage except for Coy, a deer hide wrapped around two weeks' worth of jerked meat, and the letter, tucked into a leather wallet inside his shirt.

"First time we met," said Sam, "you told me to follow my wild hair. Any advice this time?"

"One small bit," said Hannibal. "That dream, the buffalo. If you come back to Indian country, tell a medicine man. Do a sweat lodge with him, and tell him your dream."

Sam gave Hannibal an odd look. "Sweat lodge?"

"Yes."

Sam looked at friend. "I will. If I make it back."

"You will."

Sam clapped Hannibal on both shoulders. "How about another prediction? Will I see you again?"

Hannibal flashed him a big, easy grin. "For sure," he said. "When you're not looking for me."

Chapter Twenty

"OH, BROTHER, HAVE I been waiting for you. Do I ever have an idea for us."

This was Grumble. Sam could hardly believe he was with Grumble and Abby in the Green Tree Tavern. Seemed like another planet.

His trip had gone easy as sliding on goose dung. At Fort Osage they offered him a ride downstream with two other men in a good canoe. He took it. They were bearing letters to Cadet Chouteau, he to General Ashley—messengers of rival firms.

Now it was ale, wine if he wanted it. These didn't feel as alien as the chair they expected him to sit on, or the table, or the silverware. He had to resist saying, "Fancy doin's fur a mountain man."

Right on the table in front of him were fluffy white bread, sweet butter, grapes, fresh tomatoes and cucumbers, sliced melon, fricasseed chicken, turtle soup, Sam didn't know what all—even fresh oysters, brought up alive in barrels filled with seawater on the steamboats from New Orleans. A long, long way from prairie oysters, which was what mountain men called the nuts of the buffalo, and even further from an unbroken diet of jerked meat. Still, Sam wasn't ready to try fresh oysters with Abby.

She was treating him to the best luncheon in St. Louis, she said, and chuckled when he hitched Coy outside. When she asked if he wanted Cadet to join them, he said no thanks.

At first he couldn't get past the bread spread thick with butter. Then he got caught up in the grapes. He didn't know what might come next.

"Oh, Grumble," said Abby, "don't be concocting schemes until we get to enjoy him a bit. I want to know everything that happened every day since you left."

Sam wondered what she thought had happened, considering the condition of his face and his body. But no one could see, from the outside, what had taken place in his mind and spirit.

He told. And told and told. Abby and Grumble finished the first bottle of wine, and a second, and started a third. Sam drank ale until he was woozy.

He couldn't think how it sounded to them. Like old-time stories of wondrous places where there were monsters, and giants, and miracles, he imagined. He realized for the first time that he had been living a life of monstrous grizzly bears and buffalo, Indians and white men of giant wants and appetites, and miracles of life and death. He even realized, partly, that he abided in that kind of world, and was himself one of these storied men.

He felt glad beyond glad.

Abby, naturally, was most interested in the Indian women. He only knew the Crows. She bristled at how they gave their favors away cheaply, but reveled in his description of their dress. Sam went so far as to sketch a beaded bodice on the tavern's white tablecloth, bringing a very stern look from the waiter. Abby waved the fellow off.

Meadowlark was fascinating to Abby. She wanted every detail, and seemed stumped only by the idea of keeping virginity until after a certain ceremony was performed. "Their priests are as bad as our ours," she said, and was happy to know that few Crow women participated in that practice.

"Take off the *gage d'amour de votre amour*," she said.

"What?"

She looked at him in amusement. "*Amour* means love. Hand me the token of love given you by your love."

She fingered it like she could sense the sweetness of Meadowlark's feeling in the delicately tanned hide and beautiful beads.

Their merriment and reminiscing were interrupted, in the end, by a young man who came calling on General Ashley's behalf. Sam had stopped by Ashley's office first thing after they docked the canoe, but the General was out. "He would like to see you as soon as possible," said the emissary.

"Come to the Pirates' Cove tonight," said Abby, "we'll feed you supper."

"And stay with me in my rooms afterwards," said Grumble. "I'm sitting on this idea like one very restless hen."

"YOUNG MORGAN, YOU'VE done very well. Thank you."

At Ashley's nod Sam sat down across the big desk from the general. He studied the polished wood of the desk and the nameplate, GEN. WM. H. ASHLEY. Seemed like the whole was meant to make him feel like an underling. He smiled to himself. A man who walked seven hundred miles alone, escaped from Pawnees, an underling? . . .

He missed the beginning of Ashley's conversation but soon caught on to what was wanted. This wasn't conversation. The general was pumping him for information.

So he told his story again, this time angled to what would concern Ashley—beaver plews, how many they'd found and where, where they were now, relations with the Indians, the discovery of the Southern Pass across the Rocky Mountains, country where they were welcome and weren't, all that sort of thing.

"Do you consider the Southern Pass passable to wagons?" asked Ashley. In fact, he asked a couple of times.

"Sure. Pretty easy for wagons. Not steep at all."

Ashley nodded with satisfaction. "That confirms Mr. Fitzpatrick's opinion." Ashley gestured toward the letter from Fitzpatrick. Sam didn't know what it said, and wasn't about to announce that he couldn't read.

Then Ashley found out about Sam's long, lone walk. He was duly impressed in an official sort of way, though he didn't dwell on it much, as though mountain men were a different species, something like Sam's coyote, with certain remarkable talents.

Next Ashley asked about the activities of Captain Smith. He was appalled by the tale of the clawing by the griz, and at the same time impressed. Did Sam think Captain Smith a good leader?

"First-rate."

"Enterprising?"

"For sure."

"Energetic?"

"Too damned energetic." Sam mentioned the maps Diah was always making but not the month-early start to look for a pass to the Siskadee.

"Resourceful?"

"Absolutely."

"Did the men respect him?"

"Tremendously."

He noticed that Ashley didn't ask if they liked him, or if he might be too hard-driven.

Ashley also inquired carefully about Fitzpatrick, who'd apparently been appointed second in command, and gave nods of approval at each answer.

After nearly an hour of this Sam was damn near exhausted by words. He wouldn't have thought that could happen, not when he was back on the Platte and wanting to walk into an Indian camp.

"Young Morgan," said Ashley at last, "we need to settle accounts. First, I thank you for work excellently well done. I hope you want to remain in my employ. Now, what were your expenses? What did you purchase from Captain Smith?"

Sam told him what he could remember buying, and Ashley noted each item in a ledger, with a price written opposite.

"Very well. Number of plews?"

Sam told him, and he made some marks.

"Altogether you've worked one year, seven months of a two-year contract. Are you prepared to return to the mountains now?"

"I want to go home for a few days, sir."

"Home to Pittsburgh?"

"Morgantown, nearby."

"That will require a couple of weeks, I should imagine, even if your visit is short. I will be heading for the mountains as soon as I can get affairs in order. Two to three weeks. Are you confident that you want to return with me?"

"Can't say for sure, sir."

"All right, then, I shall muster you out." After various calculations, which he read aloud, he concluded that Ashley-Henry owed Sam Morgan nearly two hundred dollars. He got the exact amount out of an office safe and handed it over, plus a ten-dollar bonus for bringing the letter downstream alone. Sam had to smile at that. Ashley said that if these figures were different from Captain Smith's, they would settle up later. "I know you're honest."

"Mind you, Morgan, if you want to go to the mountains with me this season, you must come back promptly."

Sam left dizzy. He'd never touched so much money in his life.

GRUMBLE'S ROOMS WERE down-at-the-heels in a shabby boardinghouse. Seeing Sam's look, he said, "Yes, I could afford better, but I belong to the shadow world, and I don't want to feel respectable."

"At least there won't be rules against coyotes here."

Grumble gave a cursory smile and launched into his idea. It was elaborate. It was imaginative. It was clever. It was altogether a humdinger, and potentially very profitable.

On the other hand, Sam didn't feel like running con games. "It will take two days," he protested. "I probably won't get back in time to go west with the general."

Grumble gave him a look, and Sam realized he couldn't deny his comrade a bit of fun. Also, it revolved around another big acting job . . . And to hell with General Ashley.

THEY BOARDED THE steamboat separately, as class distinctions required. Grumble was the gentleman, perhaps a capitalist, or a man of leisure. Sam was the frontiersman of the lowest type, a man to be avoided by the better sort, or looked at with amusement from a distance.

Grumble set to his job right away. He headed for the bar, spotted a man of mature years, full side whiskers, and excellent clothes, and struck up a conversation. In short order, though, Grumble realized that he couldn't smell money, which he had an infallible nose for. He passed on.

He switched to a sporty young man in the outfit of a Louisiana plantation owner. Had he brought up blacks for sale? Bales of cotton to go by ship to the Northeast textile manufacturers? . . . It didn't matter. This fellow had the air of a gay blade, and Grumble did smell money.

He seated himself at the young man's table and asked if he could buy him a drink, always a good opener. These steamboat voyages were tedious, they agreed, so little to do, only women and preachers could spend all this time gawking at scenery, good job the ship afforded a wide choice of libations, a man could have a cigar, a sensible conversation, and indulge in a variety of inebriates . . . "Jameson is my name." The fellow extended his hand. Grumble shook it vigorously, a custom he didn't care for, and murmured, "Smithson, Able Smithson."

Jameson was a self-possessed, virile kind of fellow of the merchant class, it turned out, a dealer in sorghum who traveled to secure new customers. Grumble had more fellow feeling, actually, for the corrupt, patrician planters. Grumble himself was an owner of newspapers, he said, looking for a likely site for a new enterprise. He saw Jameson take in the exquisite cut of his English tweed suit, dove gray pin-striped charcoal waistcoat, and wonder how newspaper owners made quite so much money. Grumble loved dressing up—it showed off the fuller range of his talents.

As the second drink arrived, Grumble found himself wondering, Where the devil is Sam? Grumble hated male small talk.

Here came Sam now. Grumble put on a face of amusement at the rube. Actually, he was very pleased with Sam's appearance. The gauntness was genuine. The deerskin clothing was new, just what a very *back* backwoodsman would choose. The shirt front was already streaked with tobacco stains, which he and Sam had applied the night before. The boots were ripe with horse apples, carefully stepped into on the way to the levee. Altogether very artful. Grumble was proud of himself—both the conception and details were his.

As Sam passed their table, he lurched sideways but regained his balance with alcoholic agility. Passing on, he lurched again, and used his rifle butt on the floor to regain balance. Then he gave up and collapsed into the chair. He threw a rueful grin at the gentlemen whose privacy he was violating. One gent to another, we understand indulging in whiskey, don't we?

"To set it right for buttin' in like this, let me buy you both a drink," Sam said expansively. He affected not the speech of a drunken man, but of a man carefully trying to sound sober. The lad really had a talent.

"Waiter," Sam called. Now he got out a purse swollen with Spanish coins, enough to corrupt the most honest of men. Oh, how Grumble would have liked to be corrupted for the first time again.

He leapt in with his line. "Young man, you ought to be cautious about showing so much cash in public."

" 'S fine," said Sam. "I been in St. Louis, I'm used to every kind of thief, and I'd like to see one as can stand up to a mountain man." He put the purse into the hunting pouch slung over his shoulder. After the game was over, Sam would have to be careful. At least half a dozen men had noted where he kept the coins.

The waiter accepted excessive payment for three whiskeys and was off. Grumble reminded himself to sip the whiskey slowly. He liked it a little too well.

"What is it you did in St. Louis?" he asked Sam. "Mr., ah . . ."

"Name's Two Hawks," said Sam. "I sold my furs, yessiree. To that Chouteau. Two years' furs, yessirree, and prices is good. And I seen all the fast tricks the crooks in that city got to offer, sartain this child did. You know the best one?"

Grumble gave Jameson a sideways glance that said, This is going to be fun. "I don't suppose I do."

"Wagh! I was in one where a man had three cards, an old man, an old woman, and a little boy with a hoop. He slipped them cards around so fast you couldn't tell. You had to find the little boy with the hoop.

"Right truth, I thought I could find it, and was willing to bet fifty dollars. But when that hoss picked the card up, it was the old man. I put out fifty dollars more. He done the same again. But this child never keered. This beaver told that hoss, 'If you'll show me how to do it, I'll give you fifty dollars for the cards."

He ran a look back and forth between the two of them, a potent brew of childish self-congratulation and hick shrewdness. "I been practicin' it. Now I do it so fast I can't tell whar that little boy is my own self. I got the ol' cards right here."

Sam—Two Hawks, Grumble reminded himself—got out the three cards and threw them clumsily. The throw was so clumsy, in fact, Grumble wondered if Jameson might catch on, but he didn't dare look at the man's face. He frowned at Sam—you don't need any extra effort to look clumsy with cards.

"A dollar says I can pick out the little boy." Grumble counted four two-bit pieces onto the table.

"Well . . . ," said Sam. The look of greed on his face was really quite delicious. "All right." He got out the fat purse and matched the four with his own.

Grumble picked out the little boy and gave Two Hawks a tight, superior smile.

Sam was flustered. So flustered, in fact, that when he picked up the first two cards he dropped them, leaving the little boy on the table.

While Sam was bent to the floor picking up the cards, Grumble reached out quickly and bent the corner of the little boy. Then he gave Jameson a slow wink.

Sam came up sputtering.

"Twenty dollars says I can do it again."

Now Sam was really flustered, and about to snarl in anger. He poured an excess of gold coins into his palm and slammed twenty dollars onto the table.

He threw the cards.

Grumble calmly picked out the little boy again, and more calmly pocketed all the coins on the table.

"God damn it," Sam burst out. "God *damn* it."

He picked up the three cards and hurled them onto the floor. Then he started to stomp them.

Grumble put a gentle restraining hand on his forearm. "You've had terrible luck, nothing more than that. It comes with the territory." Then he gave Jameson a conspiratorial nudge. "Why don't you change your luck by changing players? Throw for my friend Jameson here."

"I'm gonna throw these cards overboard."

"Just one more time. Be a sport."

Sam bent down to pick up the cards. This was the crucial moment in manipulation of the mark, but also manipulation of the cards. Sam had to slip those three cards away and substitute another three, with the old lady corner-turned instead of the little boy.

He did it very, very well, and while pretending to mull things over.

Sam stood up and staggered one step back into the chair. He glared at them. "All right," he said. "One throw. But I ain't gonna play for chicken feed." He opened his purse and spread the entire contents on the table. It was impressive, nearly the entire two hundred he'd earned from Ashley-Henry. "I'm gonna throw for *all* I got against *all* you got, both of you."

Grumble hesitated judiciously, then put the contents of his own purse next to Sam's. It was between forty dollars and fifty dollars.

Jameson was quick to do the same. About seventy dollars or eighty dollars, Grumble noted.

Sam threw the cards, if possible, more clumsily than before.

Grumble nodded to Jameson with a half smile, smilingly inviting him to pick the winning card.

Jameson turned over the marked card. When the old lady appeared, his face shot into wonderful mottles of purple, orange, and red.

Sam seized all the coins, slurped them into his purse, and chortled loudly. Then he jumped up, cackled louder still, and held up his purse high. It was a full, resounding cackle, backwoods triumph riding high. "I knowed I could do it," he called. "Yes, sir." These words came out like slush. "I knowed, I *knowed* I could do it." And he staggered off toward the deck.

"That poor fool may not even get off this boat with his money," said Grumble to Jameson.

"Our money," said Jameson.

"Yes." He made a wry face. "I really couldn't afford that. I'm afraid my foolishness . . ."

He puckered up as though tears were imminent.

Jameson stood up. "Perhaps we'd each prefer other company for a while," he said in a disgusted tone, and headed outside in the direction opposite to Sam's.

The tears usually did the trick.

Grumble finished his whiskey, which was good.

SAM GOT OFF the boat at the next stop with all the money. Grumble traveled on one stop farther. The next day he took the first steamboat back upstream. Sam got back on.

But they couldn't divide the spoils yet.

Grumble was already buying drinks for another pigeon.

Sam was glad he'd remembered the horse manure on his boots.

Back in St. Louis, when they divided their loot equally, Sam remarked happily that he'd made nearly as much money in two days as many working men earned in a year. "Way more than I need to go in style to Pittsburgh."

Chapter Twenty-one

SAM WONDERED, ALL the way to Pittsburgh, what his feelings would be when he saw the city where he fled from the constables, then the few buildings of Morgantown. The faces of Katherine Turley (now Katherine Morgan), his mother, and his brother sailed like high, vague clouds through his mind. He talked about them with Coy quite a lot on the steamboat, but he didn't have any words to say to any of them, not yet.

All he felt when he walked down the short gangplank onto the Pittsburgh waterfront with Coy on a leash was wariness of the constables.

They don't keep arrest warrants two years, do they? said an inner voice. The old anger still smoldered, he noticed.

No, lad, said Grumble's rumble, but they remember bad boys who slug policemen.

Maybe this time Coy will fight the battle for me, he teased himself. Coy was always calm, but very protective of Sam.

They hurried through the streets until he was on the road up the Allegheny and could breathe deep again. A walk of twenty miles didn't seem like much, not anymore.

The road didn't become a two-wheel track where it used to. It had been improved considerably. And it wasn't the rainy season. So he wasn't completely surprised when a wagon came along and none other than Arthur Turley offered him a ride to Morgantown.

Turley acted like he'd never been so glad to see anyone as he was thrilled to see Sam on this fine autumn noon. He did throw a nervous glance or two in Coy's direction, sitting in the wagon bed behind them. "Will you stop to share a bite with us?" Another nervous look at Coy.

"No, I'm eager to see Ma." That seemed neutral enough.

The smith nodded sagely, pulled at his beard, and allowed as how that made sense. Ellie would be very glad to see her youngest, that was sure.

Then he turned loquacious. Did Sam know about his nieces and nephews? Why, in the time Sam had been gone Gwen had borne a boy, Betsy another boy, and Katherine a girl. Turley delivered the third bit of news off-handedly, as of no particular consequence.

Sam had a bad moment. Carefully, he asked the ages of all three. Katherine's girl, Hilda, was just eight months old. So she wasn't Sam's. Relief fluttered his insides like wind-stirred blades of grass.

"Yes, just eight months," Turley repeated idly, still acting self-consciously like this information didn't matter. Sam wondered what tales had been told about him and Katherine after he left. He hoped they'd stung Owen sharply, very sharply.

They came on a place the road had been corduroyed, and Turley turned to a subject that made him more comfortable. "These improvements sure is good. We move goods to town most always by wagon now." Sam remembered Turley had always been awkward and fearful around boats.

They talked idly, and not entirely honestly, as though they'd been friends, which they weren't. Sam had always been leery of Turley's temper. Now he made a point of calling him by his first name, Arthur. Sam was through mistering people in this world. Turley pretended not to notice.

For the next two hours Sam heard more news of the people he'd grown up knowing than he'd ever heard as a youth. Some of them he got a big kick out of hearing about. Most of them, well, he was surprised at how little he felt, one way or another.

To tell the truth, and he had no intention of telling it to Turley, he was absorbed in his surprise at how angry he was, after so long, about Owen's lies to the authorities.

Turley rattled on. The poor man was nervous. Sam considered hopping off the wagon and walking out to Betsy's place first, just to get away from Turley.

No, I need to go straight into the lion's den.

THE OLD HOUSE looked better and worse at the same time. Owen had built onto the store in front. In fact, the old parlor and front bedroom were now absorbed into the store and filled with display counters. The store was also spiffed up, doors and windows newly whitewashed, puncheon floors laid, and a handsome wooden sign out front.

MORGAN STORE

A room had been added at the back, a hasty-looking construction job with a low shed roof. Sam was willing to bet that was his mother's bedroom now.

Then he saw Katherine.

She was picking tomatoes in the garden, holding her small harvest in her pouched apron. A child wearing only a shirt crawled beside her. Hilda, Turley had said.

He walked to them. "Hello, Katherine, hello, Hilda."

Katherine started. Hilda sat and whimpered.

This time you didn't hear me come up, thought Sam. He leaned on his father's rifle, held Coy tight on the leash, and looked at the two of them. He was satisfied to see that Hilda was a dead ringer for her mother, with no sign of Owen in her face.

Katherine's face turned sour. "Oh. You'll be wanting to see your mother," she said with a show of indifference. She's in her room." She looked askance at Coy, then turned her back and bent over the tomatoes.

After a moment she realized Sam was still standing there.

Now she pointed with her free hand. "It's the new room, there." She pointed to the low place with the shed roof, as he'd known she would. "She has her own entrance on this side."

Dismissed. He nodded, gave himself a hint of a smile, and moved off.

A rap on the door brought nothing. Another rap and a querulous voice. "Who's there?"

"Sam."

He heard a thump and the door flew open.

Ellie Morgan flew into her son's arms.

THEY TALKED IN her sitting room, as she called that section of her one-room quarters. Her area was roomy sideways, if cramped for head room, a sort of self-sufficient place where you put a mother-in-law you want to see little of.

Ellie sat on the one sofa and Sam on the floor at her feet, where he was comfortable. Coy curled up next to him, at home.

Ellie Morgan looked old for her sixty years, he thought, and hard used. Today she didn't look far off, though—she was right there with him. It was a good feeling. "You've growed so tall, and so strong," she said.

She wanted to hear every story of every adventure. Though the telling had gotten old for him, he reheated the tales nicely for his mother. Felt good to tell her. He kept the brag out, and skipped over many dangers, or touched on them only lightly. His walk of ten weeks he didn't mention at all. He did tell her he'd made a good deal of money, and left her the impression he got it all from hunting beaver.

She o-o-ohed and a-ahed in all the right places, and some others. After maybe an hour's recitation she kissed him for maybe the twentieth time and told him what a hero he was. It felt good.

They hadn't spoken a word about Owen, or Katherine or his sisters, or the nephews and nieces.

"Sam, I . . ."

"Yes, Ma?"

"I did want to ask you one thing."

He nodded, smiled at her, waited.

She drew a deep breath and came out with it. "Well, you know, when you kids were growing up, we never did live near enough a church ever to go. I mean to a proper service, which I wished and wished we could, but we just never did, and . . ." She gave Coy a very odd look, like he represented all the wildness she meant to stave off, and couldn't. "I done my best for you, I did, and what I want to know is, Did you ever go to church? You know, to pay your respects."

Now Sam drew a deep breath. The desire to lie was big in his heart. "No, I didn't, Ma."

She looked so downcast, he wished he had lied. "Well, would you? Would you promise me that one thing? Go to church at least once?"

"There's a Baptist church in St. Louis." He knew she'd be horrified at the idea of the Catholic church. "A Reverend Welch preaches there. I'll go."

Relief washed her face clean, and almost young.

His heart opened to her. Feelings danced, but he couldn't help her. He wanted to embrace her, swing her, and then carry her away forever. Before he could think, he stammered out, "Ma, you want to go to Pittsburgh with me? We could rent a little house." His mind immediately frothed up a bunch of lies—I could work the river, we'd see each other every couple of months—but he couldn't bring himself to say them.

Ellie's face grew tender. "That would never be a life for you." She patted his cheek. "Never."

He breathed again.

Thump. Then steps. Coming down the hall and this way. The door burst open, and Owen filled it.

"The prodigal son returns," he said with a twisty smile.

Coy growled.

"Damn, what's that?"

Coy growled loudly and barked. Sam restrained him with the leash.

"What are you doing here?"

Sam smiled at his brother's blunt words. Good, I don't have any lies for you either.

"Settling up."

"With Ma? All right. You and I don't have anything to say to each other."

Thoughts touching on "frigging" and "your wife" scampered out of the darkness of his mind toward consciousness. He had no intention of saying that, ever. From the hints in the air, he didn't need to.

"It's you I need to settle up with," Sam said. Owen's stance got belligerent. "You told the constables some lies when I left. Said I stole this rifle, which Dad willed to me. Said I stole twenty dollars and a boat."

Sam handed his mother Coy's leash and reached into his hunting pouch. Coy burst into a short fit of barking, but Ellie held him fearfully tight.

"I never stole a thing, and I ought to collect twenty for your lies, and the trouble they caused."

Owen sneered.

"Now, I considered the boat small compensation for my share of Morgan's store and mill, plus the house and acreage. Looks worth a pretty penny to me. But here's the dollars I sold the boat for anyway."

He looked Owen up and down, considering whether he wanted to swing for the balls or the chin.

Owen stepped close enough to take the coins, saying with a sneer, "Satisfied now?"

"Almost," said Sam, pulling the coins back.

He hit Owen with a humdinger of a punch, a real lollapalooza, the best punch he'd thrown in all his life. Belligerent or not, Owen wasn't expecting it. Sam's fist caught him square on the chin. Owen flew backwards, hit the sofa next to his mother, toppled over the back of it, and collapsed in a heap on the floor.

"Now we're even," said Sam, to deaf ears.

Ellie gave a little cry and peered over the sofa at her eldest. She handed Sam the leash, ran around, and put her hand on his chest. After a moment she looked up at Sam and laughed a little. "I won't say he didn't have it coming." She chuckled.

"Guess I better go," Sam said, "before Katherine makes a ruckus, or Owen tries to tell the sheriff I killed him." He counted coins into one hand, took the leash, and gave his mother the coins. "This is fifty dollars. I don't want you to be completely dependent on Owen." After hesitating, she put it in a dress pocket.

"I'll stop and say hello to Betsy and Gwen on the way back to Pittsburgh. You ever need to get word to me," he said, "send it care of Governor William Clark in St. Louis. Sooner or later I'll get it."

She came to him and wrapped her arms around him tight.

"It's in you to wander," she said. She took a couple of deep breaths, then looked up into his eyes. "I probably won't get to see you again."

He looked back into hers. "I know."

"Stay to supper?"

"Owen won't be out that long."

"Where will you go?"

He fingered his *gage d'amour*. It meant Meadowlark's affection, and a lot more. "The Rocky Mountains. I'm a mountain man."

"Your father," said Ellie Morgan, "would have been so proud of you."

In the road Sam turned and looked back at the family place. "So long, Dad," he said. He held up the rifle Lew Morgan had given him. "Thanks. This was my start."

He looked at the brass plate on the butt, where *Celt* had been scorched. He turned the stock over and looked at the side that was plain wood. "I'm going to put my sign on this," he told his father. "A buffalo, engraved right here." He rubbed the wood with his leash hand, then held up the rifle higher, as a salute.

Then he clucked at Coy, and they were off.

Afterword

THIS NOVEL IS the first of the RENDEZVOUS SERIES, which tells the story of the fur trade of the American West from its optimistic beginning in the early 1820s to its fading in the late 1830s, when westward immigration began. Here and throughout the series I mix well-known personages of history with fictional characters. Sam Morgan, his family, and his friends outside the mountain man world—Grumble, Abby, Captain Stuart, and so on—are fictional representatives of certain kinds of Americans of the time.

From St. Louis west, historical characters dominate, and they are drawn seriously and I believe accurately. William Clark, Pierre

Chouteau, William Ashley, Jedediah Smith, Edward Rose, Tom Fitzpatrick, James Clyman, and the many others are characterized on the basis of the records of the time. Though their dialogue is necessarily invented, no substantial event involving historical characters is imaginary.

In the adventures of the mountain men in this first book, for instance, every major situation and incident is taken from accounts of the men who were there: The Ashley men had just the conflict with the Rees described here; Jedediah Smith and his men, led by Edward Rose, did indeed pioneer a fur-trading route to Crow country and spend the winter with the Crows; in the spring they crossed South Pass and discovered a beaver paradise. Even many minor incidents of this novel can be found in the journals and other nineteenth-century accounts of the mountain men. For instance, Jim Clyman ran from the Rees in the way I've pictured it, Jedediah had his horrific encounter with that grizzly bear, his brigade nearly froze and starved on South Pass, and so on.

All the mountain men except Sam, his friend Gideon, and Micajah are the men named in Clyman's journal, Ashley's letters, or other contemporary accounts.

Likewise, the America of this novel is intended to be historically accurate. I've taken pains to draw Pittsburgh, Cincinnati, St. Louis, the valleys of the great rivers, and the forests, plains, and mountains just as they were. My accounts of the Shawnees and the Crow people are also based on extensive research.

My purpose in writing the series is not only to create a tale full of adventure, struggle, passion, and other ingredients of a good story, but to lay out carefully and faithfully the history of the mountain men and their astonishing deeds. Like my predecessors, I will try to show their amazing courage, skill, and hardiness, and their devotion to freedom on the most radical of terms; I will also look carefully at their relations with the Native peoples of the West, a model the rest of the country might have learned from, but tragically did not.

Though readers are welcome to agree or disagree with my

interpretations, they should know that these stories are based on facts as I am acquainted with them, and not invented.

I hurry to add that facts are only the dry kindling of good history, or good historical fiction. My hope is to use these facts to see deeply into the mountain men and so open their hearts, minds, and spirits to the reader.

Trapper Talk

A Glossary of Terms Associated with the Mountain Men

AGUARDIENTE Liquor, especially Taos lightning, a fiery booze from Taos. Also spelled "awerdenty" and the like. See also FIREWATER.

APISHEMORE A saddle blanket, especially one of soft buffalo-calf skin.

APPOLA A way of broiling meat on a stick in the flame, like shish kabob. Also the stick itself.

ASTORIAN A fur man associated with the fur-trading post at the mouth of the Columbia River, Astoria; a member of that party, sent out by John Jacob Astor's Pacific Fur Company in 1810 (by sea) or 1811 (by land). Though ambitious as a financial enterprise and an affirmation of American sovereignty, it was short-lived as an American post.

AUX ALIMENTS DU PAYS The expression of a fur trader or trapper meaning "to live off the land"; literally, from the food of the land.

BABICHE A thong of skin, often woven into mesh for snowshoes. French-Canadian.

BEADWORK Decoration made by Indian women with trade beads, usually for clothing. Mountain men commonly wore beadwork because their women wanted them to go to rendezvous in style.

BEAVER Aside from the semiaquatic rodent that was the object of the trapper's great search and his potential bonanza, this was a word for the felt hat that was made from the underfur of the critter. It was also commonly a term a mountain man used for himself and his partner (see CHILD). More: Beaver was a word for money, because beaver pelts were a universally accepted medium of exchange. "Whose beaver you earnin'?" was asking, "Who's your employer?"

The treasure the mountain men brought back to the settlements was the beaver's underfur, which made excellent felt for hats. They also valued the poor fellow for his tail, a delicacy when boiled. All this desirability might have been the critter's undoing, some people say, except that in the 1830s beaver hats whimsically went out of fashion, and silk came marching in.

BLACK YOUR FACE AGAINST (someone) To go to war against someone. From the custom of many Plains Indians of wearing black face paint for fighting.

BOSS The hump on the back of a buffalo's neck, eaten roasted, and much favored.

BOSSLOPER An independent fur trader (from Dutch). For the various ranks of mountain men, see FREE TRAPPER.

BOUDINS A food delicacy, buffalo intestine turned inside out, stuffed with chopped tenderloin, roasted on a stick and then boiled (from French).

BOURGEOIS The head of a fur-trading party, with an implication of class superiority (French-Canadian). For the various ranks of mountain men, see FREE TRAPPER.

BUENAVENTURA A mythical river of the interior West, at first believed to run west from the Rockies into San Francisco Bay, therefore a potential route to the Pacific and so much sought.

BUFFALO-WITTED Dull, stupid. The mountain men regarded the buffalo as dim of brain.

BUG'S BOYS The trappers' familiar name for the Blackfeet, their particular enemies.

BULL BOAT A craft fashioned of buffalo hides stretched on a willow frame. Trappers liked this boat because it could be jerry-built almost anywhere in beaver country and had almost no draft.

BULL THROWER An occasional bragging word of a mountain man for his rifle, a killer of buffalo bulls.

CACHE To store your belongings in a hiding place, especially in a large hole dug for the purpose, then concealed by replacement of the sod. Trapping brigades often cached furs for later recovery. Also the hiding place itself. (From French.)

CAPOTE The usual winter coat of the fur men, made from a blanket and hooded. Also called a *blanket coat*.

CARCAJOU A word for the wolverine (French-Canadian). Among Canadian fur men and many Western Indians, the wolverine was legendary for its ferocity.

CASTOR Castoreum, an excretion of the beaver's perineal glands, the main ingredient (after drying and mixing with alcohol and herbs) of the bait for a beaver trap. Also called MEDICINE. Carried in a stoppered horn on a shoulder strap.

CHIEF'S COAT A military-style coat for giving or trading to Indian leaders.

CHILD The common way a mountain man referred to himself and his companion: "This child," he would say, meaning himself, "is fixin' to ride." Or the mountain man might say, "That child is *some*," a way of expressing admiration. The trapper used other terms the same way—*hoss, coon, beaver*, and *nigger* (a word without racial implications in this case).

COME To die. To *make 'em come* means to kill them. An expression of the mountain man applied equally to beaver, Indians, and other critters—"This child made 'em come."

CONGÉ A license or licensee for fur-trading under the French.

COMPAÑERO Companion, buddy.

COUNT COUP Though among Plains Indians it meant to recite one's deeds formally, among mountain men it simply meant to whip them, or kill them.

COUNTRY WIFE An Indian woman married, according to the custom of the country, to an Anglo fur man. Many traders, especially, had both city families and country families—sometimes a family in each of several different tribes.

COUREUR DE BOIS A French-Canadian fur trader who operated independently. Though the big companies proceeded legally, coureurs de bois ignored the regulations, roamed the wilds in small groups, and sought the furs. In many ways, sojourning among the red men, they became as much red as white.

DAMP POWDER AND NO WAY TO DRY IT An expression for a bad fix. The reference is to gunpowder.

DEPOUILLE A thick layer of fat on the back of the buffalo, valued by Indians and mountain men as food.

DOINGS trapper talk for activities, events, and so on.

DRY Thirst, sometimes for booze. "Hosses, this child's got to wet his dry."

DUPONT Gunpowder, from the name of the manufacturer. See also GALENA. The powder of the time was black, made from saltpeter, charcoal, and sulfur, then caked and tolled into grains—fine for pistols, more coarse for rifles.

ENGAGÉ A French-Canadian canoe man who paddled wilderness streams to conduct the fur trade; a trapper hired for wages. For the various ranks of mountain man, see FREE TRAPPER.

FIREWATER Booze. It was often pure alcohol cut with the water of the closest creek and seasoned with tobacco, red chiles, and whatever else pleased the fancy of the trader, according to report even snake heads. The term came from a custom developed by Indians trading with the Canadian fur men. Since the alcohol was customarily diluted, the Indians would spit the first mouthful of booze on the fire. If it flamed, they'd trade for it; if it put some of the fire out, they wouldn't.

FIXINGS Among fur men, POSSIBLES (essential personal gear), camp gear, or material needed to make something.

FLOAT STICK A stick the beaver trapper attached to his trap. If the beaver swam away with the trap, the stick showed where it was. This stick was the source of one of the best-known expressions of the mountain man, "He don't KNOW WHAT WAY THE STICK FLOATS."

FOOFURAW Trinkets, gaudy clothing, and similar show-offy stuff. What you have to give a girl you're courting, or a wife you want to keep happy.

FOOL HEN A common name for the sage grouse. The bird sits so still (for whatever reason) men can get close enough to fell it with a stick, stone, or whip.

FORT UP To barricade yourself; to take a position defensible against attack, especially Indian attack. Mountain men sometimes killed their horses and forted up behind the carcasses.

FOUR DIRECTIONS A sacred symbol of most Plains Indians, and thus of the mountain men who followed their ways. To east, south, west, and north were sometimes added sky and earth, making six directions.

FREE TRAPPER A beaver man who trapped on his own instead of working for one of the fur companies. He was usually a fellow, whether French-Canadian or American, who had begun in the trade as an employee, acquired his skills, and gone independent. Some still had to get outfitted by the big companies and so were obliged to sell their PLEWS (beaver skins) to their creditors; others were completely free. Their opposite number was the ENGAGÉ (hireling). For the various ranks of mountain men see BOSSLOPER, BOURGEOIS, COUREUR DE BOIS, ENGAGÉ, HIVERNANT, MANGEUR DE LARD, PARTISAN, PATRON, and VOYAGEUR.

FRENCHMAN Usually in the West, a métis, man of French and Indian blood. The French-Canadians preceded the Americans in the Western beaver trade, explored much of the country, learned the Native peoples, and developed many of the ways. They also brought many words to the mountain man's vocabulary.

FROZE FOR MEAT Hungry; starved; without meat for a long time, and meat was the large majority of the mountain man's diet.

FUSIL A muzzle-loading musket of the type the Hudson's Bay Company and Northwest Fur Company traded to the Indians; a *trade musket*.

GAGE D'AMOUR A heart-shaped hide pouch that hung around the neck of a mountain man, usually holding a clay pipe. Normally it was decorated with beads or quills by an Indian lover.

GALENA Lead for balls for a muzzle-loading rifle. It usually came in blocks and was formed into balls of the needed caliber by the trapper himself. Thus the phrase *duPont and galena*, powder and lead, the most critical of all mountain man possessions.

GALL BITTERS A drink popular among mountain men, water mixed with buffalo gall. Also known as *prairie bitters*.

GO UNDER To die. Said to be from the sign-language motion for dying.

GREEN RIVER A knife of the beaver men, according to much popular history. In fact it probably came to the West only after the heyday of the mountain men was past.

HAIR OF THE BEAR A mountain man expression for bulldog courage, and a high compliment—"He's got the hair of the bear in him."

HANG ONTO YOUR HAIR Watch yourself; take care of yourself. Literally, don't get scalped. Same as *mind your hair*, *watch your hair*. See LIFT HAIR, LOST HIS HAIR, RAISE HAIR.

HAWKEN A muzzle-loading rifle made by St. Louis gunsmiths Jacob or Samuel Hawken from the 1820s until the Civil War. Though popularly regarded as *the* mountain man rifle, most Hawkens probably got to the mountains relatively late in the heyday of the trade.

HIVERNANT French-Canadian term for an experienced beaver trapper or trader; literally, a "winterer," a man who has spent winters in the wilderness instead of returning to Montreal.

HUMP RIB A prolongation of the vertebrae that support the hump of the buffalo and the meat on them. The mountain men prized this meat. The *fleece* was the fat alongside the hump ribs, also thought good eating by men whose diet included little fat.

KINNIKINNICK A mixture of tobacco and other ingredients, especially dried sumac leaves and the inner bark of the willow or dogwood, for smoking. Though ceremonial among the Indians, smoking among the white men was mostly for pleasure.

KNOW WHAT WAY THE STICK FLOATS, WHICH WAY THE STICK FLOATS If you didn't know what way the stick floats, you didn't know which side was up, know your ass from a hole in the ground, etc. Same as know POOR BULL FROM FAT COW.

LIFT HAIR, RAISE HAIR To kill people, usually Indians; literally, to scalp.

LODGEPOLE (someone) To thrash someone, usually your Indian mate. Lodgepoles were the long pieces of debarked timber from lodgepole pines used to hold the tipi (lodge) up.

LOST HIS HAIR Died. Literally, got scalped, and the term was extended to other forms of death.

MAKE MEAT To kill game for eating.

MANGEUR DE LARD A beginner, a greenhorn. Literally, a man who eats pork. The French-Canadians fed canoemen pork in their corn mush on the river routes between Montreal and Lake Superior, while canoemen of the further interior were skilled at living AUX ALIMENTS DU PAYS (off the land).

MEAT BAG Stomach.

MEDICINE Castor, used as bait on beaver traps. Another meaning is to conjure in the manner of the Indians, to *make medicine*; as they adopted Indian ways, more and more mountain men did this.

MOUNTAINEER The name the mountain men first called themselves most commonly; the beaver trapper of the Rocky Mountains during the period 1822–1840.

MOUNTAIN PRICE The price for an item of manufactured goods in the West, usually at RENDEZVOUS or at a trading post. This was the price to a trapper, who would then either use it himself or trade or give it to an Indian. A mountain price might be many times what the trader paid for it back in the settlements, due to difficulty of shipment, hardship, danger, and greed. This system did its part to enrich the trader rather than the trapper.

NOR'WESTER A man of the Northwest Company, the one-time competitor of the Hudson's Bay Company for the furs of Canada and the American Northwest. The *Northwest blanket* and *Northwest gun* (or *fusee* or *fusil*), a smoothbore musket, were trade items of this fur company.

OLD EPHRAIM The grizzly bear, which was also called a *silvertip*.

ON THE PERAIRA Free, as in, "He gave me a pound of coffee on the peraira." *Peraira* was dialectical for *prairie*.

PACK A bundle of beaver hides, grained and ready for shipment to the States, weighing either about 52 or about 100 pounds.

PARFLECHE A rawhide box, usually painted decoratively, for storing belongings. Or the rawhide (hair off) such a box was made from.

PARK A natural clearing, an area of open meadows, surrounded by mountains; also called a *hole*. South Park was a paradise of the mountain men. The trappers loved this region in Colorado around the head of the South Platte River for its abundant game and generally shining times.

PARTISAN The leader of a brigade of trappers. (See also FREE TRAPPER for similar terms.)

PATRON Among VOYAGEURS and other fur men, the master or steersman of a boat.

PEMBINA The highbush cranberry of the Red River of the North. Also the name of several French-Canadian trading posts in that area.

PEMMICAN The universal preserved food of the Indians who lived on the buffalo, and later of the mountain men and other frontiersmen who learned Indian ways. Pemmican was made from buffalo meat that was dried, pounded fine, mixed equally by weight with marrow fat, and stored in PARFLECHES or sewn into other skin sacks. Often dried berries were added, especially chokecherries and serviceberries. Preserved in this way, pemmican lasted for several years.

PLEW The pelt of a beaver. The term derived from the French-Canadian *plus*, which sounds similar and meant "more," perhaps suggesting a superior hide. Among the American trappers, it became the word for any beaver skin. During the height of the Rocky Mountain trade, ordinary beaver skins brought about four dollars per pound on the open market and a prime plew brought six dollars or more.

POOR BULL FROM FAT COW A descriptive expression for a greenhorn's ignorance, from the idea that a greenhorn could not differentiate the poor, stringy meat of a buffalo bull from the fat, juicy meat of a cow. Same as KNOW WHAT WAY THE STICK FLOATS.

PORKEATER Same as MANGEUR DE LARD.

POSSIBLES, POSSIBLE SACK, POSSIBLES SACK Belongings, accoutrements, personal gear, especially camping gear. The mountain men usually carried their possibles in a sack of buffalo hide.

QUILLWORK Decoration made by Indian women with dyed porcupine quills; the predecessor of BEADWORK.

RED RIVER MÉTIS An English, Scotch, or French-Cree mixed-blood of the settlements of the Red River of the North or the Saskatchewan River in Canada. The French-Cree métis (often disliked and distrusted by early Americans) were very dark-skinned and noted for dressing entirely in black, except for a brightly colored sash around the waists of the men. Many of the fur men on the Missouri River before the Americans arrived were Métis.

RENDEZVOUS The annual trade fair of the mountain men during the heyday of the mountain fur trade, held midsummer almost every year from 1825 through 1840. As many as several hundred trappers and several thousand Indians would gather at a preappointed spot (most often along the Green River) to meet the pack caravan from the settlements. The official business was exchanging beaver pelts for powder, lead, tobacco, beads, maybe some clothing, maybe some traps or a new gun, and almost certainly some whiskey. The unofficial agenda was to have a blowout.

ROCKY MOUNTAIN COLLEGE The mountain man custom of reading during the winter, or learning to read; Shakespeare, Byron, Scott, Miss Jane Porter, and the Bible were favorites.

RUB OUT To kill. The expression may have derived from the Plains Indian sign meaning "to kill," a rubbing motion.

SAGAMITÉ Corn gruel, the primary subsistence of the French-Canadian canoemen on their annual journey from Montreal to Lake Superior and back.

SHINE, SHINING When something was terrific, the mountain man said, "That shines," or "Them was shinin' times." A converse expression was, "You can't shine in this crowd."

SIFFLEUR The term of the French-Canadian trappers for the marmot, or rockchuck.

SISKADEE The name of the mountain men for the Green River; it means "sage hen." Spelled with wonderful creativity—not only Siskadee but *Siskeedee, Seedskeeder*, and so on. This river was heaven on earth for the mountain men, who found in its valley beaver a-plenty and friendly Indians, the Shoshone. Most of their rendezvous were held near or on the Siskadee.

SOME An adjective of admiration, as in "He was some hoss." Sometimes used as an emphatic positive, as in "That hoss could shoot *some*."

SQUAW MAN A denigrating term of white people, especially Oregon Trail emigrants, for a mountain man whose wife and children were Indian.

STROUD, STROUDING A wool cloth common as a trade item in the fur trade. Named for Stroud, Gloucester, where it was made.

TAOS LIGHTNING Firewater popular among the mountain men. It was available at Taos, the closest settlement to the trapping country.

THERE GOES HOSS AND BEAVER Mountain man talk for, "We just lost everything," which they too often did to raiding Indians, raging waters, and so on.

TRAVOIS The Plains Indian equivalent of a wagon. A travois was made by taking a pair of LODGEPOLES (which you already had for the tipi), crisscrossing the small ends on a horse's back, letting the butt ends drag behind, slinging skins (or straps of skin) in between, and tying gear on.

UP TO THE GREEN RIVER to the hilt, all the way, an expression of the 1840s. On the hilt of the usual trapper knife at that time were stamped the words "Green River." To *go up Green River* was to die.

UP TO TRAP Said by mountain men of an experienced trapper, a man who knew what he was doing. Same as *up to beaver* and opposite of *don't know what way the stick floats*.

VOYAGEUR A French-Canadian canoeman. A beginning *voyageur* was called a MANGEUR DE LARD. See also ENGAGÉ.

WAGH! An exclamation of vigorous approval, admiration, wonder, etc. Perhaps from the Spanish exclamation *Gua!*, meaning something like "Gracious!"

YARN To tell a tale, probably an adventure, and probably a tall tale. Yarning was a primary mountain man entertainment. Some greenhorns mistook yarning for prevaricating: A Montana newspaper editor missed an international scoop by refusing to report the existence of the fabulous Yellowstone region—he didn't want to get caught printing old Jim Bridger's lies.

Note: This glossary emphasizes terms of American mountain men in the fur trade of the West. Those interested in more Canadian terms or terms from the Eastern U.S., or simply in fuller definitions, are referred to my *Dictionary of the American West*.

A Reading List and Sources for This Novel

The reader who wants to delve further into the history of this fascinating era of American history would do well to begin with this short and select list:

A Reader's Guide

About mountain men and the fur trade: My favorite general books are Bernard DeVoto's *Across the Wide Missouri*, Don Berry's *A Majority of Scoundrels*, and my own *Give Your Heart to the Hawks*. Journals and other writings of the time are very much worth reading—see Frances Fuller Victor's story of the life of Joe Meek, *River of the West,* and Osborne Russell's *Journal of a Trapper.* The best biography of a mountain man, perhaps, is Dale Morgan's *Jedediah Smith and the Opening of the West.* Fred Gowans's *Rocky Mountain Rendezvous* is full of useful information about each rendezvous.

Good historical fiction may be the best way to get a full sense of what people of a particular time were like. The classics about mountain men are Stewart Edward White's *The Long Rifle* and A. B. Guthrie, Jr.'s *The Big Sky.* And John G. Neihardt's epic poems about the mountain men, *The Song of Three Friends, The Song of Hugh Glass,* and *The Song of Jed Smith* are still magnificent.

About rivermen of the Ohio and Mississippi valleys: Michael Allen's *Western Rivermen* is indispensable. For a good sense of this eastern frontier, though it is written about life a generation later, Bernard DeVoto's *Mark Twain's America.*

About gamblers and con men of the nineteenth century: Robert DeArment's *Knights of the Green Cloth.*

About the Crow Indians: Robert Lowie's *The Crow Indians.*

Principal Sources

Anyone who attempts to write historical fiction about America in the nineteenth century without Howard Lamar's *The New Encyclopedia of the American West* at hand is at sea from the start. I also depended on the *Encyclopædia Britannica* and, to discover what words were and were not in use at the time, on Mitford Mathews's *A Dictionary of Americanisms,* on *Webster's Ninth New Collegiate Dictionary,* and on my own *Dictionary of the American West.*

For the mountain men and the principal action of this book I have worked with the following volumes within reach: Dale Morgan's *The West of William H. Ashley,* a superb source for Ashley's letters and other letters and documents of these years. Morgan's

Jedediah Smith and the Opening of the West. James Clyman's *Journal of a Mountain Man*, edited by Linda Hasselstrom, which offers the recollections of a key figure of the Ashley-Henry years. Hiram Chittenden's *The American Fur Trade of the Far West*, the first general history of the era. LeRoy R. Hafen and Harvey L. Carter, *Mountain Men and Fur Traders of the Far West* and *Trappers of the Far West*.

For an understanding of the Crow people: Robert Lowie's *The Crow Indians* and my several years in close contact with them.

Acknowledgments

Thanks to:

Andy Smith, my old high school classmate, who went the extra mile to help me with the look and feel of Cincinnati in 1823.

David K. Records, who helped me with the natural history of the Ohio River area.

The novelist Gregory Tobin, for help with the history of the Catholic Church in Maryland.

The poet Barney Bush, for help with the language and customs of the Shawnee people.

Dick James, for years and years of teaching me about the physical culture of the mountain men, and for emergency looks into books I don't own.

Lana Latham, my interlibrary loan warrior in this remote outpost—you're essential, Lana.

Gil Bateman, for help on the Internet and uplift of spirits.

Clyde Hall, who set my feet on the road of the sacred pipe.

Richard Wheeler, for two decades of friendship and a great, inspiring dialogue about writing and the West.

Dale Walker, my editor of nine years. You teach me, you make me write better, and you make me aspire to more.

My wife, Meredith, is the center of my living, loving, and being. It's all thanks to you, love.